THE CONJUR[...]

This is Penelope Lively for the ov[...] as well as Penelope Lively and ve[...] a breathtakingly good story. *IND[...]*

A rare, strange, vividly imagined fantasy story, reminiscent of John Masefield's classic *The Box of Delights*. Its atmosphere is beautiful and captivating, full of memorable visual images and poetic resonances, and the whole lingers in the mind long after. *SUNDAY TIMES*

Q

THE CANDLE MAN

A wonderfully engrossing book which draws the reader into its terrifying, watery world. *BOOKS FOR KEEPS*

A poet's economy and forcefulness in the use of words . . . cannot be disbelieved. *TES*

Highly atmospheric, with extraordinary descriptive passages; an excellent read. *JUNIOR EDUCATION*

Q

FINTAN'S TOWER

Vivid, unusual and well-written . . . This is a wonderful, unputdownable book which establishes Fisher as a children's writer of rare talent. *SUNDAY TIMES*

Classic fantasy fiction . . . Inventive, and well-written, it will hold eight to twelve-year olds spellbound. *SUNDAY TELEGRAPH*

Catherine Fisher has a wonderfully sure touch with both narrative and dialogue . . . as well as its sense of authenticity the story has delightful humour and gripping suspense. *JUNIOR BOOKSHELF*

Also available by CATHERINE FISHER
And published by RED FOX

THE BOOK OF THE CROW:
THE RELIC MASTER
THE INTERREX
FLAIN'S CORONET
THE MARGRAVE

THE SNOW-WALKER TRILOGY
CORBENIC
BELIN'S HILL

THE GLASS TOWER

CATHERINE FISHER

RED FOX

This volume contains THE CONJUROR'S GAME,
THE CANDLE MAN *and* FINTAN'S TOWER

THE GLASS TOWER
A RED FOX BOOK 0 09 947298 8

This collection first published in Great Britain by Red Fox,
an imprint of Random House Children's Books, 2004

1 3 5 7 9 10 8 6 4 2

Collection copyright © Catherine Fisher, 2004

THE CONJUROR'S GAME
First published in Great Britain by
The Bodley Head Children's Books 1990
Copyright © Catherine Fisher 1990

FINTAN'S TOWER
First published in Great Britain by
The Bodley Head Children's Books 1991
Copyright © Catherine Fisher 1991

THE CANDLE MAN
First published in Great Britain by
The Bodley Head Children's Books 1994
Copyright © Catherine Fisher 1994

Papers used by Random House Children's Books are natural, recyclable products
made from wood grown in sustainable forests. The manufacturing processes conform
to the environmental regulations of the country of origin.

Typeset in Adobe Garamond by Palimpsest Book Production Limited,
Polmont, Stirlingshire

Red Fox Books are published by Random House Children's Books,
61–63 Uxbridge Road, London W5 5SA,
a division of The Random House Group Ltd,
in Australia by Random House Australia (Pty) Ltd,
20 Alfred Street, Milsons Point, Sydney, NSW 2061, Australia,
in New Zealand by Random House New Zealand Ltd,
18 Poland Road, Glenfield, Auckland 10, New Zealand,
and in South Africa by Random House (Pty) Ltd,
Endulini, 5A Jubilee Road, Parktown 2193, South Africa

THE RANDOM HOUSE GROUP Limited Reg. No. 954009
www.kidsatrandomhouse.co.uk

A CIP catalogue record for this book is available from the British Library.

Printed and bound in Great Britain by Bookmarque Ltd, Croydon, Surrey

CONTENTS

Entering a door to the Otherworld is dangerous.
Time runs strangely in there – you may emerge a
hundred years later or at the same instant you entered.
Either way, you will have changed. Because the
Otherworld is the imagination, where bizarre and
beautiful creatures roam, huge buildings rise from the
darkness, difficult quests that involve a life and death
beyond the body have to be achieved.

This book contains three stories about crossing into a
perilous realm. A lost piece from a deadly game, a
candle containing a man's soul, a prisoner locked up
for centuries – each has to be recovered at terrible risk.
For me, as author, entering the glass tower was a
spellbinding adventure. I'm not sure if I've ever found
my way out. Be warned! It might be the same for you.

Catherine Fisher
2004

THE
CONJUROR'S
GAME

'And as they looked they could hear a rider coming towards them, to the place where Arthur and Owein were over the gaming board. The squire greeted Arthur and said that Owein's ravens were slaying his bachelors and squires. And Arthur looked at Owein and said, "Call off thy ravens." "Lord," said Owein, "play thy game." And they played. The rider returned towards the battle, and the ravens were no more called off than before."

From 'The Dream of
Rhonabwy' in the Mabinogion
(translated by Gwyn Jones and Thomas Jones)

To My Parents

1

The Brown Ointment

'There he is,' Mr Webster said.

'Who?'

'Luke Ferris. The chap I was telling you about. The conjuror.'

Alick stood up and had a look. Out in the street, on the opposite pavement, a thin, dark-haired man was looking in the shop windows. Just behind him trotted a white dog.

'Is that him?' Alick sat down again, and picked up the pen. 'I've seen him about before. He looks just like anybody else.'

'Ah, yes. I expect that's just what he wants you to think.' His father's mouth twitched. Alick knew something had amused him. 'Anyway, he's coming over, so you can find out for yourself.'

They watched the man cross the street, weaving between the cars. He came up to the window of Webster's Second-hand Bookshop and paused, looking in at the bright display of Christmas books and posters that Alick had spent the morning arranging. Then the bell on the shop door jangled as he came in.

It was nearly five o'clock on a late December afternoon, and the shop was already quite dark. Down at one end, the fire had smouldered into embers, and the three shelves of musty, leatherbound books that never sold, gleamed in the warm glow. Mr Webster switched on the lamp near the window. 'Cold enough for snow, Luke,' he observed.

The conjuror nodded, and gave Alick a quick glance. His

face was white with cold, and a gold earring glinted in the fire light. He wandered among the shelves, picking a book up now and again. Mr Webster searched the desk for his glasses, and Alick leaned his elbows on the counter and watched their customer.

A conjuror. And in Halcombe Great Wood that meant the real thing – not the man you saw on the television doing tricks with cards and white rabbits. And they said he was good. Well, he certainly looked at you in an odd way; as if he could see what you had for breakfast, if he wanted to. But *he* wouldn't be able to do anything about it either, Alick thought bitterly. No one could. The whole thing was hopeless.

A movement by the door caught his eye, and he saw that the white dog was lying there, watching him. Chin on paws it lay, and there was an odd smirk about its mouth, as if it found something funny.

The ashes of the fire crackled. The lights in the butcher's opposite went out. Finally, Mr Webster straightened up and slid the accounts book back to Alick with a satisfied nod. 'Good. All done.' He looked up.

'Anything you want, Luke?'

'Just these, I think.' The conjuror came and put two books on the counter, and Alick took a sideways look at the titles. *The Medicinal Properties of Herbs and Simples* was the first, and the other was a small paperback called *Poisons*. He swallowed. Perhaps it would be better not to ask after all. But it was too late; as he wrapped the books his father had already begun.

'I'm glad you called in, Luke, I've been wanting a word for a while now. It's about Alick.'

'Oh?' Alick felt the man stare at him. 'What's he been up to?'

2

'Nothing.' Mr Webster laughed, pressing down a piece of sticky tape. 'No, it's his hands. Show him, Alick.'

Feeling foolish, Alick put both hands on the shop counter and stared at them gloomily.

Warts!

They looked horrible, and dirty, and they itched like mad. There were four on one hand and three on the other, including a big hard one like a knob of dried glue on the end of his thumb. He'd had them since he went fishing with Jamie in the Greenmere, but his father didn't know about that. The Mere was strictly out of bounds – a man had drowned in it last year. The kids at school had been calling him Frog-face ever since. He was just about sick of it.

The conjuror looked down at the warts thoughtfully. 'How long have you had these?'

'About three weeks.'

'And did they just appear?'

'Sort of,' Alick stammered.

'I see. You hadn't been anywhere wet? Mucky pools? Ponds?'

'No.'

Luke Ferris nodded. 'I see,' he said again. Suddenly he smiled at Alick; Alick felt himself go red. He knew!

'I've tried everything,' his father put in, pushing the parcel of books across the counter. 'Calamine, chilblain cream, every wart paint you've ever heard of. Then the doctor gave him some nasty, white burning stuff. None of it's done the slightest good . . . That'll be eight pounds fifty, please, Luke.'

'I think,' Luke said evenly, 'that I may be able to help. It'll cost you . . . eight pounds fifty. Payment on results.'

Mr Webster laughed. 'Fair enough.'

The conjuror gave Alick another grin, and reaching into

his coat pocket, pulled out a few, small, round boxes which he scattered along the counter. Then he spread out a clean, white handkerchief and told Alick to put his hands on it, palms down. Warily, Alick obeyed. The warts itched like crazy. Mr Webster bolted the shop door, turned the sign to 'Closed' and came and leaned on the counter, filling his pipe and watching the proceedings with interest.

Humming, Luke opened one of the boxes. Immediately a sharp, pungent smell began to fill the shop, making Alick's eyes water. The dog by the door made a small noise in its throat.

'It's all right, Tam,' the conjuror said, without turning his head. Dipping one finger into the sticky, brown ointment, he carefully put a small dab of it on each of the warts, and two dabs on the large one, all the time humming and muttering words that Alick, close as he was, could not catch.

The smell made him feel dizzy, but the ointment did not sting as the doctor's had – it was just cold, like chocolate ice-cream. At last, the treatment seemed to be over; the shop was dim with a faint smoke. Luke wiped his finger clean on the edge of the handkerchief and replaced the box lid. He gathered the others up and dropped them in his pocket. Alick watched the brown blobs of ointment harden into crusts. 'Can I move now?'

'Not yet. Let it dry.'

Impatient, he kept still. Luke and his father began to talk about people they knew, and he had to wait. The smell bothered him, made him think of deep woods and wet, mushy leaves. And he felt daft, with his hands out flat like someone at a seance.

'I hope it works,' he said when the talk had stopped.

4

Luke did not answer.

'It's horrible having people stare at your hands all the time.'

For some reason this seemed the wrong thing to say. His father glared at him angrily. He couldn't see why. But then the conjuror took his hands out of his pockets and laid them down flat beside Alick's.

'I know,' he said.

It was all Alick could do not to shout out. The long, brown hand next to his had, not five fingers, but *six*! He glanced at the other. It was the same.

Luke was watching him. 'Not so easy to cure as warts,' he said.

Alick felt foolish. 'I'm sorry,' he stammered. 'I didn't know.'

'I didn't think you did . . .' Luke paused, as if he was about to say something else, then, changing his mind, picked up the handkerchief and swiftly rubbed away the brown crusts from Alick's fingers.

Mr Webster gave a whistle of amazement.

The warts were gone. Just a crumble of fine dust lay on the counter.

Alick couldn't believe it. He stared at his fingers as if they did not belong to him, then touched them, carefully. No pain, no itching – not even a scar. Nothing!

Luke had already picked up his parcel of books and turned towards the door, nodding at Mr Webster's astonished thanks.

'Oh, that's all right. But if I were you, Alick,' he added, turning suddenly, 'I'd give up fishing at the Greenmere. It's not the sort of place you'll catch anything fit to eat. Besides, it's dangerous. Your father will tell you that.'

'Indeed I will,' Mr Webster said in a meaningful way.

The conjuror smiled. 'Goodnight, Tom.'

'Goodnight, Luke. Thanks again.'

And the door closed behind him.

Mr Webster turned around and took the pipe from his mouth, but before he could mention the Greenmere, Alick changed the subject.

'I never thought he could do it!' he announced, holding up his fingers to the light. 'It's magic!'

'It might look like that to you,' his father said, instantly sarcastic. 'Luke knows a lot about folk medicine and such. But it's true I've never seen warts done as fast as that, though there was an old chap down at Swinder's End used to do them, once. Didn't you feel anything?'

'No,' Alick plumped himself on to a stool. 'Dad, why didn't you tell me about his hands?'

'Well, I didn't know you'd come out with a tomfool remark like that, did I?' his father said. 'Besides, everyone knows. Or I thought they did. Odd, isn't it?'

Alick nodded.

'Mind, he's an odd sort is Luke.'

Alick clasped his knees. 'How do you mean?'

'Well, it's not just warts.' Mr Webster crossed to the fire and began to rake it out. 'You know McCarthy, the baker? He had arthritis last year, very bad. The doctor told him he might be in bed for the rest of his life. Then his son called on Luke, and the next week the old man's in the Crown and Fiddle drinking pints. I'll bet he charged more than eight pounds fifty for that.' He straightened up and dusted his hands. 'Well now, I think we'd better go upstairs and have some tea, don't you? And a nice little chat. About the Greenmere.'

2

Greenmere

'And he did it just like that?' Jamie stared at Alick's hands. 'Get out! It's impossible!'

'It's not. Besides, Dad was there – ask him.' Alick was annoyed. 'You never believe anything I say.'

'Too much imagination,' Jamie said. 'It's all those batty old books, it is.'

'Oh shut up.' Alick felt guilty. He shouldn't be here, not after the row he had got last night. They were in the Combe, a narrow lane that ran deep into the wood; their heads bent against the bitter breeze. He pulled his gloves back on. 'It is true. And he does have six fingers. And what's more he knew I'd been at the Mere too.'

'Lucky guess.'

'No. He knew.' Alick kicked up the leaves. 'He said it was dangerous. And Dad knew then, of course.' He pulled a face.

'Was it bad?'

'Not really. Said I ought to think of other people.' And yet, he thought, here I am going there again.

Jamie must have guessed what he was thinking. 'Well, we're only going to walk past it. There's nothing wrong with that, is there? And I *must* have dropped that reel there; I've looked everywhere else.'

The Combe had been getting narrower for some time; now it was just a deep, gloomy cutting in the very lowest part of the wood. On each side, steep banks of earth towered over their heads, as if a knife had cut a deep slash in the ground and they stood at the bottom of it. In summer the

7

banks were a riot of flowers, but now, in bleak December, only a tangle of tree-roots and frost-bitten brambles poked out of the soil. High above, crowding to the edge as if to look down, were rows of golden beech trees, their leaves filling the Combe in deep drifts to the boys' knees.

They climbed up by the usual way; a zig-zag staircase of roots that stuck out of one bank. At the top, the forest was silent all about them; a faint breeze rustled the tree-tops. Far down the ranks of trees a crow 'karked' noisily and flew away.

Briskly, Jamie started down the path. 'It's all nonsense, all this stuff about the Mere. I mean, I know that chap was drowned in it, but that's just because he fell in, or went swimming and got stuck. There must be acres of mud in there. You'd never catch me swimming in it!'

Behind him, Alick shook his head. 'That man had all his clothes on. You don't go swimming like that.'

'Well, he fell. It's just the same. But these yarns about the Mere being a bad place, and people who go into the wood and never come out again – that's just stuff! Stuff to keep little kids away from the edge.'

It sounded sensible. Jamie usually did – and he was always sure he was right. Alick said nothing.

'Are you listening?'

'Yes.'

'Good!' Jamie jumped on a fallen log and raced along it, arms wide. 'There's nothing here but rabbits, and squirrels, and birds, and, er . . .'

'Foxes,' Alick put in quietly.

'FOXES!'

The thin, red shape Alick had seen loped off at the sudden shout. All at once they both burst into a fit of giggles, shoving and pushing each other and crashing noisily through the drifts of leaves.

Around them, echoes rang in the trees for miles.

Halcombe Great Wood stretches for fifty thousand acres, most of it rarely visited. Only four roads come into the Wood, meeting in a crooked X at Halcombe Cross. One of the lanes leads to Halcombe village; the other two are roads towards Gloucester and Monmouth; and the fourth, far more spindly and lost under its leaves, is the Combe, which goes only to the house at Swinder's End and then peters out in the trees. It is an ancient wood, a wildwood, riddled with lumps and humps, ruined cottages, and a maze of bridleways and tracks and paths.

Halcombe village is surrounded by trees. From the church tower, all you can see in any direction are endless dark green branches, and the cluster of red roofs like an island in the middle. And, if it is a fine day, you might see the sun glittering on the pinnacles of Gloucester Cathedral, thirty miles away.

You would also see Tolbury Tump. All the forest is hilly, but Tolbury Tump stands out; a high round knoll, bare of trees, the only bald spot in the whole of the wood. And at the foot of the Tump, hidden in a gloomy hollow of dark pines, lies the Greenmere.

As Alick and Jamie trod the thick layer of pine needles towards it, their footsteps were muffled, and the reek of weed and rottenness seemed stronger than ever. Alick pulled a face. 'Yuk!'

The Mere stank. It was always green; a scum of algae lay on the surface like a heavy velvet cloth. It never seemed to break, either – even when you threw a stone in, it was just gulped down without a ripple, and there was no sign of that sudden opening and closing. It was a mouth; it swallowed things. No one in their right minds would go swimming in there.

The boys paused right at the edge.

'Now if I listened to you,' Jamie said slyly, 'I'd be waiting for some slimy hand to come out of that lot, grab me by the ankle, and haul me in.'

Alick laughed, but it wasn't funny. 'Forget the reel. Let's go up the hill,' he said. 'It's worse down here than usual, and darker.'

'Tut-tut. Scared of shadows.'

Alick ignored that. He looked at the trees. The leaves were black and heavy; glossy. Small bright lights glinted among them. He caught Jamie's sleeve.

'Look!' he whispered. 'In the branches!'

The trees were black with birds. Every twig, every branch, bent with their weight; a feathered host, a shadow of wings and beaks and bright eyes. Alick glanced from tree to tree. There were rows of them, sitting perfectly still, looking at him.

Jamie whistled. 'Crows. Where did they all come from?'

'Don't know.' Alick's eyes moved uneasily along the branches. 'Perhaps it's some kind of migration.'

'Crows don't, daft. It's weird.'

The breeze rustled. Black barbs of feathers rose and fell.

Suddenly Alick turned. 'Let's go.'

'They're only birds.' Before Alick could stop him, Jamie picked up a handful of grit and flung it into the Mere with a tremendous splash. 'Go on,' he yelled, waving his arms.

'Clear off! Shoo!' But the birds did not move. Rank on rank they perched, hunched up in the wind.

Jamie backed away. When he spoke again his voice was quieter than usual. 'I don't get this. Let's get out of it.'

They turned, but Alick stopped so suddenly that Jamie slammed into the back of him. 'Hell!' he said.

Across the lake, sunlight was slanting into the trees, lighting up the wood. In the golden glade stood a line of horses, snorting and shifting, their pale manes lifting in the cold wind. One bent its long slender neck to the water, clinking its harness.

And on the golden horses, golden riders.

There were men with long cloaks and tunics to the knee, helmed, with spears slung at their saddles. There were women with long ropes of hair twisted with braid and gold thread; and minstrels with harps; grooms and huntsmen; falconers with their hooded hawks flapping and screeching on their wrists. Between the horses' legs, a pack of slim greyhounds twisted their leashes, growling and snuffling in the bushes.

'Mad,' Jamie muttered. 'That's it. I'm going mad.'

Alick shook his head. 'Then it must be both of us.'

Birds and horsemen eyed each other coldly.

'I'm not going to be scared of this lot.' Jamie thrust both fists into his pockets. 'Just walk slow. Back the way we came.'

'I don't think so.' Alick glanced back at the birds. 'Look at them. The way they're lined up. It's as if they're waiting for a battle. And we're in the middle.'

'Down here then.' Jamie pushed through the bushes at the edge of the Mere. 'We can get through.' The bank began to crumble gently at his feet.

'Be careful.'

'Oh, it's all right.'

Soil slipped and splashed into the water.

And then, in the wood, a horn rang out – an eerie, alarming, shattering of the stillness – and in answer, every bird in the trees opened its wings and screamed!

Jamie turned too quickly, slipped, flung out his arms. For a second he hung on the lip of the lake, then, with an enormous splash, he fell. The birds screeched; water cascaded over Alick's face.

'Jamie!'

The green carpet of the Mere was foaming and boiling. Hands and a face floundered and disappeared, bubbled up again, shouting. Desperate, Alick ran along the edge and yelled at the horsemen.

'He's drowning! For God's sake!'

Silent, unmoving, they stared at him. Their eyes were cold. One horse chewed grass, quietly.

Swearing, Alick tore off coat and boots and gloves. The water was ice round his knees; the mud of the Mere soft and cold around his feet. 'Swim!' he yelled. 'Keep up!' But the white face gasped and turned over and under, and without another thought he threw himself forward and the Mere opened its cold mouth and swallowed him.

After a black second he came up, gasping. The water was a solid weight on his clothes, pulling him down. He kicked towards Jamie; a dark commotion in the ripples somewhere ahead. Blue-lipped, breathless, he forced his arms and legs to move. They were lead weights, the effort to raise them exhausted him. The cold bit him; its teeth pierced through his fingers and bones and lungs. He grabbed at the dark heavy shape in the water, sank, swallowed green scum and vomited it out, caught a glimpse of pale sky far up over the trees.

Then the Mere put its hand over his mouth and dragged him down.

3

The Fidchell

Choking, kicking and struggling, Alick sank into blackness. But the hand held him; a thin, firm hand that heaved him up by his shirt, out of the sucking grip of the water, out into sudden wind and air and an explosion of roaring trees.

Luke dragged and shoved him to the bank. 'Get out,' he commanded. 'Hurry up.'

The birds and the horsemen were gone.

Confused, wet and gashed, Alick stumbled out on to the pine needles and slumped against a tree, gasping for breath in the bitter cold. The conjuror was waist-deep in the water; he had both arms under Jamie's shoulders and was half-dragging him to shore. Slowly they staggered out together and collapsed, breathless.

There was a moment of coughing and spitting and wiping of eyes. Then Alick got his breath. 'We'd have drowned!' he yelled furiously.

'They wouldn't help . . . they just sat there!'

He pushed the wet hair out of his eyes and crouched down, shivering. The conjuror coughed, and the gold of his earring glinted. 'Who did?'

'The horsemen . . . those people . . . riders. And all those birds screaming at us . . .'

'Were they?' Luke looked at them both. 'Then you must have frightened them. Birds don't just scream at people.'

'Ordinary birds don't.' Jamie scraped green algae from his ears. 'These weren't ordinary. They were weird. Gosh, I'm frozen.'

He rubbed his face and arms furiously.

'It was as if they could think,' Alick said firmly. 'Not like birds at all. And who blew the horn? Who were those people?'

Luke stood up and tugged his wet shirt off, then picked up his coat from the floor and flung it on, shivering. Then he whistled. As the white dog came out from the trees, Alick said, 'You must have seen them.'

Luke did not answer. Angry now, Alick persisted. 'Jamie did.'

'Thought I did.'

'You know you did!'

Jamie laughed, despite the cold and the pain in his leg. 'Yes, all right. But I was too busy drowning.'

Alick turned to Luke. 'Did you see them?'

Luke shook his wet hair. 'I think you'd better come home with me. It's too cold to hang about.' And as if he had not heard, he hauled Jamie to his feet and started off with him through the wood.

Thoroughly annoyed, Alick trailed after them. They had seen those people, the horses, the strange gold colour of their clothes. What's more, Luke had seen them too. He must have. So what was going on?

Talley was a small woodman's cottage, among the trees on the north side of Tolbury Tump. It was quite isolated, and only a narrow, overgrown track led down to it from the main road. By the time they reached the house, they were all shaking uncontrollably with the cold, and Alick's clothes stuck to him, wet and stiff with the smelly algae. He was very relieved to see smoke rising from the chimney.

Luke lifted the latch and hurried them in. While they

huddled numbly over the fire, he dragged out some dry logs and tossed them on, stirring the blaze up rapidly; then disappeared into the kitchen. A few minutes later he came back with a huge bowl of steaming water and some dark blue towels.

'Here. Get the worst off – and those wet clothes. I'll see if I've got anything you can wear.'

It was glorious to feel the hot water on their faces and bodies after the icy wind. They got as much of the green scum off as they could, then spread their clothes to dry and sat huddled up in towels next to the blaze. Jamie's ankle was swelling fast. He touched it, gingerly.

'Ouch.'

'Does it hurt?'

'Like hell. My throat is stinging too. I swallowed pints of that muck.'

'And me.' With the stinging of his hands and face, Alick had forgotten his annoyance. 'It'll be a wonder if we're not poisoned.'

'We'll catch something worse at home, anyway. Or I will.' Jamie sighed and wriggled his toes. 'I can just about feel my feet now. Funny sort of place this, isn't it?'

Alick nodded. It was a small, dark room with scraps of rug on the floor and bare rafters above. There was only one window, and the light that filtered in was dim and green from the trees outside. A dresser stood at one end; its shelves and drawers crammed with boxes and jars, dirty dishes, papers, shells, stones, books. Bunches of herbs hung from the ceiling; some were so crisp that their leaves had dropped off and lay crushed on the floor. The windowsill was jammed with dusty books, and muddy wellingtons and a spade leaned by the door. Around the walls hung branches of holly and mistletoe, and a white cat walked along the back of Jamie's chair. It was all rather untidy, but warm and comfortable. Alick liked it.

But Jamie had caught sight of something else. 'Alick,' he said. 'Look at that!'

On a table in the corner was a large black and gold chequered board, and on it was what seemed to be a chess set, but with bigger pieces than Alick had ever seen. And different. The black pieces were made of a dark stone. There were no pawns or bishops. Instead, as he noticed with a shock, there were three rows of hunched black birds with diamonds for eyes, each barb and feather accurately carved. Sightless, they glared at him.

The opposite pieces were the same size, but made out of what seemed like gold, and they glistened with emeralds and rubies and bright enamels. On this side were knights on horseback, ladies, minstrels with harps of jasper. Each was different, frozen in movement, their shields and surcoats blazing with colour; before them a row of greyhounds, cats and twisting serpents. Even the falconer was there, with his hooded hawk.

Jamie whistled. 'It's Them! Just like in the wood. And they must be worth a *fortune*! Real gold, I'll bet . . .'

'They can't be.' Alick stood up, gathered his towel about him, and padded over to the table. He picked up one of the horsemen. 'Gosh, it's heavy though.' Thoughtfully he put it down, and picked up something else. 'I wonder what this is for?'

It was a piece that stood by itself in the middle of the board. A golden tree. Tiny leaves of metal hung from it, and made a quiet, tinkling noise as he raised it. The leaves nearest the gold army were gold, and those on the other side, nearest the black army of birds, were black. He turned it round, and gasped.

'What's up?' Jamie could only see his friend's back.

'Nothing.' Alick stood very still. How could he say what he had seen – that as he had turned the tree, the black leaves were now gold and the gold, black! Was it a trick of the light? No . . . there it was again. No matter how much you turned it round, the gold leaves were always by the gold pieces. 'Come and look at this,' he began, but a growl silenced him.

Luke's dog had come into the room. It growled again, teeth bared.

'Better put it down,' Jamie muttered.

Nervously, Alick's hand moved an inch towards the board. An explosion of barks nearly made him drop the piece.

'Tam! That's enough!'

The conjuror raced down the stairs, pushed the dog aside, then came and took the tree swiftly out of Alick's hand. His six fingers closed around it, tight.

He gave Alick a peculiar look. 'Like it, do you?'

'Yes . . . I was just looking . . .' Alick could feel himself going red. 'It's not chess, is it?'

'Fidchell,' the conjuror said, putting the tree gently back on its central square. 'A very old game. Not played much now.'

And then someone laughed.

Alick looked round, astonished. It hadn't been Luke, or Jamie. The room was dark; there was no one else in it but the dog, watching him with that same smirk it had had in the shop.

'What was that?' Jamie asked.

'Owls. You hear them all the time.' Luke tossed a bundle of clothes carelessly towards them. 'Here, try these. They'll be a bit big, but they're all I've got.'

While they were dressing and giggling at the rolled-up trousers and large shirts, he stood leaning against the table, watching them. Alick felt uneasy. Surely Luke didn't think he'd have stolen that tree? And how were the pieces the same as those people . . . and the birds?

When they were dressed, Luke laughed at them, and strapped Jamie's ankle with a tight, white bandage and some stuff to stop it hurting. Then he gave them a hot drink that wasn't tea or coffee, but whatever it was it drove the cold right out, and Alick suddenly felt warm and glowing to his finger-ends.

While they were drinking it, Luke went out, and when he came back he said he had been down to the telephone box on the road and phoned Jamie's father. 'He'll be here in about five minutes.'

'Thanks. I'd never walk it.'

'Where's the dog?' Alick asked, glancing round.

'Outside.'

Alick was glad. He didn't like it. He kept thinking it was the thing that had laughed.

There was silence for a while. Alick stroked the cat. Jamie was moving his ankle, testing it. Alick noticed Luke's eyes move across the room, from door to stairs, as if he was watching someone cross the room. There was nothing there. Then, upstairs, a door slammed.

At the same time, the conjuror leaned forwards and poked the fire. 'Didn't I tell you yesterday not to go near the Mere?'

Alick was tongue-tied.

'It was my fault.' Jamie put in. 'I lost a reel. Still haven't found it either.'

Luke made no comment. Instead, he said, 'The Mere is a bad spot. There are places like that – places that have a bad effect on animals, and birds, even people. I suppose you do physics at school?'

They nodded.

'Well, there are physical causes for it,' Luke went on, staring into the fire. 'It may be something to do with magnetic forces in the earth. They affect people's nerves, make them ill, uneasy. The Chinese have a science called feng shui – it means they find out these places and then they keep away from them. I advise you to do the same.'

Something's going on, Alick thought. Something queer, that he doesn't want us to know about.

The fire made a row of strange shadows walk down the wall.

'But you live here,' Jamie objected.

'I do.' The conjuror gave him a look that wiped the grin off his face. 'But I'm different.'

Alick glanced at the hands holding the poker. He must have seen them, those riders and those birds – gold and black, like the Fidchell.

But the purr of a car up the track interrupted him. Luke got up abruptly and went to the door. 'It's your father, Jamie. Come on.'

4

The Hollow Hill

When Alick walked into the bookshop ten minutes later, Mr Webster nearly fell off his stool with laughter. 'Where on earth did you get those clothes! Oxfam?'

Alick scowled. 'They're not mine. I fell . . . well, I got wet. In a stream. Your friend Luke lent me these.' And he hauled himself up on the counter and told his father about the strange riders, and the black birds, and Luke, but took care not to mention the Greenmere.

'Talley, eh? I've never been inside,' his father said curiously, filling his pipe. 'What's it like?'

'Scruffy. All right though. All sorts of odd things. That reminds me, how do you play Fidchell?'

'What?'

'Fidchell.'

'Never heard of it.'

'It's a game,' Alick explained. 'Like chess. Luke's got a set. Jamie thought some of the pieces were gold.'

'Gold!' Mr Webster snorted as he put the bolt across the door. 'Oh, I'm sure. I suppose you want a set for Christmas? Gold, my eye!'

While his father laughed and smoked and struggled with the accounts, Alick ran upstairs and changed. He put his wet clothes in the bottom of the basket in the bathroom, hoping his father wouldn't find them. Then he came downstairs and went along the 'Natural History' shelf until he found a good bird book. That was one advantage of living in a bookshop – you had your own library.

He looked up crows. The picture showed two black, rather scruffy birds, but they weren't right. But on the next page was a raven – big, hunched, with a beak like a nutcracker. That was it, ravens. Not crows. But according to the book they were very rare. It was odd. The whole business was odd.

He put it back and looked for something on Fidchell. It was that tree that had fascinated him: he couldn't forget the way the leaves had changed. But none of the books made any mention of the game at all, until finally, in a battered old encyclopaedia without a cover, 50p in the bargain box, he found this:

FIDCHELL (or WOODEN WISDOM)

A board game, probably similar to chess, consisting of two armies of men on a chequered board. Known to have been played by the Celts, this game is mentioned in several ancient texts, and is known to have had magical meaning. No known pieces have been found. The rules are nowhere recorded. Pronunciation: *Fee*-kell.

Puzzled, he asked, 'Dad, how long ago were the Celts?'

'Oh, hundreds of years,' his father said absently. 'Before the Romans. Now don't start reading down here. We're closing.'

Hundred of years. No pieces found. It didn't make sense. Even more puzzled, he put the book back in the box, then took it out.

'Can I keep this?'

'If you want. 50p.'

Jamie telephoned that night. 'My ankle's the size of a

balloon,' he moaned. 'Stay off it till Christmas, the doctor says. *And* I'm having a bike! What's the use if I can't ride it?'

Alick laughed.

'Shut up, heartless. Listen, that Luke character is *weird*!'

'Well, I told you, didn't I!'

'Ah, but I still don't swallow all that about the warts. But those chess pieces, that was uncanny . . .'

Alick nodded. 'He saw them too . . . in the wood, whatever he said. I know he did.'

'Yes. And that means you'll have to find out what's afoot, my trusty sidekick.'

'Me?'

'Well, I can't, can I?' Jamie demanded. 'It's easy. Just watch him. Follow him. Use your brain.' He giggled, 'What there is of it.'

It was when he was crouched behind a tree outside Luke's cottage, and trying to edge his cramped feet into an easier position, that Alick realized that finding things out was cold, uncomfortable and, up to now, boring.

He ate his last-but-one bit of chocolate, and counted the chimes from Halcombe church as they rang out over the tree-tops. Five o'clock. He'd been there an hour already. Around him the forest was dark and silent; far off in the trees, a patch of moonlight showed. And it was getting colder. He thought about his supper, hot in the oven.

Then, the light in Luke's window went out; a figure came down the path, opened the gate, and moved off among the trees. Alick slipped after him, without a sound. Whatever Luke knew, he would find it out.

The moon striped the wood black and silver like a great

badger. Far down the path, Luke's figure glimmered across a patch of light and vanished into darkness again. There was no sign of the dog – which was just as well, Alick thought.

He tried to get a bit closer. It was hard to see in the dappled wood, and if Luke left the path he might miss him altogether. The conjuror was a flicker of movement ahead; he seemed to be heading straight for Tolbury Tump.

Once he was sure of this, Alick could concentrate on keeping quiet. He had cracked two twigs already, and once, Luke had looked back as if he had heard something. Flattened against a beech bole, fingers gripping the smooth cold sides, Alick watched the conjuror turn and walk on. He was more careful after that.

A few minutes later he had a shock. It was starting to snow. Tiny grains floated in the air like scraps of paper; his breath smoked as he walked. By the time they reached the bottom of the Tump and had begun to climb, there was a fine powder underfoot, crunching as he stepped on it. Luke went up the hill and Alick, back in the shadows, wondered why. The path was steeper now, twisting through tree-roots and old rabbit burrows. Finally, he came to the very edge of the trees and looked out.

The top of Tolbury Tump was a grey dome, gleaming faintly with snow. Under the precise silver ring of the moon, Luke was walking up the slope. He came to a small hollow in the hillside, where a few scrubby bushes clung out of the wind, and stopped. He looked around, cautiously. Then he turned aside and went down into the hollow.

There was a ditch along the wood's edge. Alick jumped down into it and squirmed along until he could see between the bushes. Snow swirled in his eyes. Between the flakes he saw Luke stoop. There was a noise. He listened, intently.

Tap. Tap. Tap.

The knock of stone on stone.

More snow. He wiped his eyes. What was Luke doing? and *what was that!*

It was light; bright and golden. As he stared, a great slot of light was swinging slowly open in the hillside, reddening his face and making the falling snow glitter like golden grains.

Then the conjuror stepped inside, and with a click the door was shut.

In the cold moonlight, Alick's breath made a slow cloud. He took the last piece of chocolate from his pocket and ate it, automatically, tasting nothing. Then he crinkled the silver paper. Ideas were flooding into his head. Tugging his feet out of the mud, he watched the moon as, agonizingly slowly, the cloud drifted over it. Now it was a dome, now a fingernail, now a faint line closing up at the edges. As soon as it was gone, he leapt up, ran up the slope and jumped into the hollow. Brambles whipped round him; the hole was full of thorns and scrubby rowan; a steep earth cliff overhung it. The snow was settling, but he groped round till he found a stone, and then crouched down by the one big grey boulder. Brushing the snow away he pulled a glove off and felt the surface: spirals and circles, old zig-zag lines. Then he raised the stone as Luke had done, and knocked.

Tap. Tap. Tap.

The light caught him before he could move; a dazzling slit, widening in the hollow, reddening rowan berries to globes of fire.

Crouching, he turned to face it.

Behind him a small door stood open in the hillside; the light shone out of it. He saw a long tunnel. The walls gave out the light; they glimmered golden, and hundreds of thin, golden pinnacles and pillars upheld the roof. They were not smooth, but twisted and spindly like young trees. Their roots spread over the floor, and they even had stony branches – nets of fruit and leaves on the cavern roof. There was no sign of Luke. Far ahead the tunnel turned a corner.

Alick stood up, bit his lip, and stepped inside.

5

First Move

He was standing in pitch darkness.

Alick swore in surprise; he hadn't even heard the door shut. Carefully he stretched out his hands into emptiness. Then he moved – and crack! his head hit something so hard, the tears jerked into his eyes.

'Damn!' he hissed, clutching his head in both hands. It was the ceiling. It felt cold and knobbly through his gloves. It shouldn't have been so low. Hurriedly, he felt in his pocket, found a box with three matches in, and struck one. Then, shielding the glow, he gazed around.

Slabs of grey stone, and a litter of bones and rubble on the floor. No sign of a door. There were spirals and squiggles carved on the rocks, like the boulder outside. Then the match scorched his fingers. He threw it down, bewildered. Where were the golden pillars? And where was Luke?

'Luke?' he whispered.

Echoes whispered back. He began to move, cautiously. It was difficult, shuffling a few inches at a time, trying not to make any noise on the loose stones, and keeping one hand on the clammy, invisible wall. As he went deeper into the hill it got colder, and the air grew earthy and unpleasant. Then he stopped.

He could hear voices.

They were low, and far ahead, but they were there.

He went on, carefully, and at each twist of the tunnel the murmuring grew louder, until it sounded like a few men talking quietly. One of them must be Luke. Then Alick realized he could see his hand, and the tunnel wall. And round the next bend the tunnel ended.

It was closed by a glimmering, golden curtain that fell to the floor. His hand reached out to it, and had almost touched it, when a sudden uproar of laughing and clapping froze him with terror, his heart thumping loudly and his hands clenched in his gloves.

But no one came through, and the talk went on. Music was playing too; low, subtle and strange, it drew him to the curtain – he could see a few blurred forms through it; the glow and crackle of a fire. He heard chairs being pushed back, and somewhere a door opening and closing. A smell of flowers, an impossible summery smell, wafted out.

Then there was silence.

He waited a few minutes, then carefully reached out and pulled a corner of the curtain aside.

A large hall lay before him, with a fire burning in its centre – the flames were sweet smelling and strangely smokeless. The walls were golden, the floor, chequered with huge squares of black and gold, and the same pillars he had seen in the tunnel held up the roof – their trunks twisted like ice, tinkling with frosty fruits and leaves.

Alick stepped further into the hall. At the far end, he saw three doors, all closed, and in front of them, near the fire, were two chairs facing each other across a small table. There was nothing else.

He padded across the cold floor, feeling snow drip from his shoulders. The table had a board on it. The Fidchell pieces stood there, gleaming gold and black in the firelight.

He was beyond surprise; anything could happen now. Carefully he picked up the tree and turned it. Just as he'd thought – the leaves changed colour. It was inexplicable . . . magical.

Suddenly he noticed something lying on the floor by one of the chairs. It was a fruit, like a cherry, but pure white. He picked it up and smelled it; felt its soft juiciness under his fingers, imagined its sweetness. The next minute he had eaten it.

He knew at once it was a mistake. There was no delicious taste, it was just like water in his mouth – rather sour water too. It made him feel sick. The room looked different, shadowy, in the corners, and he felt dizzy, like the time he had drunk a whole tumbler of his father's port. And there must be something wrong with his eyes, because the Fidchell pieces had all turned their heads and were looking at him; the knights amused, the ladies laughing, the dogs and horses shifting, the black birds in ominous silence. He backed towards the curtain, watching one raven unfurl its wings and stare.

The curtain was a rag of cobweb. He tore it down and plunged into the tunnel, banging and bumping himself in the darkness as the noise rang around him; laughter, low and mocking, cat-calls, whistles, the beat of wings. He ran so fast and so carelessly that he had crashed into the smooth surface of the door before he realized, and it swung open without a sound, spilling him out into the bitter cold of the hollow. Breathless, he crouched, and looked back.

In the distance, down the tunnel, shadows moved. Black, golden, they flickered towards him. He flung himself on the door and heaved, but it stayed open, unmoving – the golden light bathing the rowan bushes – and when the first horn rang faintly in the distance, he turned and fled, leaving it wide.

He crashed to the lip of the hollow, took a deep breath,

and let it out in amazement. He had forgotten the snow! The hillside was a white sheet; the air full of flying patches that muffled the moon. Reckless, he jumped knee-deep into the drifts and struggled for the wood.

Noise pursuing him, he raced along the path, coughing and spluttering. Snow stuck to his hair and eyelashes, branches tripped him; he was sure that his noisy crashing run could be heard for miles. And perhaps he was half a mile down the path before he realized what he had in his hand.

Small and enigmatic, the tree from the Fidchell board shimmered and tinkled. Without stopping, he stared at it, taking in the truth. What an idiot he was! But it was too late to worry about that now. He shoved it into the pocket of his coat, and ran all the faster.

Even so, after ten more minutes he had to slow down, clutching his aching side. He was so breathless and dizzy he hardly recognized where he was before the earth fell away suddenly in front of his feet, and below him the Combe lay silent and leaf-littered in the moonlight.

He slipped and slid and slithered to the bottom. Only then, when the sudden silence fell, did he look up. High overhead, crowding among the trees, a host of shapes gazed down at him. He saw glints of metal and gold; horses and men. And in the branches, the birds.

He said nothing. The horses clinked their harnesses; the rows of eyes did not move from him. Both sides were there, and he knew they wanted that tree. That damned tree.

It was about a mile to the village it might just as well be ten, he thought, bitterly. He tried a step forward and nothing happened. He took another, then yelled in fright and leapt back.

The spear quivered in the leaves by his foot. There was no sign who had thrown it; the dark ranks were silent and unmoving.

Alick rolled his hands into fists. 'Listen!' he shouted, and then stopped, ears catching that new, deep purr behind him. A car!

But the listeners had heard it, too. With a cry and a hiss the thin sinuous shapes of hounds and serpents poured over the lip of the hollow. Alick turned and raced along the lane, waving and shouting as the humming in the air grew. Something grabbed his coat, wrapping round his ankle; in a flurry of leaves he fought and kicked and struggled.

'Alick? Alick Webster?'

Bewildered, he opened his eyes. Snowflakes swirled in the glare of two large headlamps. Someone was leaning out of the car.

'It is you, isn't it? Have you hurt yourself?'

'Er, no. Thanks.' Alick climbed stiffly to his feet and glanced around. The Combe was empty.

'Going home? Hop in then.'

The passenger door jerked open, and Alick slid hastily in and slammed it tight. The warmth of the car, its smell of tobacco and leather, wrapped him like a blanket. The driver switched on the light.

'Hello, Vicar.'

'You're a bit wet,' the vicar remarked, releasing the brake. Alick realized that water was dripping all over the seat.

'Sorry. It's snow.'

'That's all right. Just take your coat off and put it in the back. On top of that big box will do. It's just stuff for decorating the church. That's better.'

It was. Alick felt the warmth prickle his hands and cheeks. The snow had soaked his trousers though, and the tips of his ears ached.

The car droned up the Combe in a flurry of snow. He gazed out of the window, but only saw himself and some flying branches.

'Coming to the Carol Service?'

'Yes . . . probably.'

'Good, good. That's what all those boxes are for, to decorate the little chapel at Ashton Bailey – It'll be there this year as usual – though the place is so old and damp, I wonder how the Lord keeps it up. You've seen the old tombs there? Mind if I drop you here?'

Alick nodded. The street lamps were on in Halcombe, and the bookshop window was bright with red and gold. As they pulled in, the vicar asked, 'How's the coin collection?'

'Oh fine, thanks.'

'You don't want any old halfpennies, do you?'

Alick shrugged. 'If you've got any rare ones . . .'

'Oh, I don't know the dates,' the vicar laughed, fishing Alick's coat out of a box. 'Just found a bag of them in a cupboard. Come and get them sometime. You never know, they might be worth something.'

The light was on over the bookshop. As Alick waited for his father to open the door, he wondered what time it was. And he was half-way up the stairs when he realized the pockets of his coat were empty. He had lost the little tree.

6

Inquisition

'Six ninety-five, please.' Alick pushed the book across the counter and then dropped the money in the till.

'Merry Christmas,' the woman said cheerfully.

Then the shop was empty, the first time that morning. He went over and poked the fire, and fetched more coal. Then he noticed one of the decorations had fallen down, and pinned it up with a drawing pin still bent from last year. Still no customers. He went to the window.

Halcombe High Street was full of shoppers slipping on the snow. Outside most shops it had been scraped away, but some still lay outside the houses and the empty shop, trodden down flat like dirty marzipan. A lorry was gritting the road, and the butcher was putting up a sash saying 'We wish all our Customers the Compliments of the Season.' Alick was wondering what they were, when the shop door opened with a loud jangle and Luke Ferris walked in, glanced around, and flipped the sign over to say 'Closed' in one deft movement.

'Hey! You can't do that!'

'Can't I!' The conjuror's eyes were black and he did not smile. The dog padded to the fire. Luke followed it and warmed his hands.

'Was it you?'

Alick was nervous. 'Was what me?'

'You know very well.'

Alick reddened. 'The shop's open,' he stammered, going to the door and changing the sign. 'Do you want to buy something?'

Luke drew himself up and leaned on the mantelpiece. But just then a young woman with a baby came in and asked Alick for books on Italian cookery. He tried to be polite, showing her the shelf and taking out books, and all the time watching the conjuror from the corner of his eye. Luke did not seem to move, but after a few minutes something changed in the shop. It was mustier, dimmer. Alick counted the girl's change for the third time – the coins seeming to multiply and slither from his suddenly clumsy hands. She smiled, gave him back a pound, and went to the door. The cold draught swirled the strange blue sparks in the fire to a glittering fountain. It was hard to breathe. He leaned on the counter, sleepily.

After a moment, Luke went to the door, locked it, turned the sign, and pulled the blind down on the window. Then he pushed Alick into a chair.

'Can you hear me?' he asked coldly.

Alick nodded. The voice came from a dark blurr standing over him.

'Tell me how you got into the hill.'

'. . . I . . . followed you,' he mumbled.

'Me!' Luke crouched down and clutched the chair arm. 'Last night?'

Somebody tried the door handle. Luke ignored it.

'What did you see?'

Alick didn't answer.

'Tell me!'

'Chairs. A table. A game like yours. And three doors.'

'Did you open any of the doors?' the voice asked softly.

'No.'

'But you took the tree, didn't you?'

Alick nodded, miserable. It was easier to breathe now. His sight was clearing. 'I didn't mean to. I didn't know till later. I suppose I got scared; starting to think those . . . things were after me.'

Luke was watching him carefully. 'So you ate something too. You've been very stupid, Alick. It's a long time since the Fidchell was played. And it's no game.' He drummed his fingers on the table. 'Go and get the tree. We might still have time.'

Alick felt sick. 'I've lost it,' he said.

Luke was silent for at least a minute.

Suddenly scared, Alick tried to explain. 'It might have been in the Combe . . . or in the vicar's car – it must have fallen out of my pocket. Is it . . . that important?'

Luke laughed, harshly. 'Important!' For a moment he seemed lost for words. Then he straightened. 'Alick, by taking the tree you've started the game. Both armies – the Black and the Gold – will be after it, anywhere, wherever it is. They'll spill out into the wood, into the villages, searching, hunting, letting nothing stand in their way.' He stared at the fire. 'Last time it happened here was in 1561.'

'The Black Winter?'

Luke nodded. 'Blizzards, famine, trees falling, unexplained migrations of animals, flooding. Fires, that started for no reason. Dead men, found in ditches. Portents and strange signs in the sky. That's the Fidchell, Alick. And now you've started it again.'

For a moment they were both silent. Then Luke sighed, rummaged in his pockets and brought out a small wax candle, pale green and about an inch high. 'We must find it, that's all. Have you got a mirror?'

'Upstairs.'

'Get it. Tam, go with him.'

The white dog raced up the stairs before Alick. Then it went into the bathroom, jumped on to the bath, and stared into his father's shaving mirror.

'Get down!' Alick snapped – then stared. For a moment he had seen a different face in the glass. A pale, thin, laughing, dangerous face. Then it was just the dog, ears pricked.

He took the mirror downstairs, thoughtfully.

'Your dog's one of them, isn't he?'

Luke laughed. 'What dog?'

A small white cat lay by the fire, washing.

Luke lit the candle and put it in the middle of the mirror. It had an unpleasant smell.

'This may help us,' Luke said. 'Don't speak, and don't touch the mirror.' Then, muttering something, he picked up the candle and poured the hot wax on to the glass.

The small pool was almost white; faint smoke came from it. Alick expected it to go hard, but it didn't. Bubbling and hissing, the film spread. Then he saw things come into it. First, dark, meaningless quivers, then a house, a tree, moon-light glinting on some water. Luke was staring at it, waiting.

Suddenly, the picture changed. Faint and grey as a cobweb, he saw a stone figure of a man, lying on its back. The man's legs were crossed at the ankles. His face was covered in dust. A spider ran over his chest, and a dead leaf gusted by. Then the wax was white and cold and smooth.

'It looked like a tomb.'

'Yes,' Luke said quietly. 'And I think I know where.'

The doorhandle rattled. A loud knocking startled them.

'Alick! Open up!'

36

'It's my father,' Alick said, but Luke pushed him back. 'Wait. Be at my house this afternoon. Two o'clock. Right?'

Alick nodded. 'Yes, but . . .'

The letterbox rattled. 'Alick!'

'Just be there,' Luke went on, shoving the candle into his pocket. 'We've got to sort this thing out.'

'ALICK!'

'Coming!' he yelled, opening the door. Cold bright air struck his face.

'Give us a hand, then.' Mr Webster began to tug in a few heavy boxes. 'It's damn cold out here!' He stalked to the fire. 'And the shop shouldn't be shut yet, and it's as smoky as . . . Oh, hello, Luke.'

'Tom,' said the conjuror, thrusting his hands in his pockets. 'Tam Lin, too.'

'Yes, we just dropped in.'

'His warts haven't come back, you know.'

'They won't.' Luke called the dog and went to the door. 'Merry Christmas to you both.' And with a meaningful glance at Alick, he went out and walked swiftly up the snowy street.

Alick watched him go. 'He's a daunting sort of person, isn't he? Always seems to know much more than you do.'

'Very,' said Mr Webster. 'Alick, isn't this my shaving mirror? And what's this muck all over it?'

7

The Hosting

At ten to twelve, Jamie phoned.

'Listen, Sunshine,' said the testy voice, 'how about visiting a poor invalid? I still exist you know. It's not the Black Death.'

Alick grinned. 'How's the foot?'

'Sore. Why didn't your magician friend give me some magical cure?'

'Perhaps he thought you deserved it.'

'Found anything out?'

Alick thought about it. 'Not really,' he said. 'And if I do, I'll tell you.' He knew just how much Jamie would believe of all this. Nothing.

'That reminds me,' Jamie said. 'Those birds were ravens. Did you hear it on the radio?'

'No. What?'

'About the ravens. A bird-watching chap was talking about them. All sorts of reports they'd had, of these huge black birds. Ouch, my cat's walking on my leg!'

Alick laughed, and promised to go over the next day – Christmas Eve. Then he went thoughtfully back into the sitting room.

His father was sitting by the fire. Large boxes of books were piled by his feet; he was writing prices on the front pages.

'1878,' he remarked. 'First Edition. Very good. Might get fifteen pounds for that. Your dinner's hot, and I got you one of those ghastly sticky things you like, from Thomas's.'

'Good.' Alick sat at the table, picked up his fork and switched the radio on.

'Today has seen the worst blizzard conditions in the west of England for sixteen years,' said a woman's voice briskly. 'Four feet of snow fell overnight in some parts. Roads in the Mendips and Cotswolds are impassable, and helicopters from nearby RAF Arlington have been dropping supplies and fodder to outlying farms . . .'

'Oh, very nice,' Mr Webster muttered. 'Look, Alick, if it's too bad for me to get back tonight, lock up and go to Jamie's, all right?'

Alick nodded. He had forgotten his father was going to the book fair.

'And finally, on a lighter note,' the announcer continued, 'at Halcombe Great Wood, in Gloucestershire, several curious phenomena have been reported. Flocks of large, unidentified birds have invaded farmers' fields, and residents claim to have seen packs of spectral hounds and riders streaming across the sky.'

'Ha!' Mr Webster grinned. 'After closing time!'

Alick said nothing. It's all starting, he thought. He felt rather cold.

'Oh, I saw 'em all right,' said a loud local voice. 'Great white cloudy things, like dogs, like, and horses. Tops of the trees all cracking under them. Streaming down from the Tump they were, and the whole of the wood shaking, and full of wind, and noise . . .'

Mr Webster stared at the radio. 'Sounds like Jacky Harris. I thought he was teetotal.' He poked the fire. 'Well, well. Seen any spectral hounds, Alick?'

'I thought I saw one,' Alick said thoughtfully. 'In your shaving mirror.'

On the way to Luke's he had to pass the vicarage, and on a sudden impulse he knocked at the door. He could have dropped the tree in the car; it would be easy enough to find out.

The door opened with a jerk; the housekeeper glared out. When she saw Alick, her frown cleared. 'Oh, sorry, love. We've had a few queer callers round here this morning.'

She left him in a big room with lots of bookshelves and potted plants. A clock ticked in one corner. Alick sat on the edge of the settee and twisted his scarf, nervously. Out in the snowy graveyard a black bird landed on a tombstone. He looked at it suspiciously. Was it one of *Them*?

The door opened.

'Alick!' the vicar said, dumping a pile of books on the piano. 'I thought it might be you. Now let me see, where did I put it . . .'

For a glorious moment, Alick thought he meant the tree, but the vicar dumped a small plastic bag on to the table. Coins spilled and rattled and rolled.

'There. Anything interesting?'

Alick swallowed his disappointment and sorted through the coins. 'The Maundy sixpence is nice – early, and almost mint, too. Most of the halfpennies I've got . . . um, and halfcrowns. None of it's worth much, I'm afraid.'

'Never mind,' said the vicar. He smiled nostalgically as Alick gathered up the coins. 'Used to collect moths myself, at one time. Had to stop though; takes up too much room – all those cabinets and boxes. Display yours, do you?'

Alick nodded. 'I've got a room upstairs.'

'Ah! Big old house.'

Alick buttoned his coat slowly. 'Um, there was one thing

I wanted to ask. I think I may have dropped something in your car. A little tree . . . a piece from a game.'

'Tree? Can't say I've seen it. Come on, we'll go and look.'

The car door was open. The vicar stared at it. 'Damn it! I locked that . . . someone's been in here.'

Hurriedly, he checked his car radio and glove box. 'Nothing gone though. You look for your tree, and I'll go and ask Mrs Hughes . . .' Still talking, he went back up the drive. Alick dived into the car and scrabbled under the seats, then ran his hand down gaps and crannies. Nothing. Nothing but a few golden hairs, strangely stiff and bright. He was wondering about them when the vicar came back.

'She didn't open it. Says there've been people hanging about the place though. Strangers. Still, no harm. Did you find it?'

'No.'

'It may have fallen in the boxes.' The vicar closed the door. 'I've taken them over to Ashton Bailey chapel. You're welcome to look.'

Ashton Bailey. Famous for its tombs. Stone knights, crusaders. Like the picture in Luke's mirror. 'Thanks,' Alick said, starting up the drive. 'I will.'

Twenty minutes later he was standing in Luke's house.

'They've moved!'

Luke nodded, both hands leaning on the corners of the table. On the Fidchell board the pieces were scattered, black and gold, in a confused huddle. Some had fallen over. Alick wanted to pick them up, but Luke warned him not to touch them. He was studying their positions carefully.

'I should say,' he murmured, 'that they've got the scent. See how they are gathering together?'

'You talk as if they move themselves.'

'And so they do. Not that you ever see it, however long you look. See what I mean.' He pointed to a golden knight. Alick blinked. A minute ago it had been on the other side of the board.

'So . . . who decides the moves?'

'They do. There are two players,' Luke said, 'but they can only watch. That's their fate. The game cannot be stopped till one side or other gets the tree, or . . .' he put his thin extra finger on the empty square in the centre of the board, '. . . or we put it back here. Then the board will be balanced.'

'Your tree has gone, too.'

'There is only one tree.'

Alick frowned over that. 'But I saw two. One here and one on the other board.'

Luke shrugged. 'You may have. But there is only one, and that is the one you took. This board,' he waved a hand at it, 'and the other two like it, merely show us what happens. The board in the hill is, if you like, the master board, the real game.'

'So there are two others?'

'Only three left in the world; each guarded.'

'By whom?'

Luke smiled slowly. 'And wouldn't you like to know! By others like me, those that are half of one world and half of another.' He looked closely at Alick. 'You must have guessed?'

Alick shrugged. 'I suppose so. You mean . . .' he struggled for words, 'you're related to Them?'

The conjuror grinned. 'Sort of. We have strange blood in our family. But we must get on.' He went to a drawer in the dresser and pulled out a small round box, like the one the ointment had been in. He threw it to Alick. 'Here. This is only for emergencies. Don't open it unless you absolutely can't do anything else. I'll have this.' He put a thin wand of peeled hazel in his pocket. 'I've been working on it all night. It will have the power to scatter Them over the board, and they'll take time to regroup. It may help.'

Alick pocketed the box and watched the conjuror wind a scarf round his neck. Then he said, 'I've been to the vicar's. The tree isn't there, but I found these.'

Luke took the hairs and held them up to the light. 'Well. This means they're ahead of us.'

'It's at Ashton Bailey, isn't it?'

Luke nodded. 'Now don't say too much when we get outside. The wood is full of movement; we're bound to be watched.'

Rather unhappily, Alick followed him out into the snow, the slam of the door echoing ominously in his ears. They took a short cut through a thick larch plantation that would bring them out on to the main road beyond the village. It took only ten minutes steady walking for Alick to feel uneasy. He glanced around.

'Oh, they're here all right,' Luke muttered. 'Since we left the house.'

Alick couldn't see anything, but he believed it. They began to hurry. The going was wet and difficult, the path some-times clear and sometimes blocked by drifts as high as Alick's knees. And it got dark. The darkness closed in – it seemed to ooze out of the trees, so thick that it seemed Luke was forcing his way through a black, solid resistance. The branches creaked and swished, invisible above their heads.

The feeling of oppression, of hidden watchers, was getting on Alick's nerves. 'How far to the Cross?'

'About ten minutes.' Luke sounded worried. 'I didn't think they'd start so soon. Keep close, and don't look behind you. *Don't!* Understand?'

He nodded. But from the corners of his eyes he could already see the shadows moving with them, just out of sight, like reflections that move and flicker in a grimy mirror. And then he began to feel it – the soft touching on his shoulders, a light tapping, something brushing his hair, soft and cold and clinking. He was shivering and couldn't stop.

'Luke . . .'

The conjuror stopped, clenched his fists, then turned around. He looked straight over Alick's shoulder, staring at whatever was there, calmly. At once Alick felt the coldness loosen from his neck. Something backed away.

'Further,' Luke said.

A rustle.

'Get in front of me, Alick,' Luke said quietly, and he obeyed, keeping his eyes firmly ahead.

It was an incredible relief to have Luke behind him, but as they went on, the snow splashed in his face, and he didn't know the path. Luke muttered instructions, but Alick kept his eyes ahead. Finally, the trees ended. They stepped out on to the road at Halcombe Cross.

Gaunt, misshapen, the finger of stone marked the heart of the wood. It was old, it had been a trysting-place, a market, a gallows, but the original purpose was long forgotten. Strange marks and carvings adorned it; a rough cross, and under that, pagan rings and spirals and letters from forgotten alphabets.

Alick leaned on it, breathing hard.

'Don't stop,' Luke warned.

The roads were deserted, already thick with snow. On the modern fingerpost a bird was perched, black and silent.

'Come on!' Grabbing his elbow the conjuror strode with him roughly down the road towards Ashton. Alick gasped for breath, but Luke would not slow down, and he constantly glanced over his shoulder.

And then Alick knew why. The certainty came in the silence and tension of the forest. A great host was moving after them down the white road; a crowd of shapes, creaking, and rustling and padding. Their shadows, long and black, stretched out before him. Fingers touched him again, icy coldness closing at his neck.

Suddenly, Luke shoved him ahead and whirled round on his enemies. Surprised, Alick stumbled and fell his length in the wet snow, and at once the road was aflame with an astounding brilliance and a rumbling and roaring that rang in the trees around him. He jerked his head.

Two huge white eyes roared through a torn mist. Luke stood before them, his figure small and dark, half lost in the eerie swirling smoke and the dark bulk screeching down on him.

Then the lorry swerved. With a scream of brakes it careered past them down the road and slithered to a stop.

The cab door was flung open and a head poked out. '*What* the 'ell do you think you're doing, mate?'

Luke grabbed Alick's arm and hauled him towards the lorry. Mist snaked after them.

'You drunk or something?' the driver asked, seeing them loom up in the dimness.

'No. Listen, can you give us a lift along the road? To Ashton?'

The man laughed. 'It's barely five minutes walk!'

'I know. Will you?'

'Oh, all right. Get in round the other side.'

As he climbed up the step, Alick glanced back. Something misty hung there, hardly visible. In the cab the radio was playing loudly. The driver whistled the tune cheerfully through his teeth. With a great hiss and shudder the lorry started. He changed gear noisily.

'Could've been killed, in the road like that!' he yelled above the music. 'Snow, patchy fog. Dangerous!'

Luke nodded. His face was pale; his fingers deep in pockets.

The lorry dropped them half a mile further on. When it had roared away, Alick looked at the conjuror.

'Are you all right?'

'Quite.' Luke climbed the fence. 'But we'll have to take more care. I can see how they're moving. With me out of the way, you'd be on your own, and easy prey for them.'

Alick didn't like the thought of that at all.

8

Ashton Bailey

Along the road ran a metal fence, old-fashioned and bent. Luke jumped over and began to push through the undergrowth. Alick followed, getting snow flicked all over him from the springy branches. Soon they stepped out on to a track, very straight, running into dimness. The trees above were thick and black, and withered grass poked up between frozen puddles.

'Gloomy,' Alick muttered.

Luke crossed the track and tugged ivy from what seemed to be a rock. Half smothered in the leaves was a standing stone.

'There's another,' Alick pointed ahead. 'And one over there. It's an avenue.'

'It is. This will help them; it's their sort of place.'

The weight of oppression, of being watched, had lifted from Alick. He felt careless of danger.

'Feng shui,' he said suddenly.

Luke laughed. 'Yes. A lot of good trying to tell you that, though. You and your sceptical friend!'

'Oh, Jamie's all right.' He stopped, struck by a thought. 'You made his leg worse, didn't you? On purpose!'

Luke had the grace to look confused. 'Well, a bit. Not much, though. I wanted him out of the way. Stupid of me, but I thought he might be the one to go poking his nose into things. How wrong can you get.'

Alick thought about that for a while. Then he said, 'I've always thought . . . the wood has more in it, than you can see. It's a special place.'

'It's Their place, Alick. The wood is a web of danger. We're just trespassers.'

'Like that man who drowned?'

Luke sighed, and was silent. Ice splintered under their feet. Then he said, 'I was too late that day.'

As they walked on, it grew darker. Waxy laurels sprouted on each side, their berries black and poisonous. The ditch stank of fungi and stagnation. Alick pulled the scarf over his nose in disgust, and then noticed the small square tower ahead.

'There's one thing in our favour,' Luke said, blowing on his cold fingers. 'The church.'

The gate clanged noisily behind them. Alick followed the conjuror up the path and stood close behind as Luke turned the great round handle. The door rumbled, and swung slowly open.

The chapel was quiet and empty. Bunches of fresh holly and mistletoe were piled in the middle of the floor, and next to them three large boxes that Alick recognized from the vicar's car. There were no benches; the church was derelict, and only used for the candlelight carol service on Christmas Eve – a tradition that went back to medieval times. It was bitterly cold. The famous tombs, with their figures of knights and ladies, lay under a coating of frost.

Luke went in, snow swirling behind him. 'Come on.'

He tipped the contents of the first box out, and began sifting through them. Echoes ran around the walls. Alick opened the next. Candles, hymn-books, hassocks and papers, jammed together, damp to the touch. It was as he tugged a sheaf of papers out that he heard it, the tiny, melodious tinkle.

'It's here!' He groped about at the bottom, and, with a laugh that rang in the roof, grasped the edge of a stone tomb and hauled himself to his feet, the gold and black tree glittering in his hand.

Luke sat back on his heels. He looked relieved.

Then Alick gasped, jerked his head. The stone hand of the knight on the tomb had closed around his wrist.

'Luke!'

'Be quiet!' The conjuror was already there. The knight lay on its slab, eyes closed. It was stone. Its hands were stone. This was impossible.

'It's holding me! I can't get out!'

'Quiet!' Feverishly the conjuror searched his pockets. Then suddenly he turned around.

'What's the matter?'

Luke ignored him. 'Show yourselves!' he said to the empty chapel. Nothing seemed different. But now there was a shadow outside the windows; a mass of shadows.

Luke took a step forward. He had the hazel wand in his hand. 'There's been a mistake,' he said quietly. 'You should go back. The game is over.'

'The game is just begun.'

Alick jumped. The whisper had come echoing round the walls.

'No.' Luke's eyes travelled round the room, as if he saw things Alick could not.

'Friend, it begins here.'

A rustle in the corner. Alick twisted, shouted, the door slammed open. In a whirlwind of dust and leaves, a cascade of black and gold shapes arched over them, hung, crashed down.

'Luke!' Alick squirmed in the stone grip. Stones and leaves fell on him, stuck to his hands and face, knocked him to his knees. Arms over head he clung to the effigy, hand-cuffed in stone, under the uproar of wind and dust. Luke reeled backwards – was slammed to the floor – but as he fell he raised the wand and swept it before him. Vivid white sparks stung Alick's eyes.

It ended as quickly as it had begun.

When he was ready, Alick uncovered his face. Dust and dead leaves coated the floor, and rose in clouds from his clothes. Luke was lying by an overturned box.

'Luke!'

The conjuror was still, crooked. Alick knew he would not answer. Fiercely he tugged at the stone hand. 'Let me go, damn it!' The tree was in his pocket. What if they came back for it now? But no. He had time.

Then he saw the white rod. Luke must have dropped it – it lay on the floor nearby. However he stretched, his hand couldn't reach it . . . but perhaps with his foot?

He pushed himself as far out from the tomb as he could, stretched towards the stick. Inch by inch his foot strained for it; cramps attacked his toes, the stone grip seared his skin. Another inch – and he touched. Would it roll away? Painfully, he rolled the wand, dragged it, scooped it in, until it was close enough to pick up.

A peeled hazel stick, white and thin. Now he had got it, he didn't know what to do with it. How did it work? He touched the stone glove with one end. Nothing happened. Tugging was no use; his wrist was sore and bleeding from that. A stone. Get a stone and smash it. Putting the stick in his trapped hand he bent down to fumble for a broken tile

– and fell over! It had let him go! Or rather, he thought, rubbing his aching wrist, he had gone through it as if it was sand.

He turned to Luke. The conjuror's eyes were closed, his forehead lay on the stone floor. He was cold, and shaking his shoulder had no result. Alick bit his lip. His fingers felt the conjuror's pulse. He didn't even know if it was fast or slow. That first aid class, he thought. Sat at the back and talked. What a fool.

He would have to go for help. Cautiously, he went to the door. Outside it was snowing again. The wood was a web of white driven flakes. He was on his own. They'd got what They wanted.

Alick went back. 'Please, Luke! Wake up!' No use. He didn't seem hurt, perhaps it was some sort of spell. Finally, Alick found a pencil and a scrap of paper, wrote 'Gone for help' and pushed it under the conjuror's cold fingers.

When he turned, the white dog was sitting in the doorway. It padded softly past him and sat down, then looked at him. 'Tell him I've gone on,' Alick said suddenly. The dog lay down, chin on paws. He felt stupid, and yet . . . 'I'll take care of the tree. Look after Luke.' Then he marched out into the snow, pulling the door behind him. After about ten steps, he remembered that the hazel twig was still in his pocket. Should he leave it? No. After all, They were probably still about.

Plunging hands in pockets, he began to plough up the long avenue. Gloom seeped into him with the cold and the wet. What a mess. Where was he to go? What should he do? Ahead, the standing stones began, a tall one loomed at the side of the track and a shorter one leaned opposite it. Among the flung blurs of snow, their edges seemed like faces, hook-nosed, gaunt. After a moment's consideration, Alick stepped off the track and plunged into the wood.

9

The Oak Tree

He had once been a Boy Scout for two years – he knew all about compasses and guiding yourself by the stars and blazing your trail. Despite that, in ten minutes he was totally lost. Everything was black and white, straight trees and flying snow; the sky, when he glimpsed it, a horrible dead yellow. The blizzard was almost horizontal, blinding him, soaking the front of his clothes and numbing his face and hands. He had tried to cut marks in the trees with his latchkey, but it was useless. Stumbling, he struggled on. If he kept this way he was sure to get back to the road, sure to.

The snow lay in humps and hollows; often he sank knee-deep in drifts. Blackthorn and bramble spread nets to tangle him. At one point the snow suddenly collapsed. He found himself gasping ankle-deep in an ice cold stream, and as he jerked his hands out of his pockets to balance himself, the white stick fell out and into the water. Wordless, he watched it float swiftly away.

On the bank he wrung out his socks, stamped about to get his feet warm, and put the tree in his shirt pocket inside his pullover. As he moved it, the tiny leaves tinkled, and he closed his hand over it quickly. For a second he had sensed the wood listening. The sudden silence was enormous. All around him, nothing for miles and miles but the trees, their humps and hollows, their boughs and boles and branches. He was all alone in it, and small.

It was then he heard the bang. Not very far ahead. Familiar. Normal. It took him a second to pin it down. A car door, slamming. After a second's astonishment he shouldered through the snowy bushes to his right and almost fell out on to a narrow gravel track. There in front of him, solid stone and with a warm comfortable light in its windows, was the last thing he had ever expected to see – a pub.

Where on earth was he?

Puzzled, he limped through the car park and stopped under the sign.

It creaked and swung under its coating of ice. The Oak Tree. He really must be lost. Still, he thought thankfully, they're bound to have a telephone or something.

He made his way round to the front and peered in through the window, rubbing snow from the glass. There were only about nine or ten people inside, most at the bar or sitting down, two playing darts. Boldly, he pushed the door open and went in.

The smell of beer and cigarettes struck him, and the drowsy, airless warmth of a hot room. Heads turned. He felt suddenly small, and wet and scruffy.

'Well! What happened to you!' The barmaid laughed and put down her cloth.

Alick felt the snow slide off his boots. 'I'm sorry,' he muttered.

'*And* you're under age.' She winked at a man at the bar.

'I haven't come in for a drink.'

The customers chortled. 'Don't mind her, son,' one of them said. 'She's just kidding you.'

Alick smiled, uncomfortably. He went up to the bar, hoping they'd stop staring at him and carry on their talk.

'How far am I from Halcombe?' he asked quietly.

'About four miles.'

He groaned, silently. 'Have you got a phone?'

'I'm sorry, my love,' the barmaid said. 'It's out of order. Snow, I expect. We're waiting for the engineer.'

He might have known. Nothing was going right – perhaps 'They' had even pulled the lines down. He had hoped to get help for Luke, but now he saw he was on his own.

He must have looked as dejected as he felt.

'Come over and sit by the fire, love,' the girl was saying. 'You're wet through. Take your coat off and have a nice hot cup of tea.'

He shouldn't stop; he ought not to waste time. And yet . . . After a second's hesitation, he pulled off his gloves and undid the wet thongs of his duffel coat. He needn't stay long; just to get warm.

He gave her the coat and wandered across the room to the fire. There was a comfortable armchair next to it, but he did not sit down. Better not get too cosy. As he warmed his face and hands, he thought hard. Luke had said the tree had to go back on the board – presumably that meant to Tolbury Tump. He must be six miles or more from there. In the snow and growing darkness, it would take him hours – even if he got to the road it would be choked with snow-drifts by now. Traffic must have all but stopped. Well, at least that meant his father would have to stay in Gloucester . . . if only he didn't phone Jamie's house!

Alick sighed. He would have to walk to the Tump – there was no other way. He was beginning to wish he had stayed with Luke.

The fireplace was wooden, carved with old twisting snakes and stems. Above it, a large mirror reflected the room. He looked up at it. The barmaid was hanging up his coat on a peg by the door. And as he watched he was sure he saw her hand slip out of his pocket. She hung the coat up, and went into the kitchen.

Despite the fire, he felt cold. The tree, small and hard, was in his shirt pocket; he could feel it against his chest. Was that what she was looking for?

Some of the customers were looking at him; two men at the bar. They had hard, black eyes, and high, hooked noses; somehow familiar. They leaned easily on the bar, but did not drink. They pretended to talk, but their eyes were on him. The hairs on the back of his hands bristled with tension. He knew now. 'They' were here! He wasn't certain how many, but they were here all right; watching.

A few more men came in, laughing, and went to the bar. Some dogs slipped in behind them. If the roads were blocked, how did they all get out here? Sixteen, seventeen now. Was it all of them? The fire crackled cheerfully. Steam rose from his damp knees.

'Now then, how about some tea?'

The barmaid was at his elbow, with a tray. On it was a large mug of steaming liquid and a plate of cakes – small sponge cakes with buttery icing.

'How much will it cost?'

'Oh, never mind that,' she said. 'Go and sit down . . . sit in that armchair there by the fire.' She nodded at the big chair with its soft, enticing cushions. He sighed, thought, Why not? and was about to step towards it when he glanced in the mirror.

Every eye in the room was on him.

The drinkers were not drinking, talk had died, the dart players had forgotten their game. Even the landlord was leaning on the bar, studying him.

'Go on,' said the girl, impatiently. 'What's the matter?'

56

He looked at her. Her eyes were black, bird-like. Something bright sparkled in her hair.

'Sit down!' she commanded.

Suddenly, overwhelmingly, fear washed over him. He could not move – No! Keep still, think! Knight, minstrel, king, lady and bird; they were all here. From the corner of his eye he saw the carved serpents on the fireplace rustle. He did the only thing he could think of; plunged his hand in his pocket and brought out the conjuror's box.

At once the girl dropped her tray and grabbed at him with a scream. The men at the bar leapt from their stools and flung themselves forward. But the lid was off.

It was dark, and cold. Snow settled slowly on his pullover. He was standing six inches from the edge of a sheer cliff. It plummeted down into the forest, bushes springing out from its side. As he stood there, a rock slipped and bounced, crashing down endlessly into emptiness. One more step, that's all it would have needed. One more step . . .

Ten minutes later he realized he was sitting on a stone in the snow, staring stupidly at nothing. Shock. He had to pull himself together. Getting up, he stamped about, shivering. The box was still in his hand. It was empty, but the inside was coated with black powder, like soot. He touched it gently, then realized that the stuff was all over his hands and clothes, and was blowing about in the wind. Black smudges darkened the snow.

He put the lid back on and put it in his pocket, then washed his face and hands with snow, rubbing vigorously until his skin tingled. His coat and scarf hung on a bush. He pulled them on and gazed around.

It was a small clearing in the wood, that was all. Where the door had been was a crushed trail of nettles. The whole thing, pub, fire, chair, had been an illusion, made for him. One more step and he would be lying down there now, badly injured if not worse, and those Things pawing him for the tree. No wonder Luke had been worried.

He began to march in what he hoped was the right direction. Things were bad – he must hurry. They knew where he was, but he was hopelessly lost, and had used up Luke's box. He was also cold, tired, and hungry – the memory of those cakes was a torment. And it was almost dark. He *had* to find the road.

An hour later, leaning on a tree-trunk to catch his breath, he knew he could not do it. The wood, they said, had twenty million trees, and he was blundering further and further into the middle of it. Down here among the aisles of trunks, the snow lay in drifts; dark branches overhead hid the stars. And the silence was the worst – the unbroken winter stillness. As he moved on, even his footsteps were muffled. The snow stopped, then began to freeze slowly on the ground. He was walking into trees now, and bushes, it was so dark, and the tiny threads of path led him nowhere. Worst of all, he began to imagine he was walking in circles; was sure he recognized trees he had passed ten minutes ago. Trees, trees, trees.

Until he saw the light.

Yes! There it was! Ahead of him, a little way off to the left.

A warm, red light, flickering.

But Alick was wary. Once bitten . . . he thought, and stood still in the silence, watching it. When he moved at last, it was as slowly and quietly as he could, slipping from tree to tree without a rustle in the wet undergrowth. Soon he was close enough to see.

It was a fire. From behind a thick holly bush he took a good look. The fire lit a small clearing. In the centre of the clearing was an ancient oak stump, rotten and hollow, with a great gash down its side. For five minutes he watched the flames burn and nothing stirred – finally he crept out and warmed his hands. It might be a tramp's fire. A tramp would be a relief.

Then he noticed the tracks, trampled in the snow around the oak stump. A dog's? Or a fox? He got down on hands and knees and looked closer. The crack in the tree was wide. He slipped his head in and waited to get used to the blackness. He saw the outline of a heap of straw, a huddle of what looked like fur. And then the voice spoke, close by his ear in the darkness.

'I've been waiting for you, Alick Webster,' it said.

10

Tod-lowery

Alick froze.

The bundle of furs twitched, stretched out a long thin arm, and grabbed the end of his scarf as it dangled on the floor.

'Come in, sonny. I don't bite – much.'

Tugged suddenly forward, he fell on his hands and knees into the hollow tree, and the bright light of the fire flooded in behind him. It showed a thin weaselly face, straggly hair, rusty whiskers. The creature hugged its knees with bony arms, and the fingers that held his scarf had sharp nails and were covered with short, reddish hair.

'Got the tree?' it asked casually, turning its head sideways and laying it on its knees.

Alick nodded, speechless.

The creature grinned, showing sharp white teeth. 'Good.'

There was nothing else to do. Alick crawled in and leaned back against the damp bark. The tree was dingy and smelt of wet fur and leaves.

'Tod-lowery,' the thing said, with a wink of one eye. 'That's what you call me. Chicken?'

'What?'

'Chicken. From a farm over Minsterworth way. A bit stringy, but chewable.'

Bewildered, Alick watched the creature fish something out from a corner. It was a chicken leg, badly singed.

'I don't usually bother myself, but I thought you might not like it raw. Take it then!'

Alick took it, rather unwilling.

'Eat it,' the Tod said slyly. 'It's real enough.'

It was. And delicious, since he hadn't eaten for what seemed hours – *was* hours, by now. As he chewed, he watched the creature and the creature watched him.

Finally, he tossed the bone outside and licked his fingers. 'Thanks.'

'And now, a drink.'

It was a murky-looking liquid, in a carved wooden cup. Dubious, he sipped and felt the warmth spread through his chest. As he downed the rest he tried to remember where he had tasted it before, and as he put the cup down it came to him. At Talley. It was the same stuff.

'Now,' the Tod said, 'we can speak. Tell me how you got it.'

'Got what?'

It smiled. 'The Fidchell tree, my innocent.'

The narrow eyes shone in the firelight. Whoever it was, it knew too much already. To his surprise Alick found himself unafraid. He explained how he had gone into Tolbury Tump.

The Tod nodded wisely. 'And on that day of all days. So you're the one who started it – the Fidchell.'

'You know about that?'

'Everybody does. It happens.' Seeing Alick was uneasy, it grinned, and wrapped long bony arms around its knees. 'But not for a long time now. *What* a naughty boy we've been. No wonder there's all this fuss.'

'Fuss?'

'Out there.' It nodded towards the opening. 'The wood is alive with them; swarming, like a tipped-up hive. I've heard there's been no end of trouble already.'

'It's not fair!' Alick said suddenly.

The Tod looked surprised. 'That's the game, sonny. Gold and black, sunshine and shadow. They have to be in balance.'

'And who are the players?'

The weaselly face turned sideways. 'So you don't know that either. We are innocent, aren't we? Well then, long ago, little cub, two kings played Fidchell. They played it in an iron-grey fortress, while outside their two armies tore each other to pieces. It was a battle they could have stopped, but neither of them would lose the game.'

Alick stared. 'So what happened?'

'It's said that their punishment for causing all those deaths is that they must play Fidchell until Doomsday, and only on one night in a hundred can they leave the board. Which, I suppose, is where you came in!'

'So they move the pieces?'

'Oh no. Nothing's that simple.' The Tod winked slyly. 'The Fidchell armies play their own game; the players must sit, and watch, and suffer, and not a finger can they raise to help – whatever happens.' He hugged himself gleefully. 'They'll be in a fine state watching this.'

'So am I,' Alick thought. 'What about you?' he asked aloud. 'Aren't you in it?'

'Ah, well, I'm just me. I keep out of it, no one bothers me.' He licked his sharp white teeth. 'Just as well.'

A gust of wind crackled the flames. The Tod's nose wrinkled. 'You smell of wizardry,' it said slowly.

Alick remembered the box. 'I can't smell anything.'

'But I can. What is it?'

He took the box out of his pocket, but kept hold of it.

'And who gave you that?'

'A conjuror.'

The Tod-lowery narrowed its eyes. 'Ah! That'll be the sorcerer at Talley.'

'I thought you might know Luke!'

'I know him.' The Tod grinned. 'And he knows me.'

Perhaps it wasn't such good news. Still, Alick explained about the attack in the ruined chapel.

'Oh, he'll not be hurt, not that one. He'll be about by now.'

'Can you help me to find him? Or to get to Tolbury? I'll never get through by myself.'

'Well now,' the creature scratched idly, 'I might.'

Suddenly Alick wondered if it could be trusted. After that business at the pub he should be much more wary. He put the box away.

'Forget it. I'll go myself.'

'The last one who tried that,' the Tod said casually, 'didn't get far. I found him hanging on a tree, not ten paces from where I left him. Not a pretty sight. Bloody as a dead fox.'

It pulled a flea out of one ear and cracked it.

Alick fidgeted. Then he said, 'Can we start now?'

'No,' the Tod shook its head. 'We'll wait for the moon. They're more than a handful in the dark. You go to sleep now over there. I'll call you.'

Its white teeth glittered. After a moment, Alick shuffled down into the straw. He felt tired, but didn't want to sleep; he wanted to get it all over. But the Tod was in no hurry. It lay down again, yawning and scratching and fidgeting itself, into a comfortable hollow. 'Can I ask you something?' Alick said after a long while.

'Surely.'

'Well, all the time we've been here, you haven't put a bit of wood on that fire, and it's as bright as ever. There's no smoke, either. And how did you know my name?'

But the Tod turned over, and began to snore.

Alick sighed. He hadn't really expected an answer. Through the crack in the tree he could see the snow, falling softly again, smoothing out his footprints. He had lost all count of time; it must be late, after midnight. Where was Luke by now? Was he out there in the wood, or in Halcombe, banging on the bookshop door? Or was he still lying in the cold chapel? Wondering, Alick fell asleep.

When he woke, the Tod-lowery was gone and the fire was out. A wand of moonlight came down through the branches. He sat up, stiff with cold, and felt anxiously for the tree. It was still there, chiming faintly under his fingers. Outside, something howled, long and melancholy. A fox, he thought. After a while it stopped. Then, in the silence, he heard paddings and rustlings in the wood.

He crouched, warily, watching the crack of darkness. Now he could distinguish the sound of hooves; a low thudding in the leaves, that grew louder and closer. The clinking of harnesses began to fill the clearing. Silent, his hands and knees deep in the straw, he watched them pass the crack in the tree; the pale hooves of the horses gleaming in a strange light, the paws of dogs padding past. Someone was playing a harp. The soft notes tugged at him, but he sat still, hardly breathing, every hair and muscle stiff with dread.

It took them at least five minutes to pass – all that silent, jingling troop – and once, to his dismay, a golden dog put its nose to the tree and sniffed, so that the hair prickled on

his scalp; but it padded on, and the whole glinting, shimmering army rustled away into silence.

After a few minutes he looked out. The Tod was standing
in the glade, a lean shadow. As Alick crawled out he saw the
wood was made of black columns rising from a white carpet.
And far above the branches, like gems in a net, shone the
brilliant frosty stars of December.

'Ready?' The Tod held out a hand – almost a paw, Alick
thought – and helped him up. 'Right. That was too close.
Now we go my ways, and very odd ways you'll find them.
Don't say a word . . . not for anything. If you see anything
more of Them, give me a poke in the back, but doubtless
I'll have seen them before you. Remember, not a whisper!'

'But where are we going?'

The Tod glared. 'That's a daft remark. Tolbury, where else?'

'Luke might need help.'

'You need help!' The Tod grinned. 'Luke can look after
himself. He's had plenty of practice. Come on.'

It was a journey Alick never forgot. They walked for hours,
under great plantations of trees, in a black and white world.
The Tod loped ahead, squeezing through gaps in bushes and
under sharp, overhanging rocks, climbing over scree or
following invisible threads of paths through the hummocky
snow. Often they crossed small streams that had frozen into
ice; underfoot the glassy slabs splintered; and bubbles of
trapped air slid and creaked.

Many things paused to watch them go by. Badgers, snuffling in the undergrowth; a startled deer; a white owl that
twisted its head silently as they passed. The Tod winked at
it and it flew off, hoo-hooing gently. And there was a woman,
dressed in green who came up to them suddenly out of the

trees and spoke a few low words to the Tod. As she passed beside him, Alick shivered at the iciness and the cold sweet smell that hung about her. But he was careful not to ask any questions. When they went on again the Tod grinned at him strangely, eyes and teeth a-glitter in the moonlight.

After that things grew confused. Alick lost himself; walked in a dream or a spell, vaguely aware of wading chest-high through snow (or was it leaves?), of entering tunnels and moving through holes – dark narrow holes littered with branches and rubble and insects that were too large. Size and shape seemed to change; sometimes he was sure the trees were miles above him, bushes were like forests about him, or that he was bent over, long and lean and running on hands and feet. Glimpses of his own hands showed them strange, unfamiliar. Once, at the end of a long ride of oak trees, he saw a dark bird flap ahead of them; its feathers brushed a scatter of snow from the branches. He tapped the Tod and pointed, but the Tod just laughed and shook its head.

Finally, they came to the end of the trees. With a rush, recognition came back to him, and he straightened, easing a strange ache in his back. He knew now where they were. Before him the moonlit fields dipped to the railway line where it ran deep in its cutting into the great tunnel under Corsham Chase. Beyond that, somewhere in the wood, was the Greenmere, and the bald dome of Tolbury Tump.

'Right,' said the Tod. 'You can talk now. We have to cross the field and the silver lines, and this is the hard part, for I have no power once out of the trees. They'll see us for sure.' The foxy face grinned at him. 'Good runner?'

'Sort of. Not very fast though.'

66

'Isn't that a pity. Well, take a deep breath, and do your best . . .'

'Wait!' Alick said. 'Before we start, was that one of Them, in the wood?'

'No.' Alert, the Tod rubbed its long nose. 'That was just folk, moving. Things are restless. Everyone knows the Fidchell is on. The Ellyll told me.'

'Who?'

'The Ellyll, the icy lady. She said the wood is sealed tight. Nothing can get in or out. And she's heard the sorcerer is looking for you.'

Alick's eyes widened. 'Luke!'

'Ay. I told you, didn't I? He'll be making for the Tump. Now, are you ready?'

'Yes.'

'Let's go!'

They leapt into the white field, floundering rather than running; snow to the knees. But only half-way across, and they heard the whirr of wings above them. Something blotted out the stars.

'Hurry!' the Tod yelled. Ahead, the field was sliced clean. Alick shouldered through the bushes and saw, below him, the railway lines – two tracks of silver in the moonlight. Shadows wheeled over him. He plunged over the side and slithered and scrambled after the Tod, through the stinging nettles and brambles, hitting the bottom cut and sore. The Tod loped over the rails. 'Come on,' it hissed, 'or . . .'

Then it stopped, teeth bared.

'What's wrong?'

The Tod's tongue flickered, tasting the air. 'We're too late, sonny.'

Ahead, the silver lines ran into the tunnel, a great mouth opening in the hillside, its dark entrance dripping with brambles and ferns. Inside it, was blackness; a crowded, clinking, restless, fluttering blackness.

11

Icicles

They were there all right. Horsemen – indistinct in the shadows, but the glitter of their weapons was unmistakable, all colour toned down to a ghostly grey. Pennants and banners floated above them. Shields were slung on arm or saddle-bow. And behind, deeper in the tunnel, other shapes lurked, long and sinuous.

In all the trees of the cutting the ravens came down, silently – a black snow.

'What now?' Alick muttered.

'Not much. You'll have to give it up.'

'I won't!'

The Tod grinned, its eyes on the tunnel. 'That's my boy. We'll doubtless think of something.'

A horseman was moving forward, harness clinking. Slowly his horse came on over the snow, leaving no prints, having no shadow. The rider was helmeted, only his eyes visible. Alick waited, fists clenched. He hadn't come all this way for nothing. He wouldn't give it up. Think of something!

The shining beast stopped. The knight gently dropped the point of his spear an inch from Alick's face, and left it there. The wicked steel menaced his eyes. Still he did not move.

'He wants that tree,' the Tod muttered, unnecessarily.

'He can whistle for it.'

The spear fell, its point touched his chest. Then, eyes impassive, the knight pushed. Alick felt the point push through his clothes, then shove, painfully, against his breastbone.

He stepped back. 'All right. Have the damn thing.'

Slowly, his hand went to his coat buttons. As he took out the tree, dragging each second out as long as he could, the tiny leaves tinkled in the wind, glittering gold and black.

And then, with a bounce and a flutter a raven came from nowhere and landed on the spear, weighing it suddenly down. The horse moved back, uneasy; the knight whipped up his weapon angrily.

It was then Alick had his idea. Both sides, ravens and knights, wanted the tree. To get it was to win. While he had it both sides were against him, united, but if he gave it to one side, the other would fight them for it. Divide and conquer.

Suddenly, he held the tree high, so the moonlight caught it. Every eye swivelled to it, a small, glinting, mystical object. Then he flung it, hard and fast, into the tunnel – or pretended to. Every head turned, seeking the small thing in the blackness of the sky. Alick shoved it back quickly into his pocket. but as he stared he saw to his amazement the flash and glitter of it falling from the stars high over the horsemen into the tunnel's mouth. But he hadn't thrown it!

Chaos erupted. The knight wheeled and rode. Birds and riders poured into the tunnel; shriek and howl and sword-slash rang in the cutting. For a moment he and the Tod were forgotten. And then, as they watched the black semi-circle in the hill, the change began.

Icicles grew suddenly, swiftly, without sound. Down like a portcullis they fell, like a frozen curtain, spreading and joining and spilling, hard as rock, on to the snow. Sealed with seamed glass, the tunnel's mouth was white and hard.

'Alick,' said a voice. 'Up here.'

High on the embankment, Luke was watching them, hands in pockets. Behind him a white horse nuzzled the snow.

Shoved from behind by the Tod, who was snorting and chortling with glee, Alick scrambled to the top. The horse raised his head and watched him with narrow red eyes.

Luke caught the bridle. 'Can you ride?'

'Not much.'

'It doesn't matter.' Luke swung himself up. 'Just get behind me, Tam Lin will manage us.'

'Put your feet here.' The Tod crouched and clasped its hands. Alick put his foot in, but did not jump.

'Hurry up!' the bent figure snapped.

'Luke. I didn't throw it . . .'

The Tod snorted.

'I know.' Luke was watching the tunnel. 'But you saw it.'

'He means he conjured it up,' the Tod snapped. 'Now, are you getting on this creature or not?'

Alick scrambled up. Once it felt him there, the horse turned its head and paced into the wood. The moon stroked them with brief silver fingers.

'That trick with the icicles,' the Tod declared, 'that was the best ever, laddie.'

Luke nodded, serious. 'It was risky. It could have brought the whole thing down on top of you.'

He sounded tired, Alick thought. He held the conjuror's coat with both hands.

'I didn't know you had a horse.'

'There are a lot of things you don't know,' Luke observed.

'And you've met this horse before, though he might have looked different.'

Alick thought of the face in the shaving-mirror.

'I was glad to see you,' he said. 'I was worried stiff in that church.'

The conjuror shook his head. 'You did all right,' he said. 'Tam Lin was waiting for me, that was maybe an hour after you'd gone. I found your note.' He slapped the horse's neck affectionately. 'I was sore and cold and worried. There was terror running in the wood. Trees were down on every road. You'd been seen running, and in a glamour.'

'A what?'

'A sort of spell. I don't know what they tried, but when I got there I knew you were all right, because of the box. Then someone said you were with the Tod. I stopped worrying after that.'

The Tod, loping at the horse's side, laughed, and bowed with a flourish.

'We tracked you from the lair,' Luke said. 'It wasn't easy.' He and the Tod exchanged a knowing look. 'Now, hang on. We haven't got time to waste.'

As the horse ran, the wood loomed like a black wall in front of them. Before Alick could gasp, they arrowed down a path like a crack in masonry. Clutching Luke's coat he twisted and glanced back, saw far behind them a long red form loping. The fox sped after them, bending its sly, whiskered face sometimes to lick the cool snow. Alick clung on, out of the wind, thinking of his living room over the shop, with its snug fire and the Christmas tree loaded with tinsel and coloured globes. And his father's present – a pullover and two books and a tin of tobacco – all wrapped up in the bottom of his wardrobe. If I don't get back, he thought, how will he know where they are?

'Alick!' Luke yelled irritably. 'Hold on! You're falling asleep!'

With a jerk he gripped tight, and opened his eyes. The horse slowed and stopped. Alick slipped off, thankfully, and stamped about, banging his arms against his body and rubbing the agonizing chill out of his ears. 'Sorry. I couldn't help it.'

The Tod-lowery ambled out of the trees, grinning, and Luke took it aside, talking quietly. It nodded, waved at Alick, and was gone.

'Drink this,' Luke said, crossing to him. 'It'll wake you up.'

Alick took a swig. Hot, searing liquid struck the back of his throat like a flame-thrower. Gasping, he handed it back. 'Did you make that?' he managed.

Luke laughed. 'I wish I could! It's brandy.' He took a drink and screwed the top on, his hands clumsy with cold. 'Come on. The last lap.'

The next half-hour was the worst. Despite the bitter cold, Alick found it hard to keep awake, and when he did his hunger was painful. That chicken leg must have been hours ago. And not only that – as they came nearer the Greenmere he began to feel that terror that Luke had talked about. Owls flapped about them as they rode; the trees were full of creaking wind; small animals scattered and screeched as they thundered by. On the last part of the path Luke slowed the horse. Progress was difficult. Branches had been torn down and scattered; the spilt and trampled berries were black as blood. As they went on it was harder; whole saplings had been uprooted, and finally a great bank of snow, as high as the horse's head, reared before them. They had to stop.

Luke sat there, silent for a second. Then he whistled, low and clear. The answer came from far off towards Tolbury; the eerie bark of a fox. Luke turned the horse's head. 'The wood is sealed,' he said grimly. 'So we'll have to go another way, one they might not expect.'

The horse whinnied and blew through its nostrils, then it turned off the path and pushed through some bushes.

'Hang on now, Alick,' Luke said in his firmest voice.

They came out of the trees. There lay the Greenmere, its surface shining strangely. Daintily, the horse stepped down to it, crushing the pine needles and the frosty white stalks of grass. Its forehooves clattered on the Mere. It stepped out, and the polished surface was as smooth and firm as a marble floor. The Greenmere was frozen.

Astounded, Alick gazed down. A perfect reflection of his face stared back at him. The mirror-horse below licked the tongue of its replica.

'Will it hold our weight?'

'I don't know,' Luke said. 'Anyway, we've no choice.'

'And if it breaks?'

'Don't ask.'

12

Sealed

Luke nudged the horse on with his knees. Blowing and tossing its head, it gave him an unreadable look and began to walk. The silver hooves rang on the glassy surface, and strange, wheezing sounds came from the ice, as if it would crack and splinter underneath them. Breath held, Alick waited, expecting any minute the crack, the dark star of water and the sudden toppling. But, despite a few slips, the white horse walked out into the middle of the Mere and stood there, snorting clouds of breath from its nostrils.

'Come on, Tam,' the conjuror murmured. 'Don't listen to them. That's what they want.'

The horse paced, ears pricked. Behind the splintering, Alick could hear it too, a muffled sound, like people shouting to be heard, and banging on some thick door between them and you. Angry, frustrated voices. Then he realized where they were coming from.

Beneath the horse's hooves, beneath the green glass of the ice, shapes moved. Broad hands splayed against the barrier; a host of faces mouthed muffled threats. Alick heard beaks pecking, swords hammering; he looked away, but Luke had already felt his grip tighten. 'Ease up, Alick,' he said gently. 'You're pinching.'

'Sorry.' Alick stared straight ahead. If they fell . . . If the ice splintered up like a row of green teeth and swallowed them . . . but he told himself not to think about it. It was too late now.

Then, like a pistol shot, the ice cracked. Tam Lin staggered;

Alick grabbed Luke tight. The ice heaved, jolted apart, a hand came out of it, then a sword, a body in armour, and at that moment the horse put his forehooves on the first cracked reed on the shore. At once Luke kicked him into speed, and behind them, as they rode, the Greenmere erupted with a roar and crash as if some mighty iceberg was smashing through the surface.

Over the soft wet snow they galloped, out of the trees and on to the floundering whiteness of Tolbury Tump. The sky was dark; a thin moon trailed rags of cloud.

Luke jumped down and Alick leapt after him. They fell into the snowy bushes breathlessly, the cries from the lake roaring through the wood. Luke snatched up a stone and struck it against the rock until it rang among the clamour. But the door did not open.

'Try again!' Alick yelled, but Luke shook his head and flung the stone away. 'It's sealed. I expected it.'

The crack of a twig made them spin.

'Tod?'

The long, grinning face slid round a tree.

'Still here?'

'Oh, I had to see this one through.' Tod bit its nails. 'What are you going to do?' Behind him the ring of the hollow was a mass of shadows. Luke ignored them. 'Where's Tam?'

'Here.'

Alick stared in surprise. Into the hollow jumped a tall slim boy, his white hair glimmering in the moonlight. He wore pale clothes and carried a spear; a gold collar gleamed about his neck.

'They're coming,' he said. 'Gold and black together.'

'Open the door!' Alick shouted. The tree stuck in his chest

and he pulled it out and flung it down. 'I've brought the damn thing back! What else am I supposed to do!'

'Quiet!' The conjuror put all twelve fingers together and blew on them. 'All right, I'll do it. Tod, Tam, I'll need time. Just five minutes.'

The Tod grinned, 'My pleasure. This should be good.'

'It will be,' Luke glanced at Alick. 'If it works.'

In seconds they were alone. Two sinuous streaks, one white, one red, flashed over the lip of the hollow. Growls and cries and the screams of horses rang around them. Fox and hound flung themselves on the foremost riders.

'No questions,' Luke ordered, before Alick could open his mouth. He pulled boxes of oddments hastily from his pockets. Horns rang below them; green phosphorescent flashes lit the sky.

'Take your boots off. Socks too.'

'What!'

'Do it!'

Grumbling, Alick obeyed. His feet were blue in the bitter air.

'Sit still!' Falling on his knees the conjuror dipped his finger into a box of ointment, dabbed it on the undersides of Alick's feet and then on the tops. It was icy, but Alick clamped his teeth shut and endured it. Luke worked hurriedly, humming and muttering to himself. As Alick jerked his socks back on, the backs of his hands were anointed, then his forehead, his neck, the small of his back – all were dabbed with the icy cream. When it was finished, tiny rings of cold lay on the extremes of his body. As he stood, he could feel the cross of ice creep up and join with swift, stabbing pains.

'Here! Don't forget this.' The Fidchell tree was shoved into his hands. 'Put it back where you found it!'

'What!'

'Back where you found it!' Luke yelled, shoving him to the door. Vivid green lights were flickering in the sky; the screech of a fox and the clang of swords rang down the hillside. Alick hung on to the cliffside, transfixed by cold. The strange hands of the conjuror turned him to face the rock, pushed him hard on each spread hand, each foot, on back, on head. He screamed. The rock softened, welcomed him. Its cold grip folded him in blackness. It gripped his hands, his feet; he could not turn his head. Luke was somewhere, shouting, kneeling in the snow behind him, far, far behind. Down a tunnel of blackness he was sucked, absorbed, and the rock took hold of him and tore him fiercely through.

Outside, a spear clanged against the rock.

Luke stood up slowly, and turned to face the dark ring of horsemen around the hollow.

13

The Fortress

Alick was lying in dirt and blackness. A spider ran across the back of his neck, and he shook it off as he sat up. Blood ran from a cut on his face. His body felt as if it did not belong to him, as if it had been frozen and thawed again, or gone through some extremity of pain.

The tunnel, he found, standing up, was just as it had been before, a filthy crack in the hill. But the odd thing was that he could see right through the door. He knew it was there, but as he put his hand up it sank in gently, and it was hard to tug out again.

Outside, he saw that Luke was standing with his back to him, hands clenched. A spear lay on the ground. In the dimness round the hollow clustered a great host of shadows, black and formless. Luke was speaking, but no sound came in to Alick. He saw the Tod lope up, and Tam Lin, behind him, picked up the spear.

But what now? Put the tree back, Luke had said, but still Alick hesitated. He couldn't leave them out there. Not like this. He shoved the tree into his pocket and fumbled over the door. There must be a way to open it. His fingers stubbed on hardening rock. No knob, no handle.

Already the lip of the hollow was seething with birds, rising and swirling like black smoke from a cauldron. One of them launched itself at Luke. The conjuror ducked, and Tam Lin stabbed the thing with the spear. Black feathers crashed against the rock.

A lock, a lever, anything! His hands groped. He kicked

and slammed the rock in fury. Birds were falling like black rain. The Tod bit and snapped, his lithe body twisting in the air. Luke flung his arm over his eyes.

Nothing! And after all, Alick thought suddenly, why should there be? This was no ordinary door. 'Open!' he yelled, hands flat, commanding. 'Open!'

The rock shuddered, swung; noise erupted from outside. It was a battlefield. As the golden light hit them, the birds screamed; their eyes were gilt studs in blackness. A waterfall of horses roared into the hollow.

Luke must have felt the rock move against him; he grabbed the Tod. 'Leave it! Get inside!'

They dived in beside Alick and threw themselves against the door. 'Tam Lin!' the conjuror yelled. Slowly the great rocks moved together; a white body slithered in, behind it a lance head snapped, a bird's wing was crushed. Then the line of light closed up and sealed tight. Feathers and dust settled.

For a while they sat wearily in a breathless row; Luke and the Tod bleeding on face and hands, Tam Lin smiling strangely. Finally Alick rubbed tired eyes with his sleeve.

'They can't get in now, can they?'

His voice echoed down the tunnel. Dimly he saw Luke shrug.

'Not through this door. There are other ways.'

He gazed at Alick. 'I told you to go on. We would have been all right.'

'It didn't look like it!'

'It's not us they want. It's the tree.' The conjuror tossed the Tod a handkerchief, and with a grin the creature dabbed daintily at a cut.

'Sorry.' Alick said bitterly. 'Next time.'

'I'm not ungrateful,' Luke said quickly, 'but we've lost time and that's important. Still, it's probably just as well. This part isn't likely to be easy.' He stood up. 'Come on. I'll lead, then you, Alick. Tam last, if you will.'

As they rose, the Tod clapped Alick's shoulder. 'Whatever he says,' he whispered, 'I'm damned glad to be out of *that*, little cub.'

Alick grinned. Then, hands stretched, he shuffled into the darkness. The passage was as narrow and contorted as before, but soon Alick came to realize that the twists were tighter and more sudden, as if somehow the tunnel had shifted and wriggled in the earth. Ahead, in the dimness, Luke's shadow stumbled as he felt his way; behind, the Tod kept a firm grip on Alick's coat.

Not only did the tunnel twist wrongly, but it began to run steeply downhill. Alick knew they should have reached the Fidchell hall a long time ago.

Then Luke stopped. A cool draught moved against Alick's face. 'Are we there?'

His voice rang double. Luke shook his head. 'The tunnel forks in two.'

'That's impossible. It didn't before.'

'Before, Alick.' The conjuror peered into the left-hand tunnel, his words distant. 'Since the Fidchell began, "before" is another world. Which way, Tod?'

The Tod-lowery pushed past Alick and snuffled down the tunnel entrances. 'The left is water,' he said at last. 'The right, fire.'

Tam Lin tapped the spear on a stone. 'Fire, for me.'

'No.' Luke said. 'We can't go through fire. And we must stay together.'

The pale face moved closer to the conjuror. 'You know I cannot touch the water.'

'Then you must pass over it,' Luke answered, as if he was laughing.

Something happened. Something rustled and flapped.

Then the Tod moved to where Tam Lin had been and picked up the fallen spear. A white bird sat on Luke's shoulder, preening. It sent a delicate downy feather into the darkness.

'If water is the worst thing down here,' the conjuror remarked, edging into the tunnel, 'we'll be very lucky.'

At first, the water was enough. It began after only a few steps. Alick's gloves were so wet he had taken them off, and now he could feel the walls turning slimy, and the cold trickle of moisture froze the ends of his fingers. Then his feet began to stick, squelching as he tugged them free. Something cold lapped about his wellingtons.

Grimly they trudged on, splashing downhill. The noise of the stream grew to fill the cavern, and after a while the first wave came over the top of Alick's boots and ran down in an icy cascade into his socks. He groaned.

'What's the matter?' the Tod laughed. 'Cold feet?'

Gritting his teeth, Alick watched the bird take off from Luke's shoulder and fly down the tunnel. Suddenly he realized he was seeing Luke more clearly than before; a faint light was growing ahead, and the conjuror was wading towards it. Just before it flew round the bend of the rock, the bird shone.

'We're coming out,' Luke shouted over his shoulder.

'Out where?' Alick murmured.

'Just about where we are now,' the Tod said. 'And where we have been since we came through that door.'

Alick frowned 'What?'

'Walking and standing still, my lad. They're all the same in the hollow hill.'

Trying to make sense of that, Alick waded round a rock, and stared, astonished.

Before him the stream cascaded out of the mouth of a cave and down a steep, rocky hillside. Below them a network of fields lay white with untrodden snow, and beyond those, a threatening fringe of dark pine forests stretched into the distance. The sky was iron-grey; every tree and hedgerow laden with snow, thick and heavy. A bitter wind whistled into their faces.

Alick shivered. 'It's not possible.'

'No,' said the Tod, splashing past.

'But where are we?'

'I told you. We're not anywhere – or anywhere you could put a name on.' The red paw grabbed his arm. 'Now then. Look at that!'

On the white field stood two pavilions, about a hundred yards apart, their doors facing. Each had a pennant flying from its roof; Alick could just make out the devices. On the black pavilion, a raven, and on the gold, a knight. And between the two tents, facing him on a rocky knoll of its own, a great fortress, iron-grey, its gates wide open.

No one moved in the fields or the pavilions, or on the battlements of the fortress. The windows were staring blanks. Everything seemed deserted. Far over the woods one white bird circled.

Luke was sitting on a rock emptying water from his boots. The Tod scrambled down beside him, out of the wind. Alick followed. He took off his scarf and rubbed his numbed feet, then put the wet socks back on. He could never get wetter or colder than this.

The Tod sniffed. 'Looks deserted.'

'Good. Still, nothing here is as it seems.' Luke stared down at the castle with a smile. Alick tried another question.

'Are we still inside the Tump . . . I mean, is all this inside?'

The conjuror shook his head. 'I suggest you try not to think about it.'

'He means he doesn't know,' the Tod put in.

'Do you?' Luke said.

'Nope. Come on.'

They scrambled down the hill, over rocks and scree, and when they reached the bottom the wind snatched their breath and froze their faces. Alick pulled his hood on; Luke clutched his collar. Only the Tod seemed not to care about the cold. They plunged across the snowy waste, heads bent, struggling forward. Above, the white bird circled.

The field seemed enormous. However far they trudged, the great gates of the fortress came no nearer, and to each side the pavilions swayed and flapped in the icy wind.

It was eerie walking between them. Once, Alick paused and stared at the flapping draperies of the black tent. For a second the whole billowing structure seemed a vast black bird, struggling and flapping in the snow. Then the Tod tugged his arm, and he turned to face the fortress. It was still a long way off.

'I keep thinking,' he said, 'They might come out at us from these tents.'

Luke took no notice. He stopped and listened. A low sound, barely heard, troubled them.

'Thunder,' the Tod said.

'Bees?' Alick tried.

Luke shrugged. 'I don't think so.' He began to walk faster, taking some powder from a box in his pocket and sowing it liberally before his feet.

Instantly, the fortress was nearer. In a few steps they had reached the gates.

14

The Players

The gates were wide open. Pure untrodden snow filled the courtyard. Luke paused, and Alick noticed that he and the Tod were looking anxiously along the rows of dark, empty windows. The quiet was broken only by the wind, whistling through the bare cloisters, banging a door somewhere, sweeping dry snow into corners.

'Do we go in?'

Luke nodded. 'It'll be in here somewhere. Is the tree safe?'

Alick put his hand up and touched the small lump inside his coat. 'Yes.'

Tod was looking into a doorway. 'Start here. I'll feel better out of the open.'

As he said it, Alick gasped. 'Look!'

In the faint light the white gates were closing, swinging silently together. Snow jerked from them.

'It's best to be safe,' Luke said, hands in pockets. He grinned at Alick. 'Don't want Them coming up behind us, do you?'

'No . . . Will it do any good?'

The Tod snorted, and Luke did not answer. Alick followed them up the stone steps. It was best not to be surprised at anything any more. Just shut up and tag along.

The steps were broken and dangerous. They wound upwards, past arrow slits that showed deserted courtyards below, and gardens of black, stunted trees. When they came to a corridor they walked down it in silence, and Luke flung open each door as they passed, but found only dusty, empty rooms, with broken windows and snow on the floorboards.

No living thing – not a spider, not even an ant. Only, in the last room of all, a small silver fruit, rolling in the draught.

Alick picked it up. 'It's the same as the one I ate in the Tump.' He showed it to Luke. 'Are we near it, the Fidchell board?'

'Near enough!' Luke muttered.

Suddenly he glanced towards the window, so swiftly that Alick looked too, and saw a fire burning before each pavilion, blazing eerily in the snow.

'They weren't there before.'

The Tod was hustling him out of the room. 'We must find the board,' he said to Luke. 'It must be here.'

Luke bit his lip. 'Oh yes, but would we know it if we saw it?' They walked along corridors and up and down countless stairs, through many empty echoing halls. There was no sign of the chequered board, the table, the hall with its central fire. Then at one turn in a corridor a white bird sailed in through a window and became Tam Lin tapping Luke on the shoulder.

'They've reached the gates.'

As he spoke, a heavy thud shook the slabs of the floor under their feet, rumbling away into silence. And then came shouts, the far-off clash of metal. 'Didn't take them long,' the Tod sighed.

Alick was playing with the fruit in his pocket. Quietly, he took it out and put it in his mouth. After all, the first time . . .

The taste was as unpleasant as before. He felt suddenly sick and leaned against a window; a small dirty glass pane, only as big as a book. His eyesight swam, then steadied, and he saw . . . the Fidchell board!

'Look! Down there! What does that remind you of?'

Luke squeezed in beside him. Alick felt his body stiffen. Below them was a small courtyard, paved with black marble slabs. The dust of dead leaves lay on it, but not scattered randomly – it lay in a pattern; a pattern of black and gold squares. Leaves, and no tree.

'How do we get down there?' the Tod snapped. 'There must be a door.'

They clattered down some steps, Alick last, still feeling strange and dizzy. In front of him, the others faded, their voices indistinct. Above, heavy footsteps paced the corridors.

Then Alick saw it, the small door, shimmering in the wall. He pushed it, stepped through, and heard it click behind him.

He was a figure on a black and golden board. It stretched to the horizon in every direction, flat and unending. And he was alone on it; one solitary figure under a grey sky. Somewhere was the centre, the important square. How could he find it? It would look just the same as any other. He began to walk, and the wind swept across the empty acres and snatched his breath.

Suddenly, he turned. Around him the Fidchell pieces were springing from the earth. Black and gold, glittering – bird and horseman, greyhound, minstrel – as he had first seen them at Talley, worlds and centuries ago. But this time they were the giants, and he was tiny, tiny as an ant on a chequered tablecloth. They towered above him, bestriding their squares, eyes fixed on him. All around him. He was in the middle, in the very centre.

For a moment, Alick hardly realized what that meant. Then, as they began to move, to press closer, to clink and rustle and flap towards him, he tugged the tree from his pocket and ran across the huge blackness of the square towards its centre, the very hub and axis of the great spinning board. Breathless, he felt the black and gold giants crush down on him. He held the tree, its leaves tinkled, a shiver and roar swept the falling darkness. But before they crashed over him he was kneeling, falling, and the roots of the tree touched the black icy soil.

It exploded. It shot upwards and arched over him. Huge and glittering, it erupted into leaf and branch like a firework of jet and gold. Leaves and snow and dust cascaded on his upturned face; leaves that rattled like tin in the sudden wind and uprush, whirling round a great tree, heavy with fruit and stars and birds, its branches tangling in the sky. The ground heaved and buckled; twisting boles and roots snaked around him; a cascade of leaves brushed and smothered his face and became a curtain of gold that he reached out to, and grabbed, and tugged firmly aside.

The Fidchell hall was quiet, and flooded with sunlight. Two men were sitting at the table. One leaned back in his chair, face towards Alick. The other was frowning at the board, chin on hands. A dog lay asleep under the table, and a raven on a gold chain croaked and hopped on the back of one of the chairs.

'So,' said the sprawling man to Alick, 'you're back.' The other looked up, interested. Neither seemed in the least surprised.

Alick stepped forward, and saw the tree on the centre square, exactly between the opposing armies. They all surveyed it, calmly.

The player with the raven sighed. 'It was not a long battle.'

'But some of the moves were interesting,' added the other. He glanced at Alick. 'Don't you think so?' He wore a fine fillet of gold in his hair.

Alick nodded, wary. He rubbed dust and leaves from his coat. 'Where are my friends?'

The players smiled at each other. 'They'll be here,' one said. 'The tree is back, so all the danger is ended.'

'And is the game over?'

'The game goes on for ever, secretly, here with us. You let it spill out into the world. Now you have brought it back.'

The player with the raven stood up. 'And it's time you left.' Whistling to the sleepy dog he walked over and opened one of the three doors.

Impossible breezes blew in, warm and sweet. Bees hummed in strange flowers. Alick saw an orchard, heavy with blossom. A stream ran through it, bubbling over stones, its surface a cloud of dragonflies. A white road led over distant hills.

'Where is that?' he whispered. The players smiled at each other. 'Go and see,' one of them said. 'You know you'd like to. Or perhaps you might prefer this.' Taking Alick by the elbow, he pushed him to the second door. A rose garden, in full bloom. Behind it a house of glass, its roof thatched with bright birds' feathers.

Alick shook his head. 'Where are these places? They look so . . . familiar.'

'Countries of the mind. Your mind. They are whatever you want them to be.'

'And you. Who are you?'

He knew they were smiling over his head. 'Just the players. Watching the ways of the world.'

The third door was very close. He made a picture in his mind, then reached out his hand, turned the knob, and opened it.

The sea.

The sea thundered on rocks somewhere below. Just through the door was grass, short and coarse – the top of a cliff. Not far out to sea was an island, misty with cloud and seagulls. He took a step closer. He wanted to see the water crash and foam far below. He wanted to step through the door. The player was close behind him, a hand at his back. 'Go on. There's no harm. Just for a look.'

Suddenly Alick stopped. 'No. No. I don't think so.' He turned quickly away.

'You're wise, Alick.' Luke was leaning just inside the curtain, his coat dark with water and dust. 'Don't go in.'

The players exchanged glances. 'He's seen us,' one said. 'He's seen the inside of the hill. You know . . .'

'I know,' Luke interrupted. 'But you can leave that to me. He will never find his way back in here, and if he should tell anyone of this, who would believe him?'

'Are you certain, sorcerer?'

'Quite certain.'

Alick came back and gazed down at the board. 'And if I had,' he said, 'what would have happened?'

'You know, don't you?' Luke moved aside for the Tod and the white dog. 'Nothing. You would walk to the edge of the cliff, gaze out to sea, come back. Just five minutes. But when you went back down into Halcombe you would have been away two hundred years.'

As they walked to the curtain, Alick paused and looked back. The players sat on their carven chairs, the dog asleep, the raven preening its feathers. Between them the Fidchell board gleamed, its knights and birds and ladies still and cold.

'Goodbye, Alick,' one of them said.

The other shook his head. 'He should have gone through the door, as all the others did.'

'All those tales,' the Tod said slyly as they walked down the tunnel, 'of those people who went into the wood and never came out.'

'You'll never have the chance again,' Luke added.

'What about you?'

The conjuror laughed. 'That's my business – which you are going to stay out of, from now on.'

At the entrance to the hollow, they paused. The door was wide open, the golden glow lighting falling flakes of snow. As Alick looked back down the tunnel the golden pillars stretched into the distance.

'I'll never understand all this.'

The door closed.

'Well,' the Tod grinned, 'the sun's coming. Until next time, sorcerer. And you, young one, I'll watch out for you in the wood. You're the sort that makes trouble, and no mistake.'

With a wink and a wave of its arm it was gone.

Alick and Luke walked slowly home through the wood. The white dog – or whatever it was – trotted along behind them, nosing roots and rabbit holes, just like any other dog. Light grew slowly; the first birds began to sing. Once past the Cross the going was easier; a gritting lorry had been along, strewing bright red gravel. As they came near to Halcombe the church clock chimed six.

'I'm going to catch it now,' Alick muttered.

'I doubt it.' Luke took his hands out of his pockets and blew on them. 'Your father could never have got home.'

'He could have phoned.'

'The lines were down.'

Alick thought about that. 'Good.'

'But he'll be home today. The blizzards are over.'

'Are you sure?'

Luke laughed. 'Quite sure. And Alick . . . don't follow me anywhere again.'

Alick grinned.

'And keep away from the Greenmere, unless you want more warts. Merry Christmas.'

'Merry Christmas, Luke.'

At the bookshop the key was on the ledge over the door. Alick thundered upstairs, turned on all the electric fires and sat in a huddle, shivering and tugging off wet clothes. Then he put the kettle on and went to the telephone.

'Jamie . . .? Yes, I know that's the time . . . Listen. Do you think your mother will make a pair of gloves for me, by Christmas? I know it's tomorrow! But listen, idiot, they're a bit special. They've got to have six fingers. Yes, that's what I said. Six.'

THE
CANDLE MAN

All rivers run into the sea, yet the sea is not satisfied.'

Ecclesiastes 1:7

For Joseph

1

'Well, that's that.'

The bus driver slammed down the engine cover and flicked off the torch.

'Engine's packed up – and it's not as if I hadn't warned them. The old tub barely got up Pwllmeyrick Hill yesterday.'

He pulled out a handkerchief and wiped oil from his fingers, glancing through the dimness at his last passenger. 'Got far to go, son?'

Conor shrugged, absently. 'Not really. I was born on a Monday.'

'Eh?'

'You know . . . the rhyme. "Thursday's child has far to go."'

'Oh yes.' The driver looked at him doubtfully. 'But today's Friday.'

Conor wished he hadn't bothered. 'It was just a joke.'

'Oh ay.' The driver pressed a button under a flap and watched the doors swish shut. 'Now then. I'll have to walk back to the phone at Pye Corner and get a truck out. They'll love that, at this hour.' He flicked the torch on again, lighting Conor's face. 'Want to phone them at home to pick you up?'

'We haven't got a car.' Conor swung the sports bag quickly up onto his shoulder. 'I'll walk, it's all right. It's not far.'

Dubious, the driver looked around. The lane ran down in front of them into a misty darkness; the fields on each side were flat and black. Distant trees rose against the sky.

'Are you sure? It's as dark as a cow's belly on these levels.'

But Conor was already striding off. 'Don't worry,' he called back. 'I won't be ten minutes. Goodnight.'

'Goodnight.'

Leaving the driver staring after him he walked quickly into the darkness. After all, he thought hurriedly, it hadn't really been that much of a lie. A van wasn't a car. But if he had phoned, his mother might have been too busy, and she would have sent Evan out for him. Evan already used the van as if it was his own. He would have pulled up and swung the door open and said 'Come on, son', grinning all over his flabby face.

Conor ground his teeth and marched faster. Rugby had left him restless; he began to run hard, racing in the dark lane.

After a while, breathless, he slowed down. Over the hedge on his right the sky was scarred with a line of pale cloud, its edge white with the hidden moon. The lane in front of him turned a corner. Looking back, already further away than he'd thought, he saw the dark mass of the bus slightly turned into the hedge.

As he walked around the bend he realized how quiet the night was. There were only his own footsteps, and from all around, the faintest shift of the grasses fringing the invisible reens. Gradually the hedges became thinner, sheep-gnawed; then they were gone, and he walked between black fields stretching away to the horizon, each with its network of stagnant, salt-smelling waterways.

He stopped and shifted his bag to the other shoulder. The road was lonely and empty. In the silence a frog plopped into a reen and suddenly the moon came out, flooding the lane with silver and the fields glinted under their lacework of water – water in ditches and reens, trickling over the tarmac, glittering in ponds and hoofprints and hollows, as if the whole of the Levels was a great black sponge, oozing with silver liquid.

It was so quiet. Conor stood there a moment, listening. No car had passed him. Behind, for miles, the lane was empty. He went on, hurrying a little past the clumps of stirring grasses.

At the crossroads near Poor Man's Gout he left the lane, crossed a little bridge, climbed a gate and set off over the fields, the grass squelching under his feet. It would be quicker this way, if wetter. After five minutes he came down the track to the farm called Monk's Acre, seeing a faint blue glimmer of light between the downstairs curtains. That would be old Mrs Morris, watching television. Her son would be in the pub – he usually was.

A dog barked. Conor hurried on.

Beyond Monk's Acre he crossed the dark wet land quickly. Ahead he could see the great curve of the sea wall against the cloudy sky. Not far now, he thought. And he wouldn't even be that late.

At this end of the field was a big drainage reen called Marshall's; there was a narrow bridge across it made from three planks tied up with binder twine. Even in this darkness, it didn't look very safe.

He put his foot on it carefully; the wood creaked and shifted, but he jumped hastily over, scrambled up the bank and brushed the cold mud from his hands and knees. Now he was almost home. Across the field and up the lane was the Sea Wall Inn, where his mother was probably pulling a pint and wondering where he was.

He bent and picked his bag out of some nettles. Then he dropped it again, heart thumping.

The noise had come from the dark fringe of trees behind him. The breeze brought it; a squeal, sharp and eerie. As he listened it rose, winding up to a horrible screech that made his flesh prickle; then it sank again to a long moan, barely heard among the swish of reeds. Conor stood absolutely still, sweat prickling his neck. Was it an animal? In some sort of trap? A fox could make some unearthly noises, but nothing like this. He thought of ghosts, spectral dogs, marshlights, of banshee women, wailing at the tideline before a wreck. And yet he felt he almost recognized it; it was a familiar sound, somehow out of its true place.

After a moment of struggle he moved across the field towards it, silently, into the wind. The moan went deep and hollow in the darkness. Crossing the tussocky grass was difficult; he kept stumbling, and once almost twisted his ankle in a rabbit hole, but finally he got to the edge of the trees and paused, knee-deep in nettles, trying not to breathe so hard.

The cry burst from the trees, making him jump. It screamed high, then, astonishingly, broke, became music, a tune, the wild free skirl of a jig.

Conor let out his breath in slow relief. 'You idiot,' he muttered to himself. He grinned. Ghosts. Banshees. He must be getting soft.

Edging forward, he put his fingers against the cracked bark of a willow, and crouched down.

A few yards in front of him was a small, smoky fire, burning near the edge of the reen. Next to it, standing with his back to Conor, a dark-haired man was playing a fiddle.

He was playing it quietly now, dreamily, one foot tapping rhythms into the soft mud. The music crooned and hummed in the stillness; the flames crackled on the damp wood.

Who on earth could he be, Conor thought. A tramp? Maybe a gypsy. Whoever he was, he could play. Now the music had slid back to the long eerie notes that wavered and hung, quivered and whispered. It was wonderful music; it dissolved into folk tunes and snatches of half-remembered songs, and before Conor could put names to the tunes they were gone and the fiddler was playing a strange, stately lament, wandering like a shadow through the trees.

Then, as he leaned forward to listen, Conor saw something moving in the grass near the fiddler's feet. It slithered, glinting in the brief moonlight. At first he thought it was an eel that had crawled up out of the reen; then, with a shock, he realized it was water! The green, sluggish water of Marshall's reen was streaming upwards over the bank; long, gleaming rivulets that moved silently through the grass. Already a pool was forming behind the fiddler – even as he half turned and started a new tune Conor saw the fingers of water draw back, then trickle out again, sliding ominously after him. It was uncanny. How could water run uphill?

He edged forward, staring. Was it water? He'd thought so, seeing it break and trickle, but now it seemed to him more like a hand; wet fingers reaching for the man's ankle as he played and hummed, his head low over the bow.

Conor jumped up. He shouted. The man's head whipped round. The hand grabbed.

The fiddler jerked back with a screech of his bow; he gave a yell of fury and kicked out at something that glinted and moved at the water's edge, stamping at it in rage, splashing the water high.

'Leave me alone!' he yelled, stumbling backwards. 'Haven't you done enough?'

He was not surprised; he was angry, bitter, shaking with rage. And all at once the water was gone, sinking silently back, sliding soundlessly over the bank into the stagnant reen. All around, the trees stirred their branches.

For a long while the fiddler stood still, as if getting his breath. When he spoke again his voice was calmer. 'For a moment,' he said to the darkness, 'you almost caught me. I didn't think I could come back without you knowing. I'm here to get back what you took from me.'

As if to answer him a terrifying sound rose out of the reen; a thin hiss, a bitter choking. The man waited, warily, until it faded to silence. Then he turned around, to face the trees.

'And who are you?' he asked quietly.

Conor froze. He was sure the man couldn't see him among the branches unless he moved, and he didn't want to be seen either. He wanted to get away from this madness altogether.

But the fiddler pointed his bow at the trees. 'Come on. Show yourself.'

At that moment, to Conor's alarm, the moon drifted from its lid of cloud. It glinted on his face and hands; he saw the man step forward, and in an instant of panic he turned and was running, racing hard over the wet grass, slipping and stumbling, leaping the reeds to the lane and running, running to its end, his bag thumping against him. He turned the corner and hurled himself onto a gate, doubled up and gasping for breath.

For a while the night roared and swung around him, but

slowly, as he took great breaths of the damp air, he realized he had not been followed. The lane was silent and dark; the only sounds the drift of voices from the pub just ahead; the slam of a car door. He heaved himself upright and walked wearily up the track.

The Sea Wall Inn was busy; lights blazed from its windows onto the multicoloured row of cars; a few bicycles leaned against the wall. As he walked up to the door and scraped the mud from his boots he thought about the fingers of water that had crawled from the reen. They were quite impossible, of course. But he'd seen them.

2

'So you didn't come home in the bus last night.' His mother lifted the bowl of ferns from the windowsill and scrubbed the faded wood firmly with the duster. Her short dark curtain of hair swung vigorously. He knew she was very angry.

'I did . . . like I said, it broke down. Only up the road. Just beyond Morris's.' It had been further by far, but this was bad enough.

She glared at him over one shoulder. 'You might as well have told me. You know everything gets back to this pub sooner or later.'

He tore the corner off a beer mat, irritably. That was true enough.

'There are some very odd people about these days, Conor. I've got enough to worry about, without you wandering around in the dark.' She straightened, wiping her hand on her cheek and leaving a smudge of dirt. 'Next time, phone me. I don't know why you didn't.' She gave a flick of the duster. 'Evan would have come out and picked you up.'

He glared at her, but she was already back wiping tables. Tossing the beer mat down he swung himself off the stool. 'Can I do anything?'

'Ashtrays, if you like. Or the fires.'

Cleaning the ashtrays was the one job he hated, so today, he told himself, he'd better do it just to keep the peace. He collected them up and emptied all the cigarette ends and ash into the bin. Then he washed them, wiped them carefully, and put them out again, one on each clean table. It was a peaceful thing to do.

The pub was always quietest in the morning. It was a large, rather dark room with small leaded windows on each side of the door. His mother kept it painfully clean; the brass jugs on the shelves gleamed, and every glass shone. A fireplace stood at either end of the room, with an old dark wood mantel shelf and a framed print – Tintern Abbey and Raglan Castle. It had probably been two rooms once – there was a definite rise in the floor halfway across, that strangers carrying drinks often tripped over, soaking their trousers. Now the room was smoky and dim, even in sunlight, smelling of beer and wines and the faintest tang of bacon.

Near the door were the flood marks. The highest was a dim brown smudge higher than his head, with 1863 written next to it in heavy black letters. Below that were eight other lines, at intervals, with a few others almost worn away. Each was dated, in different handwriting; 1908, 1905, 1897, 1966, 1989, this last only about knee-high. That was the only big flood Conor could remember – the tides whipping over the wall, the mud and the sandbags; having to live upstairs for a week. There had been others, of course; water seeped over in most winters and in heavy storms, but they weren't marked. And the house wasn't old enough to have a mark for the Great Flood – that had been in 1606 and had swept whole villages away.

In fact, he thought, as he knelt down at the fireplace, the whole house would have been underwater then, and as he shovelled up last night's ashes he imagined fish swimming in at the windows, swirling muddy water and great crusts of barnacles on the tables and chairs.

'Daydreaming, Conor?'

With a jerk he picked up the bucket and looked round. The big man in the doorway smirked at him.

'Oh Evan,' his mother said. 'I'm glad that you're back. The brewer is coming at twelve. Is that all right?'

'Don't you worry. The cellar is all ready.' Evan Lewis sat himself on a clean table, drying his large, hairy hands with a towel.

If I put my feet on the seat like that, Conor thought, she'd say something. Then he told himself fiercely to shut up, and took the cinders out, bringing back sticks and paper and coals.

'. . . It is your birthday after all,' Evan was saying, in a reasoning voice. 'You ought to take the afternoon off. Shouldn't she?' He looked at Conor.

'You mean on Friday?'

'That's right. I thought we could all go to the cinema in Chepstow. My treat.'

Conor made a careful crisscross of sticks on the newspaper.

His mother stood up straight and pushed her hair back. 'That's very kind of you, Evan, but I don't know . . .'

'Please Jill. I'd like to.'

'In any case I wouldn't let you pay. And who'd look after the bar?'

'Nia. Or Siân. They'd do it just for one afternoon.'

She put her arms on the bar and leaned her chin on them. 'Well . . . it would be a change. I haven't been to the pictures for ages.'

She looked round at Conor. 'What do you think?'

He put the last piece of coal on the fire and stood up, his hands black. If only he'd thought of this first. Now he was trapped.

'I don't mind.'

'That doesn't sound very keen!'

Conor clenched his fists. 'I mean I'll come, but I'd like to pay for you myself. I've got some money.'

'Wouldn't hear of it.' Evan had poured himself a lemonade shandy and was drinking it noisily.

Conor felt a wave of anger flash over him. 'I don't think you should pay for us,' he snapped. 'It's not as if we're related or anything, is it?'

'Conor!' His mother glared at him. 'Don't be so rude!' She turned. 'Yes, look, Evan we'd be delighted. I'm sure Siân will come in. Thank you very much.'

Damn, thought Conor. Now I've pushed her into it.

'My pleasure.' Evan put down his glass. 'You've got dirt on your face, Jill.' And he took out a clean handkerchief and wiped the smudge off her cheek. She went faintly red.

Conor ground his nails into his palms and turned round, abruptly. A man was standing in the open doorway, watching them.

'Good morning,' he said.

'Morning,' Conor mumbled, in a shocked voice.

He was a young man with a narrow face and black hair. He had a rucksack on his back and a violinshaped canvas bag under one arm. He gave Conor a cool, considering look.

'We're closed,' Evan said at once.

'I'm sure you are, my friend, but it's not drink I'm after. I've come about the job.'

He put a small piece of paper into Jill's hand. She stared at it vaguely, then her face cleared and she said, 'Oh I see! The advertisement.'

'It's not been filled?'

She turned and smiled at him. 'Not yet. We're looking for someone dependable for a few Tuesday nights, and possibly Saturdays – our live music nights. Just for a while. We usually have a group but the dulcimer player is in hospital and the rest are touring at various folk festivals . . .'

He nodded, and slipped the rucksack off. 'Do you want reels, jigs, ballads? Irish, Welsh?'

'That would be fine.' She hesitated 'Mr . . .?'

'Rhys. But Meurig will do.'

'I suppose you have some references, reviews, that sort of thing?' Evan said, elbowing himself forward. He folded his arms across his broad chest and looked the fiddler up and down. 'We can't employ just anyone. This pub has a name for its music.'

'We!' thought Conor.

The fiddler shrugged. 'I could give a list of people I've played for. But perhaps you should just listen and decide for yourselves.' He took the fiddle out of its bag and drew the bow across, adjusting the pegs. The low squirm of sound reminded Conor of last night. He sat on a stool and waited.

The fiddler did not disappoint him. After five minutes of the sweetest melody she could imagine, his mother came slowly out of her amazement and said 'Do you know that was absolutely wonderful! What was that tune?'

'An air I learned in Brecon once.' The fiddler watched her, his eyes bright. He smiled. 'You love music, I can see.'

'I do indeed, and I've heard plenty, but never anything like that.'

'Look, Jill, this is all very well,' Evan blurted out, 'but you need some references, something . . .'

'No.' She shook her head firmly, 'No I don't. If you can

play like that, Meurig, then welcome to The Sea Wall. The regulars will love you.'

He laughed, and began to put the fiddle away. Evan had a glowering look of annoyance, and Conor was glad. Who did he think he was anyway!

'This is my son Conor, and Evan Lewis, our cellarman. Now, have you anywhere to stay?'

The fiddler pulled the cords tight. Then he said 'Yes. The old watchtower on the sea wall belonged to my grandfather. It belongs to me now, though I haven't been there for a while . . .'

'The watchtower?' Conor's mother looked surprised. 'Then I knew your grandfather . . . he came in here sometimes. But can you live there? The sea washes right up to it – around it, at some tides.'

Meurig shrugged. 'I expect so.'

But Conor caught a sudden flicker of unhappiness on the man's face. The memory of the fingers of water groped at him.

'Well if you need any supplies, let me know. You won't be very comfortable there.'

'I'll manage.' Then the fiddler turned to Conor. 'I don't suppose you'd like to help me carry these things down?'

Oh, no, Conor thought, but his mother said, 'Of course he will' with that peculiar threat in her voice that he knew very well, so he carefully picked up the violin bag and followed the fiddler outside.

They walked along the track in silence, skirting the muddy pools. Conor gave a quick glance sideways, and saw that the fiddler was looking at him. Does he know it was me, Conor thought uneasily, or is he just wondering?

But Meurig said nothing. He climbed the steps quickly up to the top of the sea wall, and stood there, his hair and coat lifting and flapping in the wind. Conor climbed up after him.

The Severn was grey and purple; huge, a shifting, breathing mass of water, swollen right up to the base of the wall, lapping quietly. The tide was full and far out the sun glinted on moving threads of current, dark streaks in the water. Beyond, low and faint as cloud, the hills of Somerset glimmered.

About half a mile down the wall was the watchtower, tall and built of black stone, its windows blank eyes that watched them come.

As they trudged towards it along the muddy path the fiddler said, 'It won't be very dry, I suppose.'

Conor hesitated. Then he said, 'Do you think it will be . . . safe?'

Meuring turned. 'Safe?'

'Yes. You know.'

The fiddler glanced out at the estuary. 'You mean from the water?'

'Yes.'

They looked at each other for a moment. Then the fiddler smiled a bitter smile. 'I doubt it. For me, nowhere is safe, Conor.'

3

The fence was broken, and snagged with debris washed up by the tide; weed, broken boxes, wood, plastic bags. Conor kicked a rotten sack and a crab scuttled out. 'What a mess,' he muttered, watching it.

Meurig had pulled a key out of his pocket and was fitting it into the lock; he had to force it round, grinding into the rust. Even then the door would not open; the wood was swollen and warped. After a few shoves the fiddler pulled his rucksack off and threw it down.

'This will take two of us. Ready?'

They put their shoulders to the door. At the third blow it shuddered ajar, and at the fourth slammed wide, almost pitching Conor onto his face in the dark entry. Echoes hummed through the tower. Upstairs something bumped and slid to the floor.

Meurig stood there, listening.

The building smelt damp; there were pools of water on the floor and the only window was broken, a black spider of cracks sprawling in its glass. Against the curved wall a wooden staircase without a handrail led up into the dark.

'It's like a lighthouse,' Conor muttered.

'Exactly like. But to warn the land against the sea.'

Leaving the door open, the fiddler stepped in. He looked warily up the stairs. The building was quiet, except for the faint sound of dripping.

'Is everything all right?' Conor asked.

The fiddler gave him an odd look. 'Can you hear that?'

Far above them, something was moving. It slithered, wet and heavy, over a stone floor.

'What is it?'

Meurig didn't answer, but moved a few steps up, into dimness. Conor followed, one hand on the damp wall. They listened, their breath a faint mist.

The dragging stopped.

Meurig began to climb, quietly, with Conor close behind, his heart thudding. The steps were steep and slippery, they wound up around the wall, passing a few narrow windows clogged with dirt and salt. Rubbing one with his finger he saw the estuary below, gleaming brown and silver as the tide flooded it, and some gulls and oystercatchers on the thin line of wet mud. He stepped up, and banged into Meurig.

'Listen.'

There was the dripping; louder now, a slow rhythmic plopping into some pool. And again that indefinable slither, high in a room above.

Conor shivered. 'Do you know what it is?'

'It's water,' the fiddler said, grimly.

Conor shot a look at him. The man's face was a pale glimmer in the dark, a wary stillness. Conor bit his lip, and then jerked with sudden terror as something icy splatted on his cheek. Putting up his hand he felt wetness, and breathed out through gritted teeth, but when he reached up to brush the roof it was dry. Quite dry.

They went up again, step by step. After a while they came to a door on the right: Meurig opened it gently and let it swing wide.

This room had some furniture, a table, chairs, a sink.

Water dripping from the ceiling had made an ugly green stain down the wall. There was a smell of mould.

'She's taken this tower,' Meurig said, 'and it's all my fault.'

'Who has?'

But the fiddler was looking up at the ceiling. Water dripped from the middle of it, onto the table.

Upstairs must be awash, Conor thought; the roof had probably gone. 'You can't live here. Come back to the Inn.'

'It's a lot better than the place I've come from.' Abruptly Meurig turned and ran up to the top room. As his fingers closed on the latch he paused, and again Conor heard from inside that peculiar drift and swish of sound, and suddenly it reminded him of a dress, a long, wet dress, dragging along the floor.

'She won't keep me out,' Meurig muttered. He flung the door open; Conor flinched, expecting a wave, a tide of water to come rushing out and sweep them down the stairs. But the room was perfectly dry. And empty.

It was a circular room, with windows all around, full of sunlight. Meurig walked in. 'Yes I'm back,' he said.

He turned to Conor who was staring at the dry floorboards, and smiled, as if he was relieved. 'Well, this isn't too bad, is it? At least it's habitable.'

There was a small bare wooden bed opposite; cupboards, a shelf and a clutter of rubbish – a few boxes, some old newspapers, a broken chair. Conor came in, cautiously. Someone had been in here, he was sure. A tang of salt hung in the air; one window banged open. He turned a complete circle, staring out: the sea, the Levels, the hills, a far horizon right around. 'What a view.'

Crossing to the open window he caught the handle and

found it wet. A slither of water ran over the sill and down the wall outside, leaving a green stain. Conor touched it, puzzled.

'It was to watch for flooding?'

'That's right.' Meurig had thrown his rucksack down and was rummaging through the boxes. 'There was always a flood warden – they were paid, long ago, by the monastery, and then by the parish. After that, they did it for nothing. Generation after generation. My grandfather was the last. He lived up here until about two years ago – don't you remember him?'

Conor thought he did – a dark, silent man sitting in the corner of the pub. 'Yes, I was a bit scared of him. I was only a kid, mind.'

Meurig nodded. 'He was a grim man. It does that to you, watching Hafren.' He stood up, and nodded at the window. 'It's a war Conor, between her and us.' He gazed down at the estuary, all the glinting miles of tide. 'She wants the land and we won't let her have it.'

'You talk as if the river were alive.'

Meurig looked at him sidelong. 'Because she is.'

Conor was picking through the litter on the windowsill. He didn't like Meurig making fun of him. 'So where have you been these last two years then?'

'That's my business,' the fiddler snapped. 'Do you think I've been . . . My God, DON'T TOUCH THAT!'

He was across the room in an instant; he had snatched the candle stub out of Conor's hand before Conor could move.

'It's only a candle!' Conor gasped. 'An old candle! That's all! What on earth's the matter?'

The fiddler closed shaking fingers round it tight. For a long moment he said nothing. Then he said, 'I'm sorry. For a moment I thought it was something else.'

'What?' Conor snapped. 'Dynamite?'

Meurig gave him a hurt, bitter smile. 'Clever.'

He went over and opened a window and leaned out, hands on the sill, the wind ruffling his hair. He looked quite sick, and Conor, watching him, suddenly felt sorry. After a moment he went and stood next to him. He wanted to say something kind, but couldn't.

'Last night,' he said, looking towards the pub, 'I heard you playing.'

'I know you did.' The fiddler leaned back against the window and looked at him. Conor waited for an explanation, but it didn't come. Instead the fiddler turned his light green eyes back to the window and said, 'Tell me about the houses I can see. Who lives in them, these days?'

Conor shrugged. 'The same, mostly. That's Ty Gwyn, the Mostyns have farmed there for years . . . and Jack Morris and his mother live over there at Monk's Acre . . .'

'What about the house in the trees?'

'That's been empty for a few months but there's a man called John Caristan moving in now. He used to be my teacher when I was little, but he's retired these days. Came into money, my mother says. He collects antiques.'

The fiddler gazed intently at the slate roof, half visible through the blown branches. 'Caristan.'

'Yes. Do you know him?'

Meurig didn't answer. Instead he said, 'And who's this, on the bike?'

A girl was riding along the top of the sea wall from the

direction of the pub, her hair blown over her eyes by the wind. Conor looked down.

'That's Sara Mostyn. She lives at the farm. I expect she's looking for me.'

It seemed she knew where to look too, he thought, watching her jerk to a halt outside the broken fence and wave up at the window, tugging hair from her eyes and mouth. He leaned out. 'Wait there. I'll be right down.'

'Well hurry up. We're late.'

He turned to the fiddler. 'I've got to go. We promised to help Mr Caristan unpack – he's not very fit and his stuff is coming today. I'll see you in the pub?'

'Surely.'

Conor paused at the door and looked back. Meurig was still leaning against the window, looking out.

'Are you sure,' Conor said awkwardly, 'that you're all right?'

Meurig glanced down at the candle stub still in his hand. Then he threw it wearily into a box in the corner. 'I'm all right Conor. For the moment.'

4

'What about here?'

'No . . .' John Caristan ran a hand through his dusty hair. 'Sara, what do you think?'

'I think it would look better on that little table.'

With a sigh, Conor moved the vase again.

'Oh yes,' Mr Caristan said, 'that's it. What would I do without you. Now the books – they go in the other room.' He picked up a box and went out with it, peering carefully round the sides for obstacles.

'So go on. Did he say why?' Sara asked, unwrapping another vase from newspaper.

'Not really.' Conor perched on the arm of a chair, and wound a piece of string round his fingers. 'He just snatched it out of my hand as if it was going to explode. Then he said he'd thought it was something else.'

'What?'

'Exactly. But I'll tell you what Sara, he was terrified. He looked really ill.'

She frowned, tucking her hair behind one ear. 'Just a candle?'

'Yes.'

'He sounds weird.'

'I don't know.' He swung his foot, wondering whether to tell her about the fingers of water that had groped from the reen. Maybe not yet.

'Oh look at this, Conor. It must be worth a fortune!'

Out of the paper came a large Chinese jar, its sides glittering with strange pagodas and ladies in long, swaying poses.

'Not quite a fortune.' Mr Caristan came in with a tea-tray and set it down unsteadily on a packing case. 'Might take a few years' pocket money thought. Do children still call it pocket money, these days?'

They laughed, and exchanged awkward looks.

'Sometimes,' Conor said. He never knew whether or not to add 'Sir'. It sounded odd either way.

'Now that box,' Caristan said, nodding at it as he handed out a mug of hot chocolate, 'has some interesting things. Staffordshire pieces, some Meisen, the best of my Chelsea. Chelsea's my speciality – I collect it. Gorgeous stuff. Thin as eggshell.'

He dumped a spoonful of sugar in the mug and handed it to Sara.

'Do you eat off them?' she asked.

'Good Lord, no!'

'Then what's the point? I mean,' she tapped the jar lightly with her spoon, 'it must be such a worry, in case they get broken, or stolen. I drop cups and plates all the time.'

'Do you indeed?' A small frown creased his forehead; he picked up the Chinese jar smoothly and slid it onto a shelf. 'Good heavens, Sara, what a revelation to make. That doesn't do my blood pressure any good, I can tell you.'

'Well, not quite all the time.'

He sat down and stretched out his legs. 'I'm glad to hear it! The point, Sara, is that they are very beautiful objects, and I just like looking at them. And they're old, of course; from a time when things were made more carefully, by hand, not by machines. I like that. From a money point of view, they can be a bit of a worry. Hence insurance. And the burglar alarm. Have a biscuit, Conor.'

120

Conor took a chocolate digestive gratefully. He never got them at home.

'Sara?'

'No thanks. They rot your teeth.'

'You have sugar, though?'

'That's different.' She sipped from her mug thoughtfully. 'I saw you had an alarm. It must have cost a bit.'

'I can afford it now. And I deserve it, after all those years of drudgery in school!'

He looked comically at them and they both laughed, but Conor thought he meant it. He could remember Mr Caristan's class, years ago now; the constant noise, the class toughs being cheeky and uncontrollable, ignoring the timid 'Please sit down boys'. There had been one day when the headmaster had come in and roared at them all in fury. And Conor had caught Mr Caristan's look; a mixture of embarrassment and shame and bewilderment that he had never forgotten. No, Mr Caristan hadn't been a very good teacher. He must be very relieved to be out of it.

But Sara was still thinking about the china. 'Have you ever been burgled?' she asked.

Caristan looked unhappy. 'Once. About two years ago, when I lived in Chepstow.'

'What happened?'

'Oh, it wasn't very pleasant. The man was caught. I had a dog then, an Alsatian, dear old Marcus. He pinned the fellow against the wall, bit his hand too. A neighbour heard all the noise and came in. Then it was the police and the court . . . all pretty unsavoury. I almost felt for the thief, in the end.'

They were quiet a moment. The wind rattled a loose pane of glass. 'I must get that fixed,' Caristan said, absently.

Sara put down her mug and looked at her watch. 'I'll have to go home,' she said. 'It's five o'clock.'

Mr Caristan sighed, and gazed hopelessly at the stack of packing cases still blocking the hall. 'I suppose you must. Didn't get very far, did we?'

'Sara's fault,' Conor said, 'wanting to know the value of everything.'

'A collector in the making, I can see.'

'We'll come again,' she said, 'promise.'

'I'd be grateful.' Mr Caristan heaved himself up. 'I'll walk home with you both. Doctor says walk a leisurely mile a day. I won't say I might not linger in the Sea Wall, either, for a well-earned half. We'll need an umbrella, though.'

He was right. Conor was surprised at how the light had faded outside; a great mass of dark cloud was streaming in over the estuary, with a few white birds wheeling and gliding under it. Black-headed gulls, he thought, and a few terns. The fields looked bleak; the small bent trees seeming to huddle before the rising wind. Rain was already drizzling; before they had reached the corner of the lane it was a heavy downpour, pattering on Conor's hood and Caristan's umbrella, as he struggled to hold it over Sara and himself.

'Take it with you,' he said to her at the top of the drive to Ty Gwyn, but she shook her head and climbed onto the bicycle.

'Can't. Get blown off. See you tomorrow!'

And she was away, wobbling down the rutted track, the wind sending her hair out like a pennant.

'Mad girl!' Caristan called out.

Conor grinned. 'She's that all right.'

Turning, he saw the watchtower, stark against the growing

storm. A thin wisp of smoke streamed from the chimney. Meurig must have found some dry wood, at least, before the rain.

The Sea Wall Inn was a haven on autumn evenings like this. Light gleamed from every window; when you opened the door and came in, dripping with rain and windblown, you felt the thick stone walls close around you, solid and safe.

Although it was early it was already warm; the two fires were crackling over their sticks and sea-coal, and a few old men sat round a table discussing live-stock prices.

Mr Caristan heaved his raincoat off. 'What a sanctuary!' He hung it on a peg and came over and leaned on the bar, where Evan Lewis was polishing glasses. 'A half, Evan please, of your best.'

Conor left them to it and went through to the back.

'Your tea's ready,' his mother said crisply, 'but get those wet things off.'

Upstairs, he changed and then looked out of the window. Here the wall loomed close against the sky; it was higher than the house, green with slippery grass. On the other side, invisible, was the river, black by now, with the lights of Clevedon reflecting faintly. It would be ebbing, swiftly, soundlessly pulling back its power. He remembered what Meurig had said. Hafren was the name for the river – Severn in English, or Sabrina, the Romans' name for her, the goddess or the drowned princess in the water. Fierce, eager to drown and flood. So the fingers then, had been hers . . . the same, he thought, that scraped at the wall night after night, fingering the piled-up rocks and the great cement foundations. It was all crazy – except that he had seen them.

Then he saw the fiddler. Meurig was coming up the track towards the pub, hands in pockets, head bent against the wind. Conor ran downstairs, and found him in the kitchen.

'I can let you have some milk,' his mother was saying, 'and tea. Cheese, if you want it. No bread, I'm afraid, I'll need that for sandwiches – there's a darts match later . . . oh, well, maybe a few slices won't hurt.'

The fiddler smiled wryly at her. 'Thanks.'

'Will that be enough?'

'Plenty. I'll walk up to the shop at Pye Corner tomorrow.'

He glanced at Conor, and pulled some money out of his pocket. 'The weather's turned bad.'

'Perhaps you brought it with you.' She handed him some change and Conor noticed his wary look.

'Perhaps I did.'

As they went out through the bar Conor said, 'I don't think I'd fancy spending the night out there, especially tonight.'

Meurig shrugged and went out into the porch. 'It suits me.'

They stood there a moment, listening to the rain hissing on the fields and trees.

'Conor,' the fiddler said suddenly, 'did you go to see your friend, the one with the antiques?'

'Yes. Why?'

'What does he collect?'

Conor frowned. 'China. Chelsea, some of it.'

'Plates and cups? Candlesticks?'

'That sort of thing. Why?'

Meurig shrugged. 'I just wouldn't think it would be safe. He's got a dog, I suppose.'

'No. But he's got a burglar alarm.'

The fiddler stepped out into the rain. 'I'm glad to hear it. You'd better get inside. Your tea will be cold. Goodnight.'

'Goodnight.' But Conor stayed where he was, watching the man become a shadow moving into the squall, and then nothing. Now what was all that about? Meurig had wanted to know something. And, he thought, I think I've told him, without even knowing.

As he turned in the doorway he paused. In the darkness outside, just to his left, something had moved. There was a faint rustle and drip. Conor stood still, his heart hammering.

He came back out into the rain. It lashed into his eyes and down his chin, but he waited, listening. There were some bushes and brambles in the corner, and beyond them a reen, smothered with willows that hung over it. Now the wind moved the dark branches, making them sway and hunch and hiss. Behind him, from the pub, came the hum of voices, and the comforting light that streamed out, throwing his enormous shadow from his feet. But he felt afraid. The sound was behind him now; a choking hiss, and then, distinctly, a ripple of cold laughter. His hands clenched.

'Conor. Over here Conor.'

It was a fluid, cold voice, as if the rain had spoken, or something underwater had bubbled the words out.

He jumped back, quickly. Next minute he was in the porch, slamming the door behind him. He was wet and shivering, trying to think, but there was no time for that either, because Mr Caristan was there, watching him anxiously.

'Conor,' he said, 'I think I'd better have a word with your mother. Is that all right?'

Bewildered, Conor nodded. 'Yes . . . I suppose so. She's in the kitchen.'

Leading him through he was struck by the change in Mr Caristan. He looked worried, even afraid. Surely he hadn't heard the voice too? When they were in the kitchen Mr Caristan said, 'I'm sorry Jill, but it's important I have a word. Alone, I'm afraid.'

'Take this,' Conor's mother said to him frostily.

He picked up his plate and went into the bar, but thought absently about a knife and fork and turned back. As he reached the door he paused. It was ajar, and Caristan was talking, in a quick, embarrassed way. '. . . and it's not that I'd want to stand in his way Jill, not if he's making a new life for himself, but I just felt you ought to know, if he hasn't told you himself. I mean, he'd be in the bar, where there's money, and there's Conor to think of.'

'He hasn't told me anything,' Conor heard his mother say grimly. 'What has he done then?'

'Well . . .' Mr Caristan sounded unhappy, but firm, 'the fact is, that the man I just saw in the bar, Meurig Rhys, is a thief. He attempted to rob me two years ago, and was caught. In fact Jill, I should imagine that he's only just got out of prison.'

5

The sky over the church was grey; heavy with unfallen rain. As Conor glanced up at it he saw the weather vane creak round and back in the wind that spun leaves down on his face. Already the base of the wall where he sat was clogged with a wet, golden drift of them. He swished them absently with his feet.

'She was shocked, I suppose. So was I. I mean, that he'd been in prison! Then, after she'd thought about it, she said if he'd had his punishment no one should give him any more, least of all her.'

'So he's keeping the job?'

'Looks like it. I think she'll tell him she knows, though.'

Sara pulled a leaf out of her hair and dropped it on a gravestone. 'I like your mother. She's her own person.'

Conor laughed. 'You say some daft things. Whose person would she be?'

'She might be yours. She might even be Evan's.'

He glared at her. 'Him! Why him?'

'Oh, I'm only teasing, Conor.' Sara smiled her most smug smile. 'And anyway, you're the daft one. I don't know why you let him worry you. Anyone can see she's not interested in him.'

Conor turned his head and jumped down off the wall into the leaves. He put his hands in his pockets and strode off towards the church. With a sigh Sara slid down and went after him. 'Don't get all moody on me.'

'I'm not. I'm thinking.' He kicked a stone into the long

grass and a frog croaked, unexpectedly. 'Listen, don't you think it's strange that Meurig has come back here?'

'He lives here.'

'Yes . . . but he was asking about Caristan. I wish I hadn't told him so much — he must think I'm a real find. I even told him about the Chelsea stuff, and about the alarm. Do you think he's going to try again?'

'You know him, not me.'

Conor shook his head. 'I can't believe he's a thief. He's odd, but I think he's worried over something.'

They paused by the stone flood mark on the church wall and looked up at it.

'You'll just have to tell him,' Sara said firmly. 'Tell him you know that Caristan recognized him. That's all.'

Conor nodded, reading the words on the stone, as he had often done before.

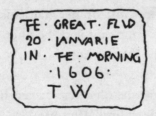

It reminded him. 'That's not all.'

'What?'

He told her, as carefully as he could, about the fingers of water that had groped from the reen, about the fiddler's anger and fear. Even as he said it he knew it sounded wild, as if he had imagined it in the dark, among the eeriness of the fiddle-wail. But she listened. And when he'd finished, she didn't say anything for a while. That was one thing he liked about her; she never said the first thing that came into her head. He knew she was turning it over, just as she twisted the one long strand of brown hair round her finger.

'It's an old idea,' she said at last, 'about the river, the spirit of the river, being alive and hungry. The Severn takes three lives a year, they say.'

He nodded, as they walked down to the gate. 'Yes but Meurig talks as if it's . . . she's real. And then there was last night.'

'What about it?'

'After he'd gone I heard something . . . someone laughing. A low, creepy laugh. From the reen. And someone said my name.'

Sara looked at him quickly, but his face was serious.

'It could have been anyone.'

They opened the rusty gate and trooped through, letting it clang behind them.

'Right then.' Sara spun around suddenly in the path. 'I'm coming with you. I think it's about time we found out what this Meurig's up to. Come on.'

The lane from the church to the sea wall ran between open fields, with the usual narrow green-coated reen on either side. A few stunted willows leaned at angles. Cows lifted their heads and watched Conor and Sara walk silently by; two cars slithered past them on the wet road. It began to rain again, and the horizon closed in, misty and blurred. When they climbed the steps to the wall they were wet already, and Conor's hands were cold with the water that ran down them.

The Severn lay churning in its shoals and currents. They knew how immense its power was. Almost the greatest tidal sweep in the world surged through it twice a day, an enormous weight of water pouring from the heart of the sea, scraping and scouring the long banks of chocolate-grey mud, roaring in at over eight miles an hour, sweeping away everything.

Now the tide was out. Before them a great scatter of birds picked and waded on the treacherous flats, daintily probing, walking with long toes that left light prints. Curlews cried, out there on the waterline; knots, dunlin, oystercatchers and gulls rose in clouds, crying and settling. Half-sunk in the mud were old groynes, and the hulks of rotten boats that the tides had bleached and split until they looked more like rock than wood; strange, petrified forms. Conor watched the birds, wishing he had his binoculars.

'Gulls,' Sara remarked.

'Black-headed. Lots of other species too.'

'I can't see any black heads.'

'It's only in summer the heads are black. Now they've just got a dot behind the eye. You can see it on that one, over there.'

'Conor,' she said, in a strained voice, 'there's someone out there.'

He looked where she pointed among the wheeling birds. Right on the water line, knee-deep in the mud, a woman was standing. She had her back to them, and was looking out at the purple-grey water; a wave ran in and lapped about her.

'What's she doing!' Sara breathed. 'She'll get stuck!'

Almost as if she had heard, the woman turned her head, looking back towards them. She wore a grey dress that seemed to drift in the tide; her hair was dark and long, blown by the wind.

A squall of rain blurred between them. Birds swirled. Then the shoreline was empty.

For a moment they both stood there, astonished, while the rain splattered into a pool at their feet. Then Sara shook her head. 'Where did she go? Let's go down.'

They ran down the steep concrete steps; at the bottom the thin stretch of shingle was scattered with black masses of drying seaweed. Down here in the hush they could hear the faint popping and bubbling of the mud, an enormous expanse stretching from the Porton Grounds to Goldcliff Point, all empty, except for the rain and the picking, wheeling flocks.

Conor put his boot into the mud; it sank and was held, gently. The mud was almost liquid.

'No one could possibly have stood out there.'

Sara shrugged, bewildered. 'Maybe there's a sandbank . . .'

'There isn't. You know that. And where did she go? Into the water?'

Sara looked at him. 'She disappeared, didn't she. Into nowhere.'

Before they came to the watchtower the sound of the fiddle drifted out to meet them, and Conor noticed again the peculiar tone it had, purer and clearer than any other. He wondered if Sara had noticed; as they walked towards the building he saw she was listening, but neither of them spoke.

Conor banged on the door. The music stopped; Meurig opened a window and looked down.

'This is Sara,' Conor said.

'I remember. Come up, it's not locked.'

When they walked breathlessly into the top room he was putting the fiddle away, wrapping it carefully. 'Damp,' he said absently, 'makes the strings slack.'

Sara looked round, curiously. A fire crackled in the swept hearth; next to it was a stack of driftwood in various stages of drying, faint steam rising from it. A few chairs and the table had been brought up; the bed, with a neat sleeping bag on it, stood against one wall.

'Sit down.' Meurig looked sideways at them.

'Sorry about the mud.'

'That doesn't matter. I tramp in enough myself.'

The fire was a fierce heat; after a moment Sara edged her chair away. Meurig came over and sat on the hearth.

'How are you managing?' Conor said, after an awkward pause.

'Fine, thanks. I walked to Redwick this morning and bought some things – enough to keep me going.' Meurig was watching them closely. 'What's troubling you, Conor?' he said softly.

Conor looked helplessly at Sara.

'You should tell him,' she said.

'Tell me what?'

Conor felt the heat rise in his face. He untwisted his fingers. 'We know,' he muttered. 'I mean, about the burglary . . . and everything.'

For a moment Meurig was very still. Then he put his arms around his knees and stared bleakly across the room. The silence was terrible; Conor had to fill it. 'Mr Caristan recognized you.'

'So I gather.' Meurig's voice was harsh. 'When?'

'Last night, in the pub.'

'I didn't see him.'

'He was standing at the bar.'

The fiddler turned his head away 'I presume he's told your mother?'

Conor nodded.

'So that's it, then.'

'No it's not,' Sara said. 'Tell him, go on.'

'Well . . . I overheard. I mean, they don't know we know. My mother told Caristan that it doesn't matter as far as she's concerned. She still wants you to play.'

'Does she now?' Meurig gave them a wan smile. 'She's a good one, your mother.'

Conor was annoyed. 'It's true then? You were in prison? You should have told her if you thought she was so good.'

After a moment Meurig got up and went to the window. 'I'm not a thief, Conor, no matter who says so. I suppose you thought I'd come to try again.'

'We didn't know . . .'

'Don't lie, Conor.' The fiddler turned. 'This is to warn me off, right?'

Angry now, Conor jumped up. 'Yes, all right! Don't try to use me, that's all. I like Mr Caristan. I don't want him robbed!'

'Neither do I.' Meurig took a tense step towards him. 'But he's got something I need. Something of mine.'

'Yours?'

'And I want you to help me get it back.'

Conor turned abruptly. 'No, I don't believe you. Come on, Sara.'

She took a step and stopped. 'Hey, I'm not on a lead, you know. I think we should wait, Conor.'

He glared at her. 'You believe all this?'

'I might, if I had a chance to hear it.'

'Listen,' Meurig said quietly, 'it's true Conor, I swear it. It's vital to me.'

133

Conor looked at him. 'So what's he got of yours that's so precious?'

The fiddler shrugged. 'You might say he's got my soul.'

6

They sat close together, around the fire. A squall of rain rattled the window; the sky darkened under the gathering cloud.

'There's always been a watchtower,' Meurig began, 'and a watcher, ever since the monks first took the land from the river, drained it, dug the reens, built the first wall. Year after year, one family, and when they died out, another. My grandfather was the last. Since then no one has watched her. I should have been here to take his place.'

He pushed a twig deep into the fire.

'What about your father?' Sara asked.

He shook his head. 'No, both my parents were dead by then. There was only me. And I was away, in Scotland . . . but I've gone too fast. The whole thing started long before then. It started the night after I was born.'

He looked at them. 'My grandfather told me what happened. It was in a house near here, down towards Magor. And it was a night like this one coming; dark, wet, and with a raging tide. There was a party, a celebration. The tower was left empty; my grandfather came, my parents' friends, there was a crowd in the house. The windows were open, moths and spray and leaves fluttering in. There was music too, fiddles and whistles, and all the house was lit up with candles and lamps.

'Late in the evening, they started the blessing. It's an old thing, a custom on the Levels; they passed a jug around and everyone drank and wished something on the baby – luck, good health, you know the sort of thing.'

Conor nodded, imagining the hot, bright, crowded room.

'Well,' Meurig went on, slowly, 'there was a woman in the corner, a dark-haired woman in a green dress. No one had noticed her, particularly. When it came to her turn she drank, and put the jug down. Then she pointed her finger at a candle that was burning on the chimney shelf. She said "The child's life will end if the candle burns away."'

They stared at him.

'A candle?' Sara said.

'That's right,' Meurig gave them a sideways look. 'It was before I was christened, you see . . . I suppose there was uproar, confusion. When they tried to grab her she was gone. The floor was awash; the tide had risen to the top of the wall and was swirling in at the door. In all the hubbub my grandfather snatched up the candle and blew it out.'

He frowned, rubbing his forehead. 'He kept it. Once or twice he showed it to me, but usually he kept it locked up, somewhere secret. I remember it was just an ordinary white candle, a few inches high. He tied a red thread round it, so as not to get it mixed up with any other, and he kept it safe. He believed in her curse, you see.'

Sara shook her head. 'It's impossible. Life can't depend on something else.'

'She has power for that, Sara. She locked my soul in that thing.'

'You mean,' Conor said, 'that if someone burnt it away, you'd just . . .'

'Die.' Meurig finished quietly. 'Such things have happened before. There are spells, curses, words that will work themselves out, because of the will of the sayer. She came for my great grandfather – drowned him miles inland. And then there was Carys Rhys, in the last century – Hafren cursed her that she should never see her wedding day. Nor did she. A wave washed her from the wall the night before it. No one even knew why she was out there.' He watched the fire sombrely. 'And have you ever thought how a candle is like a life? That the flame moves like something living, that it's warm and quick, and then it eats itself away until quite suddenly it's gone, nowhere, leaving nothing.'

'I hadn't thought of it,' Conor said.

'I have. I've had plenty of time.'

'But mightn't it work the other way?' Sara interrupted. 'I mean that as long as the candle's safe you will live?'

'Live for ever?' Conor muttered.

Meurig shook his head. 'She didn't say that, though it might have been a heavier curse than the other. No she just gave me an extra danger – burning that candle. Anyway we'll never really know, will we, unless we light it and let it burn.'

'You're hardly likely to do that!' Sara muttered.

'I can't.' Meurig shook his head bitterly. 'I've lost it.'

'Lost it!'

'In a way. I think I know where it is, but I can't get at it.'

'But you mean anyone could light it . . .'

'Exactly.' Meurig watched the flames. 'That's all I seem to have thought about these two years. Locked up in that cell, fretting, counting the hours . . . knowing I just might stop, go out, as if a hand had clenched over me . . .'

Conor went from astonishment to sudden understanding. 'It's at Caristan's! That's why you tried to rob him!'

'That's right,' Meurig said. He rubbed his cheek with one long finger. 'You see when my grandfather died I came back from Scotland, where I'd been playing, cleared my cottage, and sold it to move here. This was where I had to be. Then when I moved into the watchtower, I sorted through my grandfather's things and took a crate of bits and pieces to a junk stall in Chepstow market. Two days later I found a letter from him; it was about the candle. He told me it was in a small gilt box, and I knew that it was too late. The box had been in with all that stuff. I'd looked in it, and thought it was empty, but there's a secret drawer – the candle was in there.'

'What did you do?' Conor asked.

'What do you think! I was there next morning when the market opened, but the box was gone. Sold. Caristan had bought it, but it took me days to find out who he was and where he lived – then I went to his house.' He frowned. 'I was worried. Panicky. The place was dark; I thought he was out. The window was open. I thought it would be quick, and easy.'

He laughed bitterly. 'I was stupid. Ten minutes later I was pinned to the wall by a dog, covered in blood, with the neighbours in and the police on their way.'

'Didn't you try to explain?'

Meurig eyed him coldly. 'For a while. Until I got sick of their sarcasm.'

They were silent. It had gone dark in the room, and quite cold. Meurig got up and brought the lamp to the table. He turned up the wick and lit it with a spill from the fire.

'So that's my problem' he said. 'I can't go there again, obviously. I need your help.'

'We'll do it,' Sara said, immediately. She looked at Conor.

'Steal the candle?' he said.

'And replace it with another. He'll never know the differ ence, even if he's found it.'

138

Conor thought about it. It didn't sound too difficult. 'All right. But look, why don't you just ask him for it . . . explain it to him, I mean. He's a kindly old man . . .'

Meurig shook his head firmly. 'I tried that last time. No one believed me – why should they? And Caristan already thinks I'm a thief and a liar and probably half mad. You heard how he warned your mother. No, Conor, I can't face that. I need you to try and get it for me. Otherwise I don't know what I'll do.'

'We'll do it,' Sara said. 'We've said so, haven't we?' She scrambled up, pulling the hair from her face. 'Don't worry Meurig. It'll be no problem.'

That night Conor lay in bed, watching the thin moon outside his window, and listening to the music of the fiddle. Downstairs in the hot, noisy bar, Meurig was playing a set of reels; dancing music, that made you want to leap and shout; fierce music, full of energy. When it was finished there was a roar of voices, a beating of tables, applause. He was going down well. Conor rolled over. He felt warm, and sleepy. He was used to the voices downstairs, they were there every night, they never kept him awake. In fact they were comforting. He thought about the candle, lying in its dusty box somewhere in the muddle at Caristan's house, forgotten. Or what if it had been sold, or even found and thrown out, in some dustbin, some rubbish tip, nibbled by rats? He closed his eyes. The music had begun again without his noticing. Slow now, and dreamy, it led him deep into sleep.

Late in the night, he dreamed. Someone was tapping at his window. Turning on the pillow, he pushed the hair from his eyes and saw her, the woman from the mud flats, her long dark hair floating out, her green eyes close to the window.

'Let me in Conor,' she said quietly.

He sat up, and swung his legs out into the cold. In the dark room the gleaming hands of the clock whirled crazily round and round. He walked to the window. Water was seeping in through the gaps around the frame; a green trickle of it ran down the wall.

'Let me in,' she hissed, her face against the glass.

Reluctantly, he reached out his hands, and noticed they were wearing Sara's red gloves. Then he seized the window, and heaved it up.

The river exploded into the room, pouring in a smooth green torrent over his feet. Looking out he saw it was high over the sea wall, a glassy lake that roared in, bringing mud and drowned birds and eels and broken nets and all the debris of the estuary. It rose around him quickly up to the ceiling; he was in a cube of water, but he could walk and breath without surprise, so he went over and opened the bedroom door and drifted downstairs.

The bar was drowned and silent; fish swam through it. Chairs and tables hung, lifted at strange angles. He stood there a moment, his hand on the door, watching weed wave from the chimney, a small crab scuttling across the silted floor. Beer mats floated around him like flatfish, advertisements for Guiness stamped on their bellies. Tiny eels slid between his fingers.

She was sitting at a table near the window. For a moment she looked an old, old woman, but even as he looked her face blurred and she was young, her dress green with weed and crusts of shellfish. She beckoned to him with a long hand.

'Come and see what I've brought you, Conor.'

On the table, burning in the murky water, was a white candle. The flame rose, long and smoky, and Hafren watched it, her eyes lit with its glow, weeds and bubbles rising from her hair. It was Meurig's candle.

'Put it out!' he whispered.

She put her finger into the flame. 'Ah but I can't. I've lit it, and now I can never put it out.'

A fish swam past Conor's ear. 'Spells and curses,' it murmured. 'Words that work themselves out.'

'Put it out, please!' He could feel the heat now, burning inside him, he was hot and melting, losing himself, losing all strength. He flung himself forward, floundered, swam, struggled so hard that the bedclothes fell off him and he sat up, suddenly cold.

He waited, heart thudding.

The room was quiet; it was long after closing time. He leaned over and pulled the blankets back onto the bed. Then, quickly, he got out and crossed to the window, avoiding the creaking board so that his mother wouldn't hear him.

The window was closed tight. Outside, the great black bank of the wall rose up, high against the sky. Far along it, one light gleamed in the watchtower. He watched it for a while, oddly comforted.

7

'Slow down, Conor!' Sara bumped the bicycle over the rough track. 'If you don't I'll get on and ride there.'

Conor stopped his grim march and stared out at the pale blue sky.

'That's better.' She caught up and took out a packet of mints and handed him one. He ate it, without looking at her.

'It's Evan,' he said, after a while.

'I should have guessed!'

He gave her an angry look and walked on. 'He's found out about Meurig.'

Sara lifted her eyebrows. 'Your mother told him?'

'No. Someone in the bar. It's got round already. That made it worse, of course . . . he went on and on. Why hadn't she told him? Why were they employing a thief? They!' He kicked a stone in an explosion of fury. 'It's our pub, not his. I'm sick of him!'

After a while she said, 'They had a row, then?'

'Not even that.' Conor shoved his hands in his pockets. 'He doesn't argue with you, he just . . .' he shrugged, 'oh, you know, he just goes on, in a reasonable whine. Meurig might steal things, he can't be trusted, they should have insisted on references . . . sickening.'

She nodded, 'Well, look, forget it. It's not worth it. I take it Meurig's staying?'

'Oh yes. She says it's her decision.'

'And you worry about her! Now, did you get a candle?'

142

He brought it out from his pocket. 'From the box under the sink.'

'And I've got one too, so that whichever of us finds it can just swap and no fuss.' She grinned. 'I'll be like that spy in the film last night. Beautiful and clever.'

Conor snorted.

They walked slowly up to Caristan's house. The red creeper that massed all over the front had left a rich scatter of leaves on the path. They crunched through them to the door and rang the bell. Sara nudged Conor. 'See the alarm?'

While he was looking up at it the door opened.

'Hello!' Mr Caristan was wiping his hands on an old yellow duster; his face lit up when he saw them.

'We just thought . . .' Conor began. He glanced at Sara.

'. . . you'd still need our help,' she finished, brightly.

'Absolutely! There are about three hundred books in here, all over the place. Put the bike round the back, in the shed.'

Conor wiped his feet on the mat and took his coat off, looking around. The house was in an even worse state than a few days ago. The remains of Mr Caristan's midday meal – fish and chips by the look of it – stood on a packing case. He whipped it into the bin at once.

'My books,' he said, waving a hand.

'Why are they all over the floor?' Conor muttered.

'Well, I started sorting them, you know, but I kept dipping in, reading this and that – then I look up and whole hours have gone.' He smiled at Sara as she came in. 'And I simply have to have a few cups of tea to keep me going . . .'

They laughed.

'Well, we'll soon sort it out,' Sara said, with a quick glance at Conor.

'I hear,' Mr Caristan said quietly, 'that your mother's keeping her fiddler.'

Conor nodded. 'Yes.'

Mr Caristan shook his head. 'Well I hope she knows what she's doing. He's a strange young man. He said such odd things.'

Conor frowned at Sara. He could see Meurig had been right. Caristan would have laughed away any story about a candle.

They stacked the books and put them on the shelves, flicking each with a duster. Caristan wandered in and out, fetching more, talking, reading them favourite poems, launching into speeches about M R James and Dafydd ap Gwilym. After a while they just wished he would go, but knew they'd have to put up with him . . . Sara offered to make tea, and when she brought the tray in, at least half an hour later, she gave Conor a sharp shake of the head. Presumably it wasn't in the kitchen. They'd have to find it soon. They'd been here an age already.

Then, at about half past three, Mr Caristan went upstairs. They heard him thumping round in the room above.

'Now!' Sara said, and she whipped open a cupboard, rummaging quickly and thoroughly through the contents. Conor opened the sideboard drawers, feeling guilty. They worked quickly and in silence.

'No luck. Try the crates.'

There were a few of these still unpacked; they searched them hurriedly and even found a small gold box, but it was empty, and Conor thought it was too small anyway to be the one. There was nowhere else. On the dresser and the small tables the precious china glinted in the reddening light.

'It could be anywhere,' Conor muttered. 'Upstairs, in some suitcase . . .'

'Sshh. He's coming.'

When he came down, carrying some more books, she said, 'Mr Caristan, what would you say was the most important thing you've got? The most expensive, the most precious?'

He laughed. 'Ah well, the most important piece isn't necessarily the most expensive, Sara. But I keep my choicest delights in a cabinet upstairs. Come and see.'

Behind his back, she winked at Conor. As they climbed the stairs he thought how clever she was. He'd never have thought of that, or even known how to put it.

Caristan took them into the tiny front bedroom, with the window that looked across the Levels; miles of flat fields, lit now with the eerie western glow.

In the corner was an ornate walnut cabinet, with bowed legs. He unlocked the glass door with a tiny key.

'There we are. This is Sevres, and this is early Chelsea.'

'What about that?' Conor said, pointing with satisfaction to a small gilt-coloured box at the back.

'Oh that.' Mr Caristan chuckled, and lifted it out. 'Well, it's an example of what I was saying. It didn't cost much, but I like it. Local workmanship. Quite old too. Do you see here, the map of the estuary incised on the top? And the words look, AFON HAFREN, HEB DRUGAREDD . . . the river Severn, without mercy . . .'

'Can I see?' Conor said.

'By all means.' Mr Caristan dropped the box, surprisingly heavy, into his hands. 'Rather like a warning, isn't it?'

Sara crowded close. Conor could feel her excitement. He opened the lid, and a pang of sharp disappointment pierced him, until Caristan said, 'Now there's a secret drawer in that box, and I'll bet neither of you can open it.'

Of course, he'd forgotten! It must be the right box! He turned it, hurriedly, looking for a hidden catch, some knob.

'Oh let me,' Sara moaned, so he gave it to her.

'All right, clever. I suppose you'll find it.'

But she couldn't, and had to give it back at last. Conor shook the box and something rattled inside. Fighting his excitement he let his fingers explore the dull metal, and found a tiny crack. 'Got it!' He put his thumbnail in, and pushed. With a snap the drawer shot out. In it was a small gold ring.

'My mother's wedding ring,' Caristan said calmly. 'I keep it safe in there.'

Suddenly, frustration swept over Conor, a hot wave of anger and disappointment. He saw in an instant the cruelty of the long spell, the taunting green eyes of the woman in his dream, and hated them, hated the whole thing. His fingers clenched on the box.

'I'll bet,' he said, his voice oddly choked, 'that there was something more than a ring in there when you bought it.'

'Jewels? Precious stones?' Sara added, encouragingly.

Mr Caristan chuckled, fingering a china cup. 'Nothing so wonderful. Just a piece of old candle.'

At last! Conor thought. Sara's voice was wonderfully calm. 'I'll bet you were disappointed. What did you do with it?'

'Can't remember. Put it in a candlestick, I suppose.'

Sara flicked a look of worry, but Conor was staring past her shoulder with a grim face. She turned. On the windowsill was a vast assortment of candlesticks — some small round ones with handles, others tall and ceramic with painted flowers, or brass, in the shapes of dolphins and fish and birds. One or two looked like silver. Each had a white candle, all different sizes.

'Did you hear that?' Sara whirled and grabbed Caristan's arm, shooting Conor a swift, secret look. 'Downstairs. Someone's moving about! I heard them!'

'But the alarm . . .!'

'Is it switched on?'

Caristan hesitated, as she knew he would.

'Come on then!' She pushed him towards the door; Conor heard them running hurriedly down the stairs.

Instantly he was at the windowsill, fumbling among the clutter of candlesticks, the countless white columns of wax. Which was it? How could he even tell? Downstairs a door slammed. Sara shouted something. He tugged a candle out, stared at it, stubbed it back in. Too small, surely. He tried another. It was so firmly jammed in its melted wax it took both hands to jerk out; a blue tin candlestick fell off the window with a clang. Was this it! He didn't even know!

And then he saw on the windowsill the end of a tiny red thread. He pounced on it, sweeping the rest aside, and tugged; a slim silver fish holding a small candle in its mouth juddered and fell over. In a flash he had the candle out and in his pocket, and was pushing the substitute in when Caristan announced 'False alarm' behind him.

'Was it?' Conor turned, his hands in his pockets. 'That's a bad pun, too.'

They both laughed, and Sara grinned behind them in the doorway.

As soon as they were down the lane and around the corner,

she unclipped the lamp from the front of her bicycle. 'Right. Let's see it. Are you sure you got the right one?'

He brought it from his pocket. 'Sure enough. Remember what Meurig said about the thread?'

It was wrapped round the bottom third of the stub; a faded red thread pulled so tight that it had cut into the wax. Apart from that it was just as the fiddler had said, an ordinary kitchen candle, rather dirty yellow-white, with a blackened wick.

They stared at it through the dimness.

'What did you think of my false alarm?' she said.

'Brilliant. I wouldn't have believed it for a second.'

She kicked him absently. 'It looks smaller than I'd thought. Do you think it's been burned?'

He shrugged, 'I don't know. Perhaps Meurig might.'

For a moment they thought of all those hours and minutes the flame might have licked away; then Conor closed his hand on it tight.

'Come on. I want to see his face when we give it back to him.'

The sun had gone; the sky was an eerie purple. From the west black clouds were mounting, and a fresh wind struck their faces as they climbed the steep steps to the top of the wall and stared at the sudden sheet of water.

The tide was full, immensely full, crashing against the wall! Spray whipped in great arches over their heads as the waves roared in and back, sucking with horrible cloops and gurgles through the stones. The river was a dark expanse, churning and boiling.

'Run!' Sara called, climbing on the bike. 'Quickly!'

She began to ride and he raced after her. Great drops fell on them; the sky hung heavy and low over their heads. Ahead the watchtower was a blaze of lighted windows but, as Conor glanced down, the path was a black thread and the raging tide crashed and bubbled and crashed just below him.

A shout came out of the darkness ahead; Sara answered, and waved. As she raised her arm the bicycle wobbled; one wheel slewed to the side, and suddenly she was down, Conor stumbling over her. He fell heavily, onto the wet mud, the breath thumped right out of him, wet grass against his face. Pain shot up one hand. He jerked off it, grabbing for the candle that slid and rolled down the slope. 'Sara!' he yelled, 'Sara! Get it!'

But the hand that picked it up was wet, with rings and bracelets of gold and weed; the hand of a woman with green eyes who was there for a moment, laughing, until she blurred and shimmered and dissolved into a great green wave that fell crashing over him, drenching him so that he flung his hand over his head and cowered. As the water ran down his neck and soaked his back he clenched his empty fist and yelled with anger. She had taken the candle!

He struggled up and squirmed to the edge but someone grabbed him and hauled him roughly back. 'Leave it!' Meurig shouted in his ear. 'Leave it! It's too late!'

8

'I broke two little bones in my hand.' Conor pulled the stool up to the hearth. 'Not even enough for a plaster. It's just strapped up.'

He knelt down and put a match to the newspaper under the coals, touching it here and there with the blue flame.

'Did you have an X-ray?' Sara asked, glancing at the bandage.

'Yes. We had to wait ages. Went into town after.' He shook the match out.

It had been nice to be in Newport with his mother, and no Evan. He hadn't even minded trailing round the shops.

'What about you?'

'Nice of you to ask,' Sara said drily. 'Cuts and bruises. All over.'

He grinned; he could see one bruise shining on the side of her face.

'Want a drink?' He crossed to the bar.

She swivelled. 'Gin and orange please, plenty of ice.'

'Idiot. Is Coke all right?'

'I suppose I'll have to put up with it.'

As he was jerking the cap off the bottle his mother came in with a box and glanced at the fire. 'Oh that's better. That'll take the damp out of the air.' She came over and looked at Sara's bruise.

'Have you put anything on that?'

Sara went red. 'Butter. My nan swears by it.'

'So do I.' Mrs Jones tore open the box of crisps and pulled

out two packets. She tossed them on the table. 'Presents. Is your bike still in one piece? Why you were out cycling in all that rain and wind I can't think. Conor will be out of rugby for weeks. What good is a winger who can't catch?'

'Thanks. It's all right – I mean the bike. The wheel was dented but my dad can straighten it.' Sara opened the crisps – salt and vinegar – and watched Conor bring one drink at a time, left-handed.

Evan came in and dumped the rest of the boxes on the counter.

'Eating all the stock I see,' he said, winking at her.

She smiled, briefly. He was bald at the front, his high fore-head oddly shiny. She could see why Conor didn't like him.

He began to stack the boxes. 'And you know Conor, it's illegal for you to be served in here.' He came out from behind the bar and snorted with laughter. 'You'll get yourself banned, son.'

Conor glared.

'Oh don't tease him,' his mother laughed. 'Not now he's an invalid.'

They went out, giggling. Conor was silent with fury.

Sara crunched a crisp. 'Eat yours.'

'I don't want them. Those two are like a pair of schoolkids.'

'It must be nice living in a pub. Everything free.'

'It's only because you're here. Usually I have to pay.'

They were silent again. Then Conor said, 'I feel awful.'

'About Evan?'

'About Meurig.'

'Ah.' Sara crumpled the packet up and threw it onto the fire. It squirmed and melted into a burst of purple flame. 'So do I. He wheeled the bike home for me last night, after we'd brought you here, and he hardly said a word all the way. What a mess, Conor, after all our trouble! We had the candle in our hands! I can't believe it.'

'We'd better go and see him.' He wandered to the window and sat on the sill, looking out at the wall. 'You realize we've just made everything worse? I mean, she's got it now. She might do anything.'

Sara nodded, opening the other packet of crisps. 'Do you want these?'

'SARA!' he spun around.

'Oh all right, all right! I only asked. And she won't have burned it yet Conor. We won't find him dead, if that's what you're thinking. She's too canny.'

He hadn't thought of that. He was glad. It was a horrible thought.

A crowd of gulls was flapping and wheeling high above the watchtower. Conor looked up anxiously. 'There's no smoke. Do you think . . .?'

'We'll soon see.' She thumped on the door; the sound echoed, a dull thud, around the stairwell inside. After a moment she pushed the door open and they went in.

'Meurig?'

Echoes hummed and dripped, but no one answered. They ran upstairs quickly and noisily, as if to keep the silence away.

The top room was dark; the grey clouds outside seemed so low that they pressed against the windows. Meurig was lying on his back on the bed, staring up at the cracked ceiling. He turned his head as they came in and sat up, slowly

Sara shivered. 'It's freezing in here. Your fire's gone out.'

'Has it?' He looked absently at the cold ashes. 'I hadn't noticed.'

Conor sat down next to him. 'We came to say we were sorry about last night.'

'It wasn't your fault.' The fiddler leaned back against the wall, and ran his fingers through his ruffled hair. 'You did your part . . . but I should have realized that she'd know, that she would be waiting . . .' He shook his head and then looked at them, his face shadowed in the ominous light. 'When I saw you coming along the wall, I almost threw myself down those stairs but it was already too late. I saw her, for a moment, as she took it from you. You were lucky she didn't drown you.'

They were all silent. None of them wanted to think of what Hafren might do with the candle; what she might be doing at that moment. Conor thought of his dream; the dim flame burning in the drowned rooms and the floating weed.

'Can't we get it back?' he burst out.

'Don't be daft.' Sara was looking out of the window at the estuary. 'If she's got it it's out there somewhere, rolling around in all that water.'

Meurig gave her an odd look; Conor thought he was about to say something, but instead he dragged his coat from the end of the bed and pulled it on, and leaned back again.

'What sort of creature is she?' Conor asked.

'A water-spirit . . . I don't know. Some say a drowned princess, a force of nature. She's said to have an island, somewhere out there. Long ago the people of these parts would worship her, throw their gold and weapons to her, so that she wouldn't destroy their fields or steal their children. She remembers that; she's still hungry for it. Every river takes lives, but Hafren is the most treacherous. Three a year, man or beast. Remember the man in Chepstow, last week?'

They nodded. The man had been swept away; his body found miles upstream.

Meurig rubbed his face wearily with the back of one hand. 'She has me in her hands now. That scares me.'

Sara came over and pulled up a chair. 'You mustn't worry. Maybe Conor is right . . .'

Then she saw they were not listening to her. They were staring over her shoulder, and she turned and saw the sky grey and ominous, the sudden patter of rain.

'What is it?'

On the glass the rain moved wet fingers; they slid down, dragging, fumbling at the latch. Conor jumped up; his chair fell back with a smack, and at once the window crashed open; rain roared in on the gale. Mugs tipped and rolled, smashing on the floor. Ashes swirled up in a grey storm of spray, the sudden screaming of gulls.

Conor beat Meurig to the window, but it took both of them to force it shut. Meurig jammed the latch and wiped rain from his eyes. Then he turned, into a shocked silence.

Sara was staring at the opposite wall.

Running down it, in great brown letters that dripped to the floor, were the words:

OPEN THE SLUICES. LET ME IN.

After a moment Meurig crossed the room. They followed him, and knelt by the letters. Conor touched the O – it felt cold and gritty.

'What does it mean?' Sara said, her voice faint.

'What it says.' Meurig said. 'Letting her in. Letting the river on to the Levels. That's her price for the candle.'

'The sluices . . . you mean flood the reens?'

He nodded, and they stared in fear at the long, brown, running letters, now almost illegible. They both knew that the reens drained the low-lying land, and that excess water drained from them through sluices and gouts back into the river. If they were opened the river would run in, flooding the reens and overflowing, drowning fields and roads, running into houses, the pub, the church, and rising and rising until the Levels were a silver lake with trees and rooftops jutting through.

'You can't!' Sara muttered. 'It would mean a flood.'

He nodded. 'Exactly. That's what she wants.' He got up and stared out at the houses below. 'She wants me to betray all of them.'

9

After that, the weather got worse.

It rained all night; squalls of hard-driven spray that rattled against the windows. By morning the wind had risen to force 8, coming straight off the estuary.

Wiping the tables in the pub Conor lifted his head and saw a familiar yellow van rolling up the track, the words CALDICOT AND WENTLLWG LEVELS on its side half hidden by splashed mud. The driver came in whistling, a mass of glistening yellow oilskin. He nodded at Conor and went through to the back.

Thoughtfully, Conor drifted nearer, table by table. He caught snatches of talk through the open door.

'. . . an amber alert on the Wye, the Usk, and the Severn . . . it'll be on the lunchtime news . . . bridge down at Crick . . . road's awash, may be a burst main . . .'

Conor thought of Hafren. If those sluice-gates were open the whole of the Levels would be a drowned stillness at the next tide. But she had the candle. He flung the damp cloth into the sink angrily. If only he'd held on tighter.

Later, lunchtime customers began to arrive. The flood warning had got around.

'Tides are higher than they ought to be,' Goronwy Hughes said, lighting his cigarette with a spill from the fire. He looked over at Mr Caristan, hanging his coat up. 'You've got some sandbags, I hope?'

'Sandbags?' Mr Caristan looked at Conor. 'What for?'

'There's a flood alert. Only amber.'

'Ah,' Mr Caristan sat on a stool by the bar and ordered a whisky and soda from Evan. He smoothed his new silk waistcoat. 'That'll be way upriver, won't it? Minsterworth, Newbury . . . all those flat water meadows.' He sipped his drink. 'Now that's the kind of liquid I like.'

Evan laughed, leaning his broad arms on the bar. 'Quite right. And don't let them worry you mind. There'll be no flood here, not with the wall.'

'Perhaps it's the wall she hates most,' Conor muttered.

'Now by she,' Mr Caristan said, 'I suppose you mean the ancient personification of the river.' He winked at Evan. 'Sabrina fair, listen where thou art sitting . . . and all that.'

'I suppose I do,' Conor said sulkily.

'A poetic idea. Water as woman. The source of life . . . unpredictable.'

Evan laughed. 'They certainly are.'

At one o'clock Meurig came past the window and a moment later came in through the door. A few of the older men nodded at him. The fiddler looked worn, but determined; he grabbed Conor by the sleeve and drew him into a corner.

'Look,' he said. 'I've made up my mind. I've decided to try and speak to her. It's dangerous . . . and probably quite useless, but it's the only thing I can do now. The weather's making things worse. There's an alert out.'

'I know.' Conor shook his head. 'How can you speak to her?'

'Call her. She'll come, if only to torment me. I can't do what she wants, Conor!'

'I know that. But I've been thinking. If she can flood the

Levels – and they've flooded before, at least partly – then why does she need you?'

Meurig picked up a beer mat. 'To make it easier. Think about it. With the sluice-gates open the water level would rise slowly and silently. It would creep up. That's how she'd prefer it. No one would notice at first – there'd be no alerts, no warning – and then suddenly she'd catch them, all those people miles inland, the houses and farms and factories in Magor and Roget and Undy, where the people think they're safe. It would be a disaster! It would be the Great Flood all over again. Do you know how many died in that?'

'Over a hundred,' Conor muttered.

'Well it would be more this time.' Meurig looked at him anxiously. 'Will you come with me?'

Astonished, Conor glanced up. 'Of course I will. Sara too.'

A wan smile crossed the fiddler's face, but before he could say anything Conor's mother was there. 'Meurig,' she said. 'Look at you. You look half starved.'

'Do I?' He flipped the beer mat over in his long fingers.

'Come and have something to eat with us. No arguing. I have money invested in you.' She marched off, her dark hair swinging.

'You'll have to come now,' Conor said. 'She won't take no.'

'I've already found that out!'

They ate in the kitchen – steak and kidney pie and chips – and despite his worry Meurig ate hungrily. He and Conor's mother chatted about music, and Conor grinned to himself to see Evan wandering back and forth through the kitchen for the slightest reason, giving them brooding looks. Jealous, was he? thought Conor, stabbing a chip with his fork. Good. Excellent.

158

It was nearly half past two before they got away to Ty Gwyn, half running the whole way into the rising gale. Already the ground was very wet; great pools filled all the ruts in the track and still the rain poured steadily down. Conor stamped his boot into a puddle. 'How much of this is her doing?'

Meurig shrugged, his eyes on the green, sodden fields. 'Who knows?'

'It won't be safe, calling her up.'

'If it worries you, Conor . . .'

Conor shook his head. 'Of course it worries me. Everything does. People are always telling me about it.' He stopped as he saw the fiddler's grin. 'And you needn't start either.'

Suddenly they were both laughing, the rain dripping from the ends of their hair. From the barn Sara watched them with astonishment.

'What's up with you?' she said, stepping aside to let them in.

Conor gasped for breath. 'Nothing.' He sat weakly on a bale of straw, and rubbed his side. 'Hysteria, I think.'

Sara looked at Meurig. 'I wouldn't have thought you had much to laugh about.'

'I haven't.' Serious, all at once, he said, 'We're going to speak to her.'

'You must be mad!'

'Yes,' he shrugged. 'Maybe I am. Maybe I've got no choice. Come if you want to.'

'Of course I want to!' She pulled on her hood and grinned at them. 'I'm not sure you two ought to be let out on your own!'

They left the farm by the back lane and ran over the wet

fields. Meurig led them inland, over narrow bridges and down lanes, until Conor saw Marshall's reen in front of them, the wood on its far side. By now the rain had dwindled to a fine drizzle that hung in the air without even seeming to fall, blurring distances like mist. Water was everywhere around them, even here.

On the edge of the reen, Meurig stopped. 'This will do. She came here before.'

Sara dragged the soaking ends of hair from her cheek and looked around.

'How will you call her?'

'With this.' He unslung the bag from his back; took the fiddle out and began to tune it, quickly.

'What about the damp?'

'I'll manage. I'm used to damp.'

'Did they let you have it in prison?' Conor asked suddenly.

Meurig lifted his head. 'No,' he said quietly. 'They didn't.'

He put the fiddle under his chin and drew the bow across it. A strange note shivered into the wet air; it lifted into an odd, lilting tune.

'What's that?' Sara said.

'It's a song a man heard once as he lay asleep on a faery hill. For ever afterwards, they say, he could never play anything else. This will bring her.'

Conor shivered. The music seemed to keen and cry in the dampness about him, like a live thing; he could almost imagine it to be the voice of something that drifted in the mist, out of sight. Meurig played slowly, ignoring the rain that ran down the bow and dripped from his fingers; he bent his head down and closed his eyes and the music slid out and hung softly and eerily over the marshland.

Conor watched the reen. The water lay still under its green cloth of algae. Broken stems of reeds pierced it; brown hollow stalks of last year's cow parsley and teazle, and a half rotten willow sprouted from the bank. Then, almost unnoticably, the surface trembled.

'Look,' he murmured.

Mist formed over the water; a low swirl of it drifted up. Underneath, far below the surface, a face was watching them. It blurred and moved with the rippling reen, its eyes watched them, green and narrow.

She rose, slowly, a creature of mist and water, and her hair and dress were never still; they ran and trickled, streaming with water and weed, the algae clothing her like heavy velvet. She sat on the bank opposite, watching Meurig, and Conor saw how her dress had no end, it just ran into the reen and was water. Gold glinted at her neck; through the mist he saw pearls in her slippery hair. The fiddler stared back at her. Slowly, he let the music die, lifting the bow and leaving only echoes in the murk.

For a moment no one spoke.

Then Hafren moved, turning her gaze on Conor. He stood still, cold. Before his eyes she blurred from hag to girl to woman, her sea-green gaze enfolding him like fear. Did she know about his dream? How could she?

Meurig came forward, the bow and fiddle hanging from his hands. He kept well clear of the water's edge.

'I can't do what you ask,' he said.

A low, choked hiss came out of the mist.

'Watchman, you will.'

Her voice was fluid and rippling; it was the cold bitter lap of the waves against a flat shore.

She spread her misty fingers out in the grass; water trickled from them into the reen. 'Or I will light the wick and melt your life away.'

Her eyes moved to Sara and Conor. 'You are his friends. Warn him.'

Conor cleared his throat. 'You don't understand . . .'

'Oh she does,' Sara said quietly. 'Of course she does.'

The woman flowed into a young girl, her voice bitter.

'It was my land. They took it away. Now I will take it back. Slowly.'

'And what about the people?' Meurig snapped.

Looking at him sideways, she dissolved away into mist. For a moment she was just a drift of vapour.

'Warn them.'

'It's impossible! There are hundreds of scattered farms, people's houses, livestock . . . we could never clear them all out . . . you know that!'

Her green eyes held his.

Suddenly Meurig crouched at the reen's edge, his fingers gripping the wet grass. His face was white and despairing. 'I can't do it! I can't! Nothing will make me!'

For a moment she watched him. Then, with one finger, she touched the smooth surface of the reen. The mat of tiny floating leaves opened, leaving a dark hole of water.

Conor edged closer. Far down, burning faintly, he saw the flame. It flickered, dwindling and rising, brilliant in the dark water.

Sara reached towards it, but Meurig grabbed her. 'Be careful! It's deeper than you think.'

The water at the reen's edge sent tiny, rippling fingers towards them.

'It's just out of reach,' Sara said.

Hafren watched them. 'It is far, far away,' she murmured. 'In my own safe place, beyond the borders of the world. I will not put it out. Second by second, you are dying.'

With an effort Meurig scrambled up and turned his back. He jammed the fiddle into its bag, his hands shaking. 'Come on,' he snarled. 'Let's go.'

'But Meurig, the candle . . .'

'LET HER BURN IT!' he yelled at them. 'She can't hurt me like that! I don't even believe it any more!'

But they knew he did.

The creature dwindled, moving down into the reen. Her hair spread on the surface; vapours rose about her, marsh smells and stale air; the green fetid smell of decay. 'Choose, Meurig,' she said.

He stood there, helpless, his eyes on the flame. Then all at once Sara shoved him aside. 'All right. We'll do what you want.'

'No!' Meurig rounded on her, but she took not the slightest notice of him. She knelt on the edge of the reen, her face close to the green eyes in the water. 'He's too upset; he doesn't know what he's saying, but we'll make sure he does it. When do you want the sluices open?'

The creature in the water slid nearer. She reached up a dripping hand and touched Sara's cheek. 'Tomorrow night,' she whispered. 'At the high tide; the moon and I will come together, hand in hand.'

'But you must put the candle out first.'

'Oh, my sweet . . .'

'You must!' Sara bent closer; Conor gripped her belt. 'You must. To give us time. And to show him it's worth it.'

Hafren moved away, into the reen. She looked down, and far below her the flame in the water went out.

'Tomorrow,' her voice rippled, bubbling from the green weed. 'Tomorrow you let me in. Or I burn his life away.'

10

Meurig sat with his head in his hands watching Sara pour the hot tea into three mugs, and stir it.

'Why did you say it?' he asked at last.

'Oh you're speaking to me now, are you? I said it to give us some time.' She brought the tea over, gave a cup to Conor and put Meurig's down on the table. He ignored it.

'But I can't do it!' he said wearily.

'I know that! We're not going to do it. But we are going to get that candle back.'

They both stared at her in astonishment. She sipped the tea and laughed. 'You look like two frogs in a pond.'

Conor frowned, but Meurig almost smiled, the first time for hours. He picked up the mug and stirred the tea. 'So tell us your great plan, Sara.'

'I haven't got one. I've done my bit, lying to that creature. Now it's your turn.' She sat on the bed and wriggled back against the wall, shuffling off her wellies and curling her legs up. 'And you should have the plan. You're the watchman.'

Meurig sipped his tea and gazed at the darkness outside the tower windows. 'Not much of one.' But he was thinking, they could see.

'Listen,' Conor said. 'Before, you said something about Hafren having an island out there . . .'

'So they say.'

'Out in the estuary?'

Meurig shrugged. 'You heard what she said. Beyond the borders of the world. It's her island. It's on no map, but sometimes seamen have seen it, a landmass where there should be none. Then the mist closes down and it's gone again. It's not a real island, not like Flatholm and Steepholm and Lundy. It's . . . somewhere else.'

Conor got up and looked out of the window, but it was too dark now; he could only see his own reflection, and a few lights, towards Weston.

'How can such things be?' Sara muttered, thinking of the title of a book she'd been reading.

'I don't know. How can we know? But there are tales of men who have been there . . . old stories . . .'

He drifted into thought. Conor looked at Sara. 'We'd need a boat.'

'There's Dad's. But he'd never let us. Not without him.'

'You can row.'

'Yes, but it's not that easy. There are the tides and sandbanks, shoals, currents . . . you know what the estuary is like . . .'

'It doesn't matter,' Meurig said quietly.

Sara glared at him. 'Of course it does! We're going to get that candle, so don't mope!'

He looked at her in surprise. 'Oh, I'm not Sara, believe me. No, I mean the boat doesn't matter. I know where I can get someone to row me out, a way she won't feel us come.' He tapped the mug thoughtfully. 'But it will still be very dangerous. She could easily drown us all. So I'm going to do this by myself – I can't take the responsibility for you.'

'Meurig!'

'No.' He looked at them sadly. 'You've done enough for me already. You found the candle.'

'And lost it again,' Conor muttered.

'That was her doing. I can't bring you into this, not now. And that's the end of it, Conor. No arguing.'

And for all their nagging and asking, that was all he would say. But later, as they were leaving, Meurig pressed something cold and small into Conor's hand. 'Keep it safe,' he said in a low voice. 'It's the key to this tower. There always has to be a watchman, Conor. No matter what happens.'

He led them out into the rain, kissed Sara gently and ruffled Conor's hair.

'I'll be back, don't worry.' He looked up at the clouds, driving in over the dull sky. 'But remember, tomorrow is the highest tide. And she'll be coming.'

Conor and Sara walked silently along the wall, the wind buffeting against them. Neither wanted to speak, and they couldn't in any case, not with the wind snatching away every breath. Out in the river the tide moved with a turgid roar, spreading white foam on the mud, closer with each wave.

When they came to the concrete steps they climbed down carefully and stood in the shelter of the wall. Out of the wind it felt warmer; Sara rubbed her ears and said, 'He's not doing this without us, whatever he says.'

Conor grinned. 'I knew you'd say that.'

'We'll follow him,' she decided. 'I'll come to the pub early; we can watch the tower – he'll have to walk along the wall, and we'll see him. He'll lead us to this boat.'

'What then?'

Sara shrugged and began to walk, avoiding the nettles. 'We go with him. We'll make him take us.'

Conor nodded and then stopped suddenly in the path. 'Oh hell!' he hissed.

'What?'

'Tomorrow! It's my mother's birthday – we were going to the pictures.'

She went back to him. 'What are you going to do?'

'I don't know.' Feeling the rain he walked on, but at the gate to the farm they stopped again, and Conor picked absently at the ivy, pulling a leaf off and shredding it. 'I'll have to come with you,' he said at last. 'Trouble is, it means Evan will have to take her . . .'

'Right, I'll see you tomorrow,' Sara waved and began to run up the lane. 'And stop worrying about him. This is more important.'

Conor turned away. 'I wish I could,' he muttered.

At eleven next morning they sat in the window of Conor's bedroom, watching the dark line of the wall against the sky. Behind them, the radio spoke to their backs.

'. . . Meanwhile flood alerts on six rivers in South Wales have been increased to red; on the Wye at Tintern, the Usk, the Afon Llwyd, the Trothi, Ebbw and Severn, both at Lydney and downstream. The recent heavy rain is pouring down from the hills and a spokesman from the rivers authority warned today that coastal defences are on full alert for tonight's high tides . . .'

'They'd better be,' Conor muttered.

'Rising gales from the west and the recent strange tidal surges in the Seven estuary have added to the danger. Sandbags are being issued and the army and coastguard are standing by. Now, attention all shipping . . .'

Sara grabbed his sleeve. 'There he is!'

Meurig had come out of the tower and was standing up

on the wall, his hands in his pockets. They could see the slight bulge of the fiddlebag as it hung over his shoulder.

'What's he waiting for?'

'I don't know!' Sara snapped. 'Let's get outside, quick.'

They raced down the stairs, swept past Conor's mother and out of the door. Then, hesitantly, Conor came back.

'Have a nice time,' he muttered.

'Thanks. Are you sure you won't change your mind?'

He kicked the step. 'I can't.'

'Well, don't look like that. It's not the end of the world.' She smiled at him. 'I don't mind going with Evan, you know.'

Conor turned his head. 'That's good then, isn't it.' He went out, quickly. 'See you later.'

Sara was waiting impatiently. 'Come ON!'

He swept past her, hardly listening. They ran to the edge of the track, but the top of the wall was empty. They scrambled up, looking anxiously into the wind, but the shore was a blank expanse of purple-grey mud. Then they saw him. He was picking his way carefully along the foot of the wall, leaping from stone to stone, keeping to the solid patches of shingle and weed.

'Get down.' Conor pushed Sara back over the side of the grassy bank and slid down beside her. 'He's keeping out of sight – he must have guessed we'd be watching. See?'

Meurig had turned and glanced back; apparently reassured, he hurried on.

'We'll have to keep to this side of the wall,' Sara muttered. 'Come on.'

It was difficult, scrambling along the steep wet bank of grass, and having to keep checking too, that the fiddler was still ahead of them. After a while he scrambled over the treacherous foreshore and up onto the rocks; he climbed to the top of the wall and then over it, down the grassy slope on their side. Safe behind a willow, they watched him.

Meurig crossed two fields, jumping the reens. It was hard to follow without him seeing, and once Conor put his foot into the water with a sickening splash, but a light mist was closing around them, and that helped.

The fiddler kept east, heading towards the Porton grounds. Then he turned down a dank track back towards the estuary.

Conor and Sara stopped to draw breath.

'Where's he going?'

Sara opened the gate and let Conor through. 'I don't want to worry you Conor, but this leads to Ferryman's Pill.'

'Isn't that supposed to be haunted?'

'So they say.'

He looked at her, and at the dim track ahead, winding into mist. Dark trees twisted at each side, their boughs contorted by the sea-wind. Far ahead, the fiddler's shadow had flickered out of sight. Reluctantly, they followed.

'What does he want down here?' Conor muttered.

The mist seemed to swallow sound. The cries of gulls died away; the coughs of cows faded behind them. Down here it was silent, and dank. Water dripped without sound from black branches.

Quickly, their feet crunching slightly on the stony track, Conor and Sara followed the fiddler's shadow. Ferryman's Pill was a tiny inlet of the river, a place where mist always hung, where strange blue lights were sometimes seen at night. Marsh gas, people said, but others spoke of haunting, a grey shape that moved into the darkness. Whatever it was, Conor thought grimly, he'd rather not know. What did Meurig want with this place?

Sara caught his arm. Ahead, a shadow in the mist, they saw Meurig was climbing the wall. The wall was lower here, not so strong. As soon as he was over they scrambled up between the bushes, disturbing a heron that rose and flapped over the trees.

'Can you see him?' Sara peered over the top, her hands in the mud.

'I can't see anything,' Conor whispered.

A grey wall of mist confronted them. The tide was coming in; it had almost filled the narrow pill and was lapping the mud, but they could see nothing out there. Then, as if he had materialized out of nowhere, Conor saw Meurig. He was standing on the spit of shingle, waiting. Fog wrapped him, so that sometimes they barely saw him, and then his figure was clear, his fixed gaze staring out at nothingness.

'Move up,' Sara muttered.

Conor wriggled forward, lost his footing, and slid, with all his weight on his hands. The sudden pain of the fracture made him gasp; a half stifled expulsion of breath that hissed in the silence.

Meurig turned like a cat.

Teeth clenched, Conor waited, letting the pain ebb. Sara glared at him.

'Get up from there!' the fiddler said at last. 'Conor!'

With a bitter look at each other they stood up on the wall.

'Go back!' Meurig hissed. 'Now! While there's time!'

'We can't . . .'

'You must!' He took a step towards them. 'Sara, go back!'

It was too late. Over his shoulder they could already see

the shape moving in the mist. Drifting without a sound, like a shadow, it glided in towards the shore; a grey boat, frail as a cobweb, glinting with damp. And Conor's heart clenched as he saw the man who rowed it; an old man, his hair grey as the mist; a man who looked up and watched them, dripping with water, his face like one of the drowned.

11

For a moment no one moved. Then Meurig said, 'Come over here' without even looking at them. As they scrambled hastily down the rocks Conor stared at the figure in the boat; it watched him, unmoving.

When they were beside him the fiddler muttered, 'You're a pair of fools. Don't say anything. Leave the talking to me.'

Raising his voice he spoke to the image in the mist. 'We need to go to Hafren's island. Do you know the way to that place?'

The old man gazed back. Conor was almost sure he had not heard. It was hard to see where the grey rags he wore ended and the mist began; he seemed to fade and shimmer like an illusion of the fog.

Meurig moved forward, balanced on the sunken stones. 'Will you take us?' he said urgently. 'I'm the watchman; these are my friends. We need your help against the malice of the river. We need to be secret . . . only you can do that.'

For a moment a change came into the ferryman's eyes – his gaze moved to Conor and Sara, a quick scrutiny that made them both shiver, as if at the touch of something damp. Then he took one frail hand from the oars and beckoned.

Meurig hesitated. Then he turned. 'Come on.'

He led them over the stones, their feet slithering into the liquid mud; he climbed carefully into the boat and Sara followed, sitting beside him. Conor stepped in awkwardly, feeling the craft give and sway beneath his weight. He sat, quickly.

Now the old man was very close to them, but still indistinct, as if he might fade to nothing. Sea water dripped from his hair; his clothes were strewn with bladderwrack and tiny fronds of lichen. The boat itself was a grey cobweb, its timbers swollen and encrusted with barnacles, cracked and gashed and in places transparent. A crab scuttled through the water that washed at Conor's feet. It smelt rotten and it was. He bent forward.

'Meurig . . .'

'Quiet Conor. I warned you not to come.'

Meurig had taken something out of his pocket; he held it out and the ferryman looked at it. Then slowly, he put out one grey hand, and Meurig dropped the silver coin into his palm. For one fascinated moment Conor thought it would go right through, but the vague fingers closed about it. The ferryman put the coin into some fold of his clothes. Then he took the oars and prodded the boat off the mud bank; when it was free he sat back and began to row, with long, sweeping strokes, his wet hands tight on the wood, his face, with its remote gaze, fixed on his passengers.

Conor looked away from the drowned eyes, but the boat was moving in a solid greyness; he could see the oars dipping into the dark choppy water, but beyond that, nothing. He realized how quiet it had become. Even the foghorn sounding at Nash had faded out; apart from the creak of the rowlocks all sound was lost. They could have been anywhere.

Sara gave him a lop-sided smile over her shoulder.

'I'm all right,' he muttered. Then he said 'Meurig . . . won't she know?'

Meurig stared out into the fog. 'Can even Hafren feel the

drift of a ghost on her back? I don't know Conor. It was all I could think of.'

Conor looked past him. What was stopping the ferryman drowning them all, he wondered. How did the drowned feel about the living . . . did they feel, were they even there? Why did he still haunt the river? He longed to ask, but dared not.

The ferryman pulled the oars, rhythmically, as if he had no thoughts or feelings, and the motion of the boat became stronger; they swirled and drifted in new cross-currents; the prow lifted and fell with increasing depth. Conor started to feel very seasick. He gripped his hands tight together, feeling the saliva gather, the sweat start down his back. Oh don't let me be sick, he thought grimly. Not now.

Fog swirled about them, cold and clammy. Once a gull screamed and another answered. Water slapped against the sides of the boat. He thought about his mother and Evan in the cinema, about Hafren and the candle. He felt dizzy and was shivering, his teeth gritted tight. He felt Meurig scramble back and sit next to him, put a firm arm round him.

'Hang on, Conor.'

Miserable and ashamed Conor muttered, 'I'm all right. I'm all right.' And then, to his dim surprise, he realized the swaying had stopped.

The boat seemed to have entered suddenly onto some still sea, barely a ripple passing under it. As the ferryman rowed them on the mist began to fade, drifting in thin snatches around them, breaking up, until with magical abruptness they were in sunlight, on smooth blue water, crowds of kitti-wakes flapping and calling above them.

Conor wiped his face with his hand.

'Better?' Meurig asked.

'Great. Ready to run a marathon.'

Sara grinned. 'Where are we?'

They were nowhere. Both banks of the wide river had gone; they were floating in an endless expanse of water, and there before them was an island, its tall gashed cliffs white with screaming birds.

In the sunlight the ferryman and the boat were incredibly faint; Conor could almost see the waves through the planks that he gripped so hard. But the knot in his stomach was loosening; he raised his head cautiously, and felt the salt sting of the wind freshen his face.

They were under the island now, and the cliffs stood high above them. At any other time he would have been amazed and delighted with the birds – gannets and razorbills and kittiwakes, even puffins, wheeling and screeching and flashing into the water – but now he only cared about landing.

The ferryman guided his craft carefully along the foot of the cliffs, among the swirling eddies, and then, rounding some rocks, they saw a small stretch of shingle, with the waves washing in.

With a sweep of the oars, the ferryman drew them in, and the keel of the boat grated hard on the beach.

Meurig climbed out, knee-deep in the clear water. He helped Sara over the side, and then Conor followed, still shaky, but shrugging off Sara's hand. She grinned at him. 'All right, hero, have it your own way.'

Meurig leaned on the gunwale. 'Thank you.'

The old man watched him, and then stretched across. His ghostly fingers caught the fiddler's sleeve, and he spoke, with a voice like a whisper of frost, hoarse and long unused.

'You have paid. I will wait for you.'

Meurig nodded. 'Where?'

'Where you are.'

They waded ashore and out onto the shingle. Sara tried to wring out the ends of her trousers.

'You'll have to take them off for that,' Conor muttered.

'No chance, son.'

He looked up at Meurig, and then out to where the boat was, but the ferryman and his craft were gone; before them the sea was unbroken to the far horizon.

'I thought he said . . .'

'He did. And he is, somewhere.' Meurig turned, easing the fiddle on his back. 'Come on. Let's see where we are.'

The beach was tiny, smelling of fish and seaweed and bird droppings. At the back a thin path led up the cliff, broken and dangerous, but there, as if it had been used before. They climbed up; Meurig first, then Sara, and finally Conor, who insisted on coming last. He still felt that he'd made a fool of himself in the boat, though neither of the others had said anything. He felt better now, and drew in deep breaths of the salt air.

The path was slippery; they had to hold onto the wet rocks. Birds shrieked about their heads; their gaping throats red, beaks wide.

Sara ducked. 'They're attacking us!'

'They're not. They're just interested,' Conor said.

Meurig glanced down. 'Keep quiet. We don't know what's at the top.'

But when they got there, they found there was nothing but grass; tussocky, rough grass studded here and there with thin gorse bushes, their flowers brilliant yellow against the sky.

'Where is this island?' Sara muttered, picking a sprig of thrift and pushing it into her jumper.

Meurig stared over the waving grass. 'It's nowhere in our world.' He turned to them. 'I don't know what might happen here, even who is here, and whether they know about us. We have to get the candle and be back before the tide.'

Sara nodded, tucking her hair behind her ear.

'Where do we look?' Conor asked.

'This way.' The fiddler turned and began to walk into the wind. 'It seems as good as any.'

They walked across the island to a low hill that reared up before them, dotted with white boulders. When they reached the top they crouched out of the wind.

On the other side the island was just as bare; waving grass, and beyond that, dunes and shingle, the long waves washing in, the birds scattered on the shoreline among stones and pebbles.

Conor put both fists on the grass and leaned his chin on them. 'It's empty.'

'No,' Meurig said, his eyes searching the scene. 'It can't be.'

'But we can see all the island from here, more or less. It's not very big.'

'And it's not empty.' The wind whipped the fiddler's dark hair over his eyes and he brushed it aside. 'Look. Down there. That rock by the stunted tree . . .'

Conor gazed down at the shore. He squinted, and then opened his eyes in surprise. 'It's a cat!'

'Hush!' Meurig pulled him down at once.

The white cat sat on a rock, licking its paw. As if it had heard it lifted its head for a long moment, and looked up the hill towards them. Then it carried on washing.

Sara let out a soft breath. 'Is it hers?'

'I wouldn't be surprised.' Meurig eased a cramped knee. 'We shouldn't let it see us; luckily the wind is blowing towards us. Back off, back down the hill.'

At the bottom they sat in a hollow behind some bushes.

'A cat can't hurt us,' Sara said.

No one answered. They all knew the cat was a threat, somehow.

'The candle is here,' Meurig muttered, his arms around one knee. 'I know it is. I can feel it, close . . .'

'Then we'll have to try going round,' Sara said, 'along the shore.'

'What about the cat?'

'Hope for the best.'

Meurig gave her a wry smile. 'I'm not very good at that.'

'I'd noticed.' She pulled him up. 'But I am.'

They explored the edges of the island. Most of it was cliff, apart from the small beach they'd landed at, but when they had worked their way round to the other side they saw it was flatter, with dunes of soft yellow sand, marram and thrift growing through it. It slid under their feet, and they left great hollow footprints down the slopes. At the bottom of one Sara stopped and emptied the sand from her shoes.

'It's not going to be here,' Conor muttered to her.

'He seems to think so.'

'But he wants it so badly. He may be fooling himself.'

She stood up, and put her shoe on, balancing with one hand on his shoulder. 'It doesn't matter. We've got to do what we can.'

Meurig was already walking out onto the wet beach towards the cliffs at one end; they ran after him quickly, climbing over the tumbled boulders, their feet slithering over barnacles and limpets. In all the rock pools were tiny yellow and brown cockles, and crabs that scuttled away and buried themselves, and once or twice Conor saw things that flicked out of vision; strange fish and eels that quivered and gleamed. Then he climbed up the cracked sides of a great tilted slab of stone, and saw the cave.

It opened in the hill side like a mouth; black and silent. Below him, Sara was sitting on a rock, looking at it, Meurig beside her, his face pale.

Damp air breathed out from the cave; the tidewater ran right up into it, knocking the walls and slooping into pools with strange echoes; rolling the rattling heaps of stones.

Conor scrambled down. 'In there?'

The fiddler sucked a cut finger. 'There's nowhere else. They say the gate of the underworld is a cave like this.'

'Don't be so encouraging,' Sara laughed. 'Come on, Meurig, it'll be all right.'

A rattle of stones made them look up. 'Will it?' he muttered.

From the top of the cliff the small cat was looking down at them, its ears flat.

12

Almost as soon as they saw it, the cat was gone.

'It's coming!' Conor said, but Meurig and Sara were already scrambling into the cave. He dropped down and raced after them.

They slid and slipped on the banks of wet pebbles; the noise made Conor wince. 'It'll hear us,' he muttered; his voice ringing in the darkness above.

'Let it!' Sara's feet splattered the pods of bladder-wrack. 'It saw us anyway. Oh come on, Conor!'

The cave stank of fish. Water dripped and plopped around them, and the walls narrowed as they went further in until they could only just see the smooth rock, glistening green and purple, oiled and worn by the tide. The roof was low here. After only a few minutes they reached the back and Conor thought they were trapped. Then, in the shaft of daylight, he saw the hole.

It was a tiny doorway, no more than three feet high. It was made of three great slabs set in the wall, one lintel on top of two uprights. He crouched and gazed at them, and saw, with a peculiar shiver, that they were carved with spirals and crude waving lines, like children used to draw water.

In the hole was black emptiness. The air from it felt cold and damp.

Sara crouched beside him. 'In there?' She twisted round to look up at Meurig. 'We'll have to crawl!'

He nodded.

A click of sound made them all turn, but the cave mouth was an empty blue, screaming with birds.

'Something's upset them.'

Meurig crouched, 'I'll come last.'

'Have we got any light?' Conor murmured.

'A few matches, but we'll save those. Go on Sara.'

And she went, quickly, on hands and knees, under the lintel. Conor followed, folding himself up. He had to keep his head low, but even as he crawled through the tiny entrance the roof of the tunnel scraped against his back. In front of him, the soles of Sara's boots scuffled into blackness.

'It's too low,' he muttered, hearing Meurig struggle behind him.

'And it doesn't get any higher,' Sara's voice came back, muffled and annoyed.

They crawled deep into the cliff, down the tiny tunnel. Conor's knees quickly became sore; his palms were pitted and scuffed with the sandy grit; his right hand ached in its dirty bandage. Sometimes he could feel that the floor was smooth, paved with slabs of rock, and he thought the walls widened a little, but then it all closed in again, until at last he could feel rock on each side of him, pressing against him. A wave of panic almost overcame him. Sara in front, Meurig behind, blocking the air, and none of them could possibly turn around . . . what if he got stuck here, in this airless hole? He told himself not to be stupid. He could breathe. It wasn't stuffy. That was imagination. He'd made a fool of himself in the boat and it wasn't going to happen again.

Then he stopped, resting his raw palms, and listened.

'Sara! Wait!'

Ahead of him the shuffles stopped. Her whisper came back, irritably.

'What?'

'It's Meurig. I can't hear him.'

Conor lay down on one elbow and twisted his head awkwardly. A light shower of dust fell into his eyes; he rubbed them and hissed 'Meurig! Are you stuck?'

Something shifted in the darkness a long way back. 'Not quite,' the fiddler gasped. 'I'm thin enough. Does it get any wider up there?'

Conor rubbed at his eyes. 'No. Are you sure we should go on?'

Meurig wriggled up behind him. 'I can't see how we can go back! And I know it's here. Believe me.' He bumped against Conor's foot. 'Is that you? Go on, quickly.'

Conor sighed and squirmed forward. 'I've heard of being in a tight spot,' he muttered, 'but never this tight.'

Somewhere ahead, Sara giggled. Then she said 'Hey! It's getting wider. Oh the relief! It's getting . . . Oh Conor, look!'

He put his elbows down and hurried. 'What?'

But with a rattle and a slither she was gone, and light glimmered through a small hole in front of him.

'We're coming out,' he called back to Meurig, and then squirmed through the hole after her, spilling hands first onto a soft cold bank of sand.

He drew his knees up under him, and gazed around the cave. It was immense; a shadowy cavern high as a cathedral; its roof lost in the darkness. A peculiar light glimmered around him; a greenish, phosphorescent shimmer that rippled over stalactites, twisted formations of rock, pillars of quartz and salts mirrored in hundreds of pools of clear water. It was a chamber of mirrors and crystals, cold and secret, utterly silent.

Meurig rolled out and flexed his arms, painfully. Then he pulled the fiddle out from under his coat and slung it on his back.

They scrambled up the bank to Sara. The light confused them, played tricks with them. Gradually, they saw that the cave was not one, but a labyrinth, and behind pillars and columns, and through holes in the rock the pools reflected each other endlessly. There were banks of shattered quartz, and great curtains and solid waterfalls of stalactites, glistening white and smooth, melting and folding into each other through slow centuries of infinitesimal growth.

Sara raised an eyebrow at Meurig. 'Still sure?'

'Certain.'

His voice murmured oddly in hollow places; it came back whispering at them from unexpected corners. Drops fell into several pools, as if the vibrations had disturbed them. Conor felt that no one had ever spoken here before.

'Well,' Sara muttered, 'let's find it. That cat can't be far away.' Meurig didn't answer; Conor saw how tense he was. With a rattle of stones he climbed over the floor of the cave and the others followed. The ground was broken and shattered; the air cold. The strange light made them feel they were underwater.

The fiddler made his way over the rocks to the margin of the nearest pool; he bent over it, and as Conor came from behind he saw Meurig mirrored perfectly in the dark, clear water. 'Look,' the fiddler said, with a peculiar satisfaction in his voice. 'Her treasure house.'

And he touched the water.

Instantly, all reflections broke. Conor saw, deep in the pool, hundreds of skulls, littered on the pale sand; thousands of them, a floor of lost faces, white as ivory. Lying between them were coins, scatterings of jewellery, gold rings, torques, great necklaces of rubies. The more he looked the more he saw. Swords, some with their blades broken; silver armrings; tiny carved wooden figures all warped and unrecognizable, swollen by the sea. There were shields half buried in the sand, tarred rope, even a child's doll with one arm gone, lying on its side, smiling. Deep in the dark corners were strange, inexplicable objects; antlers and pebbles knotted together, crude stone figures of women, a piece of yellow oilskin, quite modern.

'What is all this?' Sara asked quietly.

Meurig pulled up his sleeve and plunged his arm in deep, groping for something within reach of his fingers. He touched a wooden figure and pulled it out, dripping.

'I told you – her treasures. Look at this.'

The wood was seamed and split; the figure was a woman, its long hair marked with crude slashes; a fish carved across it.

'Is it her? Hafren?'

'I would think so. An offering, probably, thrown to the river centuries ago. She's brought them here, all the sweepings of the tide.' He nodded down at the rippling pool. 'Some of it – those antlers, look, those marked stones, could have been here for thousands of years.'

Conor watched a shoal of tiny fish swim through an open jaw.

'What about the skulls?'

'They didn't just throw in objects,' Meurig said darkly. He

dropped the votive figure; they watched it float slowly down. 'Men have sacrificed to the river since before Stonehenge was built – to keep her back from the fields, to stop her drowning their cattle and their children.'

They were silent. Then Sara gripped Meurig's arm. 'Look,' she said, her voice choked.

'What?'

'There! Oh there, look, by that box! Can't you see it!'

Meurig grabbed the rock and hung out over the pool.

'Oh God, Sara!'

Then Conor saw it too. It was a tiny white cylinder of wax, half buried in the sand. A filament of red thread wound about it hung still in the water.

His heart thumped. 'The candle! Meurig . . .'

But Meurig was already swinging the fiddle from his back.

'No!' Conor said quickly. 'Let me get it!'

Meurig stared. 'Why you?'

'No reason.' Conor already had his coat and shoes off; he tugged his pullover over his head. 'Except that I lost it, so I should get it back. And the pool is very deep.'

'Conor's a good diver,' Sara explained, 'and he's got a life-saving award.'

Meurig hesitated. 'I don't know.'

'I'm going!' Conor felt he had to go. He'd been useless in that stupid boat and neither of them had said anything. If it had been Sara he knew he'd have made fun of her.

Meurig shrugged. 'All right. Be careful.'

Conor laughed. 'Don't worry.' He drew the cold, salty air deep into his lungs, put his head down, and dived.

The water was icy; it gripped him tight. Down and down he went, kicking deeper, feeling the pressure build against his nostrils and eyes and chest. Fish scattered under his hands; bubbles broke and blurred the floor of skulls, the peculiar twisted pieces of wood, the doll grinning at him. And there was the candle; his reaching fingers grasped it, scooped it out of the cold sand that lifted and clouded the water like smoke. He put his feet among the bones and pushed up, feeling the silent weight inside him swell, the pain in his ears and chest pound. Light rushed towards him; air and sound exploded into his lungs.

'Brilliant!' Sara was shouting. 'You've got it!'

He swam to the rocks and hauled himself wearily out of the water. Meurig helped him out, and Conor gave him the candle, without a word. The fiddler's long fingers closed about it, tight.

'It's not much smaller,' Sara said quietly, after a while, but Conor thought that at least a centimetre had gone, and from Meurig's shake of the head the fiddler thought so too.

Shivering, Conor picked up his shirt and flung it on, his fingers fumbling with the buttons. On the third one, he froze.

In the shadows on the far side of the cave, a stone had rattled.

They turned silently, hardly breathing, three shadows among the rocks. The entrance to the tunnel was a black gash, barely visible.

Another pebble clicked. Meurig stiffened, and touched Conor's shoulder. He nodded. He had already seen it. On the wall, moving eerily in the green underwater light, the immense shadow of the cat slipped from darkness to darkness.

13

At once, soundlessly, Meurig unthreaded his cloth bag and pulled out the fiddle, his eyes never leaving the stealthy movement on the wall. The shadow paused; they saw the cat's head turn slightly, its tongue flicker.

Meurig glanced at Conor, and gave a curt jerk of his head. They backed, foot by foot, silently from the water, until Sara sent a scatter of stones sliding and rattling. She pulled a face of disgust. 'Sorry.'

'Doesn't matter. It can smell us anyway.'

With the faintest click of pebbles, the cat had come round a pillar of rock. Since they had seen it outside it had grown, impossibly. Its white fur bristled; water beads glinted and rolled down its back. Two intelligent amber eyes watched them. Lightly, the huge cat leapt up onto a rock and crouched down, spitting and growling in its throat. It was about five feet away from them.

No one dared move. Conor was shivering with cold; he clamped his arms tight around him.

'Now what?' Sara said, barely opening her lips.

Meurig lifted the bow. Then he stood stock-still. The cat was preparing to spring. Its ears went suddenly flat; its pupils narrowed, its tail thrashed from side to side. Its gaze was fixed on Conor.

'Move!' Meurig yelled, pushing him aside. But even as Conor heard, the cat leapt. It landed with a heavy thump on his chest, knocking him flat, a spitting, scratching fury. He gasped, tried to heave it off, its breath stinking of fish, its spread claws slashing the skin under his ear. Warm blood ran down his neck.

Then the cat was gone; whirling with a snarl of rage on Sara, who turned and ran, leaping up a pile of unstable scree to a narrow ledge, the cat racing after her, silent. She flung a stone at it, just missing, and it stopped, tail swinging wildly. Conor staggered up.

'Here,' Meurig snapped. He was in a cleft in some rocks; Conor raced across and threw himself in behind.

'All right?'

'I think so. It was so quick!' He held a tissue to his neck; it reddened instantly.

'Use this.' Meurig gave him a handkerchief. 'Is it deep?'

'No, but it stings . . . What are you doing?'

'Something useless, maybe.' He stopped tuning and raised the fiddle to his chin.

'Meurig,' Sara warned. 'It's coming after you.'

The cat had turned from her; dodging another stone it prowled towards Meurig, its eyes glinting like glass in the green light.

Wedging himself in the cleft Meurig put the bow across the strings. 'Cover your ears,' he said.

'What?'

'Do it! You too, Sara!'

Slowly, he dragged the bow across the strings. A sound broke from the fiddle, a soft, unnatural hum, so quiet it was almost unheard, but the echoes in the cave took it and murmured it over and over. Water trembled. Drops fell into pools.

Conor felt quite strange; he put his hands to his ears quickly and watched the cat. It blinked, but stayed still, watching the fiddler intently. Meurig let the note drift off into silence. Then he played another; exquisitely low and soft, a long, long, languid sound.

The cat answered. Deep in its throat it made a snarl.

Half-smiling, Meurig began to play.

The music was uncanny, if it even was music. At first it seemed just a loose gathering of sounds; strange, slow notes, long and winding, humming round the cave so that echo and music merged. Conor found he could not keep his attention on the sounds; his thoughts kept sliding away, into a looming darkness and weariness, a tiredness in his arms and legs and head.

When he looked at Meurig again, he knew with a dull shock that some time had passed. The cat was sitting now, its tail out straight behind it, its eyes intelligent slits, unblinking.

Across the cave he saw Sara sitting on the ledge, feet dangling. Her eyes were empty, her arms loose in her lap.

Still the fiddle played; faint, drifting, increasingly sleepy sounds that echoed endlessly in the still green silence, until Conor felt that the cave was heavy with sound, that even the drip of water into pools slowed, became an unhurried descent of thick globules, wobbling slightly, falling into silvery metallic fluid that opened to receive them soundlessly. And blurring with the music another murmur hung in the cave; a rich, satisfying purr, drifting into warm darkness, into the comfort of fur . . .

'Conor.'

Someone had hold of him; was shaking him.

'Conor.'

Wearily, he opened his eyes. A cold hand clamped over his mouth; he squirmed.

'No sound,' Meurig breathed. 'Not a whisper. Understand?'

Dizzy, he nodded.

The fiddler stepped back and moved aside, and Conor saw the cat. It was lying curled up, fast asleep, its tail coiled tight around it; a white, barely stirring heap of fur.

He breathed deeply, trying to clear his head. He felt muzzy and dazed; his eyes were tired and it was difficult to focus. Meurig was talking to Sara quietly; he helped her down from the ledge and beckoned to Conor; he went over, lifting his feet carefully between the rubble on the floor.

'What did you do?' Conor breathed. 'I'm half asleep!'

Meurig smiled briefly. 'Something I learned. Your collar is soaked – has the bleeding stopped?'

Conor felt the handkerchief he had jammed against his neck. 'I think so. Everything seemed to stop.'

'Right.' Meurig gazed over at the cat. 'Now make no sound, none. It could easily wake up. Let's get back up that passage, quickly!'

They crept around the rocks and past the treasure-filled pools, glimpsing their own anxious, dirty faces upside down in the clear water. The cave seemed bitterly cold now, and Conor still shivered from his dive; his wet clothes clung to him uncomfortably. Once he stumbled, and grabbed a frail hanging needle of stone; it snapped with a loud crack that echoed high in the roof. They stood in terror, staring back. The cat did not get up; they could just see it, a pale smudge in the rippling green light.

At last Sara managed a wan smile. 'Next time fall over, Conor. It'll make less noise.'

'Don't worry, I'll have died of hypothermia before then.'

She grinned, and followed Meurig, but the fiddler was blocking the way.

'Come on Meurig, move.'

He stepped aside, silent.

'Oh hellfire!' Sara gasped.

Before them, the cave was flooding with a great pool of black water, lapping at their feet, rising almost visibly up the green-stained wall of the cave. Under its surface, full to the roof, they could see the tiny dark entrance to the tunnel.

Conor groaned, feeling dismay soak him like the damp through his clothes. Meurig sat down on a rock, cradling the fiddle gently. He looked distraught, almost afraid.

'The tide,' he said numbly. 'Oh God, I'd forgotten the tide!'

Sara and Conor looked at each other.

'We're trapped,' she said, after a moment.

'Looks like it.' Conor sat by the fiddler. Each of them was thinking the same thing; of the great tide surging up the river under the moon, the powerful brown muscles of the river shouldering against the land.

'Well it won't do,' Sara said quickly. 'We can't just sit here and drown, or wait until the cat wakes up. Come on, Meurig, don't get so down. I've never met such a man for gloom. We've got the candle and now we just have to get out. There must be another tunnel.'

He looked at her in affectionate astonishment. 'Don't you ever give up?'

'No. I won't.' She flung her arms wide. 'I know there's another way out. There's got to be.'

Conor didn't see why, but she had cheered him up and he felt more hopeful. You could always depend on Sara. But Meurig seemed lost in one of his bitter moods

'What sort of watchman am I?' he snapped. 'All I thought

about was the candle . . . I should never have let you make Hafren that promise. Imagine her anger . . . imagine what she'll do . . .'

'The sluices are shut and they'll stay shut and that's what's important,' Sara said firmly. 'Now come on. My feet are getting wet.'

She grabbed him and pulled him up. Already the water had risen further; looking up at the marks on the walls Conor thought that it had much higher to go – certainly higher than his head.

Meurig slung the fiddle over his shoulder. 'All right Sara, let's look. But I don't think we'll find anything.'

They followed her, keeping as far from the sleeping cat as possible. They explored the rippling green darkness, climbing past pools up to the highest curtain of hanging stalactites. Here the ground became drier; there were fewer pools and the light, as if it somehow glimmered from the water, was dimmer.

The ways they tried ended only in rockwalls or piles of rubble, until one passageway looked promising, receding into blackness.

Sara climbed up. 'There's a gap here . . . big enough to get through. It might go somewhere.'

Meurig pulled out the box of matches and tossed it up to her.

'There's only three,' she said doubtfully.

'Just use one then.'

After a moment a sharp blue crack came from her fingers, then a yellow glow; she held up the match and the flame settled, throwing her dim enormous shadow over the wall. They saw her bend into the crack.

'It's big . . . it goes on a long way.'

The flame went out suddenly and they heard her turn. 'It blew out! There's a draught!'

Meurig climbed up quickly. 'You're a wonder Sara, no mistake. I'll go first this time – if I can fit we all can.'

He slung the fiddle tight and edged in, sideways.

Sara stared after him. 'How is it?'

'Dark.' His hand came out for the box and another match spluttered. Light flared, shielded by his hand. 'It goes up,' his voice said, sounding distant. He shuffled on for a few steps, until the match went out.

'Come on,' Sara said, and climbed in.

Conor came last. He felt warmer now, though the scratch on his neck was still sore.

Inside the rocks the tunnel felt surprisingly smooth under-foot. There was certainly a breeze coming from somewhere; he could feel it on his lips and eyes.

Sara paused. 'What's that noise?' They listened to it for a moment; a dull, distant roar, and nearer, somewhere ahead, a soft swish. Odd hollow knocks came from somewhere beneath them. It reminded Conor of the sounds in the watch-tower; he wasn't surprised when Meurig answered, 'Water. The sea is all around the island remember, and far under our feet too. We're deep inside it. We'll have to feel the way now – there's only one match and we'd better keep it.'

They moved forward, into blackness. Conor could not feel the sides of the tunnel, or the roof, even when he stretched up.

'It's big.'

'Good.' Sara laughed. 'Better than the way in. We   '

A sudden, enormous crash silenced her. The tunnel seemed

to move; there was a slither of rocks, a cry, dust. Conor flung himself down instinctively; for a moment he thought the roof was coming in, but nothing fell on his taut back, though the taste of dust in his mouth made him cough.

'Sara!'

'I'm all right! What happened?'

'I don't know. Meurig? Are you all right?'

There was no answer.

'Meurig?' Sara breathed.

A rattle of stones ahead, a long fall, the plip of them in deep water. Then nothing.

14

'He's hurt.'

Conor jerked forward but Sara grabbed at him. 'Be careful! Hands and knees.'

They crawled into the dark, through dust, feeling stones and shards roll under their palms. Almost at once Sara stopped him. 'Feel it?'

'What?'

She took his hand and slid it forward over the ground. 'That.'

He felt an edge, broken and crumbling, and beyond it, nothing. It was a hole, and a big one, sprawling right across the path. Sara leaned over into the dark. 'Meurig?'

There was a movement below, a clatter of stones. Then to their intense relief, his voice. 'Keep back Sara. The edge isn't safe. It gave way under me.'

'Are you hurt?'

'Sore. I've knocked my head . . . I'm a bit dizzy. And I've taken the skin off my hands, or it feels like that.' The voice paused. 'This slope – if I move I'll slither deeper.'

'You don't sound so far down.' Conor wriggled out. 'Hold my waist, Sara, tight.'

He put his palms down the inside of the hole and stretched downwards. Then he squirmed out a bit further, until his chest was well out into nothingness. A few pieces of stone and soil fell; he heard Meurig slip and gasp.

Still they could not touch.

'I'll try going a bit further.'

'For heaven's sake be careful,' Sara muttered, her hands gripping his belt. 'If you fall in you'll pull me over, and then we'll all be finished.'

No sooner had she said it than he almost overbalanced; his hands waved wildly in mid air, and he yelled in alarm. She hauled him back almost at once, but not before his fingers had touched something warm and alive.

'I felt his hand! Down a bit, Sara, just a bit . . . that's it.' He felt the fiddler's firm grip close on his. 'Got him! All right, pull!'

He began to struggle back, Sara dragging at him. It took them five minutes of pulling, with Meurig scrambling and clawing in the darkness, until Conor's back and shoulders were an agony of stretched and aching muscles. Finally he managed to grab the fiddler's coat, and with one last effort Meurig crawled over the lip of the pit and collapsed, breathless and aching, next to Conor. They lay there, uncaring, while the echoes settled.

After a long silence, Conor sat up. 'I feel as though I've been on the rack. I'm at least two inches taller!' In the dimness he saw Meurig move his fingers gently over the fiddle. One string hummed, a soft comforting sound in the dark.

'Is it all right?' Sara said.

'I think so. Luckily it was on my back and I fell forward.' He still seemed shaken, and in some pain, Conor thought.

'Nothing broken?'

'No, just bruises.'

Reluctantly Sara said, 'Meurig, we should get on . . .'

'I know.' He stood up, unsteadily, and moved one foot carefully forward. A rattle of stones slid into distant water. They passed the hole by feeling the edge but after only a few steps they came to another, gaping treacherously in the floor. Only Sara's outstretched foot saved another fall.

Beyond that were more. At the fourth she stopped and sighed. 'Oh look, this is impossible. It will take hours, if we have to feel like this! And if we hurry we'll be down one of these deathtraps for good.'

In the silence they listened to the sound of water far below, swishing and washing in slow rhythms, filling all the drowned hollows of the island.

Then Meurig moved. They heard the crack of a match, then saw his face clearly for a moment, with a new long scratch down his forehead, lit by a small flame that slowly steadied and grew. All at once Conor could see Sara, her astonished stare, her clenched fists.

'You can't!' she gasped. 'Meurig, you can't do that.'

The fiddler gripped the candle, blood from his hands smeared red on the wax. 'No choice Sara.' He scrambled up. 'We've got to get out . . .'

The flame crackled. They stared at it in horror.

'It's too much,' Conor said.

Meurig looked down at them, his face sharp and edged with candlelight. 'Look Conor, it's me Hafren is angry with, and I have to be there when she comes. I have to. It's all my fault, my carelessness, my despair. If this is what it costs then so be it.'

'Oh put it OUT,' Sara moaned.

'No.'

'Conor, tell him!'

'I have,' Conor said unhappily. 'But it's the only way to get out. He's right.' And yet he knew how much this must be costing Meurig, and he was horrified. The fiddler's hands shook. The candle flickered.

'Hurry up then,' Meurig turned abruptly. 'Life's short enough as it is.'

With the tiny flame to guide them the dangers were obvious. Great chasms and gaps broke open across the path; holes plunged to deep pools of phosphorescent water far below, sometimes stinking with greasy black weed. Most were steeper than the one Meurig had fallen into; he had been lucky. They had to jump several, and without the faint glimmer of the candle flame they would surely have fallen.

When the tunnel widened they saw more clearly the holes that pitted it; they threaded their way between them, over narrow bridges of rock, around brims and edges. They hurried more than was safe, nervous, out of breath. In the dark the candle burned steadily, with the soft hiss of melting wax. Its light flickered up wildly over the walls; threw huge leaping shadows. Their eyes strayed to it, furtively, fearfully.

The passage led up now. They pulled each other wearily over rock falls. The air seemed to grow lighter; looking up, Conor saw far above him a ghostly gleam of daylight, at the top of a narrow chimney.

The three of them paused to stare up at it.

'What do you think?' Meurig muttered.

'Too high.' Conor looked at the tunnel that ran on into blackness. 'We'd never climb up.'

He was right, but they went on reluctantly. That glimpse of distant, unreachable sky brought back all the worry about what Hafren might be doing, far off in the estuary. Meurig gripped the dwindling stub of candle tighter, as if he could somehow make it last.

Then Sara stopped. 'Listen!'

For a long second all they heard was the splutter of the

flame. Then, far back, a tiny whisper of sound; the rattle of falling stones.

Conor looked at Meurig. 'The cat!'

'Only too likely.' Meurig walked on, quickly. 'If the water reached it then it would wake up.' He began to run, sending the flame jerking over the low roof. 'Hurry. We must be near the end.'

They ran upwards, aching, their hands and feet sore from crawling and scrambling over rock. The air grew lighter; Meurig pinched out the candle flame with a whisper of relief and jammed the stub deep in his pocket.

'How much is left?' Conor gasped.

'Enough. Look, up there!'

Unbelievably, wonderfully, the tunnel was opening. It spread to a wide track, a bank of millions of tiny shells that crunched and slithered underfoot, and then as they climbed up Conor saw the sky, blue and clear, and smelt the fresh, unmistakeable tang of salt and weed and rock pools. Gulls screamed overhead, and a yell of delight rose in his throat, but as he turned he saw far down the tunnel a lithe white glimmer racing towards them.

'Run!' he yelled.

And they ran, really ran, scrambling and falling down the bank of shingle, spilling out onto a wide beach paved with flat slabs of green rock, crusted with barnacles. Deep pools of sky opened under their feet.

Meurig glanced around. The beach was backed by cliffs, high, sheer, white with gull nests. There was no way up.

'Down to the water!'

They raced to the edge of the rocks. The sea spread a wide frill of white lace over the sodden sand; their feet cut sharp prints that filled and softened.

'Now what?' Sara stared out to sea.

'The ferryman. He said he would wait.'

'It wasn't here he left us.'

'I have the distinct feeling that doesn't matter.'

'Well he'd better be very quick then,' Conor said, glancing back.

The cat sat in the cave mouth. It licked one paw, then slid smoothly upright and paced towards them, through the barnacles and bladderwrack. Above, the birds screamed and soared.

'It won't come into the water, will it?' Conor muttered.

No one answered. Instead they all backed into the sea, feeling its cold soak their boots, drench their feet.

As the cat came on they went deeper; knee-high, swaying as the waves tugged at them, as the rough sand was scoured out from under them.

Snarling, ears flat, the cat reached the water's edge.

'What about swimming?' Sara said.

'It would surely get one of us,' Meurig staggered as a wave slapped him, 'and where would we swim?' He pulled a wry face. 'I'd like to thank you both for your help.'

'We're not going anywhere,' Sara said. 'I hope you're not losing heart again.'

'How can I, with you?'

Conor looked at them both through the spray. 'You're idiots, the pair of you,' he said.

The cat crouched, choosing. Then it stared beyond them, out to sea. Its eyes narrowed. It yowled with rage.

Meurig turned; then with a cry he twisted and dived, and even as his head came up above the water, mist was around him, a faint grey glistening, and in it Conor saw the boat,

201

and the ferryman's silent, huddled form. He pushed Sara towards it, and with a great yell, turned and splashed water furiously at the prowling cat. The cat mewed, its eyes narrowed in the foam and spray. It jumped back, and Conor felt someone grab his arms from behind and haul him up, and even as he fell into the bottom of the boat he saw the cat dissolve; become nothing but a floating patch of foam and bubbles on the incoming tide.

'Where is it?' he gasped. 'Did it drown?'

Sara dragged the soaked hair from her face and looked back at the beach. 'It's gone, that's all. Just gone.' She looked at him and grinned. 'I have to say I thought we'd had it then.'

He picked himself up. 'So did I.' Then he turned and saw the ferryman pulling the oars close beside him, and moved quickly next to Sara, lurching the frail boat.

Silent, drained of all speech, and cold despite the sun, they let the ghost-craft carry them away from Hafren's island. It dwindled, slowly, a green glint in the sparkling waves.

Conor took his eyes from it at last and looked at the others, seeing how worn and dirty they looked; how the blood had crusted on his own collar and on Meurig's hands, how Sara had a great smudge of dirt down her face. He told her about it and she wiped it off with her sleeve, irritably. 'I'm filthy all over, Conor, but I don't suppose anyone will notice out here, do you?'

The ferryman watched her, his eyes wan.

Conor turned to Meurig. 'Well we made it!'

The fiddler opened his eyes and smiled. 'We were lucky.'

'How's the fiddle?'

'The bag's waterproof.'

'And the candle?'

Meurig opened his hand. The candle, rather smaller, rolled as the boat swayed. He clutched it tight.

'Good.' Conor leaned back. The sun was warming him now, and he felt no seasickness; he was cheerful and relieved. 'We've done all right, haven't we? Considering.'

No one answered him.

'Well?'

'Conor,' Meurig said.

He sat up, took one look at the fiddler's white face and whirled round to stare back at the island.

Swollen, enormous, the cat was pacing towards them over the waves. It had become a creature of mist, its eyes shining, its huge tail thrashing across the sky, leaving drifts of cloud behind it.

Conor clutched his knees and said nothing. None of them could.

Closer, looming high above them now, the cat filled the sky, its eyes narrow, satisfied slits. It raised one paw of mist, bigger than the boat, and slowly, firmly, brought it down on them.

15

Sara screamed; Conor ducked.

But the paw passed right through them and swept up again, its claws dripping.

Furious, the cat struck again, slashing sideways with a swipe that made the air hum, and then again, angrily, bringing a strange cold tingling through Conor's body. The boat swayed as he grabbed the side.

'Keep still,' Meurig snapped. 'It's all right! It doesn't look as though it can hurt us.'

The cat bent closer; they could see its fury. Its great face snuffled against them, as if it would pick the boat up in its mouth like a dead mouse, and shake it, spilling them all out, but even as it tried it found it could not bite a ghost, and they saw its anger change to fear, almost bewilderment.

'Poor old puss,' Sara laughed. 'It's all a bit hard to grasp!'

She giggled as the great tongue of mist rasped over her; Conor saw the enormous teeth, the furry muzzle with its whiskers thick as cables, and reached up to touch it, but his hand too, passed through, and he felt only damp and cold.

'It's there, but it's not there. Or is it us? Are we the ghosts?'

Meurig glanced at the ferryman. 'Perhaps we are.'

Chilled, Conor looked up at the cat. It stood still now, watching the boat slide away. The edges of its ears and fur seemed blurred, fainter.

'It's fading,' Sara said, kneeling up. 'Can you see?'

'It's come too far from the island.' Meurig rubbed his face with the back of his hand and allowed himself a smile. 'I should think its power stems from there. It must wane the further it goes.'

Frailer now, the sky showing through it, the cat watched them go. In a few moments it was almost transparent, its shape loosening and drifting, until Conor found he was looking only at cloud; a long thin mass of it, gently dissolving until the sky was clear.

'Well!' Sara settled back, comfortable in the long rise and fall of the boat. 'Maybe we have got away with it . . . or am I speaking too soon?'

Because the ferryman had paused in his rowing; the boat dipped in a sudden trough. He turned his head and looked back, and at the same time Conor felt a breeze spring up, ruffling his hair and collar.

'What is it?' he said uneasily.

The ferryman turned, and began to row again.

'Can you tell us?' Meurig said.

The ghost-face lifted. When it spoke the voice was strained, and painful. 'She knows, watchman.'

Fearfully, they looked at him.

'The weather?'

'She is coming after you. I feel the anger in the river, the deep swelling, the swift currents. She seeks what you have there, what you have stolen.'

'Stolen!' Meurig said hotly 'How many times do I have to hear that? I've stolen nothing. Nothing!'

He bit his lip and was silent. Conor looked at Sara.

The breeze gathered, quickly; their coats flapped. Far off to the west a low, ominous bank of red cloud was rising, dulling the clear sky. The sea became grey and choppy. The frail oars sliced through it, bringing up bubbles and foam and showing the strange sinuous shapes of fish with spiny backs and gaping mouths that swam in agitated shoals deep in the murk.

Conor felt cold again. The boat seemed frailer; mist began to drift from it. He knew they were coming back to their own place at last, back to the estuary swollen with the great tide. The sky grew darker. The boat sank into troughs, plummeting with sudden speed, rising and spinning. Rain splattered on him, and he bent his head, gripping the sides of the boat.

'Will we make it?'

'No,' Meurig whispered.

As he spoke, the squall struck. Hail pelted the boat, turning it white with a stinging hiss, robbing them all of breath. A wave picked the boat up and dashed it forward at tremendous speed, leaving them all in a tangled heap in the bottom, all except the ferryman, who rowed on, untroubled. A green wave rose against them; Conor could see far into it, brown weed floating in the heart of it; then it broke to a white roar, swamping the boat and rushing through the old man's body in a crash of foam. Conor struggled up; he put his hand down and the soft timbers split under his weight; water sloshed into the pockets of his coat.

'We're sinking!'

'Don't be daft,' Sara spat over the side. 'How can you sink a ghost?'

'We can still drown!' He looked at the ferryman. 'Can't we?'

The old man nodded. 'As I did, when she dragged me down, far into the mud and places of pain.' Through the rain and the crash of spray he smiled. 'But she could not hold me. I have escaped her.'

'Then help us to.' Meurig pulled Conor up.

The mist thickened, darkness grew. Conor became aware, through the storm, of a new sound ahead of them, the thrash and slap of waves on a beach, or on the wall, the hiss and drag of shingle.

'Listen!'

'I hear it.' The fiddler caught Sara's arm. 'Are you ready?'

She tried to answer but spray drenched them all. They saw her close her lips tight and nod.

'Guard the wall,' the old man said, unexpectedly. 'Or tonight there will be more drowned faces in her pools.' He gave one last tug on the oars, and the boat pierced the green wall of a wave and slid noiselessly into the narrow pill; the land looming so suddenly out of the dark that Conor was bewildered; he had thought they were still far out in the estuary.

Sara jumped out at once, sinking well into the mud.

'Conor!'

He scrambled over the side, his hands feeling the boat's timbers become faint and cold. Water splashed to his knees; a wave roared in and soaked him, lifting the dissolving ghost of the boat. Meurig was out straight after him; together they squelched through mud and stones to the firmer shingle. When they looked back the ferryman and his boat were nowhere. The estuary churned; wide and empty; the gale drove the tide hard on the land.

Meurig pushed him on. 'Over the wall. We won't be safe until we are.'

They turned, but as Conor put his hand down he felt the vibration under his feet, the huge swelling weight crashing down on him. He scrambled up but the wave knocked him down, drenched him, left him choking in salt and mud and spume. He clung tight to the wall, not breathing. There was a long moment of green; brown weed against his face; pain. Then his head burst out into the air; he snatched a breath and gripped tighter. The wave tore at him as it went back, tore his hair and coat with what he felt sure were hands, Hafren's fingers dragging him. For a moment he thought she had him; then with a wrench he was free, water streaming from his clothes. He scrambled up, leapt the rocks and was over the top of the wall before the next wave could catch him.

It was dark here; spray filled the air. He looked for the others and saw Sara, her face splashed with mud, and Meurig sliding down the bank. They coughed and spat in shocked silence; the waves clawing the wall at their backs.

'Let's get further in,' Conor gasped at last.

Painfully they loped up the track, shivering with cold. When they reached the gate they dragged it shut behind them and crumpled in an exhausted row against the comfortingly solid wood.

Conor wiped his face with his sleeve. He was tired and achingly hungry. He realized they had been gone since morning, with nothing to eat or drink.

'What's the time?'

Sara shrugged, 'My watch is full of water. About seven? It's dark enough.'

Over the hedge a cow coughed, making them jump.

'So we made it. I never thought we would,' Conor said, grinning.

Meurig, beside him, took out the candle from his pocket and held it, a small white glimmer on his palm.

'Now what?' Conor said, looking at it.

'Home. As soon as we can.'

16

The Sea Wall Inn was ablaze with light. The waves battering the wall threw spray high above it; it clattered on the roof like white rain.

Conor tripped over a sandbag and almost fell into the bar. His mother ran out from the kitchen, wet hair plastered to her forehead.

'Oh thank God!' she said. 'Where on earth have you been? Look at the state of you!'

'Nowhere on earth, exactly.' Conor sat down at a table. He felt incredibly tired; his hand throbbed fiercely.

'I was so worried when we came back and you weren't here.' His mother wiped hair from her eyes. 'We've had to leave the van up the lane at Morris's. The road is full of water.' She threw a shocked look at Meurig and Sara, who were crouching over the fire, shivering, and became instantly brisk.

'Right. Dry clothes, hot food. Upstairs Conor, now. Sara, go into my room, you might find a few things you can wear. Meurig . . .'

'I'm quite all right Jill.' The fiddler lay back wearily in a chair, his feet stretched out to the spitting blaze.

'Nonsense. You're soaked. You'll catch your death.'

He smiled. 'On the contrary, I couldn't be better. But I am a bit thirsty.'

Evan came in, his arms round a great sack of sand. He flung it down on the doorstep with a groan, slammed the door and turned to see her handing Meurig a glass of beer. The fiddler drank and sighed. 'Wonderful.'

As Conor pushed Sara upstairs he caught Evan's sour look in the mirror and laughed.

'What's tickling you?' Sara asked.

'Nothing.'

But when she had changed into an old purple jumper and jeans, and was sitting on the floor lacing her shoes he said, 'She likes Meurig.'

Surprised, Sara looked up. 'Well, well. I thought you didn't want her to like anyone.'

'Don't be daft. I don't want her to marry Evan, that's all.'

She laughed. 'You're mad, Conor. You've no idea. She doesn't want to marry Evan. Your neck's bleeding again – and she'd tell you if you asked her.'

'How do you know I haven't?'

'Oh I know. I know you.'

Spray rattled the window. Annoyed, Conor jammed on a spare pair of socks and went to look out. A dustbin lid went clanging somewhere down the lane; the gale struck the house with gusts that rattled every door. Beyond the wall the tide was rising fast; even now, with two hours to the top of the tide, the sound of the crashing waves was louder than he had ever remembered it before.

'You're not going home, are you?'

'In this?' She scrambled up. 'I just phoned, anyway. They're all out filling sandbags; Nan says the place is like a fortress. The police wanted them to evacuate but Dad won't leave the stock. She told me to stay put.'

'But it's nearer the wall here.'

She shrugged. 'The wall's never broken yet.'

He went to the door. 'No one's ever robbed Hafren before. I've never heard waves like that.'

210

Downstairs they ate quickly and in silence, around a table pulled close to the fire, Meurig with his hands washed and carefully bandaged. Evan banged in and out noisily, humping sandbags, carrying things upstairs, treading heavily on the floorboards. Sara grinned at Conor and he shrugged.

'Hot tea.' His mother put down some striped mugs and looked at them all curiously. 'You still haven't told me where you were today.'

They exchanged furtive glances. 'Exploring,' Meurig said, cutting a potato absently into four pieces. 'Wet, dark, horrible places.'

'I can see that. You're a bigger kid than they are!'

He smiled.

'How was the cinema?' Conor asked quickly.

'Oh fine.' She collected the plates. 'I missed you though. Evan rustled toffee papers in the quiet bits. I think he got bored.'

'He would.'

Evan, as if he had heard, came through, and gave them all an irritated glance, especially Meurig. 'You won't get an audience tonight.'

'Never mind.' The fiddler looked ruefully at the damp bag on the floor. 'I don't think I'd be worth hearing.'

A crash of spray against the windows made them all jump. It hissed down the chimney. Conor's mother slammed the windows and bolted them.

'Look, the alert's gone to double red,' Evan said, rubbing his nose. 'Don't you think . . .'

'What?'

'Well, it might not be safe to stay here. The police said . . .'

Jill faced him, angrily. 'This is my house and I'm not leaving it. Not for some village hall in Magor. We've had floods before, if it comes to that.'

'It was just a thought, Jill.'

'Well if you want to go . . .'

'Oh Lord no. Of course I don't.' He nodded, reasonably. 'I understand how you feel. I'll finishing moving the things upstairs.'

'Thanks Evan.'

Thoughtfully, Conor helped Meurig take the dishes out to the kitchen.

'Are you staying?'

Meurig shook his head. 'I'm going to the watchtower. I need to see how things are. I'll be back though.'

Listening to the roar of the waves Conor said, 'It'll be dangerous. Don't think you're safe just because you've got the candle.'

'I know. But I need to see the wall, how it's holding. I'm the watchman . . . it's about time I watched. Like I said, I've thought too much about myself.' He took something from his pocket. It was the candle. He looked at it. Then, deliberately, he held it out. 'I want you to keep it for me. I daren't take it out there.'

Appalled, Conor took it, silently, and put it into his pocket. The small stub felt cool and slightly clammy. 'Don't be long,' he said, lamely.

Meurig buttoned up his coat. 'Believe me, I won't.' Then he opened the door and slid out into the storm.

When he was gone they worked quickly. The rest of the sandbags were dragged and hauled and flung against doors and windows; shutters were nailed tight; valuables carried upstairs. Outside the gale roared; with still an hour to go the windows were awash with spray. Beyond hearing, like a pounding deep in his head, Conor felt the relentless throb of Hafren's anger, never pausing, never giving in.

At half past ten a crash on the back door made them all turn. Someone banged on it again, hard, and Conor ran to it, thinking it was Meurig, but when the bolts were shot back Mr Caristan stumbled in, rain streaming from his new yellow waterproofs. A small avalanche of mud and water streamed in with him.

'I'm so sorry,' he muttered, fumbling with the zip of his coat. 'Look at the mess!'

Jill smiled bleakly. 'There'll be plenty more later on, don't worry. Another orphan of the storm?'

Sheepishly, he unzipped his coat. 'I'm afraid so. Despite all the warnings I didn't really get enough sandbags . . . it's foolish, I know. I moved all my china to the loft. I was, just, well . . . I couldn't stand it, sitting there, you know, all alone in the house.' He rubbed his hair. 'It was as if I could hear voices. Voices in the wind, screaming . . . fanciful, isn't it? And water began to seep under the door into the hall – as you know the house is in a bit of a hollow. In short, I got scared.' He laughed, nervously. 'I just wanted a few friendly faces. Drown in company, you know. Do you mind, Jill?'

Conor grinned at Sara. His mother shook her head. 'You're a real hero,' she said, not unkindly. 'Well there's plenty of room here. Come by the fire before the rain puts it out.'

'I know I'm a nuisance,' he muttered.

'How's the track out there?' Evan asked.

'Oh knee-deep, I'm afraid, and in some places higher. And

213

the waves! I could hardly get along against the spray, even right under the wall. They must be tremendous.'

'No way out then, even if we wanted to.'

'We don't want to,' Conor growled.

Half an hour passed, slowly. When everything was done they sat in the bar, listening to the fury of the storm, watching the flames hiss and sink under the constant soaking spray that sloshed down the chimney. Finally, they went out. Conor fingered the candle, wondering about Meurig. If he had been swept away they wouldn't even know.

Water had been seeping through the sandbags and under the door for an hour or more; now it lay over the flagstones, trickling down the step into the kitchen. An enormous thump outside made Evan slide the shutter nervously aside.

'Shed's blown down.'

Mrs Jones shrugged, her feet on a chair. 'That happens in most winds.' She dragged the hair from her cheek and winked at Sara. 'The men are nervous. I think we'd better move upstairs.'

As they climbed up Conor muttered. 'I wish Meurig would hurry.'

'He'll be all right,' Sara said.

They went into his bedroom and put the light on, but almost immediately it crackled and sparked and flicked off. None of the switches would work.

'Blast!' Evan snapped. 'Now what?'

'Candles.' Conor's mother came in with three, already lit; their flames threw enormous shadows, making the room alien and unfamiliar. Conor sat on the bed, watching Evan try the radio. 'That won't work. It never does in a storm. Interference.'

'There must be some way we can find out what's going

on!' Evan said desperately. 'What are the coastguard doing? What's the storm warning? We're just marooned here.'

'We've no choice,' Conor said briskly. He was enjoying himself now; the big man was nervous, and he knew it.

Evan paced heavily, creaking the floorboards. Mr Caristan sat uncomfortably on the end of the bed.

'Oh sit down Evan,' Conor's mother snapped.

'I just wish we could *do* something.'

'I'll bet Meurig's doing something,' Conor said maliciously. Sara pursed her lips at him, and he turned and opened the shutter a crack. 'Just look at it out there!'

The night was a roaring blackness. Water blurred the glass; it was impossible to see anything, but they could feel the building shiver and crack around them, the noise of the wind rising to a shriek above the banging and clatter of objects down in the yard. Then Conor caught a movement below and whirled round. 'It's Meurig! Quick!'

He and Sara hurtled down the dark stairs. To his astonishment the kitchen was already knee-deep in water; it rose against his Wellingtons and an empty cardboard egg box bumped his leg as he dragged back the bolts of the door. Meurig slid in, a torrent of water with him. He was drenched, and they knew by his look things were serious. He pushed past them to Conor's mother.

'You'll have to leave.'

'No . . . I can't.'

Meurig took her hands. 'Listen Jill, the wall may be breached, there's a real danger. If it is, this house will be flattened; the sea will surge in and batter it to pieces, you know that. You're too close and way below sea level. Come to the watchtower. It's the safest place. This is what it was built for.'

Unhappily she looked at Conor, then briefly round the kitchen.

'We'd be swept away out there,' Evan said. 'It's madness.'

Meurig ignored him. He waited, until she looked up at him.

'We'll come,' she said.

A shutter crashed; rain splattered their faces. Outside, the wind screamed, like a jealous girl.

17

Conor's coat was still soaked; he pulled it on hurriedly and shoved two packets of crisps from a box into his pocket. Meurig waited by the door; when they were all ready he said, 'Keep together. Keep hold of each other. Once we get in the lee of the wall the wind is less powerful, but the spray is crashing like hail; it's hard to breathe, let alone see.'

'Yes all right,' Evan said impatiently. 'I think we know that.'

Meurig gave him an amused look. 'Right. Go last then, will you?'

For a moment Evan looked as if he would argue; then he shrugged and pulled on his hood.

Meurig unbolted the door. 'Ready? Here goes.' With a sudden jerk he pulled it wide. Water roared in over their knees. 'Dear God,' Mr Caristan whispered.

Staggering, half blind, they waded out, climbing over the sandbags. Evan struggled to shut the door, but the force of the water was too great; he left it and grabbed Caristan's arm.

'It won't shut!'

'Leave it!' Jill pushed Sara on. 'Leave it!'

Meurig had been right. The wind was a wild, battering pain; it slammed them across the car park hard against the fence, and they had to grip the wooden posts and drag themselves along. In the open track it was worse; crossing to the wall Conor fell twice and had to be hauled up, dripping, from the water. He reached shelter with all the breath knocked out of him, soaked again.

Meurig glanced along the line, hair in his eyes. 'All still here?'

Sara laughed, leaning back against the wet slope of the wall. 'This is crazy! Look at the spray!'

Above them the sky was white; sea water fell like hail, drenching them all. Conor felt the wall vibrate, terrifyingly close.

'It's shaking! It moved!'

Wet soil slid under his fingers; fragments of soil slid and trickled. 'Meurig!'

The fiddler was there, his face a mask of rain. 'And up there,' he yelled.

The top of the wall showed a tiny cleft, with a trickle of tide pouring from it. It was small, but they knew it would grow, that Hafren would work it with her wet fingers, dragging down the soil, washing out the roots of the grass, undermining the stones till they slipped and settled and the flood burst through.

'What can we do?'

He saw Meurig shout something.

'What?'

A gust of wind knocked the fiddler against the wall. He picked himself up and hung onto Conor 'Sandbags,' he yelled in Conor's ear.

'Plenty at the pub! But what about . . .'

Conor flung a glance at his mother. If they took bags from the pub the damage would be worse.

'It doesn't matter!' she yelled. 'If the wall breaks there won't be a pub! I'm coming back with you.'

'You're not! Evan will come. Get these youngsters to the tower, please Jill!'

After a second she nodded, and grabbed Conor's arm. 'Let's go.'

They ran, splashing through the mud and seeping flood-water. Halfway down Sara said, 'Where's Caristan?'

Conor looked back. A figure in oilskins waved them on. 'He's coming.'

The watchtower was almost invisible in the storm, all but the windows, high up. Meurig must have left the oil lamp lit, for it glowed up there, a pale square of hope. And the waves leapt up at it, great crashes of spume, slithering down the sheer walls in long sheets of bubbles and foam, and Conor thought, as he ran towards it, that for a moment they were hands, not small, as from the reen, but huge; long, white-nailed fingers tearing at the tower.

Then they were through the spray, and fitting the key in the lock.

Inside, they climbed the steps out of the water and sat slowly, taking breath.

'I can't feel my ears,' Sara moaned.

'I can.' Conor rubbed his. 'I wish I couldn't. We've got to get that door closed.'

He splashed across, and the figure in yellow oil-skins slid in and helped him. Together they forced it shut and slid the bolt, feeling the swollen wood strain and crack.

Then the man took his hood off, and they saw it was Evan.

Astonished Conor said 'I thought you'd gone to help Meurig?'

'Caristan went.'

Conor was silent. He heard his mother and Sara move behind him. 'Evan?' his mother said, her voice sounding strange in the echoing tower. 'But Caristan's an old man.'

Evan pushed past her, filling the narrow stair. 'He was gone before I could stop him, Jill, so I came on to look after you. It's a tomfool idea, anyway.'

'Not if it saves the wall.' She whirled round, angrily.

He shrugged and climbed up. Conor looked at Sara and raised his eyebrows. He followed his mother up in silence.

Meurig had left the fire burning, and the lamp lit on the table. The room was wonderfully warm and hushed. The sea might tear at them, but the strong walls were stone, and thick.

They sat down for a while, thawing themselves, listening to the storm. Conor sat next to Sara, steam rising from his knees. He put his hand in his pocket and took out the candle, holding it hidden. Such a small, ordinary thing. Feeling the fire warm it, he pushed it back.

At last his mother lifted her head. 'Here they are!' She ran downstairs; after a time they heard voices, echoing footsteps. Evan sat waiting at the table. He unfolded his arms and leaned back in the chair. Conor thought there would be a row, but when Meurig came in he went straight to the fire and said nothing. Mr Caristan gave Evan a sharp look and pressed his lips tight; he took off his waterproof slowly.

Sara got up and helped him. 'Is it done?'

'As well as we could. Wet sand is unbelievably heavy. My back will never be the same. But we've plugged the gap, and it will be slower to widen. The tide is at the full now. It may make all the difference.' He went to the fire and Conor moved aside. 'Thank you Conor. Very kind.'

For a while no one spoke. It was strange, Conor thought, how a group of people could all be thinking the same thing, and yet none of them wanted to say it. But it hung in the air like a bad smell. Evan had been scared.

Meurig and Sara were angry, and Caristan too polite to say anything, but how did his mother feel? What was she thinking? He looked across at her, as she sat on the bed staring at her wellies, her straight hair masking her eyes.

She glanced up, gave him a quick smile, and stood. 'This won't do. Have you got a kettle, Meurig? Let's have some tea.'

When it came the tea was hot and strong, in two chipped mugs that had to be shared. Mr Caristan looked at his and shook his head. 'When I think of all that beautiful china down there . . . Do you think it will survive?'

Meurig shrugged. 'If the wall holds we'll all survive.'

'I'll make you a small present of a few items,' Caristan said. 'A rather sweet Coalport . . .' He stopped, and stammered '. . . that is . . . if you want it.'

Meurig frowned. 'Thank you.'

Conor knew they were thinking of the burglary. He grinned into his mug.

'About that business . . .' Caristan said suddenly.

'It was my fault,' Meurig said shortly, 'but I wasn't trying to steal anything.'

'No . . . no indeed. But no hard feelings, eh?'

Meurig gave him a sharp look. 'No. It's all finished now.'

There was a short silence.

'The tide must have turned by now,' Sara said, at last.

'Yes.' Meurig stared into the fire. 'But the wind is still a gale. She may well have clawed the wall away. The storm would drown the noise.'

'Who's she?' Evan held the mug and sipped from it noisily. It was the first time he had said anything for a while.

Meurig shrugged, easily. 'Did I say she? I meant the river, of course.'

Later, they tried to sleep. Conor's mother curled up on the bed, and the rest made themselves uncomfortable huddles on the wooden floor. With his head on one of Meurig's pullovers Conor lay still, listening to the crackle of the flames, the moan of the wind. The pullover smelled of woodsmoke; it made Conor remember the night he had first seen the fiddler by the reen, and the fingers of water that groped and slid. Now she was tearing at the tower, and he, inside her enormous fingers, was tiny.

The floor under him shuddered as a great wave crashed against the wall; down below him, through the floor he could hear the strange sloshing and knocking and trickle of water in the base of the tower. He closed his eyes and thought of the inn, drowned as in his dream, his clothes floating out of the wardrobe. Then he saw the wall, buckling and weakening, soil sliding from it, the cat's great white paw tearing it down, licking at it with a tongue of foam, licking him too, and biting his arm. He shrugged it off, but it grabbed him again with its soft mouth and shook.

'Wake up,' Sara breathed.

He rolled over and sat up, quickly.

The room was dark; the fire had sunk to a glimmer. The sky outside was slightly pale, as if beyond the clouds the morning was coming. His mother, Evan and Caristan were asleep, dim breathing shapes, but Meurig's blanket was empty.

'He's downstairs.'

'So?'

'He's talking to someone.'

Silent, he stood. They crept between the sleepers, slipped

222

out of the door and closed it softly. The stairwell was damp; the water below slapped and knocked on stone.

'Hear it?' Sara whispered.

Voices drifted from below, quiet and distorted.

Conor went down the dark steps carefully. 'Did you see him go?'

'No. I just heard.'

Lamplight flickered below on the green walls, showing Meurig's long shadow. He turned, quickly, the oil lamp in his hands. 'Who's that?'

'Only us. Who were you talking to?'

'He was talking to me.'

The voice, cold as winter, came from the open doorway. The waves washed in, and she stood waist-deep in them, her dress storm grey, swirling into the tide.

He came closer; Meurig jumped up a step and Conor noticed the lower ones were wet. The tide was ebbing.

'I was wrong.' She stepped closer, in the quavering glints and rippling reflections on the walls. 'I will need to watch you.'

'It's my job to watch you,' Meurig muttered.

She came one step out of the water; it streamed from her dress and sleeves and down the long weed-strewn hair. 'You have your life now. But remember, the spell is on you and can never be put out. You will never be out of my reach. We are bound, watchman, each to each.'

'I know that,' he whispered.

'Your friends,' she hissed, 'must be cleverer than they look.'

'Thanks,' Sara muttered drily.

A wave surged in and splashed right up over Meurig; he leapt up the steps, water running from his pockets.

'Do you think I would have it here? I will put it some-where where you'll never find it!'

With a shock Conor retreated back up the steps. He had forgotten he had the candle in his pocket! He felt cold.

The creature smiled; a twisted, uncanny look. 'Where is there I cannot come? Bury it, and I will send threads of myself smaller than worms through the soil. I will watch from every reen, puddle and pool. Every drain. And I will not tire, candleman. This wall will wear away under my hands. Year by year I will unpick it with my fingers.' She sank into the water, her hair spreading. 'I have all the time I need. Men die. I will always be here.'

It was true and they knew it. She drifted under the water, the pale oval of her face rippling for a moment under the floating foam. Then a wave washed over her, and she was gone.

18

The mud on the floor of the bar was inches thick; it coated the fallen stools and made a heavy brown stinking layer over the cold ashes of the fire. Jill hauled the shutters open; the bleary, grey light flooded the room.

'Dear God,' she said, 'look at it.'

And yet they all knew they had been lucky. The shutters had held, and apart from a few slates, so had the roof. In a week the mud would be cleared, and apart from a new green flood mark, which Conor would label with the year and the date, they had survived the river's anger. But if there were flood marks on people's hearts, Conor thought, Meurig's at least would be scarred.

But they'd made it. And it would be the same in all the houses and farms on the Levels this morning; clearing up, and being thankful that the wall still loomed over the sodden fields.

Mr Caristan had already gone, hurrying to his precious china. He'd even shaken Meurig's hand and said, 'I meant it, you know, about the Coalport.'

Meurig nodded. 'Thanks, but I'd probably only break it.'

Mr Caristan tried not to look appalled. 'Well, it is meant to be used,' he said bravely. 'And it's thanks to you I've still got it.'

'Thanks to both of us.'

Mr Caristan looked pleased, and shy. 'Maybe, in a little way, I may have helped.'

When he was gone Meurig turned to Jill. 'Look, can I borrow Conor? It won't take long – about an hour.'

She wiped her fingers on a rag, absently. 'If you like. But get him back because there'll be plenty to do here for days. And don't forget you're playing here tonight.'

'We're not opening!' Evan looked at her in surprise.

'We certainly are.' She pulled her boot from the mud. 'It takes more than a foot or two of sea water to keep the Sea Wall closed, I can tell you. Last time we had a flood we could only serve spirits for a week, and that did wonders for trade.' She put an arm round Sara and smiled. 'You should be getting home. They'll be worried.'

'I know. Thanks, Mrs J.'

Evan went into the kitchen, shaking his head. Conor followed Meurig and Sara to the door. 'I won't be long.'

'Fine.'

He lingered for a moment in the room. 'You'll be all right for now?'

His mother looked up at him in surprise. 'Look Conor, I can manage. I do run this pub myself, you know.'

He nodded, drily. 'I know.'

'There you are then.' She came over to him, and leaned her hand against the doorpost. Then she said, 'Floods don't just wash things away, do they? They leave things behind them as well. And they tell us a lot about our friends, don't you think?'

'I suppose so.'

'Well they do. So don't worry.' She brushed the damp hair from his forehead. 'It's all over, and we're all still here. And I'm the licensee, Conor. I'm in charge. You're a funny old worrier. Don't you know by now I can look out for myself?'

He smiled, and looked down. 'Yes, I know you can,' he said, and he turned and ran out after Meurig and Sara, ran

226

hard down the splashing track, wanting to shout and jump and yell in the blustering wind. He hurtled past Sara and whirled, running backwards, 'Come on! Let's see the damage!'

Racing up the steps, not caring whether they followed, he leapt to the top of the wall and the wind struck him, and he stared out with wet eyes at the great banks of brown, popping mud and far beyond it the distant silver line of the Severn, where flocks of waders formed their glittering, wheeling clouds.

She had gone. She had withdrawn, shrunk to a narrowness far off, and as always he was astonished at the speed and reach of her, how she could drown such a vast expanse of land twice every day, at the power of the moon and the tide.

They walked along to the place where the gap had begun. Meurig crouched and looked at it. The gap had been clogged with bags; below it the soil had seeped slightly, leaving a hole the size of a fist. 'That will have to be repaired properly,' he muttered.

Sara said, 'What happened, with Evan? He said . . .'

'Never mind what he said.' Meurig stood up and they followed him along the wall. 'He was scared, that's all. Caristan was scared too, but the difference was, he stayed. Makes me sorry I didn't try harder with him in the beginning . . . None of this might ever have happened.' He turned to Conor quickly. 'You've still got it safe?'

Conor put his hand to his pocket but Meurig said, 'Not now. Not here.'

'He's got the candle?' Astonished, Sara leapt down the steps and opened the farm gate. 'You trusted him with that!'

'Apparently.'

'You're mad!' she said firmly. 'I'll bet he even forgot he had it.'

They watched her run up the drive, waving.

'Did you forget?' Meurig asked quietly.

'Of course not.' Conor jammed his hands in his pockets and changed the subject. 'Where are we going, anyway?'

'Newport.'

'Like this!' He knew he was filthy; there were clots of mud in his hair and his clothes were damp and stiff.

Meurig strolled on to the bus stop. 'Who cares?'

On each side of the lane the swollen reens lay green and replete. Pools spread over the track; twigs and drowned worms floated in them. When the bus came they flagged it down and sat at the back, the only passengers. It wandered slowly through the wet lanes, the driver talking all the time over his shoulder about the storm. Spray hissed from the tyres and ran down the windows.

In Newport they got off.

'Where now?' Conor said. He still couldn't see what Meurig was up to, but it was obvious the fiddler had some plan.

For answer Meurig looked up at the the huge building in front of them, the Royal Bank of Wales, all marble facade and stucco magnificence.

'In there?' Conor said, appalled.

The fiddler nodded. He pushed open the plate glass doors and walked in boldly, across the immense, echoing hall, leaving a trail of mud over the plush, plum-coloured carpet, straight to a window marked Enquiries. Conor trailed reluctantly behind.

The cashier looked up. 'Can I help you?'

Meurig brushed muddy hair from his eyes. 'I've got some

property – very valuable property,' he snapped. 'I want to put it in a safety deposit box and keep it here.'

The girl's eyes widened. She flicked a glance at the fiddler's torn, drenched coat, the frayed sleeve of his pullover. 'I see.'

Conor fidgeted. He was sure people were staring. One kid with her mother giggled and pointed. He pulled a sliver of weed off his neck and jammed it in his pocket.

Meurig filled in the forms the girl gave him, quickly and carelessly. At the part where it said 'Nature of Valuables' he wrote 'one candle' in his spiky script, signed it, and pushed it back across the counter.

The girl read it; her eyebrows shot up.

'I'll just check this with the manager, sir.'

'You do that,' Meurig muttered.

They watched her cross the floor to a thin man in a grey suit; there was a hurried conversation. The man stared at them.

'Are you sure you want to do this?' Conor muttered. 'I mean, you wouldn't have it with you . . .'

'I know.' Meurig watched the manager stalk towards him. 'But where could be safer than here? I can't think of anywhere else.'

Down in the vaults, the manager rattled his keys, selected one, and after a dubious look at Conor, lifted out a small metal box with the number 77 painted on it in white. He brought it to the table and opened it. Then he stepped discreetly away.

'Wait!' Meurig said quickly. 'Listen. No one will have access to this, will they? No one at all?'

The man looked hurt. 'I assure you sir, the boxes are never opened by anyone except the owners. You will have the key. Your . . . valuables will be perfectly safe.'

'I hope so,' Meurig said desperately. 'It's just that . . . what I keep in here is very, very precious. It's a matter of life and death.'

The manager looked at Meurig as if he was mad. 'It'll be safe, sir,' he stuttered.

Meurig sighed and nodded to Conor; Conor took the candle out and gave it to him. The fiddler rolled it in his long fingers. 'Well,' he said softly, 'rest here and don't torment me any more.' He put it in, closed the metal box and locked it. Then he turned to the manager, who had been watching curiously. 'All yours.'

As the box was lifted they heard the candle roll inside, a small ominous sound, but Meurig turned firmly and marched through the thick iron doors of the vault and back upstairs.

Out on the street, they sat for a while on the plinth of a statue, looking, Conor thought, like a pair of tramps. He hoped none of the girls from school would come by.

'That's used up all my money,' Meurig said at last.

'I've got enough for the bus.'

'Then let's get back.' The fiddler stood up. 'You've got your mother to help and I've a fiddle needs tuning.'

'Meurig,' Conor said quietly. 'Look. Over there.'

The fiddler turned.

On the opposite pavement, outside the fishmongers, a small white cat sat washing. Its eyes were amber slits. It watched them intently.

'Coincidence,' said Meurig, after a moment.

'It might not be. She'd want to know where it is!'

'Let her.' Meurig turned and walked away. 'We've beaten her, Conor, at least where the candle is concerned. The wall we must guard for ever, but she'll never torment me like that again.'

Conor walked after him. Then he stopped and glanced back. The cat licked a paw and flicked out its claws and washed them, one by one. Then it got up and stalked off, towards the river.

Fintan's

Tower

The author gratefully acknowledges the financial assistance of the Welsh Arts Council during the writing of this book.

HERE

. . .yg kynneir or peir pan leferit
Oanadyl naw morwyn gochyneuit . . .

. . . my first utterance, it is from the Cauldron
that it was spoken.
By the breath of nine maidens it was kindled . . .

The Spoils of Annwn

For Toady and Moly

1

The Green Baize Door

'We're closing,' the librarian said, looking up at the clock, 'in exactly three minutes. Books or not.'

'All right.' *Keep your hair on.* Jamie tipped out a promising title from the shelf, then pulled a face and pushed it back. Why didn't they ever get anything new? Every week it was the same old tatty plastic jackets full of boring-looking kids with anoraks and torches – no ghosts, or astronomy, or crusaders. What he wanted was a book that was different.

'Two minutes,' the librarian snapped.

Junior Fiction was in a dim corner by the window that looked down into Grape Lane. Rain ran down the glass and streaked the dirt. Jamie pulled up a stool and glared at the rows of books. Come on, there must be something. It was three weeks since he'd last found a new one, and that had been about a tribe of intelligent rats who took over the London Underground. Well, they might have been intelligent, but whoever wrote the book wasn't . . .

The street door flew open; a big, red-haired man splashed in, his mac glossy with rain. He marched straight up to the desk.

'We're closed,' the librarian said. She didn't even look up.

The man wore a tartan scarf that covered half his face. His eyes were small and rather bloodshot, with no expression. Deliberately he reached out, took the Biro from her fingers and snapped it into two pieces, his eyes never leaving her face. Then he flung the pieces into the metal bin one by one; two loud explosions.

Jamie held his breath.

Arms folded, the librarian surveyed the stranger. 'There's a button under this desk,' she said firmly, 'which rings a bell in the police station.'

The big man put both hands down flat and leaned over. 'Don't waste my time, woman,' he growled. 'I'm here to see the Name in the Book.'

To Jamie's surprise the librarian blinked. She took off her glasses and her eyes were green as glass and glinted in the shadows. 'Oh, I see,' she said slowly. 'I see. Well, you should have said before, shouldn't you. It's over there, through the green baize door.'

The man smiled, rather unpleasantly, and picked up his streaming umbrella. He crossed the library and pushed through a small door that Jamie had not noticed before; it was in a dark corner behind some shelves. The door swished shut, silently. A chill draught swept across the room, ruffling the pages of some books.

Jamie turned back to the tatty jackets. The librarian found another pen and carried on writing; the clock ticked on towards half-past four; rain tapped and rattled on the window. Listlessly, Jamie flicked the pages of a manual on hang-gliding. Then he froze.

'I wonder, my dear, if you could help me. They are saying that the Name is in the Book.'

This time it was an oldish man in a tweed coat. He was short, and had a small, clever face with a stubbly grey beard. His scarf, tucked in out of the rain, poked from between his second and third buttons, and he carried a large canvas bag.

The librarian shrugged. 'Another one. You're late.'

'Oh, I've come a long, long way. I gather from your remark that I am not the first.'

'No. Now hurry up please, we're closing. Over there through the baize door.'

Intrigued, Jamie watched the old man walk eagerly between the shelves and open the door. It swung silently behind him.

Far off, the church clock began to chime the half-hour; water gurgled down the drainpipes outside. The librarian hummed to herself, licking a paper label. Jamie watched the door. Neither of the men had come back. What book were they looking for? They couldn't both borrow it. And what was all this about a name?

Then, on the last stroke of the clock, the door from the street was hurled wide, and a tall, fair-haired man burst in through a squall of rain. He flung himself at the desk; Jamie had a sudden shiver of anticipation.

'Listen!' said the man breathlessly. 'I've got to see the Name in the Book!'

A gasp came from Junior Fiction. The man spun round like a flash, but no one was there.

The librarian waved the sticky label. 'Green door. Better hurry.'

The stranger raced across the room and disappeared with a slam and a draught.

Right! Jamie thought. He stood up, pocketed his tickets and walked over to the desk. The librarian glared.

'Are you still here? Out! We're closed.'

Jamie rolled his hands into fists in his pockets.

'I hear,' he said, 'that the Name is in the Book.'

'What?'

'The Name is in the Book.'

She wrinkled her eyes up and pushed out her bottom lip. For a moment Jamie felt almost afraid. Something cold nudged against his heart. But all she said was: 'If you say so. The green door, in the corner.'

His heart thumping, Jamie followed the trail of wet footprints across the floor. When he reached the door he looked back. The librarian was looking after him with a particularly unpleasant smile.

'Good luck,' she said. 'You'll need it.'

On the other side of the door was a dark, damp landing, so damp his breath made a cloud in the air. To his left, a narrow wooden stair ran down into darkness, and a tiny window in the wall let in some bleared light.

He padded softly down. The steps were slimy, and they sounded hollow under his boots. At the bottom was a short passage, with puddles on the floor. Down here the walls were stone, icy cold under his fingers. Ahead of him was an archway, and through that he could see a room, empty, except for books. Books on shelves, books stacked in toppling towers on the floor, books fallen from broken chairs; all of them covered with years of dust and grime and webs.

His fingers found a light switch, and after a moment's silence, he pressed it. Weak light gleamed from a bulb in the ceiling.

No one else was in the room, but a trail of footprints led past a big wooden table to a door in the opposite wall. Jamie crossed the room and unlatched it. Rain splashed his face. He was looking out into the alley at the back of the building; putting his head out he could see an old iron lamppost halfway down in the darkness, dropping a pool of light on to the wet cobbles. Tiny arrows of rain flashed across it. He looked the other way. No one. It was silent, just a wet crack between the houses.

So why had they come, those three strangers? Stepping back into the basement he closed the door and went over to the table.

On it was a book. One book, by itself; smaller than most of the others in the room. The cobwebs had been wiped off it. The cover was of plain black leather, with no title, just a single tiny picture in the centre. He put a finger on it; it was hard and shiny as if made of glass, or enamel. It showed a bright blue sky and a landscape of tiny fields, hedges and hills, all in deep lustrous greens. Far off on the horizon was something grey, a dark tinge in the glass.

Jamie opened the book. Inside, on the first clean white page, a name was beautifully written in italics:

James Michael Meyrick

He stood there, stiff with surprise, reading those three familiar words over and over. Who had written his name? Who knew that he would come down here? After all, he hadn't known himself until that sudden daft idea upstairs.

Then the truth struck him like a sharp pain. The Name in the Book. It was his.

After a moment he thumbed through the rest of the pages. They were blank. For a second he thought he had glimpsed something, and turned back, but no, each page was white and empty. It was a thin book, only about fifty pages in all. Carefully, he laid it down. It fitted into the dust, in a square of clean desk. That meant . . . well, it must mean it had lain there undisturbed for years – until now. Those three had opened it, and read his name. He put out a finger and gingerly flicked the cover open again, half hoping it might have gone away. But there it was. And underneath, in the same spiky letters:

Take me home.

Suddenly, Jamie snapped the Book shut, stuffed it into his inside pocket and unlatched the back door. In the alley rain gurgled in culverts and drains; the sky was dim between the overhanging houses. He stepped outside and slammed the door. Pulling on his hood, he shoved his hands deep in his pockets and splashed through the pool of light from the lamppost, and away into the dark.

2

Book Fair

'What's this?' Jennie tapped the Book with her pencil. 'Don't tell me they've actually got something new!'

'It's not a library book.' He looked over but it was already too late. She had opened it and was flicking through the pages.

'Mmm. I see what you mean. Nice pictures though.'

'Pictures?' Jamie threw down the wool he had been tangling round the kitten and jumped up. 'What pictures?'

He took the book from her and looked through the pages, carefully. They were empty, just as they had been yesterday and this morning; even those three words he thought he had seen were gone. There was just his name, familiar and faintly mocking.

He turned his head. 'Which picture did you like best?' He tried to keep the eagerness out of his voice. Jennie shrugged over her homework. 'Oh, I don't know. The one at the back, I suppose – the tower with the figure on top.'

'What figure?'

'Well, look for yourself, Jamie. A gargoyle thing, a sentinel. And that light in the top window.' She became immersed in the fate of Sir Thomas More.

Jamie sat himself down on the step and leaned against the open door. In front of him the garden rolled smoothly down-hill; out of sight in the willows at the bottom he could hear the Caston Brook running down to the bridge. The grass was thick with leaves; wet blackened masses of them lay clotting in the kitchen drain, and in heaps against the wall. Rooks clung and squawked in the elms.

It was all wrong. Who had written the words, and how had they vanished again? He thought vaguely of invisible inks, heat treatment, mysterious cosmic rays.

He got up and wandered down to the brook. It was narrow here, and the trees met overhead and dropped their leaves into the fast brown water. There was a hole in the bank that he thought might be a rat's. The kitten came after him, dragging a trail of wool through the grass.

He sat on the bank and examined the picture on the Book's cover, for at least the tenth time. What was that dim mark on the furthest hill? It seemed nearer than before. It looked like a house, or . . . Struck by an idea, he ran into the house and came back with a magnifying glass. Lying full length in the willow leaves, he held it carefully over the tiny enamel.

It was a castle. Small, and greeny-grey, but complete. How could anyone paint that small? Even the battlements were perfect, and that faint point of light shining from the high window. Then, with a jerk, he gripped the magnifying glass tight. The light had gone out! He looked again, but the window was dark.

'Jamie!' His mother stood over him. 'Get up off the grass, will you. This just came.' She threw down a small brown envelope, which was addressed to him in delicate spidery writing. 'I'm going into the market now. Want anything?'

He shook his head absently and opened the envelope. A card fell out.

BOOK FAIR

THE OLD TITHE BARN

SMITHY STREET, CASTON

THURS. 29 OCTOBER, 10.A.M.

'It's about a book sale,' he said, puzzled. 'Who'd send it to me?'

'Well, you read books, don't you?' His mother came and took it. 'That's today. You can walk down with me, if you like. You might find some cheap paperbacks, or something.'

While Mrs Meyrick searched for her purse, Jamie ran upstairs. He wanted to put the Book away, but as he moved he thought he saw something inside and fumbled hurriedly with the pages. There! The words were written on a page near the centre, in the same writing:

I would be careful if I were you.

It was incredible. Who was writing it – it couldn't write itself, could it? He fingered the back of the page – no magnetic strips. Nothing in the paper. Nothing. 'Careful of what?' he whispered. But the rest of the pages were blank.

With a kind of fear he locked the Book in the cupboard at the side of his bed, then hid the key in its usual place in the hole in his mattress, under the pillow. There was a place for it there, but he had to be careful or it slipped down among the springs and was difficult to get out again.

The warning – if it was one – stuck in his head as he ran downstairs and saw his mother waiting in the porch. Was it possible the Book meant it for him? He shook his head. The thing couldn't be alive. It was just paper. His mother was waiting in the porch. 'Come on,' she said. 'Before the coaches start.'

Like most of the houses in Caston, theirs was an old building, its front black-timbered, with white plaster making strange uneven squares and crosses. The porch was carved with grotesque little goblins that squatted and leered at callers – the milkman always said theirs were the ugliest in town, and that was saying a lot.

Caston High Street turned and twisted for half a mile; its houses were humped and huddled and squeezed together, their upper storeys jutting out over the cobbles and the narrow pavement that sometimes disappeared altogether. Cars roared along the one-way system; as Jamie passed the post office a coachload of tourists swirled dust into his eyes.

At the Market Hall his mother stopped. 'Don't spend too much, and don't buy rubbish. We've enough old books in the house as it is.'

'All right.' He watched her march through the doors into the dim hall with its stalls of bananas and leatherwork and home-made cakes and love spoons. His mother never walked anywhere; she marched, and dragged you with her.

Now he could dawdle. Already the tourist shops by the church were putting out their racks of postcards and tea towels with leeks on, and the Welsh words for bread and cheese, and already one or two early visitors were photographing the almshouses with their leaning doorways. He took the short cut through Pike's Alley, then through Quiver Street and Llywelyn's Street, and came out by the bridge, where the Caston Brook swirled underneath with fish in its green hair. If you put in a cork at the garden at home, it took two and a half minutes to get here; he and Jennie had tried it more than once with a stopwatch.

The Tithe Barn was over the bridge and up a short muddy lane. It was probably the oldest building in the town, but somehow or other the visitors always seemed to miss it. It stood remote and quiet in its weeds; jackdaws stole its thatch, and a barn owl nested in a hole in the eaves.

He pushed open the heavy door and went in. It was usually silent and empty, but this morning there were tables and bookshelves all around. The noise of talk echoed in the roof.

'Ten pence!' demanded a small girl behind the door, and when he gave it to her she handed him a pink ticket. 'Thank you.'

Each stall was jammed with books, most of them old and musty. After a while Jamie realized that most of them were too expensive for him, but there were one or two that he wished he could afford. The sweet, old-fashioned smell of them hung in the air; he began to enjoy rummaging in the dusty boxes and hearing the talk of folios and first editions.

It was at the stall in the corner, while he was looking at a picture of Saturn in an astronomy book priced two pounds, that he sensed someone watching him. He peered over the top of the page.

An old man sat on a stool, eating a sandwich. Their eyes met.

'Like it?' the man asked.

Jamie nodded. 'Bit expensive though.'

The man took another bite. He wore a pullover with a hole in the sleeve and black mittens with no fingers. His face was small and brown, with a short grey beard.

'Interested in books, are you?'

'Depends what they're about.' Jamie put the book back. Then he said, 'Weren't you in the library yesterday?'

The old man smiled. 'Ah, so you know about that. And you should, shouldn't you? It's your name that's in the Book.'

Despite all the noise and chatter around him, Jamie felt uneasy. Bewilderment with the whole thing bubbled up in him. 'Listen,' he said, 'can you explain to me about that Book? It's driving me mad. It has things written in it sometimes, and then, at other times . . .'

The old man nodded. 'Ah yes. I know all about it. The Book, you see, is your companion. It tells you the way, and the dangers.'

'The way to where?'

'Other worlds. Have you got it with you?'

The sudden question took Jamie off guard. 'Now? No, I haven't.'

'That's a pity.' The man fingered his stubbly beard. His eyes were bright, like beads. He pulled a card from his pocket. 'Look, my name is Morgant. Come and see me, at this house, tonight. We can tell you what you want to know.'

He turned to a customer who was holding a fivepound note, and began to count change out of the apron round his waist. 'Don't forget. Come tonight. Once the Name comes, there is little time to lose. We only have until the eclipse to get ready.'

'For what?' Jamie asked, bewildered.

'To rescue the Prisoner.'

3

The Man in the Lane

Jamie walked up the High Street with the Book in a plastic bag under his arm. It was half-past seven, and raining again; the goblin gargoyles over the houses were spouting mouthfuls of water down gutters and drains. Low grey cloud pressed on the town. At the corner a grinning wooden imp spat splashes on to his neck.

The High Street was well-lit, but Hanging Dog Lane was always black. It was an inky slot in the wall of houses, as if one of them had shuffled aside and left this thin, damp, evil-smelling gap. It led down to a labyrinth of alleys, back door-ways, steps up and steps down, and blank walls with dingy windows no one looked through.

Jamie stopped at the corner. He distrusted this lane, the smell of it and the damp; it reminded him of thieves and cut-throats and a story he had once read of a creature that flopped down on travellers in the dark. His fingers touched the old man's stiff blue card.

THE WATCH-HOUSE

HANGING DOG LANE

CASTON

GWENT

Glancing once at the bats that flickered over the house-tops, he stepped in.

The cobbles were wet, and slippery. The alley was so narrow he could easily put his hands on both side walls, and once out of the lights from the street he felt his way forward cautiously. No wonder it was an unpleasant place. The gallows had been down here somewhere, where they had hanged pickpockets and horse-thieves – and even a dog, so the story went, for stealing meat. Owen Hadley in school said the dog walked, even said he'd seen it. Black and velvety, with eyes like lamps; it slithered past your legs or padded after you without a sound.

Jamie stopped; his footsteps died into silence. Silence settled like dust on ledges and slates and sills. No padding. Well, after all, he thought, Owen Hadley had the biggest mouth in the school. And you'd never catch him down here at night.

Looking up, he saw that the stars were coming out, glittering in the ragged clouds. The dark houses leaned above him as if they had their heads together, gossiping.

Something made him turn and look back up the alley; there in the entrance, framed against the light, a man was standing. He was thin and tall, and he was looking down into the darkness of the lane, with his head slightly tilted, as if he was listening.

Jamie held the Book tight. Noiselessly he slid against the wall, not wanting to be seen.

The man waited, then stepped forward. His shadow grew huge in the rectangle of light, but as he came deeper into the alley the darkness swallowed him up; he became just a glimmer in the blackness.

'Jamie?'

Jamie jumped; the soft voice had run along the wall, echoing in pipes and gutters.

'I know you're here, Jamie. I saw you come in.'

The footsteps were quiet, but nearer. Frozen, Jamie stared into the shadows.

'I won't hurt you.'

He was close! Jamie's heart thudded; he began to edge away, silently sliding his feet over the slippery stones. A drain-pipe swung as he touched it, and clanged against its rusty bracket. At once a cold hand came out of the darkness and grabbed him.

'Listen,' the voice said. 'I want to talk to you.'

Jamie struggled and squirmed in panic. 'Let go of me!' he yelled, and the Book slid out from under his arm and they both lurched at it. Rain began to fall in large heavy drops.

Suddenly Jamie shoved the stranger backwards so that he crashed into the wet wall. Before he could get up, Jamie grabbed the Book and ran, sprinting up the alley with the rain in his face.

The lane twisted sharply; in the dark he ran into a wall, jumped down some steps and darted into a tiny courtyard full of dustbins. One dim lamp hung on the wall, lighting a ragged cinema poster. Jamie raced over to a doorway, threw himself in against the wood and listened. At first he could only hear his breathing and his heart thumping; then, in the stillness, a limp and shuffle in the lane. Footsteps came down the steps and paused; he could see a shadow stretched out in the lamplight.

'Listen, you little wretch,' snarled the voice. 'If I have to come and find you, you'll be sorry!'

There he was, standing in the lamplight, one hand on the wet wall. For the first time Jamie saw him clearly: a very tall man, with hair of a strange shining gold; dark angry eyes and a nose hooked like an eagle's beak. It was the third man from the library.

Puzzled, he was about to move when he felt sudden

emptiness behind him. A small cool hand slid round and clasped itself over his mouth.

'Not a sound,' the old man whispered, 'or he'll hear. Inside, quickly.' Jamie was drawn back into the dark, and saw the door close. The old man bent down and slid the bolts across. 'Did he see where you went?'

'No. At least, I don't think so. Listen . . .'

But the old man's hand tugged his sleeve. 'Not here. Upstairs.'

The stairs were wooden and twisted round on themselves, and creaked underfoot. Morgant led the way; they climbed up past two landings, both dusty and carpetless, and still up. Breathless, Jamie heard the old man puffing. 'Nearly there . . . it's the watch-tower.' As he spoke he pushed open the door at the top and Jamie followed him into the room.

It was small, and octagonal; in each wall was a window of thick leaded glass, tinted blue and red and green. In the middle of the floor stood a circular table stained with rings and scorchmarks, and sitting with one arm sprawled across it, eating a large greasy hamburger, was the big red-haired man from the library. Number one and number two. So they're all in it, Jamie thought.

'Ah.' The red man swallowed a mouthful of bread. 'He's come! Good!' He grinned, nastily, and Jamie remembered how he had broken the librarian's pen.

'Sit here.' Morgant dusted a chair with a red handkerchief. 'Gavan, this room of ours is a piggery.'

The big man snorted. 'Has he got the Book, though?'

'He has. Now, Jamie, this is . . . Mr Gavan. Thank you for coming here – it must have been difficult.'

Jamie perched on the chair. 'Well, I wanted to find out about my name.'

'Ah yes.' Morgant put his elbows on the table and joined his fingertips together. 'But first, I'm a little worried. Who was your friend outside, the one who was chasing you?'

'I don't know. Isn't he with you?'

'With us!'

Jamie shrugged. 'Well, I just assumed the three of you were together. He came into the library after you . . .'

'*What!*' Gavan almost choked.

'Quiet,' Morgant snapped. 'Jamie, listen, this is vital. You mean there was a *third* man?'

'Yes.'

'And he looked at the Book?'

'I suppose so. He went down there. And outside, he knew my name.'

Gavan took a swig of beer from a mug. 'He's lying! There couldn't have been!'

Morgant glared at him. 'Will you save your breath to eat!' He turned back to Jamie. 'What does he look like?' He waggled his two joined fingers. 'Exactly, mind.'

'Very tall. Blond hair, dark eyes – brown, I think.' Jamie watched them both curiously. 'His face is narrow, with a hook nose like a hawk. He's younger than you, with a black coat . . .'

'Damn!' Gavan pounded the table so hard that Jamie jumped. 'It's that hellcat Cai! The worst of them!'

He stormed over to the window and glared down.

Morgant shook his head. He did not seem as surprised, Jamie thought. 'This is a serious problem,' he explained. 'We know this man, we've had dealings with him before. He is very dangerous, and quite unpredictable. His name is Cai. He wouldn't stop at bloodshed. If he'd got his hands on you out there . . .' Again, he shook his head.

Jamie thought of the angry face in the lamplight.

'I really had no idea,' Morgant went on, 'that anyone else had seen the Book after us.'

Jamie fiddled with the corner of the bag. 'Yes, but I don't get it. If he wanted the Book . . .'

'He could have taken it from the library? Yes, but you see, Jamie, your name is in it. The Book is useless without you; he wants you as well. The time is coming when the way between the worlds will be open; it will be easy to pass through. When this is so, the Book reappears and it bears a name. That person is the Book's Keeper for that time. But look' – he held up a hand to ward off Jamie's questions – 'why should I waste my old voice, mm? We'll let someone else explain. Gavan, the light, please.'

The big man jerked the curtains across and brought an oil lamp to the table, shoving the dirty plates aside. Shadows leapt and scurried over the ceiling. Morgant drew the Book from its bag, reverently, and placed it on a stand. He opened it at a clean white page. On a small saucer nearby he placed a pinch of grey powder from a gold box, and dropped a match into it. With a puff the powder ignited; it flared harshly. Gavan leaned closer; Jamie could smell incense and tobacco and leather.

'Now,' Morgant said, 'are you ready?'

Jamie nodded, but the question was not for him. Unravelling itself across the page like a black thread, the answer wrote itself swiftly:

I am ready.

4

Directions

The dim light from the oil lamp flickered; their three huge hunchbacked shadows rippled on the ceiling. Jamie let his breath out slowly. 'It's amazing!'

'Quite.' Morgant gave him a small smile. 'But I think you will be seeing stranger things soon. Now, you must do the asking. The Book will only answer you, or rather, will only give you the information we need. Here is a list of questions I have prepared.'

Jamie looked at them, then at the Book. 'Where is the Prisoner?' he said.

The Prisoner is in Fintan's Tower.

It wrote itself quickly, each letter beautifully formed.

'Good,' Morgant chuckled. 'But we knew that. The problem is, the Tower is never in the same place twice. Ask it how we get in.'

'Yes, but who's this prisoner?'

'I'll explain all that later. Come on.'

Jamie hesitated. He had half a mind to argue, but Gavan gripped his shoulder. 'Ask it!'

Ruffled, Jamie shook him off. 'All right! Keep your hands to yourself!' He turned back to the page. 'They want to know how to get to this place.'

The Book did not answer at once. Then it wrote:

The way to the Summer Country is long and perilous.

Between the stones on the Harper's Beacon there is a door.
It will be open when the sun's eye closes on the day of
Samain. But take care! Few return from that country.

'Excellent.' Morgant seemed to take no notice of the warning.
'That part will be easy. And once we are in that country?'
    But the Book, when Jamie asked it, was keeping some of
its secrets.

I cannot yet say.

Gavan scowled. 'Make it say!' His fingernails, cracked and
dirty, drummed on the table.
    'That would be foolish. We have plenty of time.' Morgant
seemed highly satisfied; he leaned back in his chair and said,
'Now, Jamie, you say you have questions of your own. Ask
away.'
    Surprised, Jamie turned to the Book. 'What I want to
know is . . . well, who is this prisoner?'

His name is Gweir, the Book wrote promptly.

'Great. And why is he locked up in this place?'
    There was a pause; this time the writing unrolled more
thoughtfully:

The reason is lost in time. Some say that at three days old
he was stolen from between his mother and the wall. The
truth may be that he went with the Emperor to steal the
Cauldron, and was captured.

'You're a mine of information,' Jamie remarked. '*What* cauldron?'

Even the King of Annwn's Cauldron. Dark blue it is: there are pearls about its rim. Nine maidens guard it night and day. A liquid can be brewed in it. Whoever drinks of this becomes –

'Stop,' Morgant said quickly. 'That's enough now, Jamie. We haven't got all night.'

'I was interested.'

'Yes, well I can tell you about the Cauldron another time. That too is in Fintan's Tower, but it is not important.' He sighed. 'We must only think about the rescue; about Gweir.'

Jamie glanced at him curiously, at his small face, shadowy in the lamplight. It was that phrase in the Book. If the answer was lost in time, how long had this Gweir been in prison?

'Time,' Morgant said suddenly, as if guessing his thoughts, 'is a mystery. Each world has its own times and seasons.'

'Did you know Gweir?'

'Gweir is my brother.'

For a moment the room was cold. A draught moved the curtain and ruffled the pages of the Book, showing briefly that one of them was deep blue and covered with tiny, shining stars. Jamie held them still and turned back to look for it, but as he had guessed, it was gone.

'The Book gives nothing away,' Morgant remarked. 'Sit down, Gavan. Stop hanging over us like a cloud.'

The big man went round the table and flung himself on a chair. Jamie was glad. He quite liked Morgant but Gavan got on his nerves. Heavy and oppressive. A cloud was right; a storm cloud, full of threat.

'I still don't see what all this has to do with me,' he said aloud. 'Why is my name in here?'

'You were chosen; no one knows how. But it means, Jamie, that we need you to find Fintan's Tower.' Morgant made a small sweep with his hand. 'Will you come?'

'To the Harper's Beacon?'

'Apparently. And wherever the door leads.'

'To the "other worlds"?' Jamie shrugged. 'What does that mean?'

'There are dimensions within dimensions,' Morgant said dreamily. 'They lie behind each other like layers in mist; the world that is, the world that was, the world that might be. When the mist is around you, you can still see, although from a distance all is grey.'

Jamie was silent, thinking about it. Gavan gave him a leer. 'He's scared witless.'

'No,' Jamie said thoughtfully. 'I'm not. And I'm used to the hills. But won't it take much longer than a day?' He was wondering how the old man would manage on the steep wet slopes.

'Oh no. Maybe not so long. So that's agreed.' Morgant rubbed his hands together. 'Let us have something warming to celebrate.' He went to a small cupboard in the wall and brought back a tray with three glasses and a jug. The drink, when he poured it, was a ruby red.

'Something of my own. Not too strong.'

Jamie took a sip and coughed till the water came into his eyes. 'Very nice,' he managed.

The red-haired man downed his in one gulp and poured

out more. Morgant tapped his hand. 'That's enough. We have work to do. Now, Jamie, listen to me. You must remember you are in great danger at every moment. This man Cai is out there, somewhere. He will not give up; you may not see him, but he is both resourceful and cunning. Gavan will escort you home tonight.'

Jamie put the glass down again. 'I'd forgotten about him. Where does he come into it?'

'Obviously, he wants you to take him to the Tower, not us. He is a well-known thief,' Morgant said. 'I believe his aim is to steal the Cauldron of the King. It has certain . . . powers.'

Gavan snorted. 'Leave him to me.'

Morgant smiled. 'Now, on your way, Jamie.'

Halfway down the stairs Jamie paused. 'You haven't said when. And look, when we find your brother, well, he'll be guarded, won't he? They won't just hand him over.'

Morgant gave a quiet chuckle. 'The Book will advise us. As for when, the day after tomorrow, of course. Samain, when the doors of the Other world open. Allhallows Eve. We will meet at nine o'clock in the morning on Caston bridge, and be home before dark. We will see the sun's eye close and open.'

Then Jamie stepped out into the rain, and heard the bolts slam behind him.

Gavan hardly spoke all the way home. He walked huddled in his greatcoat and scarf, a huge shadow. Passers-by had to step off the pavement, as he wouldn't step aside. He didn't seem to care about cars either. Once, as he stepped into the road, a blue Volvo pulled up with a screech; the owner slammed his horn furiously but the big man just strode on, his eyes glittering in the lamplight. Warily Jamie kept an arm's length between them. Their footsteps rang loudly in the emptying streets. Sometimes he glanced behind, but the alleys and corners were dark and full of doorways. If anyone was there, he couldn't see them.

But half an hour later, when he was closing his bedroom curtains, he saw something that turned his skin damp. Opposite the house, in the doorway of the florist's, someone was standing. Who was it? He watched for a few minutes but the shadow did not move, and his feet were too cold to stay there. Puzzled, he let the curtain fall and climbed into bed.

Before he put the light out, he took the Book from under his pillow and opened it. 'Are you awake?'

Yes.

'The Tower. What is it, exactly?'

It is the Fortress of Frustration, the Fortress of Carousal. It is the Eerie Place.

'And this Cauldron, if you drink of it?'

If you drink from it you possess all knowledge.

'Worth stealing, then.'

Certainly.

And pondering that, he fell asleep.

5

In the Barn

'He's been there all morning.' Jamie's mother dropped the net curtain and went back to the stove. 'Just leaning against the wall.'

'Probably waiting for someone.' Mr Meyrick turned a page of the *Welsh Veterinary Bulletin* and wiped butter off it with his knife.

'For two hours? It's as if he's watching the house.' She broke an egg into the pan.

'Perhaps he's a policeman. Perhaps Jamie's robbed a bank.'

Jamie chewed his toast and kept his eyes on his book, but the words were a blur and his heart was beating so loudly he could hear it. 'What does he look like?' he asked quietly.

'Rather sinister.' Jennie had gone to see. 'Tall. Fair. Long black coat. A bit like a Russian spy, really.'

It was him. Once in the night Jamie had woken and lain awake, listening to soft footsteps under the window, up and down, in the silence of the street. But the Book's no good to him, he thought, panic rising inside. It's no good to him without me.

'What are you doing today?' his father asked, folding the paper and getting up. The stray puppy in his lap jumped down grumpily.

'Um . . . nothing much.'

'Good. I've got surgery all morning, so take a walk out to the farm, will you? Your uncle's promised me a whole load of stuff – vegetables mostly – if we can collect it. Both of you could go.'

Jennie frowned. 'I'm supposed to be revising.'

'Ah, get on. You're daydreaming half the time.' Her father picked up his coat. 'Besides, the walk will do you good.'

Jamie bit his lip. He'd have to go – he didn't want to be left alone in the house – and the Book would have to come too. Leaving it would be too risky. But how could he get out, without Cai seeing, and following? He put down the astronomy book and went upstairs.

Gently, he moved a corner of curtain.

The stranger stood, leaning, arms folded, in the shadows of the alley opposite. He was looking up at the window, with a thin, sarcastic smile. Jamie jerked his hand back, then sat on the carpet and opened the Book. He was surprised at how cold he felt.

'Listen, how am I going to get out?'

The page was empty. No writing appeared.

'I'm asking!'

Use your initiative, the Book scrawled.

He closed it with a clap of disgust and went down to the kitchen.

His parents had gone. Jennie had her coat on, and was tucking the ends of her trousers into wellingtons.

'Those boots have got a hole in,' he told her absently.

'No, I had a go with the puncture kit. They'll be all right.' She took off her reading glasses and tugged the trimmed ends of hair off her face. 'Ready?'

'What about the washing-up?'

'Mam said she'd do it. She'll be back later.'

'Jen.' Jamie perched on the table. 'Let's go out the back way. Over the stream.'

'Why? We're going to the farm, idiot.'

'Yes I know, but . . .' Jamie pulled a face; would he really have to explain all this? 'It's that man out the front. He's . . . waiting for me, and I don't want him to see me. There was a scrap . . . a kid in school. That's his brother.'

Jennie took the clip out of her mouth and pushed it into her hair.

'You little thug. Have you told Dad?'

'No. And you mustn't either! Oh, come on, Jen, it won't take much longer.' He opened the back door. 'I just don't want all the fuss.'

'Coward. Infidel. Recreant knight.'

But she came with him, down the garden to the brook, which was flowing fast and cold this morning, after the rain, and littered with leaves. They splashed through and clambered up the opposite bank, through black brambles and bracken to the field at the top. There was a small gap in the hedge, made by pushing through it, year after year; beyond that was a ploughed field with a footpath along the edge. They followed the muddy track along the hedgerow, bright with haws, to the gate at the end; it wound along the bank of the stream to Caston Bridge, under a line of old willows with branches that stuck out like witches' hair. As they crossed the bridge Jamie looked down into the water rippling silently between the dark cutwaters. The field was an empty square of furrows. No one was following.

They threaded the alleys and lanes to the High Street, and waited impatiently to cross. Tourist coaches and lorries roared through the narrow street, whipping Jennie's hair into a whirlwind. She waved to a friend from school.

As they ran across, Jamie's eyes darted along the street. It was crammed with shoppers, but there was no sign of the tall, sinister figure. Surely he'd be easy to spot.

Colliding with a woman, he stammered an apology, almost dropped the Book, and was hauled by Jennie into Hanging Dog Lane. 'What did you do to that kid in school, anyway?' she asked, striding out in front. 'I wouldn't have thought you'd be much good in a fight. And can't you go anywhere without something to read!' He muttered something, uneasily. He had forgotten they would be coming this way.

Hanging Dog Lane was almost as dark as it had been the night before. Through the crack between the rooftops the sky was already grey with drizzle. They jumped down the steps and began to pass the small courtyards at each side. At the entrance to one Jamie stopped. 'Hang on a minute.'

He went down, over the cobbles. Maybe he should knock, and tell Morgant about the house being watched.

But the door was not there.

He stopped short, astonished, and glanced around. It was surely the same yard, with the rubbish bins and that poster flapping on the wall. But the doorway he had hidden in was gone; the dingy bricks were blank. He ran a hand over them, feeling their dampness. And the watchtower too! Above his head was just an ordinary roof, with two gulls screaming on a chimney.

'Come on, slug!' Jennie was watching him curiously. 'What's so special about that wall?'

'Nothing.' As he pushed past her he wondered what had happened to the world since the Book had come into it. Where had that room been, with its red and blue leaded windows? But after all, there was a maze of alleys in here: it may have been the wrong one. But he knew it wasn't.

The lane to the farm at Llanfihangell went slowly up a long

steep hill; anyone following would have been easy to see on the black road. He and Jennie plodded on between the wet hedges, muffled up against the cold wind that blew in their faces; above them the sky was the colour of lead, stretching to the dark, huddled hills. Far up over the wood a buzzard swung on its wide, stiff wings.

Near the top of the hill a track branched off to the right, down through a plantation of fir trees to the farmhouse in its lonely hollow. Out of breath, Jamie paused and eased a corner of the Book that was digging into his ribs. Rain pattered loudly on his hood. He turned and glanced back, and saw, far behind, a small dark figure striding up the lane.

Cold, Jamie clenched his fists. At this distance it could be anyone. He strained his eyes in the grey drizzle; there was something about that flapping coat and hurried step that terrified him. But how would he know? Jamie wondered. How could he? He turned and hurried after Jennie.

She was swishing the branches with a stick, and whistling. The track with its deep ruts wound its way down through the gloomy trees, and then with a twist that always surprised him, brought them out into the farmyard. The gates were shut, he noticed, and both the cars were gone.

'Hello! Anyone about?' Jennie poked her head into the outhouses and tried the back door. 'Bother. No one here, after all that trek. Shall we go in?'

Jamie was looking back up the track. 'Better. It's starting to rain.'

The key was in the soil under a stone under a flowerpot; trebly safe, Aunt Clare always said. They opened the door and found the kitchen dark and silent. Emperor, the big grey cat, was snoozing on a sofa by the sinking fire. The table was a clutter of bills and papers and on the mantelpiece was a note written in blue eyebrow pencil:

> Jennie. Your mother phoned to say you were coming. Fruit and veg in kitchen. Potatoes in the barn. Lock up after you.

'She's gone to Abergavenny,' Jenny realized. 'To the market.' She went into the kitchen and began opening cupboards.

Jamie put some logs on the fire and sat down; the cat climbed thoughtfully on to his lap. He turned over the newspaper on the table – there was a paragraph headed ECLIPSE. He read it carefully.

> ... As readers of our regular Astronomy column will know, there will be a total eclipse of the sun on Saturday afternoon, 31 October, beginning at approximately 12.30 p.m. and lasting until within minutes of sunset, although the actual time of totality will be only two minutes. The eclipse will be visible from the whole of Wales and is already attracting interest from occult groups as well as astronomers, because it takes place on Hallowe'en, the ancient magical night of Samain. According to local white witch Ceridwen Hughes, this is the night when the barriers between the natural and the supernatural worlds grow thin, and ghosts, demons and faeries walk our roads and woods ...

'Potatoes!' Jennie shouted from the kitchen. 'Get them, will you?'

. . . and, she says, it is a time of great danger and peril to anyone out after dark. So all you astronomers beware!

'Jamie! Come on!'

He dropped the paper with a sigh, and heaved the cat aside. So that was what the Book meant by the sun's eye closing. He might have guessed it was something like that. And 'white witch Ceridwen Hughes' certainly cheered you up.

A gust of wind snatched the door from his hand and flung rain in his face; he ran, coat huddled on, over the slippery cobbles of the yard, through the stable and the downpour from its corrugated roof, into the barn. The door swung behind him.

The barn was dim, and quiet. Water dripped here and there from the roof; it smelt of straw, and tar, and the autumnal earth.

The potatoes were at one side, stacked in sacks; he waded through the straw towards them. The sound of the rain was hushed; he could hear the pigeons shuffling outside, and the faint squeak of a mouse in the stacked bales. As he hauled out a sack, there was a rustle in the dimness at the far end of the loft. He stopped, the hairs on the backs of his hands prickling with sudden alarm.

'Who's there?' he said quietly. The rafters creaked. The echoes of his question hung in the air like dust. For a long moment he waited, listening intently to every tiny sound. Rain spattered under the door; a tin can rattled over the cobbles outside. In the barn, nothing moved. But suddenly Jamie could see him.

It wasn't much, just a shadow in the dimness, quite still,

but it was a man's shoulder and arm, black in the blackness. He kept his eyes on it, backing away noiselessly, feeling his scalp prickle and grow hot with each step. Straw rustled as his feet passed through it. Then the shadow moved. 'Jamie,' it said.

Jamie turned, slammed through the door, hurtled across the wet yard and burst into the kitchen. 'Jennie!' he yelled breathlessly, pulling the bolts across. 'He's there! He's in the barn!'

He whirled around and the words died in his mouth. Jennie was sitting in the armchair by the fire. Leaning against the table, with his arms folded and his mocking dark eyes turned to look at him, was the the third man from the library.

6

Cai

For a moment there was silence. Then the man said, 'Don't make a fuss. Come in and sit down.'

His voice was quiet, with a soft, old-fashioned accent. Moving to the nearest chair, Jamie glanced at Jennie. He was relieved to see her glaring back at him. 'Fight! There's a lot more to this than a fight,' she muttered. 'Will someone tell me what's going on?'

The stranger ignored her. 'You're a difficult person to get to talk to, Jamie,' he said. 'Put the Book on the table.'

Jamie hesitated. The man was leaning casually against the table, hands deep in the pockets of his dark coat. He seemed to have no weapons. If I ran, Jamie thought . . .

'Don't be stupid. You wouldn't even get to the door.'

Cai straightened; Jamie was shocked at how tall he seemed. His eyes were cold and amused. 'Put the Book down,' he snapped, 'or I'll take it myself.'

It seemed to have gone very dark in the room. The fire crackled over the new logs, and the cat licked itself contentedly. Jamie pulled the Book from his inside pocket and laid it, carefully, on Aunt Clare's check tablecloth. It was in a bag because of the rain; drops of moisture slid down one corner and soaked into the material.

The tall man smiled, bleakly. 'Well, that's a start.'

'It's no good to you without me.'

'So you know that much.'

'Yes.' Jamie rolled up his fists. 'And I'm not asking it anything for you.'

Cai shrugged; his eyes narrowed. 'I can see they've told you all about me. I might have known.'

With a sudden snatch like a striking snake, he had hold of Jamie's arm. 'But then I need to know where Fintan's Tower is.' He tugged the Book from its cover and flicked it open. 'Ask it! Or have they done that already?' He grinned at Jamie's scared look. 'Yes, of course they have. Morgant never did waste any time.'

Jamie glanced at Jennie. Her face was white and bewildered, but her hands were moving under the table. Slowly, inch by inch, she was opening the drawer where the knives and forks were kept. He squirmed in the man's grip. 'Let me go! You can't make me tell you anything!'

'Oh no?' Cai dropped his arm and stood back.

Jamie rubbed his aching wrist angrily. 'You're a thief!'

A spark of surprise and fury kindled in the man's face. He glanced at Jennie, who froze, and then back to Jamie. 'I didn't want this. But if you're going to be that stubborn . . .'

Suddenly, he raised his hands. The air crackled, grew hot, and Jennie gasped. Between his narrow fingers a ring of light hung in the air, and as his hands moved slowly apart the ring widened; became a clear, spinning circle of white fire blazing in the centre of the room. Jamie stared at it, fascinated by the pure emptiness; it was as if a circle had been cut out of the air, and he could see through.

At first the whiteness was unbroken – then, all at once, something was in there. It was a landscape of fields and trees, not a still picture but a real place, as if he was looking at it through a peephole, or a circular window. It was raining there too; the sky was steel-grey and he could see storm clouds piling up over the hills. In the foreground was a lake, its cold ripples lapping the shingle; and out on the mist, as if it rose out of the water, he could see a great fortress glimmering in the dull light. Flickers of lightning played silently over the waves. He had seen it before; it had been tiny then, in bright enamels on the Book's cover, but here it was huge, rain-lashed, gleaming wet, with one lighted window high up near the battlements. This was Fintan's Tower, and the way to it lay through the door on the Harper's Beacon, when the sun's eye was closed.

He did not hear himself say the words. When he could hear at all it was only somebody laughing, and a voice shouting, 'Jamie! Jamie!' over and over. His sight cleared; Jennie was shaking his shoulders. He was cold and rigid and stiff; the white ring was gone and it was Cai who was smiling, his strange shining hair falling over his eyes.

'You told him!' Jennie said. 'Whatever he wanted, you told him. Are you all right?' She gripped his arm again and shook it; he saw the handle of the knife in her sleeve.

'Yes . . . yes. I'm OK.' He fought the strange confusion away and glared at the man over her shoulder. 'All right! So now you know. Now clear out and leave us alone!'

The man shook his head, still grinning. 'It's not that easy. I'm taking this with me.' He picked up the Book and closed it carefully. 'And as you were bright enough to point out, it's useless without you. So you'll have to come as well.'

Jennie stiffened. From the corner of his eye Jamie saw the handle of the knife slide down into her palm.

Cai lounged against the table. 'She can stay here. Come on, Jamie, don't make it too much work for me. You've seen what I can do.' But he stopped as Jennie turned round. She held the knife out firmly; the sharp edge of it glittered in the firelight.

'Listen,' she said, in a cold harsh voice that Jamie barely

recognized, 'I don't know who you are, and I don't know what that Book thing is all about. But my brother and I are going home. Now. So please get out of my way.'

The stranger's face flushed with rage; for a moment he looked so angry that he couldn't speak. Jennie grabbed her brother's arm.

'Come on.'

'Wait!' Cai jerked forward. He seemed to be forcing himself to keep his temper. 'Wait. Listen to me. Have they told you what is in the tower?'

'You mean the Cauldron?'

His eyes narrowed. 'You know about that!'

'All about it.'

Jennie tugged him towards the door, but Cai leapt after them.

'Put that stupid thing down!' he stormed. 'You're not going to use it.'

'I will!'

Furiously the man lashed a chair out of his way. 'Will you let me explain!'

'You don't need to, I know all about it!' Jamie yelled. 'I know about the Prisoner and the Cauldron and all about you!' And he tugged the last stiff bolt back from the door.

'No! Come here!' The man flung himself forward and grabbed Jamie's arm. 'Listen . . .' Suddenly he swore and stumbled back, clutching his hand. Blood welled from a deep cut across his knuckles. 'You little vixen!'

'I'm sorry, really I am.' Jennie was white and shaky; Jamie could feel her trembling. 'But you should have left us alone!' She slid the knife on to the table and then picked it up again.

The man gave her a shrewd look; his temper had vanished. Quickly he snatched a white handkerchief from a pile of

Aunt Clare's ironing and tied it round his hand; a crimson stain flushed slowly through the fabric. Then he glanced at them and said quietly, 'Did you never think it might all be lies, Jamie, all those things they told you?'

His hand on the latch, Jamie paused.

'They told you they want to rescue Gweir, didn't they? Well, it's a lie.'

'Open the door, Jamie,' Jennie said quickly.

'Listen to me, Jamie! They want the Cauldron for themselves. That's all. They don't care about the Prisoner, they'd leave him there to rot! They're using you to get what they want!'

Slowly, Jamie let the door swing open. A gust of wind swept in and crackled the flames in the hearth. Then he turned around and faced Cai. 'But *you* want the Cauldron.'

'No! At least . . .' A flicker of something passed over the man's face. 'No. I don't.'

Jamie shook his head. 'I don't believe you,' he said. 'After all, you would say that.'

'Of course he would!' Gavan blocked the doorway, his head brushing the lintel, his great coat flapping like a cloak. He brought a huge heavy hand down on Jamie's shoulder. 'Out! Go home. I'll take care of this.' Roughly, he bundled them both out of the door.

'So Morgant's sent his little lapdog, has he?' Cai smiled in cold fury. 'How pleasant! How enchanting!'

Ignoring him, Gavan glared down at Jamie. 'Clear out,' he growled, jerking his head towards the lane.

But even with Jennie tugging him, Jamie held back. 'I can't. He's got the Book.'

Like a bear, Gavan swung back, his arms hanging loosely at his sides. Cai lounged against the table. 'Oh dear, now you've confused him. That's a lot for him to take in. Is this your idea of a generous rescuer, Jamie?'

'Let's have it,' Gavan growled.

He lurched forward.

'Careful.' Cai's voice was soft and lazy. 'Remember what happened to Palug's Cat.'

The Book lay between them on the table. Suddenly, before anyone could move, Jamie darted under Gavan's arm, ran across the kitchen and snatched it up. The room exploded into sparks of white flame; the shape in his hands writhed and buckled and burnt him. Then he staggered back, dazzled.

Cai was gone. The room was empty but for a faint, fragrant smoke and the Book, hot and smoking in his hands.

'Stupid thing to do!' Gavan muttered, pushing past him to look around. 'He could have killed you. I would have got the Book, without that.'

'Yes, but where did he *go*?' Jennie came in and stared at the table.

'Oh, he's up to all sorts of tricks.' Gavan shrugged 'Notorious for it. Cunning as a snake. I suppose you didn't tell him anything?'

His small red eyes fixed suddenly on Jamie.

'Well . . . he knows where Fintan's Tower is – at least, what the Book said.' Alarmed at the man's face, he added, 'Well, he *made* me tell him!'

The big man stormed over and kicked the door open furiously. 'Made you! You've got legs, haven't you! You could run!'

'Yes, but . . .'

'Oh, save it.' Gavan threw an evil look over his shoulder. 'Save it for the old man. And he won't like it either. Not one bit.'

7

Eclipse

Jennie sat back against the tree and gazed at the brook flowing past her feet. A shaft of late sunlight slanted through the leaves on to the water, lighting up the tiny stones and gravel, and the flash of a fin. Leaves swept by on the current like small leathery coracles.

'You had a lot of nerve,' Jamie said, 'with that knife.'

'Mmm.' She threw a stone in, thoughtfully. 'So that's it. It's all a very odd story. And you say this Book actually tells you things? That's impossible. It's some kind of trick.'

'I thought so at first, but it's not. I'll show you.' Jamie opened the Book at random on his knees and asked it the first question that came into his head. 'Who is this man Cai, anyway?'

The Emperor's foster brother, the Book wrote.

'Wow.' Jennie touched the page with her finger. 'Impressive. What Emperor?'

'Tell her,' Jamie said.

Arthur, of course. Cai is a Master of Fire and Water. He can last nine nights without sleep. A wound from his sword no one can heal. He fought nine witches: they say he laughed as he slew them. He is a Harper, a Smith, an Enchanter. He killed Palug's Cat.

'Palug's Cat?'

Yes. Nine score warriors would fall as her food.

Jennie giggled. 'It talks in riddles!'

'Oh, you get used to that.' He read the page again. 'I don't like the sound of this. He scares me.'

'Well, if he killed some kind of leopard that tucked into, um, 180 people as a light lunch, then he's no joke. As we know. Look, Jamie, seriously, I'm coming on this jaunt. If Fintan's Tower is real, I want to see it. You'll need help. And,' she muttered quietly, 'I know he's on your side, but I don't like that thug Gavan, either.'

Jamie watched the kitten dipping its paw into the stream. He'd known she would say that. And in a way he was glad, because he didn't like Gavan either. It made you think . . .

'You know, back there, at the farm,' he said, 'if Gavan hadn't have come in . . .'

'What?'

'Well, I almost – for a moment – believed him. Cai, I mean. What if Morgant is stringing us along?'

Jennie shrugged. 'One of them must be lying.'

'Mmm.' After a moment he turned to a clean page and said, 'Listen, what does Morgant really want? Does he want to rescue Gweir?'

The Book drew a complicated scroll. Then, inside, it wrote:

Who knows the secrets of men's hearts?

The next morning they were ten minutes early at Caston Bridge. The street outside the house had been empty, but then Cai already knew where they were going. The wind had been rising all night, and they had dressed warmly in pullovers and waterproofs. Jennie had brought some sandwiches and a flask of hot tea; these were in a small rucksack with the Book. 'We take turns to carry this, mind,' she had said, loosening the strap against her shoulder.

Now, she kicked her boot impatiently against the stones of the bridge. 'I'm freezing! Where are they?'

'Here.' Jamie saw them turn the corner, the small old man with his hands in his pockets; Gavan with the canvas bag under his arm. They were talking, Gavan's head bent down to listen. Then they laughed.

'Is that him?' Jennie said in a low voice.

'Yes.' Jamie frowned. 'Keep alert, Jen. I want to know what's really going on.'

As he came up, Morgant stopped in mock surprise. 'What's this? Two of you?'

'If she can't come, I won't either,' said Jamie, firmly.

'Tut, nonsense.' Morgant smiled. 'Just my little joke. I wouldn't dream of sending you back, my dear; Gavan told me about your adventure yesterday. It was a very brave thing to do, if you don't mind me saying so.'

'I don't know,' Jennie said. 'I was just scared.'

Morgant nodded. 'He is a dangerous man. He will be angry now, and we will have to be even more careful. It's a great pity he managed to find out so much.' He smiled then, and his small black eyes gleamed at them. 'Now then. We have to be at Harper's Beacon by noon. Shall we go?'

They crossed the bridge and followed the road out of town, turning off into a muddy lane that would take them up into the hills. At the turning Jamie couldn't help looking back, but the bridge was empty, and the street deserted.

It was a long walk, through the rustling end-of-autumn countryside and the mild, damp air. They travelled mostly along footpaths and wet, rutted tracks that climbed slowly towards the grey bulk of the hills; the Mynydd Maen they were called. Harper's Beacon was a great mound on the end of the range, made no one knew when; an old barrow, some said, or a motte with deep ditches. A circle of standing stones crowned it, grey and leaning in the wind. Once, resting against a tree for breath and glancing up there, Jamie was sure he could make out tiny figures moving around among the stones. He shouted to Morgant, who came hurrying back.

'Ah yes.' Morgant took a telescope from his bag and focused it carefully on the hill top. 'Yes, well, I expected this, of course. The path of the total eclipse is not that broad, you see. Every hill on it will have observers – people watching, you know. Astronomers. The higher up, the better for them – clear air, and so on. They won't make any difference to us. They won't see what we're looking for.'

'The Fortress of Frustration?'

Morgant threw him a quick glance. 'I see you've been making enquiries of your own.'

'A few. It doesn't explain much, though.'

Morgant smiled. 'Only if you know what to ask. But we won't find the Fortress up there, remember. Just the door.'

Puzzled, Jamie watched him walk on towards Gavan, who was idling impatiently along the lane. Jennie nudged his back. 'Carry this for a bit. It's your turn.'

It was harder to walk with the rucksack on. After a few more miles he was plodding and daydreaming, head down. They were climbing steadily now, up the lower slopes of the hills, stopping every now and then to catch their breath.

Below them the countryside spread itself, golds, russets and greens. They could see great woods, dappled brown and red as the few leaves left on the trees crinkled and decayed. The hedgerows were speckled with berries, and on a ploughed field in the valley a crowd of lapwings and gulls followed a single yellow tractor.

Gavan, at a signal from Morgant, began to keep dawdling behind, peering into bushes and copses at the side of the lanes. Once Morgant looked back and Jamie saw Gavan slightly shake his head. Jennie had noticed too. 'They're looking for him,' she whispered.

Jamie nodded. 'I know. And what's the use? He could be up there watching us come.'

The last part of the climb went up a steep, stony track between hedges of blackthorn and stunted oak, all bending one way in the bitter wind. The track was full of puddles. Jamie splashed through them, his chest aching for breath, the wind in his face becoming colder. Then they climbed a stile, and stood on the springy turf of the open hill. Above them, bare rock jutted out, and they clambered up over it, down into ditches scraped red by rabbits, through the snagging, coconut-smelling bushes of yellow gorse, until they stood up breathless on the bare, eroded mound of the Harper's Beacon.

The wind struck them like a roaring wave. Coat flapping, Jamie stared out at the hills, miles of them, briefly stroked with light as the sun broke through the fine cloud. Ebbw forest, all moving shadow, and beyond that the mountains of Powys and Herefordshire, in the dim blueness of the horizon.

'Look at that!' Jennie shouted. Her hair streamed out behind her, whipping itself into fantastic shapes.

Jamie nodded, and turned.

Behind him the stones of the prehistoric circle rose like a crown on the hill top, gaunt and ominous.

They took shelter from the wind in the ditch; there were about a dozen people there already, setting up telescopes and expensive-looking cameras. Around the stones some hippies squatted, colourfully dressed; one girl was singing to the sound of a flute. Jamie couldn't help wondering if she was white witch Ceridwen Hughes.

'Quite a crowd,' Morgant observed. He drew them away to the seclusion of some large rocks, and sat down.

Gavan took a flask from his pocket, unscrewed it, and took a long, noisy drink.

'Now,' said the old man, straightening his legs with a sigh, 'the Book, Jamie. I think I know what will happen, but we must be sure.'

Swallowing a mouthful of cheese sandwich, Jamie pulled the Book out and opened it. He stared with surprise. The page was covered with a picture of a wolf, its snarling head turned to him, yellow eyes glaring fiercely. For a second he was sure he caught his own reflection in those eyes; then the wind ruffled the paper.

'Turn back!' Jennie gasped, and he did, but there was no sign of the picture.

'What was it?'

'Hmm.' Morgant put the tips of his fingers together. 'Interesting. I'm not sure. But ask it about the Tower, Jamie.'

Jamie crouched out of the wind. 'We're on the Harper's Beacon,' he said, feeling like someone on the radio. 'What now?'

Wait, the Book wrote. *Wait until the sun's eye is fully closed. You will see between two stones the door into the Summer Country. Pass through it and come back before the sun's eye opens even a little. You have only the twinkling of an eye.*

'You mean while the total eclipse is happening?' Jamie shook his head. 'That's impossible. The sun is only blotted out fully for two minutes. How can we go in, find the Tower, rescue the Prisoner and get back in two minutes!'

The Book did not answer.

'Time,' said Morgant, 'moves differently. I warned you. Once in the Summer Country we might have days, or even weeks, while here it is just the twinkling of an eye.'

They were silent a moment. Then Jennie said, 'Well, if I'd known, I'd have brought a change of socks.'

The eclipse began on time; the cloud had been hazy but began to clear to the west. It was too dangerous to look directly at the sun, but one of the men nearby let Jamie look through his telescope, which had a coloured filter on. 'You need that,' the man told him. 'Look at it without that and it could blind you.'

It was a peculiar sight. The sun was a pale globe, a lemon balloon with dirty spots on it, and something had already begun to take a bite out of one side. Infinitely slowly, the black disc of the moon was creeping across. It took over an hour; he and Jennie took it in turns to watch, fascinated by that rolling blackness. Morgant observed carefully, taking notes in his spidery handwriting; Gavan sat huddled in his greatcoat, slumped out of the wind, drinking and dozing.

Once or twice he got up and stamped about, to the annoyance of the astronomers.

Soon, even without the telescope, they could see it was getting darker. The sky slowly became deep blue and dusky, and a chill breeze sprang up round the rocks, flapping papers and clothes. The hippies formed a ring and began to circle, hand in hand among the stones. Carefully, Jamie packed the Book away. The sun was a pale crescent now, dwindling quickly. Around him cameras were clicking, and people were murmuring in excitement.

'All my life,' muttered the man with the telescope to his neighbour, 'all my life I've been waiting for this.'

Second by second, the sun's eye was closing. Light narrowed to a sliver; shadows stood out sharply on the ground, so that each blade of grass had its own, and those of the standing stones were black. Birdsong stopped, as if the birds thought night had come, and the lights in the houses down the valley began to flicker on.

And then, from the east, Jamie saw it coming, the black shadow of the moon racing towards him over the countryside, hurtling over the woods and villages and up the slope of the hills until it swept over his face in perfect silence, and the sun went out.

In the stillness, they stared upwards. The sky was full of stars. The sun was black, and around it great tongues of fire flickered, an eerie glow flaring out like the petals of a ghostly flower. Cameras whirred and clicked. Someone chuckled in the silence.

Jamie felt a tap on his shoulder and turned, impatiently, from the awe of the sky. Morgant pushed him towards the mound. 'Look.'

In the strange, purple dimness the two nearest stones were black, and between them in the air something shimmered and twisted, hardly seen. Through it there was a deeper darkness. Without a word he scrambled up beside Morgant and watched as Gavan stretched his arm out into the shimmer, and saw how it dissolved and disappeared. Gavan slid into the emptiness. One by one, silent as shadows, they followed him, slipping between the stones and vanishing into darkness. Jamie was last. He took one last look at the black sun, and stepped through.

'Here, son, take a look.' The man with the telescope tore his eyes from the sun and glanced around. 'Where did they go?' he asked his neighbour. The neighbour shrugged, showing a glint of bright hair under his dark hood. 'Who knows?'

But in half a second he had gone too.

THERE

Tri lloneit prytwen yd aetham ni idi
Nam seith ny dyrreith o gaer sidi . . .

Three shiploads of Prydwen we went into it;
Save seven none returned from the Faery Fortress . . .

The Spoils of Annwn

8

The Black Wood

Jamie stepped between the two stones and almost fell into someone's waiting hands.

'Keep still!' Gavan muttered in his ear. 'It's dark here.'

It certainly was. Even the wan eclipse light was gone; in this place it was cold, and black, utterly black. He felt Jennie shiver next to him. 'Where are we?' she asked.

There was a crisp splutter and a blue flare came out of the darkness, lighting Morgant's small face and beard. He bent and lit a lantern from his pack and waited till the light turned yellow and steadied. An oily smell came through the darkness, and mixed with it the sharp scent of pine needles and wet bark.

'We're in a wood,' Morgant said after a moment. He moved the lamp about carefully, and they glimpsed black branches silhouetted against his face. 'Yes. The trees are thickly crowded.'

Jamie looked up. A black interlace of twigs webbed across the sky; he could hear the thick canopy rustling softly, and through it caught the gleam of starlight. Wherever they were, it was deep midnight.

From their left came a great crashing and crackling; something seemed to be forcing its way through the undergrowth. Then Gavan's voice came from a distance: 'Over here. It's clearer this way.'

They followed, stumbling blindly over logs and brambles. Jamie was last; as he moved he caught a whisper of sound behind him and whipped round. His yell of fright brought Jennie and Morgant scrambling back.

'He was there!'

'Are you sure?'

'It must have been him. Just a shadow, reaching out . . .'

'All right,' Morgant said quietly. He raised his voice; it came out of the dark and echoed strangely among the invisible, crowding trees. 'Can you hear me, Cai Wyn?'

The wood rustled, but there was no answer.

'All this patience will do you no good,' Morgant went on calmly. 'If you come too close, no one will reach Fintan's Tower. I'm sure you know what I mean by that.'

The forest was silent. Then, not far off, someone laughed.

'Look out, Jamie.' Cai's voice came softly out of the darkness. 'Remember what I said.'

Morgant jerked them away. 'Come on. He's too close.'

It took them about ten minutes to struggle to a clearer part of the wood, and with the noise they made, Jamie thought, anyone could have followed them. His eyes began to get used to the darkness; once in the clearing, he could make out the tall tree-shapes crowding round, and the wet grass glittering in the starlight. It was the stars that astonished him most. 'They're all wrong,' he muttered to Jennie. They were bright, and scattered like glittering dust in peculiar patterns.

'Look at your watch, Jamie.' Morgant was beside him; as they walked he tugged up his sleeve.

'But that was the time the eclipse started! It's stopped.' The faintly green hands stood still at two minutes to three.

Morgant chuckled. 'It hasn't stopped – not quite. If you watched it for a few hours you might see it move a second. But each one is long, very long.'

'So we have the two minutes of the eclipse – until my watch shows three o'clock?'

'Exactly.'

'And that might be days?'

'Who knows?'

'And what happens if we don't get back in time?' Jennie asked quickly.

'Well, that would be very unfortunate. Who knows when the door would be open again, mm?' In the dimness behind the lantern Gavan chortled. Morgant ignored him. 'But it won't happen. We have plenty of time. Now, this seems to be a path of sorts. Perhaps we should enquire of the Book?'

But the Book just wrote *Get out of the wood* in a laconic scrawl across the page, yellow in the lamplight.

'I think we woke it up,' Jennie giggled.

Following the path in the darkness was not easy. Morgant went first with the dull star of the lantern in his hand, lighting the undergrowth and throwing black, leaping shadows against the boles of trees. Jennie walked behind him, then Jamie, his thumbs under the chafing straps of the rucksack. Gavan came last, noisily, the canvas bag tucked effortlessly under one arm. Behind him, the wood was silent.

The path began to slope steeply down, winding between the damp tree trunks. They slithered and clattered over slippery stones as they walked, and sometimes had to use their hands to scramble over rocks, or had to squelch through sudden patches of deep mud. Gavan stumbled along clumsily, often treading on Jamie's heels, sometimes stopping and staring back. But the path remained a dark notch between the trees. Wherever he is, Jamie thought, with a delight that surprised himself, wherever he is, *you* won't see him.

Gradually, the sky grew lighter, and the stars faded. But the wood stayed silent; there was no bird-song, or rustle of small animals. It puzzled Jamie when he noticed it. And in the growing light he could see the trees along the path were beeches, but their trunks and bare branches were black, as if a great fire had swept through the wood and charred it. It was a desolation; no leaves, no buds. A wood of black, twisted shapes.

There was no sunrise. The dull light grew around them, revealing a grey sky faintly tinged with copper. When it was quite light Jamie glanced back up the rocky path behind him and found it empty. Alarmed, he called the others, and they waited for Gavan to catch up. When he came he was smirking.

Morgant glared at him. 'Where have you been? We should keep together.'

The big man grinned. 'Just been making a few arrangements. For our sarcastic friend.' He pulled a coil of rope out of the bag and showed it to them. 'A few little accidents to slow him down.'

Morgant smiled; Jamie looked at Jennie. He felt uneasy, and the feeling was growing the further they went.

As she turned, Jennie pointed down the track. 'Look. The light is different.'

They walked on and found that the wood ended suddenly, and before them lay an immense grassy plain, rising, it seemed, to a distant horizon. Nothing moved except the grass, bending and whispering in the breeze. There were no birds. The coppery sky was still and ominous.

'I suppose we have to cross this?'

'I fear so,' Morgant said thoughtfully. 'There's no telling how far the Tower may be. Perhaps just over this plain. But let's sit for a while and eat, shall we, here at the edge of the trees. It seems we have a long walk ahead.'

He nodded curtly to Gavan, who tossed their bag down and flung himself beside it. Jennie sat down next to Jamie. 'How's the time?'

'Oh, fine. Took us three seconds to get this far.'

'In that case,' Morgant mused, 'we may only have two or three days. It's less than I had hoped.'

Jennie shook her head. 'It's weird. Look at this place. No birds. No sounds. Not even any sun. Just grass.'

The loneliness of the scene rolled over them as they ate; the grasses swished themselves in the slight breeze. Jennie finished the last sandwich, then poured out the dregs of the tea, screwed up the flask and put it back in the rucksack. Never mind socks, Jamie thought, they should have brought much more food.

Suddenly Morgant said, 'Jamie, I have an idea. It would be safer, you know, if you gave the Book to somebody else to carry. At the moment, if our enemy should make some attempt to abduct you and he well might – he'd get both you and the Book. I think we should split you up.'

The idea chilled Jamie. He knew it made sense, but it increased his uneasiness.

'Jennie can carry it then,' he said, after a moment.

'No,' Morgant said quietly. 'No. I think I should. That would be best.'

In the silence the grasses swished. Jamie laughed, awkwardly. 'Yes, but I'm the one whose name is in it. Doesn't that mean—'

'Come on!' Gavan growled. 'Do as he says!'

'It's only common sense,' Morgant added. 'I'm sure you think so, Jennie?'

'I don't know.' She fiddled with her shoelaces and threw

a frown at Jamie. He could tell she didn't like this. 'No . . .
I don't want to.'

Morgant made a swift sign; at once Gavan grabbed the
rucksack and pulled the Book out.

'Hey!' Jamie jumped up, but the big man shoved him back
and tossed the Book to Morgant.

'Thank you. Now it's really for the best, Jamie. We can't
lose both you and it.'

Furious, Jamie watched the Book vanish into the bag.
Morgant did the straps up tidily and then stood up. 'And
now for another brisk walk. Follow me.'

And he strode off through the grass.

At first Jamie lagged behind, trying to get a quiet word
with Jennie, but Gavan kept too close. Jamie was furious
with himself, and very worried. Up until now he hadn't realized how reassuring the Book had been; without it he felt
strangely alone, and rather helpless. Distrust nagged at him.
Did Morgant want it just to keep it safe? Or to keep him?
He began to wonder about them. Where had they come
from, after all? What did he really know? Everything they
had told him could be a lie.

Brooding, he thrashed through the grass. It seemed to go
on for ever; a sea of soft swishing around their waists. When
he looked back, the wood was already a low black huddle
on the horizon; on either side as far as he could see, the flat
grasslands filled the world. How could Cai follow them over
this? He'd be seen, surely – or was he subtle enough to crouch
and run and merge with the ripples of colour and shadow?
Or perhaps Gavan's trap had stopped him. Jamie remembered the farm, the man's cut hand, his anger. If he was badly
hurt he might be more dangerous, ready to leap up from the

grass any minute. But somehow, Jamie had begun to suspect that would not happen.

On and on the grasses waved around them. They plodded silently through the long hours of the morning. When the voice came, it seemed to wake them from sleep.

'Travelling far, strangers?'

Jamie's head jerked up; Gavan swore and spun round.

A man sat in the grass, half-hidden. He had a brown, dirty, pleasant face and straggly hair; his clothes were a patchwork of browns and greens. Behind him a small grey donkey grazed.

'Where did you spring from?' roared Gavan. Jamie knew that if the man had not spoken, they would not even have noticed him.

The brown man laughed. 'I asked first,' he said.

'We seek Fintan's Tower.' Morgant came back and looked at him with interest.

'Indeed? Well, just keep walking, friend. Fintan's Tower stands before you.'

The way he said it made Jamie feel it was right there, but when he turned his head there was only empty grass to the horizon.

The man smiled; it seemed to annoy Morgant. 'Thank you,' he said abruptly, and turned and walked on.

The stranger eyed Jamie and Jennie. 'I think I know you,' he said. 'Jamie.'

Astonished, Jamie stared. 'How did you know my name?'

The man winked. 'Ah. And what's your business at the Fortress? Are you in any need?'

'Well . . .' Jamie looked round furtively, 'I think we might be—'

'That's enough! Our business is our business.' Gavan pushed them both in front of him hurriedly.

'Hey!' Jennie said angrily. 'Don't shove!'

But catching their arms with a grip like a vice, he pulled them away.

Looking back, Jamie saw the man still sitting there, watching, and chewing a blade of grass. He raised a hand, with a mocking sort of smile. Soon the grass hid him from sight.

That afternoon the weather worsened. Low dark clouds rolled over; it began to drizzle, and then to rain heavily. Soaked through and hungry they stumbled on, into the coppery dimness that was closing round. Lightning flickered once or twice, and thunder rumbled far off in the west, the echoes rolling for miles over the endless tundra.

They became shadows to each other: dark shapes in the falling rain. It was only after one blue crash of lightning that the shadow that was Morgant stopped suddenly, arms wide to keep them back. They clustered around him, and saw that at his feet the plain ended, and a cliff, seamed with ravines and shattered rock, plummeted into darkness. And there, far out in the invisible country beyond, one tiny light flickered and shone in the rain, a white, pure spark like a star, and it might have been nearby, or miles away . . . they couldn't tell.

'Look,' said Morgant. 'That light is on Fintan's Tower.'

9

Down the Cliff

'It's for your own good,' Morgant said again.

Jennie fingered the end of the rope. 'I don't want to. Why should we be tied in pairs? If one falls he'll pull the other down. It's a crazy idea.'

'Stop whining and tie it on!' In the rain Gavan's temper had worsened. 'Why did we bring her?' he yelled at Morgant. 'We don't need her!' His small eyes bulged; rain plastered his hair to his face.

'Shut up,' Morgant barked. 'Tie it on, girl, and hurry. The rocks are slippery now, and this rain will make it worse. You will be with me and your brother with Gavan. We need to keep together.'

White-faced, Jennie tied on the rope. She flung a look at Jamie and hissed, 'I *hate* them!'

He bit his lip. She was right; they should never have come. Morgant knew. He knew they suspected him; knew as well as they did that the ropes weren't for safety, but to keep them prisoner. For all his sticky politeness, all Morgant wanted was for them to get him to the Tower. And it was too late to break free.

Gavan swung himself over the cliff edge; they heard him scrabble about on the wet rocks. 'All right,' he yelled, his head suddenly reappearing. 'It's not bad. Rocky ledges and a narrow path.'

He vanished again. Jamie climbed down carefully, and Jennie followed. Morgant was last. The wind flung rain at them, their numb fingers slipped on the stones. In the growing darkness each step was a danger; scree slithered about under their feet, and small showers of stones trickled and clattered down on to rocks far below. How high the cliff was it was impossible to tell, but it seemed very high to Jamie. Behind him, he heard Morgant slip and cling and curse.

There was a path of sorts, but it was broken and disused. Often it vanished altogether, and they clung to narrow toeholds and knobs and corners of rock. The rain swept across the miles of dark land below and slapped them against the cliff; water ran from above in trickles and torrents down their sleeves and into their hair, soaking them to the skin. Twice they had to leap dark empty clefts in the rock, toes stretching out over nothing, only half-seeing the other side.

But it was on an easy stretch of the path that Jamie heard Jennie shriek behind him; he turned to run, but the rope held him tight. 'Gavan!' he screamed. 'Wait!'

The big man wiped rain out of his eyes, but instead of turning back he leaned against a rock, grinning. Quite suddenly Jamie was afraid. The rope was looped around his waist; he tore it over his head and turned. Far up the slope Jennie was shouting – but before he had gone two steps, Gavan was on him.

Jamie bit and struggled but, laughing, Gavan held him, huge arms like a bear's tight around his chest, till, savage with fury, Jamie brought his heel down and stamped, hard, on the man's foot. Gavan roared, and staggered back, lost balance; and with a shove Jamie was free, and racing up the steep track. He hurtled round a rock and flung himself flat on the stones, grabbing at the rope that was slithering over the edge. In a flicker of lightning he saw Jennie's hands, and then her face, white in the blackness as she hung on to the loosening branches, hauling herself up. She screamed and slipped, but before the rumble of the thunder came he had grabbed her arm and was pulling, heaving her weight towards him. Rain beat in his face and blinded him. Then she was kneeling next to him, breathless, on the narrow, streaming path, staring at Morgant, who had watched it all and had not moved an inch.

'You just stood there!' she yelled, as soon as she could speak. 'I was shouting to you and you just stood there! You loosened the rope! You wanted me to fall!' She was shaking with fury and shock and the cold of the rain.

'My dear girl . . .' Morgant began.

'It's true!' Jennie screamed. 'You never wanted me to come! You want Jamie by himself so you can use him to get to the Tower!'

Behind them, Gavan fumbled up the track. Morgant let out his breath slowly. His smile was sickly. 'You're just a little overwrought, my dear,' he said, in a voice that was iron-hard. 'It's understandable. Now I think we should all be roped together, with the two of you in the middle.'

Gavan picked up the ropes.

'No.' Jamie jerked back; his foot sent stones over the edge. Jennie grabbed him. 'Be careful!'

'Look at them,' he hissed. 'Look at their faces!' Suddenly he lifted his head and shouted at the top of his voice, 'Cai!'

'Silence him!' Morgant snarled, jerking forward.

'Cai!' Jamie yelled. 'You were right!'

A crack of lightning split the sky wide open. For a shocking second they saw each other as white faces; the hot, sulphurous crackle of electricity scorched them, and the ropes in Gavan's hands leapt and jerked. As he held them the ropes shivered and twisted and burst into flame; they were two snakes with tongues and eyes of fire writhing over his chest, and there were others, a nest of them, swarming over the rocks and his legs and wriggling inside Morgant's coat.

Gavan roared and beat at the burning snakes; Jamie tugged Jennie out of her shock. 'Come on!' he yelled, and pushing past Morgant they ran down the wet path, through a maze of rocks, scrambling over scree and bushes, until they swung themselves over into a narrow crack in the rocks and scrambled hastily down.

In the narrow, echoing place at the bottom, their breathing sounded like a crowd of runners. They squatted against the wet stone and let the sound fade, gradually. Far in the distance thunder rumbled.

'Did you see?' Jennie whispered at last. 'Those ropes . . .?'

The rattle of stones made her stop. They pressed themselves into the darkness. Someone was following; they could see him, scrambling down the cliffside like a black spider, stealthily, with only the tiniest trickles of sound. He dropped lightly to his feet and stood in front of them. Pressed into the shadows, they made no sound, and Jamie thought they were unseen, until the man spoke.

'I wondered when you'd come to your senses.'

Jamie knew the voice. He felt Jennie's hand tighten on his arm but he stepped out, and she followed.

'About time,' Cai said.

'Oh, I know, I know!' Jamie squirmed in self-disgust. 'It's all my fault. I was wrong all the time, trusting those two . . .'

'And now you trust me, I suppose?'

Jamie didn't answer

298

'You turned those ropes into snakes, didn't you?' Jennie whispered.

A glimmer of lightning showed them his sharp grin. 'Yes. Not a very—'

He glanced up, then flattened himself instantly against the cliff. Far above them on the path they heard footsteps slithering and ringing on the rocks, and then voices, in a bitter, hissed argument. Slowly the sounds moved away, echoing in crevices. When they were gone, Cai moved. 'In here,' he whispered.

The ravine narrowed, and as they groped their way into it it became a long thin cave, running back into the cliff. Inside, it was black, and damp at first, then turned and twisted back until the walls were dry and they could no longer see the dim entrance.

'Right. This will do,' Cai's voice said.

Around them, the cave began to brighten. They saw him crouching with his hands spread out, and under his fingers a glow, a flicker of flame and sparks, and there was the fire; logs blazing and crackling and roaring out heat without so much as a wisp of smoke. Jamie noticed the long red scar across the man's knuckles. Jennie looked at him, raising her eyebrows; he shrugged, and crouched beside her. The heat rubbed like a cat against their numb fingers and faces, till they tingled and glowed.

Cai sat back lazily against a rock and watched them, his knees bent up like a grasshopper's. 'Have you got anything to eat, vixen?' he asked.

Jennie went red, and shook her head. 'We've eaten it.'

'That's a pity.' He pulled a face. 'Well, first of all, we'll stay here for tonight. The cliff paths are too dangerous in the dark. Then tomorrow we'll have to try and get to the Tower before them.' He stopped, seeing the look on Jamie's face. 'What's the matter with you?'

Jamie folded his arms around his knees and laid his head on them in desperation. 'It's not that easy. They've got the Book. They took it off me.'

Cai stared at him in horror for a moment, tore a hand through his hair, then leapt up and stormed round the cave. 'Nothing but trouble from start to finish!' he snarled. 'Why didn't you trust me from the beginning, you little idiot? I could tear you limb from limb!'

'I'm sorry,' Jamie snapped, 'but it wasn't my fault. They told me things . . . and you scared me.'

'Scared you? How could I have scared you?'

'Well, you're doing a good job now,' Jennie muttered.

The fire flared up and danced on Cai's sharp face; he sank down with a groan and ran his fingers through his hair. 'I suppose they didn't tell much more than the truth,' he said, after a while. 'Most of the things they probably said about me are true – Morgant is clever. But the Book! We need it, and they need you.'

'To get to the Tower?'

'And after. You want to get home, don't you?'

Jamie took his wet coat off and felt the warmth invade him. In that case they'd have to get it back. He didn't fancy waiting a thousand years or so for the next eclipse.

Cai was brooding, huddled up over the fire. Jennie said, 'Well, let's steal it back. Right now, when they don't expect it. It's dark, and Morgant's got a lantern. They'd be easy to find.'

Cai stared into the flames. 'It's too risky. The cliffs are wet and full of broken rock. They'd hear you coming.'

'But not you, eh?'

He looked up suddenly and grinned at her. 'Don't worry. Tomorrow we'll try it. Dealing with Morgant and his charming assistant would give me a great deal of pleasure.'

Warm through, Jamie arranged his coat around his shoulders and leaned back against a large rock. The cave roof was low and smooth, and in the firelight the floor beneath them felt dry and sandy. The echo of their voices murmured away into quiet; somewhere a drop of water plopped into a pool. He felt comfortable, and glad they would not be moving for a while. Stretching out his legs he said, 'Tell us about the Book. I mean, where it comes from. I don't know anything about it.' A slight tinge of longing for it came to him, and he wished he could feel its smooth black cover under his hand.

'You wouldn't.' Cai spread his long fingers over the fire, and it roared up to lick them. 'No one knows very much about Hu Gadarn's Book.'

'Hu the Strong?'

'That's right. Long ago, they say, he brought his people from the land called the Summer Country, and taught them how to plough the land, how to grow crops and make songs. Some say he was a giant, or that he is immortal. He sailed away in a ship of glass, and no one knows where he went, but he left behind him a book that would tell its guardian the way to the Summer Country. The book is your Book; this is that country.'

'It's not very summery,' Jennie remarked.

'No, and there's a reason. But the Book appears each time the way to this world is open. How it chooses its guardian is a mystery. But it will only answer to you.'

Jamie frowned. 'So Gavan and Morgant . . .'

'Will get nothing. Or,' Cai laughed, 'curses.'

Jennie giggled. 'I can just imagine the Book writing PUSH OFF in nice big capitals.'

'Do they really want to rescue Gweir?' Jamie asked quietly.

Cai's smile faded. 'No. But I do.'

'He's not Morgant's brother, then?'

Cai snorted. 'Is that what he told you? Of course not. The cunning old liar! Morgant has no interest in Gweir. But we have to rescue him. In a way, it's my fault he's a prisoner at all.' He stirred and gazed ruefully into the fire. 'I'm sorry to have to tell you both, but I've been to Fintan's Tower before. And the last time I came I had the same reason as Morgant has now. I came to steal the Cauldron.'

10

Theft

Jamie let out his breath and glanced at Jennie. 'I knew it was that.'

'I think you should explain,' Jennie said. 'You can't ask us to trust you until we know everything. What is this Cauldron, anyway? Why is it so important?'

'Ah, the Cauldron of the King.' Cai leaned back. 'Hasn't the Book told you . . . or perhaps Morgant wouldn't let it?'

He mused for a moment, his face a web of red light and leaping shadows. Then he said, 'The Cauldron of the King of Annwn is kept guarded in Fintan's Tower, by the Nine Maidens. It is kept safe because it is a hallowed thing; it has many powers, but most important among them is that it can give knowledge. If the Cauldron is filled with certain herbs and elixirs and kept boiling for a year and a day, whoever drinks of the liquid within it will have all knowledge and all power. You can see why Morgant wants it – and why we can't let him have it.'

'Yes.' Jamie was thoughtful. 'Yes, I can.'

'Well, many years ago, the Emperor heard of the Cauldron's power; he decided to try and get it for himself. We fitted out an expedition of three shiploads of men, and sailed here, at a time when the way was open.'

'Sailed?' Jennie interrupted. 'From where?'

Cai frowned. 'Logria. Don't interrupt. Morgant advised the Emperor that it was a good thing to do; I'm afraid to say I agreed. Some of the others didn't, even then.'

'And what happened?'

Cai shrugged, as if he disliked remembering. 'The whole thing was a disaster. Three shiploads came, and only seven men went back; I was lucky to be one. Unfortunately Morgant was another. As for the others, they were lost, or killed as we fought our way out. It was a nightmare; Fintan's Tower is a maze of sorceries, of corridors and strange chambers. Nothing can be trusted there – even my memory of it is confused . . .' He shivered, as if trying to shake something off. 'We fought against wraiths and shadows. And Gweir, of all of us – Gweir, whom I was supposed to look after – was captured. I'm not sure how; some said afterwards that he reached the Cauldron and touched it, and melted into air. Since then his cries have echoed through the land of Summer. Once, wherever he walked flowers sprang up, birds sang, the weather was warm. Since he has been in Fintan's Tower the Summer Country has mourned for him, as you see it now.'

Jamie thought of the black, twisted trees, the empty grass.

'This Emperor,' Jennie said slowly. 'Where is his court?'

'I told you. Logria. The Island of the Mighty.'

'But that's an old name for Britain.'

'Yes.' Cai looked at her sideways. 'Britain is Logria. The land of the real can also be the land of the unreal. As one coin can have two sides, each different. Logria is the underside of Britain.'

'But . . .'

Cai held up his hand. 'That's enough. No more questions. Time is getting on and you should sleep.' And as he refused to answer anything more, they had to make the best of it. Wishing he was not so hungry, Jamie settled himself on the sandy floor, tried to make a pillow of the rucksack, turned and squirmed to get himself comfortable. And while he was still listening to Cai's and Jennie's voices, and thinking he would never fall asleep, he fell asleep.

Breakfast is a difficult thing to do without. 'Hot porridge,' Jamie muttered. 'Piping hot in a blue bowl.'

'Toast, dripping with butter.'

'Bacon and eggs.'

'Oh stop it!' Jennie said crossly. 'It only makes things worse.'

Jamie stopped rubbing his arms, and staggered to his feet. 'I'm stiff too. My legs feel as if they're bruised all over.'

The fire was out, and there was no sign of where it had been. Cai was coming back down the cave, his footsteps noiseless on the sand.

'I've found them,' he said, squatting down. 'It wasn't hard – our friend Gavan leaves a trail like a herd of horses. And they're still asleep . . .'

'I wish I was,' Jennie muttered.

'. . . which will make it easier for us. Come on, and listen now, Jamie.' Cai caught his arm irritably. 'Remember, they want you as much as we want the Book. If you think you are in danger – vanish. Forget honour, forget me, even forget the vixen here. Just go!'

He nodded, but caught Jennie looking at him. 'He won't,' she said. 'Just you watch.'

As they came out of the cave the sky was still dark, with a faint greyness tingeing it. The stars were fading, and the intense cold of the air made them shudder. Silently, Cai led them up to the cliff path, and along it for about ten minutes, often walking warily ahead to make sure it was safe. In the early dawn nothing moved but themselves. The rocks were frosty and slippery underfoot. They could barely see the country they were coming down to; a thick white fog clung to it, masking all but the tops of a few hills. As they went down into it, the air grew damp and thick about them, and their breath smoked.

When they left the path they seemed to have come almost to the bottom of the cliffs. The undergrowth here was thick and tangled; black brambles and thorns were coated with a spiky fur of frost. Quietly, they shouldered through. Cai stretched out and bent back a bough; then he motioned them forward. They saw the red glow of a fire; a little way from it Gavan was sitting, his back against a tree, his legs stretched out in front of him. He was snoring gently. Morgant was a dark huddle by the fire; his knees were drawn up under his coat and they could see the corner of the canvas bag poking out. His left arm was tight around it.

'The Book's in there,' Jamie whispered to Cai.

The tall man nodded. Then he pushed them back a little way and crouched down. 'Here's what we do. I'm going to see to Gavan. When I've finished, you and I, Jennie, will try to get the Book. *If* we're lucky we might get it without waking them. If we separate, meet in that little copse down there.' He nodded over Jamie's shoulder. 'See it?'

'Yes, but—'

'But nothing.' With a swish of branches he was gone.

Jamie and Jennie waited, trying not to make a sound. They were so cold that they wanted to shift about, and Jamie's right foot began to go to sleep. Then they saw him.

He had worked his way round to the opposite side of the clearing; his dark shape flickered through the mist until he stood behind Gavan's tree. Jamie stiffened. From the greyness behind the tree a rope of fine silvery stuff was sliding out, slithering along the ground. It wound over Gavan's sprawled legs, ran over his body and slid around the tree trunk. Round and round the rope moved, over his shoulders, under his arms, cocooning him in its soft, silent web. Once he shifted, sleepily, but the rope ran gently around his neck and went back to Cai.

When it was finished, Cai crept stealthily back.

'Now, vixen. You try to get the Book. If Morgant wakes, leave him to me. You just grab the bag and go.'

She grinned at Jamie, and shoved the rucksack at him.

'Good luck.' He watched them through the drifts of mist; they emerged quietly from the bushes and Cai squatted by Morgant.

Jennie went round him, and got down on her hands and knees. Jamie could see how still and white she was. She went a little closer, until she was crouching by Morgant's side; if he had opened his eyes he would have seen her. Carefully, she reached towards the bag, caught hold of a corner of it, and tugged, ever so slightly. Jamie held his breath. Morgant did not stir, but the bag would not come; even in his sleep he held it tight. She glanced at Cai, who made a signal in the air with his hand; Jamie saw her nod, and begin, infinitely slowly, to undo one of the straps. It was impossible! She'd never get it out! He was holding his breath; around him the land was silent. Only the wind rustled the branches and lifted the ends of Jennie's hair as she inched the leather tongue from the buckle and a dark hole showed itself in the canvas. Gently, oh so gently, she slid her hand inside.

And Morgant moved! Before Jamie could yell a warning the old man was up and shouting to Gavan; he held Jennie tight and Cai was sprawling in the bushes as if he had been hurled aside. Gavan shuddered and woke; he tried to leap up, but the ropes held him. He scrabbled and tore at them furiously. Jamie watched Cai pick himself up painfully and rush at Morgant, but the moment he touched the old man, Morgant snatched up a branch and flung it; as it brushed Cai's shoulder it burst into flames. The clearing was a confusion of noise and mist and sudden smoke; Gavan roared and fought with the shining ropes. Jamie saw one snap, then another; then Cai dragged Jennie away and they were running, crashing through the bushes.

'Get after them!' Morgant screamed, his voice raw with anger, and with a mighty, snapping heave Gavan was on his feet and gone. In the silence that remained, Morgant turned. He was breathing hard. His small black eyes gazed coldly into the bushes.

'And you, Jamie,' he said quietly. 'Where are you?'

Ice-cold, Jamie held himself still. Morgant came nearer; Jamie forced himself not to move. He could outrun him, but it would be too easy to get himself lost. Morgant waited, a small grey man in the dawn. Then he said, 'You're quiet, but I can hear you. I can hear your breath, I can hear the creaking of your boots. I can hear the blood in your veins and the air in your nostrils. I am Morgant, Jamie. I left Logria to seek power, and I have it. Come out, Jamie.'

Despairing, Jamie bit his lip. And then a voice behind him answered his prayer.

'You can't hear anyone but me, friend.'

And the small brown man with the donkey brushed past him and strode into the clearing.

11

The Man from Yesterday

Morgant was as surprised as Jamie. He glared at the stranger. 'You again? Where did you come from? Are you following us?'

The small man smiled and patted the donkey's neck. 'Our paths certainly seem fated to cross. Were you looking for someone else?'

Morgant frowned into the bushes, then turned away. 'I suppose I was mistaken.' He stopped, and shot a swift glance at the man over his shoulder. 'I thought this country was empty. Are you one of the people of the Tower?'

The infuriating smile did not waver. 'This is my country.' The man rubbed the donkey's ears and it nuzzled him. 'As far as it is anyone's, that is.' But as Morgant turned in disgust to follow Gavan, the stranger said, 'One thing, friend.'

Morgant stopped, but did not turn.

'Fintan's Tower is a centre of great peril. Its treasures are forbidden. I think I should warn you . . .'

'Warn me!' Morgant snapped.

'. . . to go back where you came from, and to cease to feed this hunger that torments you. What use is knowledge, if you do not have wisdom?'

For a second Morgant turned his head. He looked puzzled, almost shaken.

'Who are you?' he asked.

The stranger smiled. 'Your conscience,' he said.

For half a moment Morgant stood. Then he pushed into the frosty bushes and Jamie heard him rustling away.

Slowly, Jamie stood up and brushed the white melting ice from his knees and hair. The small man watched him. 'Come,' he said. 'Let's find your friends.'

'Why didn't you give me away?'

The man laughed. 'Come on. This way.'

The copse that Cai had pointed out was not far, but they went along the base of the cliffs first, and round in a wide circle before they approached it. Under the branches were deep drifts of crisp, golden leaves up to Jamie's ankles, but between the aisles of trees the place seemed deserted.

'Jennie?' he murmured. 'It's all right.'

A noise behind made him turn; he saw Jennie's legs slither through the branches, then she dropped down lightly and grinned at him. Morgant's bag came down with a thud, and then Cai. They looked at the stranger warily.

'You're the man from yesterday,' Jennie said. 'We asked you the way.'

'That's right.' He sat himself down comfortably on a fallen trunk and smiled at her. 'I didn't like the look of what I saw; I thought it would be wise to keep an eye on things. Just as well, wouldn't you say?'

Cai scowled. 'Did you see me too?'

'No, I didn't, and that makes you quite remarkable.' The man waved his arm. 'But I know who you are. Cai the Cantankerous. Cai the Fair. Arthur's brother.'

Jamie thought that would make him angry, but Cai just grinned. 'And your name?'

'Doesn't matter. Have you got what you wanted?'

Already Jennie had Morgant's bag open, and now she pulled out the Book. 'Yes. It's this.'

She handed it up to Jamie, who opened it.

Hello, the Book wrote amiably.

'Hello,' Jamie said, a strange warm relief filling him. 'Are you all right?'

Quite, thank you.

'And guess what.' Jennie looked up at them hesitantly. 'There's food in here.'

'Let's have it,' Cai said at once.

She pulled out a small cheese wrapped in cloth, and some bread and apples. Cai picked up one of the apples and bit into it. 'Go on. You're hungry.'

'But it's stealing.' For some reason Jennie looked at the stranger. 'Isn't it?'

'I don't care,' Jamie said, squatting down to the bread and cheese. 'They stole the Book; they deserve it. Anyway, we can always leave them some, if you're that fussy.'

But in the end there was not much to leave; once they started eating they found out just how hungry they were. Guiltily, Jennie hung the almost empty bag on the branch of a tree. 'They'll find it,' Cai said grimly. 'Morgant has ways.'

The stranger ate nothing, but watched them, smiling and chewing his blade of grass. When they were ready to go he said, 'Now I'll come with you for a while. I know where the Tower is, and I know that every step of the way you will be in danger. The man Morgant has a hunger in him for glory; he has an evil smile. The other one is a roaring furnace. Watch your backs, my friends.'

He led them out of the copse and down a narrow track that ran through scattered woodland and gorse. The mist had lifted by now, but the sky kept its usual coppery tinge. Jamie found himself wishing for the sun, and glancing at his watch he found nearly half a minute had passed. He tried to think of the astronomers on the hill top moving infinitely slowly, as if in some slowed-down film, but it was too bizarre. There was no sign of any pursuit but, as Cai said, the trail of four people and a donkey was one even Gavan could find. They moved swiftly, carrying nothing with them but the Book, in its rucksack.

The stranger led his donkey in front, rubbing its neck and chatting to Jennie, who walked beside him. Jamie heard her ask him the donkey's name. Behind them came Cai, wrapped up in his dark coat and unusually thoughtful.

They walked a long way, down small valleys and up again to bleak hilltops, through a wood where the trees were all interlaced above their heads, down a path beside a river that roared and foamed over stones and jutting rocks. And still the land was silent, with no birds, no fish, not even an insect on the path; just the faint murmur of the wind and the drip of melting frost.

Just as Jamie was getting tired, they came to a place where the river plunged over a waterfall, and the path, too, ran steeply down.

They sat down to rest in the trees, and Jamie took the chance to ask Cai, 'How do we know he's taking us the right way?'

'Don't you trust him?' Cai asked lazily.

'Well, yes. I mean, he didn't tell Morgant I was there . . .'

'So don't worry.' Cai watched the stranger's small greeny-brown figure approach through the trees. 'The Tower is nearer than you think.'

The small man came and crouched beside them. 'It is

time,' he said, 'that we spoke with the Ancients of the world.'

Cai shrugged. 'There's no need . . .'

'Still. We should let them see what time is, and what wisdom is.' He took the Book from Jamie's bag and held it open, and with a shrug and a movement of his hands Cai lit a fire which crackled before the spread pages. Jamie felt Jennie crouch next to him.

'Time,' said the stranger, 'is mystery. A moment may be eternity; eternity a moment. Look.'

On the page was a bird, small and black. It stepped out of the Book into the flickering flames.

'Speak of the Prisoner,' Cai said softly. 'Arthur's messengers seek him.'

'I am old,' the bird said. 'I have sharpened my beak on the anvil every evening, until now it is as small as a walnut. I have not heard of this Prisoner. But there are those older than I.'

On the next page was a stag, grazing. It took a mouthful of flames from the fire and chewed them thoughtfully. 'I am old,' the stag said. 'I have known a sapling grow to an oak with a hundred branches and dwindle to a red stump. In all that time I have not heard of the Prisoner you seek. But there are those older than I.'

Silently, the stranger turned the page. An owl grew to huge size, preened one feather into the flames. 'I am old,' the owl said. 'I have seen three forests rise and fall in this same valley. I have not heard of the man you seek. There are others, however, older than I.'

Cai nodded, the owl flickered into darkness. An eagle glared out at them through the smoke and flames.

'Speak of Gweir,' Cai whispered. 'Arthur's messenger seeks.'

'I am old,' the eagle said. 'I have pecked at the stars from a mountain top, and time has worn it away till it is not a handsbreadth high. I know nothing of him. But there is one older even than I.'

Almost fearfully, Jamie saw the page turn. With a flick of its tail a salmon swam out into the heat and smoke. 'Listen,' it said. 'Once as I swam by the walls of the fortress in the lake, I heard wailing and lamenting on the far side of the wall. It was a man in sorrow. Seek your Prisoner in the Fortress of Glass.'

The pages were empty; the fire crackled.

Slowly, the stranger closed the Book.

Jamie sat back with a sigh. 'It's amazing,' Jennie breathed, chin on fists. 'I'm not even sure I heard those things – were they written or did I hear them?'

The small man shrugged and gave the Book back to Jamie. 'Who knows.' Jamie had opened the Book. On the page was written:

Fintan's Tower is before you.

'What do you mean?'

Stand up, it wrote, *and look.*

So he did.

Through the trees he saw soft, spreading countryside, and beyond it the peaks of distant mountains. Something glittered through the trees. He went forward a little, shouldered through the low branches of conifers, then reached out and pulled the greenery gently aside.

In front of him was a great lake, its surface clear and rippled, reflecting the sky. And out on the water, as if it floated there in the rising mists, he saw a tower, curiously shaped, gleaming with a pale, greenish light. The mist from the lake drifted across it; he caught glimpses of dark windows, and a great door lit with torches, and one light, high up near the battlements, where the tower sprouted turrets and balconies and staircases. There it was, as he had seen it in the ring of fire that day in the farm kitchen. Fintan's Tower.

Jennie had followed him.

'It's huge,' he said.

'Yes.' She gazed out at the lake. 'Jamie, have you thought about what will happen when we get there? What's going to stop us ending up prisoners ourselves?'

With a sigh Jamie let the branches swing back into place. 'Don't ask me. The future, you might say, is a blank.'

When they came down from the trees the path grew wider and firmer, until it was a great road running down in a long curve to the shores of the lake. As they trudged along it, afternoon turned slowly into evening, and Jamie felt his hunger come creeping back. He hitched the bag up on his shoulders and glanced behind. No sign of pursuit. They had travelled quickly.

'Not long now,' the small man said, and as Jamie turned he saw that they had nearly reached the water, and that the road ended abruptly at the lake's edge, among sedges and black, broken reeds.

'How do we cross?' he muttered to Cai.

Cai shrugged. 'Boat.'

'But what if there isn't . . .?'

'There will be.'

And there was. Jennie tugged a rope hanging in the water and pulled it into sight; a small, slimy-looking wooden boat, with a strange high prow. There were no oars.

The small man ruffled the donkey's ears. 'Good-bye,' he said. 'And good luck.'

They stared at him. 'Aren't you coming?' Jamie asked.

'No. This is your business – and yours,' he added, glancing up at Cai. 'Not mine.' He took the Book from its bag under Jamie's arm and opened it. 'What do you think?'

Your place is elsewhere, the Book wrote, to Jamie's astonishment. *I will look after them, as far as the enchantments of the Tower allow.*

'Good,' the stranger said. 'I leave it with you then, for the moment.' And he turned the donkey's head and began to lead it slowly back up the road. 'Be careful. Look ahead and look behind, and above all, look within.'

'Goodbye,' Jamie said sadly, and Jennie echoed him.

'I'll tell the Court I saw you,' Cai said.

They saw the man was laughing; he waved his arm but did not turn around.

'What do you mean?' Jennie asked. 'Do you know who he is?'

'The Book answered him.' And Cai nodded down at the words that Jamie was already reading on the white page.

Goodbye, Hu Gadarn, the Book had written.

12

Fortress of Frustration

'Careful!' The boat swung round perilously as Jennie stepped in; she sat down hastily.

Jamie came last, grabbing Cai's cold hand as he stumbled.

'Good,' Cai said, and leaned back, easing out his long legs.

'Yes, but how do we row? There aren't any oars.'

Cai grinned. 'We don't need them.' As he said it, the boat began to move. It turned slowly, so that the prow faced out across the misty lake, and then, as if it was carried in a strong current, or pushed by invisible hands, it moved out over the water.

The silence was uncanny, broken only by the soft sound of ripples under the prow. In the growing gloom the lake smelt of weeds, and dank, rotting vegetation; the water was dim with shadows and icy to the touch, and when Jamie leaned over the side he saw only his own reflection swaying on the surface, and the impossibly large crescent of the moon above him. Slowly, the lakeside fell away behind them.

Looking back, Jennie said, 'Is that Hu, there by that tree?'

A shadow flickered among the bushes at the edge of the lake. Someone was looking after them.

Cai scowled. 'I doubt it,' he said.

Suddenly the mist was around them. White and faintly glistening, it was damp against their faces; it left chill drops on their clothes and the wooden boards of the boat. Everything became blurred, difficult to see, and when they spoke their voices sounded louder than usual, so that they almost whispered. Slowly, the boat drifted into whiteness that

317

sometimes opened to give glimpses of dark water or a sky full of stars, and then closed over them again, with its frosty, moon-white web.

Gradually, they began to hear water lapping not far ahead; the boat seemed to drift more slowly. Kneeling up, Jamie stared ahead into the mist; it shimmered and drifted apart, and for a second he saw clear water, and the mighty bulk of a wall reflected high over him.

'Look!' he gasped, but they were already staring up at it; the battlements and turrets and smooth embrasures that seemed to lean out over their heads. Silent and far up on the topmost pinnacle, a man leaned over and watched them. Then the mist closed in, and the tower was lost.

'Someone saw us,' Jennie whispered.

'Sentinel,' Cai muttered. He seemed uneasy. 'It happened before.' Then the boat bumped against something hard, and stopped.

Carefully, Cai manoeuvred himself over the side; he dragged the slimy rope from the water and looped it round a jutting crag of what seemed like ice. Jamie clambered out after him, and Jennie followed, handing out the bag.

They found themselves standing on a slippery, jagged surface. In front of them, so close they could touch it, a great wall rose up into the mists, made of some smooth-looking greenish substance. Jamie took his glove off and felt the surface; it was smooth, with seams and bubbles of air trapped inside, icy to touch, with that echo of green light. It was made of great blocks fitted tightly together with no gaps between.

'It feels like glass,' he muttered. 'A tower of glass.'

And they walked on glass, smooth in places; in others

jagged and broken, its edges wickedly sharp. Careful not to slip and cut themselves, they followed Cai along the base of the enormous wall.

Soon they came to steps cut from the glass, and climbed up them. Great torches flared on each side as they came under the shadow of the walls. The door, when they reached it, was equally huge, but wooden and bound with great bronze hinges. It was locked, but the key stood in the keyhole.

'Now look,' Cai said, turning. 'I don't know what will be waiting for us in here. We have been seen; that was only to be expected. Expect anything; be ready for anything. And don't forget those other two charmers are behind us. Keep close, don't wander off, above all, guard the Book.' He paused, and looked at Jamie narrowly. 'I suppose you won't let me take care of it?'

'Sorry, no.' Jamie gripped the straps of the rucksack. 'I think it would rather be with me.'

Jennie giggled. 'You make it sound as if it's alive.'

'I think it is.'

Still, they made him go in the middle, and Jennie came last, although Jamie knew she was nervous about things coming up behind her. When they were ready, Cai turned the key and pushed open the door.

It moved slowly and heavily, with a low rumble; he shoved it wide, and as it banged against the wall they crowded behind him to look in. The corridor in front of them was dim and draughty. Tiny swirls of dust and ice stirred over the floor.

'Looks empty.' Jamie's whisper echoed down the walls.

Cai stepped inside, and peered ahead. 'We're not that lucky. Come on, and leave the door open. We may want to get out in a hurry.'

There was a faint greenish light in the passageway, as if moonlight was filtering in through the thick slabs of glass, but as they crept further in it faded to a glimmer, until Jamie could just see Cai as a blackness moving in front of him. When it became too dark to see at all, they stopped. The rustles and whispers of their progress died away, and everything was utterly silent. Fintan's Tower gave no sign of life.

'I'm going to try a light,' Cai's voice said, after a moment. 'Get ready.'

For a second nothing happened. Then a small ball of fire grew in the darkness; its own light showed them it was balanced at the tips of his fingers. With a sharp flick he sent it wobbling through the air in front of them, its glow lighting the passage a pale unsteady yellow. They saw a smooth floor and walls turning a corner not far ahead. Cai walked on stealthily, his feet making no sound on the slippery floor, and Jamie followed, trying to be as quiet. At the corner, Cai sent the light round first, then, waving at them to keep back, peered after it.

Then he tore his hand through his hair and groaned.

Jamie pushed him aside and looked. It was a crossroads. In each direction a passage led away, as dark and cold and damp as the one they were in. Each disappeared round a corner. Each was identical, and silent.

'It's a maze,' Jennie muttered over his shoulder. 'Look, shouldn't we try to mark our way, or something? Otherwise we'll never be able to get back out.'

'String, you mean,' Jamie said.

'Or breadcrumbs, if we had any.'

'Quiet!' Cai snapped. The ball hovering over his shoulder

crackled and spat; his cold fingers twitched the bag from Jamie's shoulder. 'Ask that!'

Grinning at Jennie, Jamie opened the Book. 'Can you tell us the way?'

To his astonishment the page turned black. If there was any writing, he couldn't see it. He turned the page and asked again, and then again, but each page was black and useless. Cai snatched it from him and riffled through it, then threw it back in disgust.

'What use is that!' he stormed, quietly. 'Just when we need it!'

'What's wrong with it?'

'The Guardians have silenced it!'

'Or perhaps it's just asleep,' Jamie said, to hide his worry.

'Idiot. Perhaps it will wear off,' Jennie suggested. 'Anyway, I don't think you should lose your temper over it.'

With a withering look, Cai marched off into the left-hand tunnel, hurtling the globe of light through the air in front of him.

Jennie pushed Jamie after him. 'He's just picked this one at random. It won't be long before we're lost in here.'

It soon seemed to Jamie that she was right. The passageways became an endless labyrinth and they just seemed to be going deeper and deeper and getting more confused. They passed turnings, tried a left one, then a right one, went down corridors to blank walls and then came back; but nowhere were there any doors, or rooms, or windows, or, most important, stairs.

'It's the stairs we need to find,' Cai muttered, as they paused for breath in the centre of a web of openings. 'We need to climb up, probably to the top, where the light is. It's where Gweir will be.'

'But surely,' Jennie objected, 'he'd be in a dungeon, or something.'

Cai snorted, and Jamie said quickly, 'It's a tower, Jen. The safest place would be at the top.'

'All right, clever. And he won't be guarded, I suppose?'

'He'd better be,' Cai said grimly. 'I'm just in the mood to deal with them.'

It must have been five minutes after that that they heard the noise: a great clap of sound rumbling in the air, and a vibration that seemed to shake the solid glass slabs underfoot.

'What was that?' Jennie grabbed at Jamie's arm.

'Ow!'

'Sshh!'

Stiff with dread, they let the rumbles die away into silence. When they were quite gone, Cai still waited, listening. Finally, he walked on.

'Well, what was it?' Jennie asked.

'I think,' he said quietly, 'that it was the door. Someone closed it.'

It had to have been Morgant and Gavan, Jamie was still convinced five minutes later. That meant they were in here too, going round in this maze, like mice in a laboratory. Maybe even round the next corner their shadows would be lurking . . . the small shadow of Morgant and the grey hulk that would be Gavan. And if not them, the Guardians Cai seemed so wary of. The people of the Tower – who were they? Who was Fintan? It occurred to him that they should have asked the Book a lot more questions, and now it was too late and they were in trouble.

Cai obviously thought so too. He had fiercely forbidden talking, and had moved a few metres ahead, edging up to every corner and listening cautiously. The cold seemed to be getting worse; the glass was like ice; their breath began to float about them. We're getting deeper and deeper, Jamie thought. Colder and colder. The walls were blue and green, bubbled and seamed, translucent thick ice. He paused and put his face close to them, brushing away the frost of his breath. Surely there were things trapped deep in there, like flies in amber. Surely he could see hands and faces, the curve of fingers round a sword hilt, the paws of some beast? As he moved, the images twisted and blurred, grew and shrank; he thought he saw the frozen pelt of a wolf, its mouth open in a snarl.

Jennie thudded into his stillness.

'What's the matter?' she whispered.

He shook his head and pulled her on, thinking of the lost men of the Emperor's expedition. They had come with force and met it, it seemed. He began to be afraid of Fintan's silent Tower.

Cai was waiting for them. He caught Jamie's arm. 'Look,' he breathed.

Ahead, the corridor ran smoothly, and at the far end of it was a door: a large, strong wooden door, with metal hinges and a key in the keyhole. The globe of light bumped against it gently and bounced back, like a bubble.

'Oh no,' Jennie muttered. 'It's the way we came in. We've been going round in circles.'

'Rubbish,' Cai said sharply. 'This is what we've been looking for all along!'

13

Fortress of Carousal

Pressed flat against the wall, feeling its damp chill through his coat, Jamie watched the dark slot of the door.

Jennie's breath tickled his ear. 'He's been gone ages.'

'A few minutes. Less.'

'Perhaps they've got him.'

'Him? I pity them!'

A shuffle in the doorway froze them; then Cai's tall shape blocked the gap. 'All right,' he said. 'But keep very quiet.'

He moved aside to let them through, then closed the door with a soft click.

Jamie stared before him in surprise. The globe of white fire still hung in the air, but the room had its own light. A long wooden table ran down the centre, and on each corner of it was a candlestick with seven slim candles, their wax guttering into grotesque shapes and dripping in pools on the polished wood. The table was loaded with food: dishes of apples, great haunches of meat, steaming fish, hot stews and bread, strange fruits and sweetmeats. The mingled smell of herbs and ginger and lemon drifted around them.

'Is all that real?' Jamie whispered, after a while.

'Oh yes,' Cai said. 'Real enough. It depends what you mean by real. Are you real?'

Jamie glanced at Jennie, and grinned. 'Of course I'm real.' He went over and picked up a soft red strawberry and sniffed it. 'Smells great. Can we eat it?'

'No!'

'I knew you'd say that.'

Cai crossed the room, snatched the fruit away and flung it down. 'Leave it. It's here to delay us, or ensnare us, or worse. I've seen what would happen if you ate it, and it isn't pleasant. Now this is far more important.'

He pushed them hurriedly towards the corner of the room, and through a small arch they saw a tiny thread of stairway that led up, twisting tightly round on itself.

'This is it. Now keep close. There's no way of knowing what's up here. You, vixen, keep your eyes open for anything behind you.'

She pulled a face at Jamie, but he saw she was worried. 'I'll go last, Jen, if you want.'

'No you won't.' Cai tugged him back. 'You'll go in the middle and keep quiet. She'll be all right. She . . .' He stopped, his gaze fixing over their shoulders.

The candles were out. The table was white with dust and cobwebs – thick, hanging webs, centuries old. The food – if you could still call it that – was a brown sticky mess on the plates.

'*Yuk*,' Jamie said, too loudly.

Cai grabbed him; it was too late. The echoes rippled round the room; rang above their heads in the spiral tunnel of the stairs. And at once, somewhere far off in the depths of the Tower, they heard a sudden snatch of noise – voices, music, laughter – cut off at once as if an undiscovered door had opened and closed again. And in the stillness that followed, their ears slowly caught it, a new sound, a soft padding and snuffling out there in the labyrinth of corridors, and then, echoing round the miles of twists and corners and passage-ways, a long, eerie howl, as if some creature like a dog had been locked out in the dark.

For a moment none of them spoke. The sound chilled their spines and fingers. Then Jennie said, 'They've let something loose. It's looking for us.'

Cai whipped around. 'Change of plan. I'll go last – Jennie to the front. Move!'

They raced up the stairs, slowing a little as they lost breath. Like the walls, the steps were glass, damp and slithery, climbing steeply. Cai, who seemed not to get breathless at all, urged them to hurry.

'I am!' Jamie gasped. His chest ached, and the Book banged heavily about in its rucksack and bruised his shoulders.

The higher they climbed, the colder the air; touching the walls froze their fingers. Then Jennie stopped dead.

'Empty space!' she hissed back.

Cai jerked to listen behind him. 'Go on, but carefully!'

They crowded to the top step and looked into the emptiness. It was a great dark hall, enormous and deserted. High up on one side were tall windows; through them they could see the occasional glimmer of the moon through clouds. A cold wind blew in. The globe hung over their heads, a tiny spark of light in a cold echoing place.

Without a word, Jennie began to walk forward, her quiet footsteps crunching the frost on the floor. They followed her, one at each side, eyes alert for any movement in the shadows; the moon, travelling through the clouds outside, slid a long wand of light across the hall and stretched shadows behind them.

At the far end was a dim structure; they walked swiftly towards it. As they came close, Jamie thought he saw something move, and stopped with a hissed warning. After a moment they went on. By now the globe of light had drifted ahead of them; it showed three shallow steps of green bubbled glass, and as it rose over the steps, magically there were globes of light everywhere, hanging in the air, each identical and moving as one.

Cai looked astonished. For a moment Jamie was too bewildered to understand. Then he realized.

'Mirrors!'

Around the platform the glass walls were polished in places to a gleaming sharpness. As Jennie walked up the steps, she flashed into the mirrors; nine Jennies, identically dirty and dishevelled, glimmered in the shadows and half-darkness. And in the ninefold light of the globe they saw what the great, round dark thing in the centre was: an enormous cauldron, made of some heavy, dark-blue metal, chased and patterned all over with thin gold lines whirling and twisting so the eye couldn't follow them. Around the rim were huge pearls, with strange, stick-like letters carved under them. The whole thing hung from three chains of mighty links, each the size of a hand; the chains ran upwards into the roof and were lost in the darkness, as if they hung from the sky itself.

'So that's what it looks like,' Cai said, almost to himself.

Something in his voice made Jamie turn and look at him. The moonlight caught his hair and it gleamed; his eyes were dark in the shadows of his face.

'You still want it!'

'Want it?' Cai let out his breath in a gasp of laughter. 'Think of knowing everything, Jamie, everything that's been and that's still to come.' The nine globes seemed to sparkle and crackle around him; his long hand grabbed Jamie's shoulder. 'Knowing all wizardry; being such a master of sorcery that in all Logria no one could outwit you. To know yourself. Anyone would want that!'

'I wouldn't.' Jamie squirmed out of his grip and leapt up two of the steps. 'I don't. I don't want to know everything – not all the horrible, dark, wicked things, all the fear and evil. You'd know those too, wouldn't you? Besides, we're not here for the Cauldron, we're here for Gweir – or had you forgotten?'

Cai glared at him furiously. 'Of course I haven't!'

'Well, shut up about the Cauldron. We're not going to steal it.'

'I don't know *how* to steal it,' Cai snapped back. 'Besides, if you touch it . . .' He gasped, jerked round and saw Jennie on the platform. 'Jennie,' he yelled, his voice rising in panic, 'don't touch it! *Don't touch it!*'

Her hand on the dark-blue rim, she stared at him in horror. And as they watched, she faded; her outline shimmered and became a shadow filled with pale smoke that slowly drifted away into the open spaces of the hall and dwindled into nothing.

The platform and the mirrors were empty.

And somewhere below them, in the maze of passages, that long howl sounded nearer.

14

The Prison of Gweir

Cai snapped out of the shock first. He tore the rucksack from Jamie's shoulder, threw it down on the floor and tugged out the Book.

'Ask it! Ask it quickly!'

Below them the howl came again, and then a sudden, urgent yelp. 'It's got the scent,' Cai said grimly.

Jamie jerked the Book open. 'Please tell us where she is . . . what's happened to her. Please try – it's coming up the stairs!'

The black page rippled, turned grey, then back to black, as if it struggled with its own nature. Then tiny white letters crammed themselves hurriedly together at the bottom of the page.

I shouldn't, they have forbidden me, but . . . the other stairs. In the corner to your right.

He had barely read them before they blinked out.

'In the corner – over there!'

Cai was already moving; Jamie grabbed the bag and raced after him. Behind the Cauldron it was dark and dusty; Cai sent the globe of light spinning ahead of him.

The staircase was broader than the one they had come up, but hidden behind a jutting slab of wall. They threw themselves up, two steps at a time, Jamie with the Book still gripped tight under his arm. Cai ran quicker; he was soon out of sight round the twisting pillar, his footsteps ringing over Jamie's head. 'Wait!' Jamie gasped. 'Wait for me!'

The footsteps turned; Cai thundered back and hauled him up with one long arm. 'We can't wait!'

'Then go on ... I'll have to ... catch breath. Just get Jennie.'

In the silence between his gasps, they heard nothing. Below them the stairs were empty.

'If anything comes, shout.'

'What do you think I'll do ... dance?'

Cai grinned, thumped him on the head and was gone, sprinting lightly up into the darkness. The globe drifted after him, and blackness closed in.

Jamie sat on the stairs, bent double with the ferocious stitch in his side. He tried to breathe slowly, felt the sweat on his back turning cold. It was quiet; the pattering of Cai's feet was almost lost in the layers of stone over his head. It sounded so far off he was alarmed and stood up to follow, and it was then he heard something else.

Breathing.

It was coming from just below him, somewhere down in the darkness. He stood still, ears straining for the faint sound, his eyes fixed on the wall twisting down out of sight. Yes, there it was – quiet breathing, almost panting, as if some creature was climbing up the steps towards him, in no hurry, but moving easily and stealthily. Now he could catch the pad of its paws, and a few small clicks against the glass. A shadow flickered on the wall.

It was too late to shout. He moved up, walking backwards, step by step, soundlessly. Any minute, it could leap round that bend. After four steps he paused. The stairs were silent.

It hasn't gone, he thought. It's sitting down there, listening, sniffing the air.

His heart pounded – he could hear it. The stairwell was black and empty and nothing moved but a thin cold draught of air that tickled his cheek. He brushed at it, then glanced up.

In the glass wall above his head was a door; infinitely carefully he edged up two more steps and pushed at it. The door opened.

At once the padding began, swift and close. He hauled himself up through the door and closed it with a hurried click, pressing himself against it, gasping in the bitter cold. No wonder – he was outside!

The moon dragged a trail of cloud behind it; the strange stars glittered in a black sky. He was standing on a tiny broken parapet with no edge, and below him – far, far below – the black water lapped at the base of the wall, its surface streaked and silvered with the shifting moonlight.

His breath smoked. Behind him, something flung itself against the door with a thud that jarred him forward; he braced himself in terror and pushed back, arms rigid between the doorposts. If it opened now, it wouldn't matter what came through, he would fall, down and down, to the icy water and splinters of deadly glass. It was snuffling now, scratching and growling under the door. The wind whistled round the corner of the Tower and flapped his coat. In a sudden giddiness, he felt the whole world turning slowly under him; glimpsed the moon in its eerie procession through the torn, silvery clouds.

Then he gripped tight, and looked up.

From somewhere above him in the fortress a light must

be shining; he could see its glimmer stretch far out over the water. And as he stood there, he was sure he could hear someone shouting – no, wailing; wailing and crying out loud as if in some terrible trouble. As the wind shifted, it was gone. Had it been Gweir, lamenting in his prison? Or Jennie, in hers?

Behind him, the door was silent. The creature might have gone by now; in any case he was stiff with cold. He tugged the door open, and then, when nothing leapt at his throat, he slid inside, shivering. The stairs seemed empty. Uneasily, he closed the door and began to climb, and then, not far above him, he heard a low savage growl – a vicious sound. Panic struck him. Suddenly he tore up the steps, round and round, hurtled out into a dark corridor, raced down it, turned the corner and stopped dead.

The corridor was lit with torches, red with leaping flame. An enormous black wolf crouched between Cai and himself. Wisps of smoke and icy air drifted from its skin; its paws left frost marks on the glassy floor. Cold seemed to pour out of it, a numbing, aching cold, and its cunning eyes were blue shards of winter sky. The size of the creature amazed him, and he backed warily towards the stairs. But the Wolf had not noticed him; it was watching Cai. Already one of the torches on the wall was out and a mass of icicles hung from it; as Jamie watched, the Wolf swung its great head aside and growled a breath of icy air at another torch. It snapped out in an instant, the charred wood frozen to a glittering black lump.

Cai was taller, as if he had drawn himself up. With a snap of his fingers he relit the torch, and it scorched up with a great hiss of steam.

The Wolf's eyes went yellow in the light, and its jaws hung open so that Jamie could see its long blue tongue slavering over teeth sharp as icebergs. It slunk stealthily through the shadows.

'Come on,' Cai was muttering. 'I'm not going anywhere.' His yellow hair shone in the flames, and the very air around him seemed to crackle and shimmer. He had a long gleaming sword in his right hand, its edge smouldering red. Jamie wondered where it had come from.

Head low, the Wolf prowled on. Cai taunted it, his voice bitter with scorn. 'Come on, come and look at me, devil's lapdog! I'm Cai; have you heard of me? I'm the one who cut nine witches into shreds on Ystafinion! Do you think I'm worried about you?'

Ears flat, the Wolf snarled. Ice dripped from its teeth and froze on its jaws. Cai's figure flickered in the flames; he jerked forward, his voice low and mocking. 'Scared, little dog? Cai the Fair, Cai the Furious, slayer of monsters! Creep back to your dunghill while you still can!'

Like a shadow, the Wolf leapt.

Cai dropped. It landed and turned, but already his sword had flashed in a red arc, and as it struck the beast's flank the metal hissed and scorched; the Wolf roared with fury.

Jamie jerked back; the corridor was suddenly coated with ice and the breath on his lips had frozen. Eyes white, the Wolf snarled and slavered, twisted, struck out. Cai leapt, but the heavy paw slashed him; he gave a yell of rage and struck back, missed, and staggered out of reach. The torches died, and for a second both fighters were just shadows in a dim green crack; then the flames burned up like an inferno, roaring and licking the roof.

'Come on, hell-puppy!' Cai yelled, his face twisted with anger. 'Palug's Cat would have eaten you for breakfast!'

Enraged, the Wolf flung itself silently through the darkness, and was on him before he could move, its teeth snapping and tearing at his throat, its icy breath frosting his face. Jamie gasped as they toppled and struggled; Cai cried out as the cold struck him. His sword arm was trapped; he waved the other and sparks lit the air; the Wolf yelped, twisted and bit at them, but still the man could not tug the sword free, and to his horror Jamie saw that ice was encasing them, a hard glass forming on their bodies and splintering as they struggled. The very air was aflame. Cai kicked and yelled with fury; the Wolf bit and tore at his arms and throat.

It was then Jamie moved.

He grabbed a torch from its bracket on the wall and ran forward, yelling and waving the flames. The creature jerked up its head and saw him. The eyes in the black mask narrowed; it growled and lurched at him, and he felt its shocking breath freeze the wood in his hand, numb him, coat his face and eyes with pain and hard white crystal. He dropped the torch and fell, half-blinded, on his hands and knees. The Wolf's breath was on his hair and its paws scrabbled at his neck, and as he beat it away, yelling, a vivid sword-flash burst out of the darkness, a sheet of flame that scorched the air as it passed. The Wolf screamed; its body writhed and collapsed on top of Jamie, knocking the breath right out of him; he smelt the cold, wet stench of its fur against his face. Something icy dripped down his neck. Then Cai heaved the heavy pelt off him, caught hold of his arm and pulled him up.

In a sudden echoing stillness the lamps were burning blue.

Then slowly the light steadied. For a long moment they gazed down at the black huddle.

Finally, Cai spoke. 'Stupid thing to do,' he said.

Jamie stared. 'You were in trouble!'

For a moment Cai's savage look swung on him; then the tall man shrugged. 'Trouble! I was just playing with it.'

'You ungrateful . . . boastful . . . unspeakable *idiot*,' Jamie spluttered. 'I wish it had killed you!'

'No you don't.' Cai grinned at him. 'Now come on. What we want is over here . . .'

Cai's arm was bleeding, Jamie noticed, and as he himself bent to gather up the Book the pain in his crushed ribs and shoulders made him wince. He was tired and aching and furious with Cai for his mockery.

'All that boasting,' he stormed. 'You were goading it on. It could have killed us both!'

'It didn't need encouragement for that.' Cai glanced at him narrowly. 'If a creature becomes angry enough it will become rash. Like you.'

Jamie shut up.

The prison door was made of a strange, hard crystal; Jamie had a shock when he realized it might be diamond. They turned the great key and heaved, both together, and even then they could only force the slab to a six-inch gap.

'Who's there?' asked a scared voice from inside.

Cai paused and grinned, wiping sweat from his face.

'Us!' Jamie said, relief shooting through him. 'Are you all right?'

'Yes!' Jennie's arm came round the door and touched him. 'A bit giddy. I just . . . was here. But get this thing open, will you!'

It took them a while, but finally the gap was wide enough even for Cai to squeeze through.

'What's going on? What was all that noise?' Jennie asked, taking in their bloodstained clothes and Cai's torn arm. But neither of them answered. They were staring at the boy who sat on the floor in the corner of the dirty cell: a boy a little older than Jennie, with hair the colour of corn and a smooth, serious face. He smiled up at them and moved a hand, and even that small movement clinked the gleaming glass chains that held him, wrist and ankle, to the wall.

'Cai,' he said, without any surprise. 'I was sure they would send you.' He frowned. 'I think I should warn you . . .'

'We know all about the Wolf.' Cai went forward quietly and knelt by the chains, tugging at the shining, slithering links.

'There's no lock,' Jennie said. 'I've looked.' She threw a worried glance at Jamie. 'What wolf?'

'Explain later.' He had been shaking his watch; the glass was smashed and he didn't know whether it was broken. About twenty seconds to go. Would it be enough? His heart sank at the thought of the long journey back.

Cai had the red sword in his hand; it seemed to come out of nowhere. He raised it and slashed at the chains, hard, with grim anger, and the glass shattered; shards flew out as he struck again, and one hit Jamie's cheek.

Painfully, Gweir stood up. He was thin; his hands were white as paper.

'Can you walk?' Cai asked, with stifled fury in his voice.

'I don't know.' The boy shuffled a few steps, rubbing his wrists. 'Yes. But not swiftly.'

'On my back.'

Hurriedly, Cai bent, and swung the boy up gently, then motioned Jennie in front of him. 'Go on! We may get out before they come. Hurry!'

They leapt the icy, sprawled carcase of the Wolf, its cold eye still staring upwards, and raced between the torches into the darkness, hurtling down the stairs, round and round at reckless speed, past the door where Jamie had hidden, down to the dark twist of the wall, and there was the Cauldron, huge and dusty on its platform in the empty hall. Jamie sped past it, but something reached out and grabbed him. As he stumbled, a foot shot out and Cai went sprawling over it, he and Gweir and Jennie a tangle on the floor. Cai groaned, and tried to struggle up, but a foot in his chest shoved him back.

'Lie still!' Gavan growled. 'Or I'll break your scrawny neck.'

15

The Wisdom of the Cauldron

The grip on Jamie's collar loosened; Morgant shoved him forward out of the shadows and looked at them all with a smile on his narrow face. He looked greyer here, and smaller, his beard glittering with crystals of frost. 'I see you found our lost friend,' he remarked. 'I must say, I hardly expected it. Very resourceful of you.'

'How did you get here?' Jennie snapped.

'Easily, my dear. Boat, the same as you. As for the unpleasant vulpine, our fierce friend here took care of that.'

Cai gasped as Gavan kicked his arm.

'Stop that,' Morgant said.

Gavan's head turned. 'Let me. Let me crush him. I'm sick of his insults and his arrogance. Let me finish him!'

'Just try,' Cai muttered through his teeth.

'I'm afraid we just haven't time for your delicate feelings, my friend.' Morgant came forward and took Gavan's elbow and pulled him back. 'Besides, we would hardly want the Emperor after our blood because of any damage to his precious foster brother, would we? No . . . the truth is, they don't matter any more. They've served their purpose. They can go.'

He bent down, smiling, and said it again, very clearly, as if he was talking to infants. 'Do you hear? You can go.'

For a moment they were all too astonished to move. Then Gweir scrambled up, and Jennie helped Cai, who shook her off. 'What are you planning, old man?'

'My business. Yours is to take the boy and go home, quickly, before the ways are closed. Now's your chance. I won't stop you.'

For a second Cai hesitated. Then he caught Gweir's arm and started with him down the hall. 'If that's the way you want it.'

'No. *Wait*!'

Cai stopped. Everyone turned and stared at Jamie, who was clutching his rucksack in the shadow of the Cauldron. He planted his feet stubbornly and said it again. 'Wait! I'm not going – and neither should you. You know what they are going to do now. You know as well as I do!'

'I'll do as I like!' Cai snapped. 'We came for Gweir and we've got him. Unless we leave now, we'll *all* be prisoners!'

'He's right,' Morgant put in, nodding.

'I don't care!' Jamie swung to Cai. 'You know what the Cauldron is – you told me yourself. All knowledge in time and space. Are we going to leave that for them? For him! Imagine how he'd use it!'

'But Jamie,' Jennie put in, 'they can't steal it. Look at the size of the thing; it's enormous, and you know if you touch it . . .'

'I *know*, Jen! But they wouldn't have come this far without some plan.' He turned to Morgant, suddenly. 'You have, haven't you? You've come here for the Cauldron and you know exactly how to take it!'

For a moment even Morgant seemed taken aback. Then he shrugged. 'Perceptive, Jamie, as ever. Yes, I am going to possess myself of the Cauldron.' He glanced around at their faces. 'My plans have been laid these many years, since only seven of the Emperor's Court limped home from the three shiploads that set out. I realized then that force of arms was not the answer. The answer was magic, deep and dark. And so I searched. No one, not even Merlin, has searched as I did. I worked, and planned, and studied old books; I spoke with smiths and druids; I walked hour after hour under the stars, seeking the lore of hags and witches and anyone who might advise me. Oh, the Emperor would not have liked it, Cai, but I did it. Rune stones, ogham sticks – all the forbidden things . . . I have consulted and connived with them all. And they gave me what all the Court of Logria could not. They told me how to steal the Cauldron.'

Jamie was cold. 'Whoever is here just won't let you take it!'

'Ah yes.' Morgant spread his hands. 'And who is here?'

'You can't be such a fool,' Cai said, marching back, 'as to think this fortress is empty?'

In the dimness Morgant shook his head. 'Perhaps they are waiting to see what I will do. What about you? You will not stop me.'

'We're staying,' Jamie said.

Morgant's face was dark; there were hollows around his eyes. His hunger for the Cauldron shocked them. 'Are you now?' he whispered.

'Yes,' Jennie muttered.

Behind her, Cai glanced at Gweir. The boy shrugged his shoulders. 'A prisoner learns something of his captors,' he said quietly.

But Morgant did not hear him. He turned, waved Gavan away from the Cauldron and stood before it, arms wide, his black, gleaming eyes fixed on the pearls and the dark-blue rim. Then he began to speak.

He began quietly, and slowly grew louder. The words were

strange and foreign: a chain of harsh syllables, ugly words, not to be spoken. But Morgant chanted them firmly; and as his voice rose, it seemed to Jamie that the sky outside the windows grew darker, as if great clouds were rolling over the moon. Morgant's eyes were closed; the words poured out of him, ringing in the roof and walls with hissing, sibilant echoes. He spat them out of him like a snake.

The hall was black; sparks of light crackled around the Cauldron. As Jamie watched, it shivered and rippled, and still the words came, piling noise on noise, venom on venom, unbearable! His hands were over his ears, he was shouting and twisting to get rid of the shrieking, but it was inside him, building up to a terrible crescendo that burst in his head like a roar of pain.

He couldn't see but he leapt forward, grabbing at Morgant's tensed shape, dragging him down, away, anything to stop the unbearable syllables ringing in his head. Somewhere Cai was shouting, flames were flashing, but still Jamie hung on as the old man twisted and struggled and shoved him away. Jennie came from nowhere, but she too went sprawling, and Morgant staggered up, hands clenched, the muscles in his neck and face taut with triumph. In the spasm of the last words, he writhed, and reached out, and gripped the Cauldron.

And he did not vanish!

For a split second Jamie could not move; none of them moved. Morgant tightened his grip on the cold blue metal and laughed. He began the words again, and Jamie was filled with despair; but even as he started, Morgant faltered and stopped.

His smile faded. He twisted, moved this way and that, tried to pull his hands away; his face became a mask of unbelief and cold fear.

'He's caught!' Jennie whispered. 'He can't pull free of it!'

Gweir chuckled, in the shadows. Jamie turned and saw Cai's grin, saw Gavan lying flat on his back, beating off the globe of fire that flamed perilously over his eyes.

'Lie still,' Cai muttered, 'or I'll break your brawny neck!'

Morgant still twisted and pulled, panic in his face. 'Let me go!' he hissed furiously, but the Cauldron only caught his words and hummed them round and round the metal hollow in a murmur of despair.

And at once the hall was full of light.

It came from everywhere, in through the glass walls, making them pure gleaming slabs of crystal, making Jamie feel suddenly small, and grubby, and exposed. Into each of the nine mirrors around the Cauldron stepped a woman, identical, with a wolf at her side, appearing from nowhere with breathtaking suddenness. They were all tall, black-haired; their clothes were green as glass, and though they were reflections, he realized with a shiver that they each moved in a different way. Four on each side; one behind the Cauldron, and it was she who spoke.

'This place is not without its Guardians, strangers.'

Morgant bowed his head in silent fury.

'We are Fintan,' the woman said, her voice clear and cold and young. 'We are the ninefold, the three times three who guard the Cauldron of the King of Annwn. Some of you,' she added, glancing at Gweir, 'know us already.'

They all spoke, Jamie thought, but with one voice. Just one.

'You have trespassed here,' the woman went on. 'You have killed one of our beasts; you have released our Prisoner; you have sought to steal the Cauldron of the King.'

'No!' Cai shouted, coming forward. 'Not the last. If you have been watching all this, you know that.'

Their eyes turned on him, cold and appraising. 'Once before, Cai,' the woman said, 'you came here for that reason.'

'Not this time.' Cai pointed to Morgant. 'There's your thief. The rest of us, apart from this –' he nudged Gavan with his foot – 'didn't want it. The boy tried to stop him. You saw, Fintan. Don't pretend the Guardians of Knowledge are ignorant.'

For a moment Jamie thought they would be angry, but they made no sign. After a pause the woman said, 'You are still hot-headed, my friend. We have seen everything that has happened here – everything – since you came to this place. We have seen who is guilty, even in their thoughts, Cai Wyn.'

Cai looked startled. Then he pulled a wry face and said nothing.

The eyes of the women turned to Jamie. 'Come forward,' they said quietly.

Reluctantly, he stepped towards the Cauldron, but not too near. He tried not to catch Morgant's eye.

'Because of your action in trying to stop this,' Fintan said softly, 'you will be allowed to go from here.'

'But what about the others? What about Gweir?'

She smiled. 'The Tower must have its Prisoner.'

'But why?'

'Perhaps you should ask your friend.'

Slowly, Jamie turned and looked at Gweir. 'What do they mean?'

The boy smiled an old smile and shook his head. 'All who seek the Cauldron seek its power.' He glanced sidelong at Cai. 'That was the reason we came, all that time ago. We came for knowledge. And my punishment was that they gave me what I had come for. They allowed me to know. All the sorrows of the worlds, Jamie; all the darknesses and evils and their results – I have seen all that, as well as all that is good. That is why you heard me keening in the darkness. Now I know that knowing is not enough. I have learned wisdom, at last. That is why the Tower must have its Prisoner. It must teach him to open his heart.'

He smiled at the nine women. 'I have learned, Guardians. Now release me.'

The nine identical faces looked out on him, proud and compassionate. 'You have learned,' they said. 'Now others must.'

Suddenly, as one, they leaned forward, the wolves snarling and uneasy. They breathed softly, and at once a fire was kindled beneath the Cauldron, a strange fire of blue flames that flickered around Morgant's ankles without hurting him.

'No!' he roared. 'Not me! Listen to me, Guardians. I have power! I'm cunning in magic! I will not be imprisoned!'

'You were wrong twice,' the voices chanted. 'Neither force of arms, no, nor sorcery, will gain you wisdom. But suffering may.'

Smoke rose from the Cauldron; whatever was in it boiled and bubbled. Points of light glimmered in its depths; faint flickers of colour and shape moved in the scented smoke.

'Jamie!' Morgant writhed and struggled. 'Help me! Don't leave us here to rot!'

Jamie squirmed. 'Does he have to . . .?' he began.

Fintan smiled. 'Yes. His heart is closed and black; both of their hearts. It is time they learned, Jamie.'

The smoke grew thicker. Morgant swore and cursed in fury; Gavan rolled himself up and held his head. Cai pulled them back as the wolves howled and snarled in the dimness. Then, slowly, the smoke cleared. Morgant was gone. Gavan was gone. The mirrors were empty.

Seconds later, the fortress had gone too.

16

Return to Logria

Fintan's Tower just winked out of existence.

It left them standing on a glassy outcrop in the lake, in a bitter wind that swept over the water, ruffling their coats and sleeves, and snatching their breath. In front of them the sun was rising, an unsteady red globe, flushing their faces. They stood in shock for half a second, then Jamie looked at his watch. The hands had not moved.

'It *has* stopped,' he whispered. 'Jen, we'll never get back!'

For a moment he had a vision of wandering for centuries in that desolate winter landscape; then Cai tugged him out of it.

'The boat! Quick!'

At least that was still there, drifting and bumping against the glassy rock. They grabbed it and climbed in. Jennie pushed off and the boat turned itself, moving out over the water.

Jamie broke the silence. 'What happens now?' he demanded.

Cai shook his head gloomily. 'It will take us a day, at least, to get back to the wood. Far too long. Resign yourself, Jamie.'

'Poor Morgant,' Jennie said suddenly, gazing back at the glassy green knoll.

'He deserved it.'

'Yes, but still . . .'

Cai shrugged. 'Don't worry about him. Worry about us.'

'He will be all right.' Gweir smiled at her. 'I promise you.'

The boat forged on, its prow whitening the waves. Spume and spray made rainbows over them and soaked them. Gweir trailed his hands in the water, his face to the wind as if he could never have enough of it. Cai tugged his dark coat round him, easing his stiff arm.

Slowly, the sun rose and the sky lightened. A flock of swans flew in from the south, circling low over the waves. Jamie stared at them. 'Look! Birds! Those are the first we've seen.'

He did not notice Gweir's private smile.

The swans splashed down into the water with a great rush of wings. Fish leapt out from under them, and suddenly, on the shoreline, the bird-song began. From tree to tree it sprang, and from further back, from the woods and valleys and grassy plains, a million whistles and warbles and sharp, piping notes.

Astonished, Jennie stood up in the boat. 'Look at it!' she muttered. 'It's all coming to life!'

In the warm glow of the sun, the lake and the sky were scattered with birds. Each tree on the lakeside was full of their movement, and among the reeds flocks of waterfowl fed and swam. Dragonflies dipped over the surface; squirrels climbed in the branches; wasps and bees crawled and hummed on the open lips of flowers. Almost as they watched, the trees were unfurling their leaves; the green web spread itself so rapidly that already the valleys in the furthest distance were emerald coverts in a yellow sweep of cornfields.

'What's happening?' Jamie yelled. He already had the Book open; spray splashed on to the page and he wiped it off with his hand. The Book shot tendrils and sprigs of greenery across its margins; drew quaint flowers and strange double-headed birds brilliant in blue and gold and red. Starting with a huge illuminated letter, it wrote:

The Prisoner is released!

Despite his worries, Jamie laughed. 'Fine! And what about us?'

The coloured inks ran riot across the page.

Fear not! See who awaits you!

The boat hit the shore with a bump, and Jamie looked up.

On the edge of the bank above them, Hu Gadarn stood, birds on his shoulders, a grin on his face, his rusty clothes as green as the leaves, as if he, like all the Land of Summer, had felt the change and the magic of release.

'Good!' he roared, and the birds flew up from him in a storm of feathers. 'Up you come! Quickly!'

Jennie was hauled up on to the bank; the others scrambled after her. Cai pulled an apple from a tree and tossed it to her. She bit it and giggled as the juice ran down her chin.

'No time to waste,' the small man said. 'The way is closing.'

'But it's too far!'

Hu laughed. 'Nowhere is too far. But first, Jamie, I'm afraid you have something of mine.'

He had been expecting it, but that didn't make the shock any easier. Reluctantly, he gazed down at the Book, its cover smooth and black, the small glass landscape set in its centre. And there they all were, five tiny figures by a blue enamel lake, and he could even just make out a miniature Book in one of their hands. With a rueful smile he opened the pages.

'I suppose I have to say goodbye.'

Goodbye, James Michael Meyrick. The spiky letters unrolled swiftly.

'You know, you could keep the Cauldron.' Jamie looked up. 'I'd settle for this any day if I could.'

Hu smiled.

'Oh, I know,' Jamie went on hurriedly. 'I know I can't, I know it has to go on, that someone else will need it. But . . . I suppose I've just got fond of it. It's as if there's a person in there . . . almost. Do you know what I mean?'

'Yes,' the small man said. 'I know.'

Jamie turned back to the Book. 'Thanks for helping us.'

The pleasure was all mine. This is for you.

A page detached itself and slithered out into his hand. It was blank.

I remember my friends, the Book wrote. *If you are ever in need, ask what you will and I will answer. But only once! Whatever is written will always be written. It may be in ten years or in fifty. I will reply. Good luck, Jamie.*

Slowly, Jamie closed the covers and handed the Book over to Hu, then folded the stiff page and put it in his inside pocket. It crackled there, reassuringly.

Hu looked at Cai. 'You will go with them?'

Cai shrugged. 'As far as I can.'

'Good. My best regards to the Emperor.' He held out his hands. 'Farewell, Jamie, Jennie, Gweir, son of Summer. Remember Hu Gadarn.'

As he stepped back, the light faded; the landscape dimmed.

Shivers of mist passed in front of them, as if for a moment the world was blotted out. Hu's shape darkened, grew, became hard; when Jamie put his hand out he felt rock, and he gripped it in a sudden giddiness of swirling patterns under his eyelids.

When he looked up again the sky was dark blue; the sun a black orb with a corona of fire. A high wind flattened his hair; the stone under his fingertips stood as tall as a man.

Jennie caught his elbow. 'The eclipse!' she murmured.

And as they watched from the hilltop, the sun's edge burst from its prison with a sliver of gold and flame that shot pain into their eyes, and they jerked their gaze away to the dim landscape and the black umbra hurtling silently away over the fields and the far hills.

A dog barked; birds sang as if it was morning. Steadily, the sun opened its eye. The astronomers straightened, applauded, slapped each other on the back; the rocks rang with their voices and the sound of the fiddle. Sunlight glinted on Cai's hair. They stood silent in the eruption of noise; no one even noticed them.

'Two minutes,' Jennie marvelled, finally. 'That's all it took.'

'It was really two days,' Jamie said.

'Neither.' Gweir gazed out at the hills, misty with coming rain. 'It was an eternity.'

Cai laughed. 'All wrong. It was just the twinkling of an eye.'

Jennie looked at him. 'And where is this Court of yours? How do you get home?'

'I am home.' He grinned at her look of confusion and thrust his hands in his pockets. 'First, little vixen . . .'

'Oh, stop that!'

'. . . First, we walk with you back to Caston. From there
. . . Well, let's just say it's not far. Logria never is. Under the
leaves, in the reflections of a pond, you might just see it.'
He waved his hand vaguely at the winter country below
them, at the farms and woods and the traffic on a distant
road. 'Logria is out there.'

Jennie stared at it, and shrugged. 'If you say so.'

Over her head, Cai grinned at Gweir and Jamie. 'Come
on,' he said. 'Before it rains.'

Author's Note

Some readers may be interested to know that many elements in this story are very old indeed. There are in existence fragments of a poem which date back to a thousand years ago or more, and which seem to tell of an expedition made by Arthur's men to steal a magic Cauldron from the Otherworld. The poem is known as 'The Spoils of Annwn' ('Preiddeu Annwn') and I have quoted it in the text. There are other stories too, of Arthur stealing a cauldron and releasing a prisoner. I have brewed up all these ideas and tried to make a new story from them.

Cai, of course, is the Sir Kay of the later 'King Arthur' stories, but in those his character sinks to being a bully and a fool. In the really old tales he is a hero and a wizard, and so I have made him.

And no, I don't know what Palug's Cat was, and I don't suppose by now anyone else does either!

CATHERINE FISHER

THE SNOW-WALKER TRILOGY

From the swirling mists and icy realms beyond the edge
of the world came the Snow-walker Gudrun – to rule the
Jarl's people with fear and sorcery. No sword is a match
for her rune-magic and it seems the land may never be
free from her tyranny. But there is a small band of outlaws
determined to defeat Gudrun and restore the rightful Jarl.
This trilogy follows their quest from the first terrifying
journey to meet the mysterious Snow-walker's son, to the
final battle in the land of the soul thieves.

This book includes:

The Snow-walker's Son
The Empty Hand
The Soul Thieves

'A spell-binding story, sure to kindle the imagination'
TES

'An outstanding piece of fiction'
NEW STATESMAN

RED FOX
0 099 44806 8